A Traitor in
Skyhold
John Bierce

A Traitor in Skyhold

ISBN: 9781081898038

This one goes out to r/fantasy. If it weren't for that wonderful bunch of nerds, I wouldn't be getting to write about wizards for a living.

CHAPTER ONE

Docks

Hugh of Emblin was, unfortunately, very easy to embarrass. It took remarkably little to turn him bright red.

His girlfriend, to Hugh's regret, delighted in doing exactly that.

Avah took her time in kissing Hugh goodbye, ignoring the catcalls and whistles from the crew of the *Moonless Owl,* as well as a few dockworkers. Not to mention his friends, the traitors.

Avah finally ended the kiss. "I'll see you in a couple months, when the *Owl* stops by Skyhold again," she said.

Hugh just nodded, still blushing. Avah hugged him again, then turned to climb back aboard the sandship.

Sabae, Talia, and Godrick joined Hugh at the edge of the dock as the *Owl*'s mages called up winds to carry them out into the desert. Alustin hadn't been able to make it out to see the ship off with them— he'd needed to meet with the Skyhold Council about something, and the meeting had been running for hours already. The apprentices watched the sandship sail away until it crested a dune and dipped out of sight.

The *Moonless Owl* had arrived back at Skyhold several days ago. Classes weren't supposed to resume for another few days (not that Alustin had ever stopped training them over the summer), so they'd taken the opportunity to show Avah, and Godrick's more-than-friends-but-not-quite-boyfriend Irrick around Skyhold, while the rest of the crew loaded and unloaded cargo.

They'd spent the rest of the summer following the incident in Theras Tel traveling across the Endless Erg. The *Moonless Owl* had visited port cities along its edges, hidden oases deep inside mazes of rock, and ancient ruins jutting out of the massive dunes.

The highlight had probably been their encounter with Chelys Mot, a turtle that dwarfed even the sphinx Kanderon Crux. The only larger creatures Hugh had ever seen were the dragon Indris Stormbreaker and her mate Ataerg— or at least Ataerg's corpse. The immense turtle had been surprisingly friendly, and quite willing to tell them a great many stories over the couple of days they'd spent visiting with him.

Watching the great turtle swim away through the dunes like they were water had been fairly astonishing.

To Hugh's great relief, the summer had been, after Theras Tel, largely dragon-free. There had been a couple sightings of dragons flying in the distance, but none had approached the sandship.

Even Talia had finally started to get a handle on her seasickness, and she had actually started to enjoy herself.

Spending time with Avah had been the highlight of Hugh's summer, though. Even if she did delight in embarrassing him. And even if her family— especially her grandmother— enjoyed it even more.

Talia kicked Hugh's boot after a minute or two of watching the dune the *Owl* had passed over.

"Are we just going to stand here all day?" the short redhead demanded. Unlike the other three, she hadn't managed to tan at all in the desert sun, just burning whenever she forgot a hat. Ironically, the blue spellform tattoos all over her body didn't do anything to protect her from sunburn, despite being intended to enhance fire magic and protect her from the same.

"Give him a second," Sabae said, rolling her eyes. The tall girl's branching scars stood out more than usual with her tan— she'd been dark-skinned to start with, but she was almost as dark as Godrick now, and her lightning scars were now visible from a considerable distance away. Her hair had gotten even lighter in the desert sun, and you could hardly tell that it wasn't white except when up close. "I think he's still recovering from that kiss."

Godrick chuckled at that. The massive youth's goodbye with Irrick had been considerably more circumspect than Hugh and Avah's. Somehow, he'd put on even more muscle over the summer, and Hugh was fairly sure he'd grown in height a little bit as well.

Hugh, of course, was as short as ever. At least he was still taller than Talia.

"It's fine," Hugh said, rolling his eyes. "I'm feeling hungry, anyhow."

The four of them wandered back through the crowded dockyard. There were a couple dozen other sandships in the docks, many of which were offloading other students returning to Skyhold for the new school year.

Hugh eyed a couple of students that looked rather confused and uncertain as they debarked from a large three-runnered sandship nearby. He was tempted to offer to help them find their way, remembering how lost he'd been when he first arrived at Skyhold. It'd taken him nearly an hour to work up the courage to ask for directions. Before Hugh could start towards the new students, however, an older mage debarked the ship and lead them away.

"Me da's supposed ta be back before classes start back up," Godrick said.

"I'm already feeling the bruises," Hugh muttered. Godrick's father, Artur Wallbreaker, was even bigger than Godrick, and he had a habit of cheerfully slapping people's backs hard enough to wind them. And cheerfully hugging them until they thought their ribs would crack. And nearly crushing their hands when he cheerfully shook them.

Talia snorted. "Your dad would fit right in with Clan Castis," she said. "Apart from being three sizes too large, at least."

Along with their reputations as deadly fire mages and belligerent warmongers, Talia's clan were also notoriously short.

Hugh knew better than to suggest a link between their height and belligerence, though. At least around Talia.

"He's a perfectly reasonable height, yer all just way too short," Godrick said.

Sabae coughed pointedly.

"Well, Sabae's only a little too short," Godrick said.

Talia kicked Godrick's shin.

The foursome bickered cheerfully as they wound their way through the crowded docks. Sabae suggested they cut across the sand to get past the crowds of sailors, mages, and dockworkers, but Talia refused on the grounds of having spent entirely too much time in sand over the summer. That, at least, saved Hugh the trouble of objecting, since he'd rather not walk where a sandship might run them down.

Hugh was idly glancing back out into the desert where the *Moonless Owl* had vanished when Talia elbowed him.

"Look who it is," she whispered.

Hugh glanced over to see Rhodes Charax debarking from a particularly grand sandship. Hugh came to an abrupt halt. Rhodes had made Hugh's first few months at Skyhold a living hell— he'd seemed to enjoy nothing more than tormenting Hugh at every opportunity.

Rhodes glanced their way, then seemed to notice Hugh and the others. He stopped in his tracks and stared at them.

The moment seemed to stretch on and on, until it was finally cut off by Sabae grabbing Hugh by the wrist and pulling him forward. "Come on, Hugh. Don't waste your time on him."

Talia was making a quiet growling noise, and Sabae grabbed her by the wrist as well.

"Let's get some food, ah'm starving," Godrick said. He'd positioned himself between Rhodes and the others.

After Sabae had dragged them out of sight of Rhodes, she let them both go.

"I wasn't intending to fight Rhodes or anything," Hugh said, rubbing his wrist.

"I was," Talia muttered.

Sabae shot Talia a dirty look, then shook her head. "Food sounds like a great idea, Godrick."

The four made it about fifty feet before Hugh tripped over a book.

It was, apparently, made entirely of green crystal, save for a striped orange-red stone in the front cover. Faint intersecting spellform lines radiated out from the stone, and a leather strap connected to each end of the spine.

Hugh couldn't have explained it if he tried, but he was fairly sure the book was giving him an irritated look.

"How does that thing keep following yeh everywhere?" Godrick asked.

Hugh shrugged as he picked himself, and the book, off the ground. The book seemed to move slightly out of sync with gravity as it hung from its strap. When he slung the strap over his shoulder, the book weighed far, far less than he'd expect a book made of crystal to weigh.

"It only ever seems to move when no one's looking at it," Hugh said. "And it really doesn't like being left behind when I go places."

The crystal book had started its life as three separate items in his possession— a blank spellbook Sabae had gifted him for his birthday, the labyrinth stone that had somehow gotten bound up in his warlock contract with Kanderon Crux, and the aether crystal she'd given him to bond with.

He still wasn't sure how the labyrinth stone had managed to bind itself to the book and the aether crystal, but he wasn't really sure about much when it came to the labyrinth stone. Kanderon and Alustin had both been particularly cagey about answering Hugh's questions about it— not particularly unusual for either of them, but certainly irritating.

Supposedly, a bound aether crystal would be incredibly useful to its wielder. Kanderon's wings were her aether crystal— though she still hadn't told Hugh how she'd lost her wings in the first place.

The only effect he'd noticed thus far from bonding with the crystal had been his eyes turning from brown to the same shade of green as the crystal spellbook.

The four of them were arguing about whether to eat at one of the cafeterias— which were free for students— or one of the restaurants near the docks— which were most certainly not free, but served considerably better food— when a tall, lanky figure waved them down.

Alustin usually had a slightly distracted, cheerful look on his face, but Hugh, Sabae, and Talia's teacher was distressed at the moment.

"Is everything alright? Did the meeting go well?" Sabae asked him when they drew closer through the crowd.

"No, it definitely is not," Alustin said, "and no, it most certainly did not."

Alustin's office hidden in the library was crowded with bookshelves, piles of books, loose books, papers, half-completed letters, and scrolls. The walls that weren't covered in shelves held huge chalkboards, and even the floor was a single, massive chalkboard, covered in spellform diagrams and notes. A single origami golem in the shape of a sparrow was aimlessly bouncing off the ceiling, clearly near the end of its lifespan.

Hugh could tell that his spellbook was watching the golem intently, for whatever strange reason.

The four apprentices sat in immense, over-stuffed armchairs surrounding Alustin's massively oversized desk. The chairs were large enough that Godrick had plenty of room in his, and Talia and Hugh looked like children in theirs. The armchairs had countless rips, tears, and patches, and stuffing leaked out of a number of holes— but they still remained in better condition than the desk, which looked like it had personally fought in a number of wars over the course of centuries.

Alustin, meanwhile, paced back and forth, muttering to himself. When Talia demanded to know what they were waiting for, he just muttered something inaudible and waved his hands.

Finally, after a solid ten minutes of waiting, Artur Wallbreaker ducked his way into the office, shutting the door behind him. Artur looked almost exactly like an older, more muscular version of Godrick, with the same dark skin and curly hair, albeit with a beard and ample grey in his hair. He looked tired and travel-stained at the moment.

"Da!" Godrick exclaimed, bursting out of his seat. "Ah didn't know yeh were back already!" He darted over to his father, and the two embraced roughly.

"Ah've missed yeh, Godrick," Artur said. "Ah hope yeh behaved yerself fer Alustin this summer. Speaking of which, what's with tha urgent summons?"

Alustin strode over and shook hands with Artur. "It's good to see you, Artur. I only wish my own apprentices were as well behaved as Godrick," he said. "I'm sorry to call you in so soon after your arrival, but I'll try and make this as quick as it can be, so you two can catch up."

Hugh couldn't help but notice Alustin flex his hand gingerly after the handshake ended, and he winced in sympathy. He'd had the experience of shaking hands with Artur before, and it was certainly a memorable one.

Alustin strode back to the desk and rolled up his sleeve. A banded spellform tattoo began darkening into visibility on his arm, and he seemed to shove his hand into empty space. A moment later, he pulled out another oversized armchair, which dropped several inches to the ground with a thunk.

Artur settled the chair to the side of the desk next to Godrick, waving a greeting at the others. Hugh waved back, relieved at not having been crushed in a massive hug.

Alustin collapsed into his chair and stared at the ceiling, saying nothing for a moment.

"So…" Artur said.

The lanky paper mage said nothing for a moment, then he sighed and looked down at them. "We have a traitor on the Skyhold Council."

CHAPTER TWO

Unwelcome Revelations

Everyone started asking Alustin questions at once, to the point where Hugh couldn't make out a single word anyone was saying. Alustin was taken aback for a moment, then he gestured for silence.

"Give me a chance to explain, please," Alustin said.

"It'd best be one good explanation," Artur said, leaning forwards in his chair.

Alustin sighed. "Before I do, I need to ask your son a question."

Godrick gave Alustin a confused look.

"Godrick, have you told your father anything at all about the specifics of Hugh's relationship with Kanderon?" Alustin asked.

Hugh stiffened. He'd never actually thought about whether Godrick would have shared anything about…

"No, ah haven't," Godrick said, an angry look on his face. "Ah wouldn't betray Hugh's trust like that."

"What are yeh goin' on about?" Artur asked. "And what does it have tah do with me boy?"

"Hugh, may I have your permission to share the details of your situation with Artur?" Alustin asked.

"Would you actually respect his decision if he said no?" Talia demanded, glaring at Alustin. "You've already let Artur know that there *is* a situation without asking Hugh, so…"

Alustin opened his mouth, then shut it. "You're right," he said finally. "Hugh, I should have talked to you privately first, and you have my apology for not doing so."

Hugh blinked, then shook his head. "It's fine, I actually don't mind. But what about Kanderon?"

"Kanderon was, in fact, the one to suggest bringing you four and Artur in on things, so you don't need to worry there," Alustin said.

Hugh rather doubted he would ever entirely not worry about the massive sphinx or her temper, but that did alleviate his concerns quite a bit.

"Ah have no idea what yer all goin' on about," Artur said.

"Hugh," Alustin said, "is a warlock, and he has pacted with Kanderon."

Artur's jaw dropped open. "He what with who now?" The massive battlemage gave Hugh an incredulous look. "Tha High Librarian doesn't hold reins with that sort a' thing. She's never pacted in all her centuries at Skyhold."

"Not, at least," Alustin said, "until it was the only way to save the lives of four promising students— including your son."

Alustin told Artur everything then— how he'd figured out that Hugh was a warlock, how he'd come to suspect the demon Bakori's manipulations, how they'd been hunting for a suitable entity for him to contract with, how Hugh had contacted Kanderon when the four apprentices had gotten stranded down in the labyrinth, and how the contract between them had been formed.

The big stone mage had been one of the mages who had gone down into the labyrinth to rescue the apprentices, so Alustin skipped over much of that part of the story.

"As interestin' as this all is," Artur asked after Alustin had finished, "what, exactly, does this have ta do with there bein' a traitor on tha Skyhold Council?"

"Outside of this room, there should be only five people that know the truth of Hugh and Kanderon's contract,"

Alustin said. "Kanderon and the rest of the Councilors on the Academic sub-council. And this goes double for the specific details of the contract. When we were in Theras Tel this summer, however, Indris showed that she very clearly knew about both Hugh's contract and at least one specific detail from it."

"What?" Hugh asked. "What detail?"

"Indris gifted you a book. She specifically told you that it was to pay off your yearly obligation to your master— which is one of the clauses of your warlock contract." Alustin said.

Hugh thought back to the ceremony. He remembered the red paged book, of course, but most of what people actually said during that ceremony he had forgotten in a haze of anxiety at being in front of a crowd that large.

"So you're saying that someone on the Skyhold Council works for Indris?" Sabae asked. "And why exactly are you telling us all this?"

"Not necessarily working for Indris, no," Alustin said. "Other powers have ended up with information about Skyhold that they shouldn't have way too many times over the last few years. If it weren't for that, maybe we could have believed that Hugh or one of the others had let themselves talk about it where they could have been overheard. They messed up this time, though, as outside those of us in this room and Kanderon, only the Academic sub-council members have access to the details of Hugh's contract."

"So you're saying that someone is selling secrets, then," Sabae said. "That's a problem, sure, but I still don't understand why you're telling us all of this."

"It's… not just a matter of someone selling Skyhold's secrets," Alustin said. "We think it might be considerably worse than that. We think that Bakori might be influencing someone on the council as well."

Almost everyone in the room started talking at once again.

Hugh froze in his seat, his heart trying to climb out of his chest. If Bakori was influencing a council member, then he wasn't safe here. He needed to get out of here. He needed to...

Talia's hand grasped his wrist and squeezed hard. Hugh winced, shooting a surprised look her way. Talia gave him a resolute look, slowly letting go of his wrist.

Hugh took a deep breath, and forced himself to calm down as Alustin quieted everyone else down.

"Earlier today," Alustin said, "the academic council met for their first session of the school-year. Kanderon brought up a measure to allow Hugh to do his second-year final test in a different labyrinth, as she judged it too risky to put Hugh in the same labyrinth that Bakori hides in. She proposed the labyrinth under the gorgon capital, given our fairly close relations with them these days."

Alustin seemed distracted for a moment when he mentioned the gorgons, then he shook his head.

"The council voted against the measure. Not only that, some of the members actively expressed their disbelief that Bakori was even in the labyrinth at all."

"That hardly seems like a convincin' argument for one of them bein' controlled by a demon," Artur said.

"Influenced, not controlled. Bakori can't control anyone directly, merely influence them. Sending whispers into their dreams, altering their feelings about choices that they don't feel too strongly about, that sort of thing," Alustin said. "And no, that's not why Kanderon believes Bakori was manipulating one of the council members— in fact, she could smell Bakori's influence. She couldn't, however, tell who it was on, but it seems like a reasonable bet that whoever it is likely has been selling Skyhold's secrets as well— weakening Skyhold only helps Bakori's goals. Skyhold council members are all long standing, trusted members of Skyhold, and there have been few betrayals of the sort in its history."

"Couldn't all a' them been influenced by Bakori?" Godrick asked.

"Kanderon doesn't think so," Alustin said. "She believes that no more than one of them was affected. Unfortunately, all three of the council members who voted against the measure have quite legitimate reasons for voting against Kanderon, so that doesn't help us much."

"Why does Bakori want Hugh back in the labyrinth?" Talia asked. "Revenge?"

That sounded likely to Hugh. He doubted Bakori was fine with having wasted an entire year's worth of work trying to manipulate Hugh into pacting with him.

"More likely he's trying to use Hugh's connection with Kanderon to attack her. For all the advantages pacting offers both to the warlock and their partner, it also conveys certain weaknesses," Alustin said.

This didn't significantly cheer Hugh.

"So someone could attack Hugh through Kanderon?," Sabae asked.

Alustin gave her an odd look. "Anyone powerful enough to take Kanderon alive would be more than powerful enough to squash Hugh like a bug without needing to resort to such measures. The reverse is far from true."

"So we ignore the council entirely," Talia said. "Why should we listen to them? Why does Kanderon, for that matter?"

"Because," Alustin said, "like it or not, they have the power to back up what they say. And, as powerful as

Kanderon is, even she would be hard pressed to stand up to the other mages of the council combined, let alone the combined might of Skyhold. She's the most powerful mage in the mountain, but she's not invulnerable. Besides, she helped found Skyhold. She's not going to casually violate its charter."

"Then we leave," Talia said. "Does Hugh really need to study here? We could travel up to my clan's territory. You could teach us all up there."

Alustin gave her a wry look. "I have to admit, something vaguely along those lines had crossed my mind. It's a bit premature for anything like that, though, and Skyhold seldom lets anyone break ties with them so easily. No, for now we just need to practice caution."

"Is that why you're telling us all this?" Sabae asked. "Just to warn us?"

Alustin shook his head. "No, actually, I expect you all to help us catch the traitor."

At this revelation, no one made a sound, save for the malfunctioning origami golem knocking over a pile of papers atop a bookshelf.

Finally, Artur spoke up, his voice thick with anger. "Why, exactly, are yeh havin' a bunch of children dip their hands inta a boilin' pot that most full mages would be best keepin' out of?"

"They're already involved," Alustin said. "I highly doubt Bakori has forgotten Hugh's friends. I'm also certain he means only ill towards them. What's more, I'd hardly call them children. They've all proven themselves more than capable over this summer."

"What's that supposed ta mean?" Artur demanded.

"Did you hear about the events in Theras Tel over the summer?" Alustin asked.

"Just somethin' about Ataerg turnin' on Indris," Artur said.

"Well, to make a long story short," Alustin said, "these four were instrumental in foiling Ataerg's coup."

The huge stonemage just gaped at Alustin, then at the apprentices. Before Artur could speak, Alustin raised his hand. "I'll tell you the whole story afterward, I promise."

Alustin turned back towards the apprentices. "Up until now, you've really only been training as battlemages. Kanderon and I, however, have been grooming you as prospective Librarians Errant. While Librarians Errant are required to be capable combatants, there is considerably more to the role than merely fighting. We intend to keep you on the fringes of the investigation where it is safer, but it will provide you with experience in some of the other skillsets that Librarians Errant require."

Sabae snorted. "You mean spycraft."

Alustin gave her a pained look. "I'd hardly use such crude terms to describe it. Kanderon's commands bring us to bear against a diverse range of tasks that..."

Artur chuckled at this. "They're spies, thieves, and treasure hunters. They do Kanderon and the Council's dirty work, whenever and wherever it needs ta be done. It's one a' the worst-kept secrets in Skyhold."

This honestly didn't surprise Hugh— the four of them had basically suspected something of the sort for some time.

Alustin sighed. "Regardless of how you want to describe it, yes, we're training you as candidates, and Kanderon is strongly in favor of danger as a teaching tool. Furthermore..."

As the pause dragged on, Hugh grew quite worried about that furthermore.

"Well?" Talia finally demanded.

"Furthermore," Alustin said, "events this summer have led to a situation that requires a mobilization of the majority of the Librarians Errant. We'll be in the field as often as not this year. This includes myself, and even Kanderon. And you won't be able to join me this time. So as much as it pains me to admit it, your assistance isn't just a training exercise. We'll actually need the help."

"What," Talia said after a moment, "could possibly be more important than uncovering a traitor in the Skyhold Council?"

Hugh found his mood sinking even lower, and his attention drifted inwards. Without Kanderon and Alustin around all the time, he had a feeling that life at Skyhold was going to be a lot more complicated. He certainly felt much less safe from Bakori without them around.

"Well?" said Sabae. "Are you going to answer her?"

Hugh felt his spellbook twitch, and a hint of what seemed like confusion came from it. It seemed to stare at Sabae for a moment, then at Alustin, albeit directly through his desk. Gradually, its interest seemed to fade, and Hugh felt its attention focus back on the sparrow origami golem.

Curiously, Alustin looked relieved at the question. "I actually can't tell you, no."

Artur glared. "And why am ah here, exactly? Do yeh expect me to come harin' off with ye on this mysterious quest while yeh have me son in over his head in intrigue?"

"Actually, no. We've got the mission more than handled on our end. I called you here because I can hardly in good conscience involve Godrick in all this without clearing it with you first," Alustin said. "For another, I need someone I can trust to watch over my apprentices while I'm gone."

Artur stared at Alustin, still scowling, but not as intensely. "Ah'm not saying no, but ah'm not saying yes, either. We need ta have a long, long talk first."

"I believe the four of you were planning on getting lunch," Alustin said, dismissing them.

As the four of them left the room, Hugh doubted he'd be able to make himself eat much. He'd really, really been hoping for a quiet, peaceful year, but life seemed to delight in keeping that out of his reach.

As he passed the origami golem, fluttering aimlessly through the air, Hugh's spellbook abruptly made its move. It lunged up through the air, yanking Hugh almost off balance as it closed its pages around the sparrow-shaped construct. He would have fallen if Godrick hadn't caught him, but the spellbook merely put off a feeling of contentment as it chewed.

Hugh just glared at it.

CHAPTER THREE

Class

Artur did eventually agree to allow Godrick to join the investigation and keep an eye on the foursome whenever Alustin needed to leave Skyhold. Hugh gained the impression from Godrick that Artur was mostly irritated at being surprised, not at the request or the danger involved.

Given how much less Alustin would be here to teach them this year, Hugh and the others were being enrolled in a lot more classes than they had been last spring.

All four of them had physical and combat training scheduled immediately after breakfast. Alustin planned on running that as often as he could, though Artur would be taking it over when needed.

After combat training, they had shared math and history lectures that alternated by day, followed by lunch. After that… things got a bit weirder. They had another shared class, cryptography— codes and codebreaking, essentially. Then they all split up for separate classes in the afternoon.

Talia had a class with a fire mage that specialized in, of all things, crafting puppet shows for children entirely out of flame— Alustin thought that this was her best bet for learning to control her own dream-based illusions, which only ever generated images that looked to be made of flame. Along with that, Alustin had convinced one of the few dream mages that sometimes resided at Skyhold to help instruct her, both to improve her use of dreamfire and out of hope that she might learn other uses for her dream affinity.

Curiously, Alustin had chosen not to find a bone mage for her to work with— he had just muttered something about them not being helpful. Instead, he'd reserved a large, shielded room for her to test her odd bone affinity— he was supplying her with large amounts of different animal bones to test, with a huge checklist of data for her to gather. Given how many bone spells affected the caster's own bones, it was clear why Alustin didn't want Talia learning those. That clearly wasn't a safe option for Talia, unless she wanted to blow herself up. Hugh didn't see why a bone mage couldn't teach her other things, though.

Sabae had an introductory healing class— something usually intended for first years, but given that she'd refused to use her healing affinity last year, she didn't have a ton of choice. After that, she had a sort of rotating seminar designed to help her progress with her unique magic techniques. Alustin would be taking charge of it whenever possible, but he had found a number of mages willing to try to help her out, including a noted expert on spellform-less casting, as well as several water mages. Alustin wasn't having her move forward with her lightning magic yet.

Godrick's schedule was by far the simplest— he was going to be spending most of his time working with his father, given that they had close to identical affinities. Artur's iron affinity was more than close enough to Godrick's steel affinity that it wouldn't cause problems. There weren't, unfortunately, any scent mages in Skyhold currently that could help him out.

Hugh had two main classes, other than the lessons scheduled with Kanderon whenever she was available. One was a spellform construction seminar attended mostly by journeymen mages. While Alustin was quite capable at spellform construction, he had about reached the limit of his knowledge that would be useful for Hugh— much of the rest of his knowledge was focused on glyphs, paper magic, and the like. Hugh was, however, warned not to tell anyone that he was already doing improvised spellform construction. Standard spellform construction was deemed dangerous enough as it was.

Hugh's next class was a ward class run by a somewhat reclusive wardsmith named Loarna of the Vault that lived deep in the bowels of Skyhold. Alustin wouldn't give him any more details than that, merely smiling ominously.

Finally, all four of them were enrolled in a class together that met every Fourthday afternoon. It was simply titled "Intermediate Library Filing Skills," and Alustin refused to share any details about the class with them.

To Hugh's delight, Alustin told them not to bother with attending the start of year assembly. It was, in his words, 'an utterly superfluous waste of time that literally no-one involved enjoyed.'

Of course, Alustin wanted them to use that time for training instead.

By the third day of classes, Hugh was close to falling asleep on his feet. It was common knowledge that your second year at Skyhold was much more difficult than your first, but Alustin, unsurprisingly, took this much further than most masters.

Physical training every day was absolutely brutal. After the events of the summer, Hugh definitely understood why Alustin demanded it of them, but that didn't make running miles every morning any more fun— even less so when Alustin informed them that they'd start having to do it while carrying progressively heavier buckets every day. There was also mention of obstacle courses, climbing, and a few surprises that Artur had in store whenever he took over the class.

Godrick grinned at that last one, but he wouldn't tell the others anything.

Combat training was grueling as well. There were plenty of magical training exercises planned— starting with target practice and moving up to more complex group scenarios. To Hugh's surprise, hand to hand combat training was being added as well— before, only Sabae and Godrick had trained in it at Skyhold, though Talia had plenty of combat training from home.

Hugh was fairly sure he wasn't going to be enjoying it very much.

Math and history were, well, math and history. The biggest challenge was just staying awake in their exhaustion. They clustered in the back of the classroom and took turns poking and kicking each other awake.

There was one other major challenge, at least for Hugh— all the other students kept looking at them and whispering to one another. There had already been plenty of rumors about them going around after they had escaped the labyrinth at the end of last year, and the rumors apparently only intensified over the summer, especially among the sizable population of students who had stayed at Skyhold.

It seemed that rumors about what had happened in Theras Tel were also spreading rapidly, which Hugh really didn't need. Even the instructors seemed unduly interested.

Thankfully, Godrick was more than happy being the face of the group— he'd been friendlier with a great many more people last year than the rest of them. Hugh had absolutely no interest in talking to a bunch of strangers. Talia was infuriated by the lot of them— when she'd seemed a failure as a mage last year, they'd all ignored her, only to start paying attention now. Sabae didn't seem overly concerned one way or another— according to her, she'd learned to deal with stuff like that back in Ras Andis.

Cryptography was… interesting, to be certain. Their instructor refused to tell them their name and went concealed at all times with a thick hooded robe and gloves. Their face was concealed behind magical shadows, and their voice was magically altered. Hugh had no idea what gender they were, even. The only thing that he could tell was that they were short and fat— and Sabae claimed that they were stuffing their robes to make themselves look that way.

The actual coursework in cryptography wasn't as difficult as Hugh had anticipated. They were learning about the fundamental principles of encryption and the like. They hadn't even started on any actual codes, yet, though apparently the first ones would be fairly simple.

Hugh didn't trust that it would stay easy, though.

CHAPTER FOUR

Eccentric Faculty

Hugh was more than a little nervous on the first day of his spellform crafting course. It was his first class without one of his friends alongside him in quite some time, and it would be alongside journeyman mages, for the most part— students who, rather than hiring out as battlemages or whatever other specialization after completing their first three years, instead chose to continue their education. Other than a few specialized disciplines like enchanting and healing beyond basic field medicine that required those extra years, journeyman mages tended to be those who delighted in magic for its own sake, or wanted to push boundaries.

Alustin was surprisingly ambivalent about becoming a journeyman mage. While he had done it— you couldn't take apprentices at Skyhold unless you'd completed your journeyman years, among other things— he didn't actually consider it to be that advantageous for many mages. Most battlemages, for instance, didn't need to know precisely how their spells worked, they just needed to be able to perform them reliably and quickly— especially if they were serving in an army.

When Hugh arrived at the classroom, he found himself numbering among only a dozen or so students, only three of which appeared to be apprentices like him.

The instructor was already waiting for them in the room. Every inch of exposed skin on the grey-haired, stocky older mage was covered in complex metallic spellform tattoos. He took his time staring at each and every student in turn. The look on his face said he found all of them wanting.

"My name is Emmenson Drees, and I'll be teaching you spellform construction. I accept no students without a personal recommendation from a Skyhold instructor, and only then if you already have a requisite minimum skill at spellform construction."

Emmenson glanced around the room again, the sour look on his face growing more pronounced. "I'm sure all of you consider yourself brilliant and above your peers. That's hardly an accomplishment, since most of your peers think hurling a fireball straight ahead requires magical skill, and could likely be replaced by a goat without many people noticing a difference in their spellcasting."

Someone in the front of the classroom snickered, and Emmenson fixed the unlucky soul with a glare. "I have a lot more patience for them than I will for any of you. I will have more respect for most of them than for you. The reason most mages merely use spellforms out of a book or memorize them is that they *work*. They're time-tested, reliable spells that don't explode two castings out of seven, only work in warm weather, or get shorted out by loud noises."

Emmenson rapped his knuckles on the desk of the student that had laughed. "You all, however, think that you are cleverer, more talented, and just better than everyone else. Enough so that you think you're capable of creating worthwhile spells. I doubt most of you will ever pass the level of being able to meddle with cantrips, however. One or two of you might be good enough to eventually develop spellforms for specialized, one time jobs."

He paused and looked around the room. "None of you, however, will ever be good enough to craft one of those mundane, day-to-day spells that students like you disdain so much. Those pedestrian fireball spellforms? They're tried and true works of art that you'll never even approach. In all my years of teaching, I have had exactly three students who reached that level. None of you will ever get there."

The students around Hugh held varying mixes of shock and anger on their faces. One journeyman to Hugh's right, a woman with hair nearly down to the floor, spoke up in irritation. "Who do you think…"

"Quiet," Emmenson said, sounding more bored than anything.

"I-" the woman started, only to be interrupted by Emmenson snapping his fingers. The tattoos on his hand flared slightly, and the journeyman abruptly went silent. Her mouth was still moving, but Hugh couldn't hear anything.

In fact, Hugh couldn't hear almost anything at all, except for Emmenson's voice. Even his breathing and heartbeat sounded curiously muted.

"I have absolutely no interest in hearing what any of you have to say. If you have any questions, you may write them down for me and leave them on my desk, and I'll answer any I find worthwhile during the next class. If you have any comments, you may keep them to yourselves. I teach this class for two reasons only— because the Council demands it of me, and for the vanishingly rare chance that I might actually find a worthy student amongst you all."

Hugh noticed that the journeyman's hair was twitching, apparently on its own.

Emmenson strode up to the front of the classroom. "While in my class, you may not test a new spellform without my prior approval. If you test one without it, you will be expelled from the class. If I hear of you testing a new spell on your own time, it had best be with your master's approval, because otherwise, you will be expelled from the class."

Hugh started to raise his hand at that, but then he quickly lowered it and began rummaging in his pockets for paper and something to write with.

"If you miss a class without an extremely good reason, you will be expelled from the class. If you make a habit of being late, you will be expelled from the class."

His spellbook, apparently deciding to be helpful, flipped itself up onto his desk from the floor, where he'd left it. Thankfully, it seemed to be covered by whatever sound suppressing spell Emmenson was using. The spellbook opened up, and sandwiched in between its crystal pages was a blank sheet of paper. A slightly chewed looking sheet of paper. Hugh was fairly sure it was identical to the paper that the book had been filled with before it became crystalline.

Hugh looked up to see Emmenson looking his way. The mage cocked an eyebrow at him, but didn't say anything.

Hugh set his quill pen and sealed inkpot on the desk, but he didn't do anything with them just yet.

"Even if you don't get expelled, I fail most students. I do not do so out of cruelty or for my amusement, but simply because you will not meet the expectations I have for this class. My standards will be clearly laid out, and I will be utterly fair about them, but I will not compromise on them."

Quite a few of the students around Hugh looked a little queasy.

"If you wish to drop this class now, you may do so without any difficulty. The academy is more than aware of how much I demand, and they're happy to assist you in finding a subject better suited for you. And rest assured, it will be better suited to you than this. And don't think that I'm merely being rough on you now to weed out the unsuited— I'm being kind, given that it's the first day."

Emmenson glanced at the door, which swung open at his look. He then turned his gaze expectantly on the students.

Almost immediately, a couple of students began to leave. Emmenson just waited patiently. Another student eventually got up and left, followed in swift succession by two more.

Hugh, seeing that Emmenson wasn't moving on just yet, began to write.

Eventually, after no one else chose to leave, Emmenson resumed. Hugh noticed that he didn't even glance at the door when he released the spell holding it open— which wasn't at all necessary to do, but most people had trouble not looking at the results of their spells.

Hugh was the only apprentice left in the room— only journeymen had stayed otherwise. He also noticed that the journeyman with the long hair that seemed to move on its own was still there, though she looked incredibly frustrated.

Emmenson raised his eyebrows as he looked over the remainder of the class. "You lot are harder to scare off than usual, I see. Well, let's begin."

Almost everyone in the class left questions on Emmenson's desk after the class let out. Once out of the classroom, sound resumed like normal, and Hugh could hear the other students complaining to one another about Emmenson.

Hugh was just happy he had a class where there was no chance of him being called on to answer questions in front of everyone.

A couple of days before the first meeting of Hugh's wardcrafting class, an origami golem in the shape of a bat delivered itself to the door of Hugh's hidden room in the library. When he unfolded it, the sheet of paper only contained directions to a classroom inside Skyhold.

Which, in turn, had led him today into a hallway that, so far as he could tell, didn't contain any doorways, nor anyone else.

Hugh spent a few moments double-checking his directions, but he was definitely in the correct hallway. Maybe the directions were incorrect?

For a moment, the idea flashed through his mind that perhaps the note was encrypted somehow, and he was supposed to solve the code to find the correct classroom. He quickly dismissed it, however, as a product of having just left cryptography class.

Hugh frowned, and started to walk back down the hallway. Something about this wasn't right. The classroom should be halfway down the hall on the north side, but the wall was just blank there.

As he turned his head, he thought he saw something out of the corner of his eye for a moment. He jerked his head back, but there was still nothing there.

Maybe…

Hugh tried simply reaching out towards the wall where the door should be, but met only the granite of Skyhold with his hand. So it wasn't an illusion, then.

He frowned, then walked back to the end of the hallway. He rested his hand on the north wall, then closed his eyes and started walking forward. About halfway down, the wall vanished beneath his fingers. Hugh smiled and stepped through without opening his eyes.

Only to find himself in an empty classroom, save for Hugh and the desks.

No, there was a letter lying on one of the desks. He walked over to it, seeing that it had his name on the envelope.

Hugh reached out to grab it, but then stopped himself, turning to face the door again, curious.

There, right above the door, was a ward. Hugh immediately recognized it as a ward intended to divert attention from the door. It was much more complex than the attention wards Hugh was familiar with, though— those only worked when people didn't know something was there. They wouldn't deter an active searcher.

Hugh lifted up his spellbook, intending to copy down the ward. When he opened it, however, there was no convenient sheet of paper for him to write on.

"If you're no good to write in anymore, you could at least supply me with paper when I need it," Hugh told the spellbook.

The spellbook somehow managed to give him a stubborn look.

"Maybe I should write in you, then, see how you like it," Hugh said. He strode over to the lecturer's podium, dropping the spellbook on it and getting out his quill and ink.

Its pages somehow looked even more obstinate now. Hugh frowned. "Alright, you asked for it." He lowered the quill pen to the page to start writing.

The ink just ran straight off the book.

Hugh sighed. "Are you actually good for anything at all, or did I just manage to ruin you?"

The book seemed offended. Hugh rolled his eyes and moved to shut it, but the book refused to close.

"Fine, be like that," Hugh said. He turned to pick the letter off the desk, only to have something poke him in the back.

He turned, only to see his spellbook floating off towards the door.

"Now what?" Hugh demanded. The book stopped a few feet away from the door, hovering open at chest height and somehow staring at him expectantly.

"This is ridiculous," Hugh said, but he walked over to the book. The book stared at him for a moment, then it switched its attention to the ward above the door, and then looked back at him.

Not only did Hugh have no idea what the book wanted him to do, he still had no idea how he could tell what the book was feeling or looking at. It hadn't moved at all since it had reached the spot it was now hovering in.

"Look, if the ink doesn't stick to you, how am I supposed to write in you?" Hugh asked.

The book, seeming exasperated with him, abruptly began turning pages. They didn't bend like paper, but they weren't rigid, either. They were somewhere between sheets and panes.

They were also absurdly strong. Even Godrick hadn't been able to tear one out this summer, and the book had bit Hugh hard when he kept trying after that. The edges were considerably less sharp than those of paper pages, however.

The book finally came to rest on a pair of pages near its front cover. There was writing suspended within the pages—easily visible flaws within the crystal. The writing was from when he was planning out his explosive wardstones for his sling— which reminded him that he needed to rework the ward designs so that they would be less likely to randomly blow up while he was carrying them around. He was lucky he hadn't been injured by one blowing up in his belt pouch in the labyrinth.

The book shot him an impatient look, and he focused back onto it.

"What are you trying to tell me?" Hugh asked.

The book seemed to sigh, and then the words and diagrams inside… *moved.* Hugh blinked in surprise as they reformed into a crude drawing of him drawing in the book with… his finger?

The drawing collapsed back into its constituent words and diagrams, and the spellbook flipped its pages until it reached a blank one, then it stared at him expectantly.

Hugh shrugged, then reached his finger out and pressed it against the page, drawing the first line of the ward above the door.

Nothing happened.

Hugh sighed and started to pull his hand back. The instant he did so, the book snapped shut on it. Not hard enough to hurt, but enough to keep his hand from moving.

"Alright, fine," he told the book irritably. The book slowly opened, releasing his hand. He frowned, then poked the book with his finger again. Nothing happened— he might as well be trying to use a quill without ink.

A quill without ink... Hugh smiled, then tapped into his mana reservoirs. He didn't channel the mana into any spellforms, but instead just reached out with his finger again, dragging it across the page.

It left a perfect line in its wake.

Hugh smiled and started to draw.

It took a few minutes to get the hang of it, and he made quite a few errors during the process. Partway through, he realized that he could actually erase the lines like chalk just by running his fingers over them and willing them away, which helped the process go much faster.

After he finished drawing the ward, he closed the spellbook and slung the strap over his shoulder, after which the book stopped hovering and fell against his hip. Possibly a little harder than strictly necessary. He glared at it, then strode over to the desk his letter was on.

And just kept staring.

Eventually, he felt a twinge of impatience from his spellbook.

"It's warded," Hugh told the book. "Look at the wax seal— that's a ward stamped into it, around the border of the sigil."

Presumably, the sigil belonged to Loarna of the Vault, the wardcrafting professor.

"I recognize part of the ward— it's meant to destroy the letter if the wrong person breaks the seal. It's one of the basic wards. I don't recognize a lot of the rest of the spellform components, though."

The spellbook somehow managed to emulate a bored yawn. Hugh rolled his eyes and turned back to the letter.

Part of the ward seemed to be designed to interact with other wards. If Hugh was reading the spellforms correctly, moving the letter past the other ward would destroy part of the text of the letter, but he wasn't sure what ward it was describing. Maybe the one under the door?

Hugh grinned and looked underneath the desk. Sure enough, there was a corresponding ward below it. He barely recognized half the markings in the ward, but he didn't need to— he could at least tell that the ward was mainly just built to interact with the other ward. He stood back up, grabbed the letter, and cracked the seal right there on the desk without moving it from inside the desk ward.

Hugh unfolded it and removed it from the desk, and smiled when nothing happened to the text inside the letter.

Then he frowned again.

All the paper contained was a date and time— the date and time of the next wardcrafting class, in fact— and another location in Skyhold. Below it was a homework assignment. He was supposed to write about all the wards he'd encountered during this class, as well as their purposes.

From what he was guessing, the homework assignment would have been the part that would have been burned off by the ward.

Hugh was preparing to leave the classroom when a thought occurred to him. He crouched down and began looking under the other desks.

There were wards almost identical to those under his desk under each of them. Curious, he tried to feel the tops of some of the other desks to see if there were letters hidden there, but his fingers somehow slipped away from the desk in the air above them.

Strange.

If Hugh had to guess, there was a letter atop each desk, each only visible to their intended recipient. Which actually lead to another question— shouldn't he have seen some of his other classmates by now? He was fairly sure he wasn't the only one in this class.

Curious, Hugh strode out of the room and looked down the hallway, seeing nobody in sight. He started to walk down the hallway, then stopped, feeling like something was off. Why had he started down the hall at such an odd angle? And, come to think of it, he had definitely meandered quite a bit on his way through the hallway the first time.

Hugh pulled out a piece of chalk, then began dragging it across the floor as he walked down the hallway. When he reached the nearest intersection, he stopped and looked back at the line.

It was the least straight line he'd ever seen. It wavered, twisted, made U-turns, and even looped at one point. He must have gone twice as far as he actually needed to go to get down the hallway, and he had hardly noticed it.

Hugh grinned, then stepped back into the hallway. He touched one wall with his outstretched hand, then stretched his other hand out as far as it could go.

Then he sprinted down the hall.

Within a few paces, he felt his outstretched arm smack into a couple of people, and after about ten paces, he crashed right into someone.

The attention ward in the hallway collapsed, unable to keep the students' attention off of one another any longer.

There were about a dozen students in the hall, most looking quite confused. Only one of them had a letter from the room in their hand already that he could see. Hugh was guessing they were mostly journeymen, but there looked to be a few more apprentices than in Emmenson's class.

The student who he'd crashed into pulled himself to his feet and glared at Hugh. "Indris' claws, that hurt. Watch where you're going, kid."

"I couldn't see you, so that wouldn't have helped," Hugh replied, still pleased with himself for figuring out the existence of the attention ward concealing the students from one another— even if he still couldn't tell where it was placed. He did notice that the door to the classroom was still concealed from the outside, however.

The other student just glared at him and grumbled, until he noticed Hugh's spellbook. His eyes widened.

"You're the Stormward!" he blurted.

Hugh gave him a weird look, suddenly uncomfortable. "What?"

"It was you!" the student said. "You were the one that saved Theras Tel from the storm this summer! I was there! I mean, I didn't see you while you were there, but I saw the battle and the storm and everything, and everyone kept talking about your spellbook carved from solid emerald!"

Hugh started backing up nervously. "It's not emerald," he muttered.

"What are you taking this class for?" the other student asked. "Shouldn't you be teaching it or something?"

Most of the other students were looking at them now. Hugh was really starting to regret breaking the attention ward.

"I… I've got to go," Hugh said. He pivoted and sprinted off.

Alustin had most certainly been correct about the need for physical training.

The other three had similarly unusual classes, for the most part. Sabae's healing class was the only normal, apprentice-filled class any of them were taking. It was mostly focused on emergency response and battlefield medicine— healing affinities were incredibly useful, but quite limited without an extensive knowledge of anatomy and physiology, as well as many years of training.

Only enchanters and one or two other mage disciplines required as much training time as healers, and since Sabae was training primarily as a battle mage, she simply wouldn't have time to become a full healer, so battlefield medicine was as far as she'd be going— though that was still a particularly intensive training program.

Her other class, the one-on-one seminar, Alustin had held himself. He wasn't planning on leaving on one of his mysterious missions for a couple weeks yet, apparently. They weren't doing anything new at the moment— just helping Sabae finish mastering wrapping her wind armor around her entire body. The most difficult part was, according to her, making sure that she could still breathe through it. Hugh didn't see why that was a problem   the armor was made of air, after all— but apparently it was.

Talia seemed somewhat disinterested in talking about her classes. When asked, she just said they were going fine, then changed the subject. Hugh suspected that meant that her tutors weren't making any progress with her dream affinity.

Talia's spellcasting limitations were a good bit more challenging to work around than Hugh or Sabae's— while she was incredibly powerful in a few focused areas, she'd been almost entirely unable to progress outside of those areas.

And while Talia was quite happy with those areas— especially considering that they all let her fight more effectively— she was still quite sensitive about her limitations, so Hugh decided not to push her.

Her independent study, however, Talia was quite happy to chat about. It consisted entirely of her exploding various animal bones and recording the results. Hugh was fairly sure Talia could spend weeks setting fires and causing explosions without ever growing bored.

Godrick's training with his father was apparently going great and was closely paralleling Sabae's. He was mainly working on extending his stone armor across his body. He was more secretive about it than Sabae, though— Sabae's techniques wouldn't be useful to anyone other than her, while Godrick was using his father's armor spells, which were a closely kept— and much sought after— secret.

CHAPTER FIVE

Intermediate Library Filing Skills

Sabae glared at Alustin, then punched another book out of the air.

"This is the most poorly named class of all time!" she yelled at him. Alustin just kept smiling and casually stepped out of the way of a swooping grimoire.

Sabae snarled, then detonated the wind armor around her legs, sending herself hurtling towards Talia, who was armed only with a net and was being mobbed by a flock of spellbooks. Talia could hardly use dreamfire without destroying the books, which would defeat the whole purpose of the exercise.

After Sabae dispersed the flock with a series of gust strikes, she took a moment to check on the others. Hugh had somehow ended up on one of the floating pathways in the center of the Grand Library, hunting down a particularly elusive bestiary. His weird crystal spellbook was badly savaging an innocuous-looking book. Godrick, meanwhile, was wrestling a tome that looked like it weighed more than Talia.

"What are we actually supposed to be learning here?" Sabae demanded of Alustin.

"Intermediate Library Filing Skills," Alustin replied, sidestepping another attacking book, before casually snatching it out of the air. He strode over to the nearest shelf and shoved the book in an empty space without looking.

"I thought you were training us up as Librarian Errant candidates, not librarians!" Talia yelled, trying to disentangle a panicked spellbook from her hair.

Hugh screamed something incoherent in the distance, and Sabae looked over to see him dangling above the apparently bottomless abyss in the center of the library, holding onto the bestiary in one hand and his spellbook's leather strap in the other. All three were sinking rapidly through the air. Sabae spun up her wind armor around her legs again, preparing to try and reach him, but the three started rising rapidly through the air. He'd probably just cast a levitation cantrip to reduce his weight.

"This really shouldn't surprise you, but dealing with books is still a big part of being a Librarian Errant," Alustin said. "While we might be Skyhold's intelligence service, cover stories work better when they're actually true. Just a moment, please."

The spellform tattoo band on Alustin's arm flared into visibility, and sheaves of paper flooded out of it. They hovered for a moment, and then Alustin sent them hurtling towards Hugh. They swiftly latched onto his legs, whereupon Alustin began pulling Hugh and the two books back towards the ledge.

"Help!" yelled Godrick, who was being dragged towards a gap in the railing by the massive book he'd been wrestling.

Sabae sighed and windjumped towards him.

Once the group had finished subduing the rogue flock of books and reshelving them— a task made much easier by the origami golems sent by the Index to help guide them to the right shelves— Alustin gathered them together at a reading area that jutted out over the abyss in the center of the Grand Library.

Of course, you'd have to be insane to drop your guard in here for a bit of reading time.

The Grand Library was impossibly large. It was roughly shaped like the inside of a hollow, square tower— if that tower were a mile across and at least four miles tall.

Sabae was confident that the mountain Skyhold was carved into wasn't actually large enough to contain the Library, and Alustin and Hugh had confirmed that there was spatial trickery at work— something akin to Alustin's tattoo, but on a much, much larger scale.

Books were shelved along balconies that wrapped around the wall, connected by spiral staircases, ramps, and ladders. The balconies looked small from a distance, but Sabae knew that some of them went back quite a distance.

You could spend a lot of time exploring the Grand Library without seeing the massive empty space in the center.

In said abyss floated countless rows of hovering shelves, islands that contained reading nooks, bookbinding stations, and even a small forest with its own miniature sun on one. Glowcrystals were scattered liberally throughout the library, but it was so huge that the space still seemed dim and foreboding.

At the bottom of the abyss was a thick, faintly glowing blue mist. Sabae knew that it contained the Index, a massive magical construct created by and linked to Kanderon Crux. The sphinx's lair, a massive hovering crystal dais, was located below even that, but Sabae had no idea if she was down there or not. Or, for that matter, how the massive sphinx got in and out of this place. While the Grand Library was massive, all the doors she'd seen to it were human sized.

While the flock of books had been irritating, they hadn't been overly dangerous. If the four of them hadn't been trying to avoid as much damage to the books as they could, they could have easily wiped them out.

The same, however, was hardly true of the rest of the library. It was, apparently, nearly as dangerous as the labyrinth at times, and quite a few librarians and visitors died in it every year. Alustin had forced them to memorize a list of recent victims as their punishment for sneaking in last year, and many of the entries had ranged from terrifying to nauseating.

"There's a property of the Grand Library that few know about," Alustin said, once they'd all settled down into armchairs in the reading area. "It's extraordinarily hard to scry on anyone in here. This is one of the few spaces that it's safe to discuss sensitive topics you have access to, other than my office, Hugh's room to a certain extent, and the labyrinth. And since the whole point of inducting you into all of this intrigue this early is to keep you all out of the labyrinth, I'd advise staying out of there."

"Just to an extent?" Hugh asked, looking slightly miffed. There wasn't much Hugh would challenge a teacher on, but Sabae knew how proud he was of his ward work.

"Any common scrying attempt into your room would fail," Alustin said, "but blocking a specialized affinity like my farseeing attunement or a few others would require massively overbuilt wards, which would draw entirely too much attention."

"Like there's not enough attention on us already?" Hugh muttered irritably.

Alustin pulled a thin book from his tattoo and tossed it underhand to Hugh, who barely managed to catch it before his spellbook grabbed it. Hugh shoved the spellbook off his lap, and it fluttered away irritably.

"That should provide you with a set of ward modifications that won't prevent the more specialized scrying methods, but it will warn you if someone is attempting to do so," Alustin said. "Just be careful to pay attention to them when talking in your room."

Sabae tapped her fingers, staring vaguely off at one of the islands floating in the Library abyss. She could tolerate the attention a lot better than Hugh could— every member of the Kaen Das family had to deal with it to one degree or another in Ras Andis— but something about all the attention they were receiving had been bugging her quite a bit lately.

"I don't get it," she said. "How are we supposed to make worthwhile spies if literally everyone knows who we are? My grandmother was quite clear about the best spies being entirely boring and forgettable. You and the other Librarians Errant seem exactly the opposite, and you seem determined to keep throwing us in situations that will throw us into higher and higher profile."

Well, Sabae hadn't known any other Librarians Errant until this week, but she'd been doing her research since returning to Skyhold.

Alustin smiled at that. "That's the trick, Sabae. The known Librarians Errant are supposed to be noisy and visible to people who are paying attention. They're lodestones for attention."

"Wait, the known Librarians Errant?" Sabae asked.

"There are a considerable number of our members who keep much, much lower profiles," Alustin said. "On top of that, the overwhelming majority of the missions we're sent on aren't spywork at all, but are in fact entirely on the level. If anyone tries to interfere with all of our missions, it will cost them considerable political capital, and give Kanderon and the Council room to push back against them. And most of the actual espionage that high visibility Librarians Errant like myself engage in is either just making covert pickups from embedded agents or... more active missions that require a somewhat aggressive skillset."

"Like assassinations?" Talia asked, leaning forward in her seat. She seemed a little too excited by that thought.

Alustin winced. "We try to avoid those as much as reasonably possible. A reputation as a legitimate order with a rumored tendency to dabble in espionage is one thing, but if we were to gain a reputation as assassins, we'd find ourselves welcome in far fewer places."

"Ah still don't understand why would anyone let yeh in their city anyhow, if they know yeh're spies." Godrick said.

"Well," Alustin said "Among other reasons, the true purpose of the Librarians Errant is hardly so well known as your father made it out to be. He's always preferred to make knowledge seem less valuable than to have people realize how intelligent he is. As for those who do know or suspect, they're not sure who among us are spies, and they'd rather have a known threat to watch than an unknown one. In addition, Skyhold doesn't have any true enemies— it would be prohibitively costly for most nations and city-states on Ithos to attack, and we strenuously seek to maintain as much neutrality as we can."

"Why do we even need a spy service if we're trying to stay neutral?" Hugh asked. "Quit that!" This last comment was addressed to his spellbook, which was attacking a nearby grimoire.

"We still control a significant amount of territory and resources," Alustin said. "We're at the center of what is likely the densest region of aether on the whole continent. We're above the largest labyrinth on the continent as well, and the goods that are won by the adventurers that survive delving its depths are worth more than the entirety of the exports of some major cities. We have literally thousands of trained mages, as well as Kanderon, one of the mightiest beings on the continent. She might avoid the public eye as much as possible, but everyone who is anyone knows who she is. We've got wealth, we've got power, and you can't have those without there being trouble. Nobody is ever truly neutral."

"What about Emblin?" Sabae asked. "They claim to be neutral, and I've never heard anything that might say otherwise."

Hugh shot her an uncomfortable look— he really didn't like talking about his homeland very much.

"Emblin can say they're neutral all they want, because nobody dares attack them," Alustin said.

Everyone looked taken aback at this. Alustin looked around at them and then sighed. "I would have at least expected Hugh to get this one. Emblin might be relatively poor and undeveloped, but it's in a stable and severe mana desert. Its aether is only dense enough to maintain a very small amount of magic before being drained, and it refills very, very slowly. Given how reliant almost every military on the continent is on mages, this puts them at an almost crippling disadvantage inside Emblin. The only nation that could likely overcome that disadvantage easily would be the Havath Dominion, and they're all the way across the continent from Emblin."

"Not," Alustin added, "that I have any doubt they've already developed plans for doing so some day."

He shook his head as if clearing it and moved on. This was hardly the first time Sabae had seen Alustin react poorly to even his own mention of the Havath Dominion— there was clearly some sort of history there, but she didn't know why he seemed to hate them.

Not that he was in any select company. Havath claimed to be the legitimate inheritors of the mantle of the Ithonian Empire, and they'd engaged in numerous wars of conquest and expansion over the past century, absorbing numerous city-states and smaller nations. Several times their expansions had only been beaten back by large coalitions of their neighbors.

Sabae recalled hearing something from her grandmother about their battle tactics being unusual, but couldn't remember the details, or why that might make them better suited for attacking Emblin, of all places.

If Havath didn't keep acting like they were doing their conquests a favor, the hatred so many had for them might not have been quite so intense.

Sabae realized she'd missed the last thing that Alustin had said, and turned her attention back to him. He had started to tell the others about lamplighters— operatives who tended to safehouses, prepared supply caches, and otherwise kept operations running on a logistical level.

There was something funny about this whole situation, something bothering her like a loose tooth that she couldn't stop poking with her tongue. She couldn't for the life of her figure out what, though.

She knew the whole "Skyhold is neutral" line was nonsense— Skyhold had spent most of its history claiming that it wasn't actually a city-state, merely a school, and that it was neutral, but its actions throughout history completely put the lie to both. That wasn't what was bothering Sabae, though.

Hugh and Talia might trust Alustin completely, but Sabae still had reservations. Or, rather, she trusted Alustin with her life, but she far from trusted him to be honest with them.

"Hugh, I don't think your spellbook is attacking that other book," Talia said, grinning.

"What do you mean, not attacking, it's…" Hugh started, then turned red when he realized what Talia meant.

Sabae glanced over at the books, sighed, and turned her attention back to Alustin.

CHAPTER SIX

Gifts

That Fifthday, a sandship from Theras Tel arrived bearing gifts.

Or, rather, rewards.

Indris had seen fit to bestow Hugh and the others with said rewards in thanks for their assistance in the battle against Ataerg, but they hadn't all gotten them at once. Hugh had… well, he hadn't intended to ask for a boon. Rather, he'd just frozen up in front of the crowd, and Indris had been amused enough to offer him a future boon.

Hugh really had trouble imagining that he'd ever get around to working up the nerve to call in the favor, nor did he have any idea what he'd ask a dragon for.

Sabae had requested the return of an amulet that one of her ancestors had lost in a bet against Indris— something about a contest over control of a storm or some such. Hugh was fairly sure the amulet was enchanted, but Sabae wouldn't say anything else on the matter.

Alustin had requested a book that Hugh had only briefly glimpsed— a log of grain shipments to the Ithonian capital, or something of the sort. Hugh had no idea why Alustin had wanted it— perhaps just for its extreme age?

It was Talia and Godrick's rewards that were being delivered today, however.

Talia had requested the bones of Ataerg. This had been a slightly ridiculous request on her part, but Indris, apparently not having any interest in mounting her traitorous mate's bones in her halls with the bones of her other rivals, had agreed.

It had taken until now for what remained of Ataerg's massive corpse to be removed from the ruined neighborhood he had died in and stripped of its flesh, but the first shipment had finally arrived. The hold of the sandship was almost entirely filled with bones. They'd also brought Ataerg's skull. Even badly damaged as it was, the skull was still so huge that it couldn't fit down into the hold without disassembling the deck, and so had instead been hauled behind the ship on a massive sled.

Kanderon had *not* been pleased about having to arrange to store the bones. She'd only acquiesced when Alustin reminded her that Talia's strange bone affinity might have unusual interactions with dragon bones, which possessed a number of magical properties, even beyond their freakish strength and lightness.

Despite the sheer amount of attention the partial skeleton got while being unloaded, it was Godrick's reward that most excited them. He'd requested an enchanted sledgehammer, to replace the more mundane one he'd lost during the coup attempt.

The enchanting process could often take months, but Indris had apparently moved the hammer to the top of the list for her enchanters.

After they hauled the crate away from the ship to an empty stone pier nearby, the four of them clustered around the hammer's crate as Godrick opened it. They'd been bugging him to tell them what kind of enchantment he'd requested ever since he met with the enchanters, but he'd refused every time.

"Alright, *now* are you going to tell us what it does?" Talia asked, irritably.

"Nope," Godrick said. He leaned out of the way of Talia's jabbing elbow and smiled. "Ah'm gonna show yeh."

Godrick cracked open the crate, revealing a sledgehammer even more massive than his last two. Intricate spellforms covered the blunt head of the hammer and raced down its wooden shaft. They weren't merely carved into the hammer— it was as though someone had worked copper wire deep into the very metal of the hammer during its forging, and as though tendrils of oak had grown through the yew of the thick handle, all in the precise shapes of spellforms.

Godrick picked up the hammer and took a few steps back from the others, making sure he had plenty of clear space around him. He balanced it in one hand for a moment, then swung it gently a few times to test its balance.

"Well?" the redhead demanded, crossing her arms over her chest. Godrick grinned at her, clearly enjoying her impatience.

Godrick limbered up for a moment, then reared back and slammed the hammer full force into the stone walkway in front of him. As it descended, Hugh could see the spellforms on it begin to glow slightly. The ground actually cracked with the force of the blow, and rock chips went flying.

And none of it made a sound. The impact was completely silent.

"What just…" Sabae began, but cut off abruptly. Hugh looked at her and realized that she was still moving her mouth, but nothing was coming out of it.

Hugh tried saying something, and he could feel his vocal cords vibrate, but no sound came out of his mouth. He clapped his hands, but it was perfectly silent as well.

He wasn't deaf— he could still hear sounds from the docks, the wind, and the sand drakes making nuisances of themselves among the riggings of ships— but Hugh and his friends were completely silent.

Godrick grinned, and then the faint glow of the hammer cut out. "Neat, huh? Ah had the idea after," he glanced around to make sure no-one was nearby, and lowered his voice, "all that sneaking around me and Talia had ta do in Indris' palace. Woulda made things a lot easier. It's also got ah secondary enchantment ta make it harder ta break."

"I would have expected you to request an enchantment to make it hit harder, maybe, or set itself on fire," Hugh said.

Godrick just gestured at the cracks in the ground. "Ah can already hit plenty hard, especially when ah put magic inta mah swings."

Hugh shrugged at that as Godrick crouched down and began resealing the cracks in the stone with his magic. Hugh couldn't help but think about Emmenson Drees, who he'd been guessing was a sound mage, unless his sound dampening abilities were just provided to him via his spellform tattoos.

One of the ship's crew came jogging up and handed a letter to Sabae. "Captain almost forgot to give you this letter, miss."

Sabae thanked him and opened the letter.

"Stealth is important to a warrior," Talia said. "When fire mages fight, the first one to spot the other is usually the survivor."

"What if they start the battle in plain sight of one another?" Hugh asked.

Talia shrugged. "They usually both die."

Hugh blinked at that, and Godrick seemed almost as taken aback.

"Ah can't imagine duels in your clan are very popular, then," Godrick said.

Talia smirked. "Not especially, no."

"Oh, crap," said Sabae. Her face had gone pale enough that the branching scars on her cheek had become almost invisible, and she clutched to the letter like she was afraid it would try to bite her.

"What's wrong?" Godrick asked.

Sabae took a moment to collect herself. "It's from my grandmother. She's, uh… she's coming to visit Skyhold."

"Why is that an 'oh crap' thing?" Talia asked. "Aren't you and your grandmother close?"

Sabae started pacing. "I mean, yes, but that's not the problem. The problem is that she never leaves Ras Andis. She's needed there. It's storm season, for storm's sake! The coast will start getting hit by hurricanes any week now. On top of that, this would be the equivalent of Indris deciding to randomly pay a social visit to Skyhold. It's just not done!"

"Save with a' load a' pomp and ceremony," Godrick agreed, looking slightly taken aback.

"Though I suppose the rest of the family could probably handle the storms just fine, my oldest aunt is probably going to head the family after grandmother passes, but it's still the first time she's left Ras Andis since…"

Hugh was fairly sure Sabae was going to pass out if she didn't stop to breathe soon.

"And considering how tense the trade war with Yldive has gotten, I don't know…"

Talia growled, stomped over to Sabae, reached up to grab the taller girl's shoulders, and started shaking her. "Calm down before you work yourself into a lather! I've seen chased rabbits more relaxed than you."

"Deep breaths might help," Hugh offered. He found offering Sabae's own frequent advice back to her slightly amusing, though he was mostly just concerned at the moment.

Sabae took a moment, then seemed to get a little control over herself. "Sorry about that," she said eventually. "You can let go of me now."

Talia didn't let go of her. "What are you really stressed about, Sabae?"

Sabae didn't say anything for a moment, just gently pulled Talia's hands off her shoulders. "I…"

Sabae drifted off. After a few moments, Talia cleared her throat, and the taller girl's attention returned to them.

"The only reason that I can think of that grandmother might be visiting is if she's finally arranged a marriage for me," Sabae said in a rush.

Before anyone could say anything, Sabae took a few steps back from Talia and spun up her wind armor around her legs. "I have some homework I need to do," she said, then windjumped away from them towards Skyhold.

Talia stumbled backward in the blast of wind, and quite a few sailors and dockworkers stopped working to stare at Sabae hurtling through the air.

No one said anything for a moment, then Godrick sighed. "This year just keeps getting more an' more interestin', don't it?"

"Is interesting really the word you're going to go with?" Hugh said, not taking his eyes off Sabae's retreating figure, which had just landed in the sand off the docks, before blasting off towards the nearest entrance into the mountain. "Because I'd probably pick something stronger."

CHAPTER SEVEN

Silence and Sand

They didn't see Sabae again until dinnertime at their usual cafeteria, where she refused to talk about what she'd said, beyond insisting that everything was fine.

According to Alustin, Sabae's grandmother had let Kanderon know she was coming in the spring.

And she'd left all the arrangements to Kanderon, who was less than amused. Which in turn had Hugh less than thrilled for his first lesson of the year with Kanderon the next day.

Firstday started off well enough, though Sabae was still determinedly avoiding speaking of her grandmother. Hugh, used to Sabae being the most confident and collected member of the group, was somewhat at a loss as to how he could help.

Classes were less of a challenge, at least. He had Emmenson Drees' spellform crafting lecture that afternoon before meeting with Kanderon. He'd expected Wardcrafting to be his favorite class, but he received far too much attention from the other students in there for his liking.

Emmenson started off the class by reading the few written questions he found worthwhile. Well, after completely dampening sounds other than his voice in the room. Hugh's questions, slightly to his surprise, were among them.

"When you told us not to test new spellforms, were you counting wards?" Emmenson read. "And…" Emmenson stopped reading from the paper. "I'll answer the other question after class, it's of rather specialized interest. Fascinating, but hardly germane to the rest of the class. Wards, though— now that's a worthwhile question. My prohibition on unapproved spellform testing applies neither to wards nor enchanting. Does anyone know why?"

Several students shook their heads silently.

Emmenson grinned. "You're learning quickly. It usually takes classes at least a couple of weeks before they stop trying to answer me. Wards and enchantments, though— the simple answer is that I'm not qualified to teach you about them, so I'm not going to try."

Hugh could see the journeyman with the long, twitching hair roll her eyes.

"There is, however, a more in-depth answer," Emmenson said.

Hugh, anticipating a lecture, opened his spellbook and placed his finger against the page.

"All spellforms— for spells, glyphs, wards, and enchantments alike— fundamentally serve the same purpose of guiding mana in specific patterns that generate effects. Each does it in an entirely different frame of reference, however. Spells operate in reference to the self, wards operate in reference to a spatial location, and enchantments operate in reference to the properties of the material they're worked into. This radically alters the behaviors of the patterns of each major spellform type during construction."

Emmenson began pacing. "While none of the three major types of spellform are what any sane person would call safe to tinker with, wards tend to be the safest of the three to alter, and basic ward construction and alteration ends up being taught even, to a small degree, to first years. Most mages never advance past there, though some students," Emmenson glanced at Hugh, "advance far beyond that level. It grows much more dangerous with more advanced wards, and wards that are left unattended for long periods of time tend to decay, often becoming significant hazards. There are quite a few mages who make their livings entirely by cleaning up the mistakes of other wardcrafters as well as old decaying wards."

"Spells are the next most dangerous type of spellform to tinker with. There's a very, very simple reason for this— because they're referencing the self. If you're crafting a projectile spell of some sort— and no reason why you should, we have countless effective variants already, crafting more is merely a vanity project— and you mess up the targeting lines of the spellform, well, it's quite likely that the projectile aims towards you instead of away from you. Or the spell just collapses and dumps all of its energy back in your body."

Hugh shuddered a little at that image.

"Enchantments are by far the most dangerous of the three, for the simple reason that they are the most likely to fail. Missing a simple flaw in the metal you're constructing your enchantment out of, for instance, can disrupt the flow of mana through the spellform. Only the most patient, cautious, and perfectionist of mages make successful enchanters. The rest tend to blow themselves up very quickly."

Emmenson gave the class a wry look. "Though you'll seldom find me giving you any sort of credit, I'll give you the benefit of the doubt in assuming that you won't be attempting wardcrafting or enchanting without knowing what you're doing. Or, if you do, it'll be the responsibility of your teachers in those topics, not mine."

Emmenson tapped on the chalkboard, and a ripple spread out from the point of impact, cleaning all the chalk dust off from the board as it spread. Emmenson took out a piece of chalk and began to draw. "Some of the more perspicacious of you might have noticed that I mentioned glyphs along with the three main types of spellforms. Glyphs are commonly treated as a tool for inferior mages— simple guides to channel mana into for those who can't handle memorizing spells."

A complex spellform was taking shape on the blackboard. "While this is often true, this is hardly always true. Quite a few highly effective battlemages make extensive use of glyphs."

Hugh couldn't help but think of Alustin there.

"For our purposes, glyphs are interesting thanks to their relative safety to tinker with. They generally operate around the same as spells, but instead of referring to the self, they define the self as the material they're drawn on. A glyph failure is significantly safer than a spell failure— it can still be highly destructive, but you can remotely activate many glyphs from behind cover. There are a few important differences in their construction when compared to spells, however, which include…"

As the rest of the class filed out, Hugh waited to speak to Emmenson Drees. As they did so, Hugh flexed his sore finger— he hadn't missed recording any of the lecture. His spellbook's new ability let him write far faster than he'd ever been able to with a quill.

Once the rest of the students exited, Emmenson pulled out Hugh's questions again. He glanced at them briefly, and turned to Hugh. "Alustin already apprised me of your situation in regards to overflooding your spellforms, and he showed me some of the spellforms you've been using to compensate for that. Your work is… rough, but passable. You approach your spellform designs cautiously, which is good. You're quite welcome to continue tinkering with cantrips, it should be safe enough for you at your skill level. My prohibition remains, however, for actual affinity-based spells. They're generally built to handle a lot more power than cantrips, so you should encounter fewer of them that need reworking. If you do, however, bring your corrected spellform designs to me before testing them."

Emmenson started walking towards the door. "I trust that answers your question sufficiently." He snapped his fingers, and sound came back just in time for Hugh to hear the door shutting.

Kanderon was still fuming about Sabae's grandmother when Hugh met with her out in the Erg. Without much preamble, she began testing Hugh in the way she had again and again this summer— by growing crystals below the dunes outside Skyhold, then launching them upwards at Hugh. He had to sense them while they were still forming, then either dodge, block, or divert them.

Hugh was a little rusty at it, but it hadn't been that many weeks since he'd done it last, and Kanderon was fairly distracted herself, so she only managed to hit him once with a glancing blow to the shoulder.

Eventually, Kanderon decided it was enough, and ceased launching quartz chunks at him. He happily stopped to catch his breath, laying down in the cool sand on the shaded part of the dune.

"I've put it off long enough, Hugh. Time to take a look at the form your aether crystal has taken," Kanderon said.

Kanderon loomed over the small dune. The sphinx was a solid seventy-five feet from her nose to the base of her tail, and her massive crystal wings extended far to either side of her. The blue crystals of her wings weren't all contiguous— many of them floated in formation with the wings, as though held there by an invisible framework.

The wings were Kanderon's own bonded aether crystals, and her eyes matched their color— just as Hugh's eyes now matched his spellbook.

Hugh snagged the book from where it lay on the sand and carried it over towards her. The book seemed hesitant to approach the sphinx, and tried to pull away, but Hugh grasped it firmly by the spine and hauled it over.

"Has it exhibited any abilities so far?" Kanderon asked.

Hugh nodded and began telling her about everything it had done so far. When he'd finished, Kanderon frowned.

"Aether crystals shouldn't have personalities," she said. **"That, I think, can entirely be attributed to your labyrinth stone."**

She poked the orange-red stone embedded in the spellbook's front cover with her massive claw, a surprisingly delicate action. Hugh could feel the spellbook's indignation.

"If I thought I could remove it without damaging the crystal and likely you, I would, but that's out of the question now. And the abilities it has presented so far are useful, but hardly of the level you'd expect from a fully bonded aether crystal."

The spellbook felt even more irritated for a moment, then spat a wad of chewed up paper at Kanderon. Hugh tensed, expecting her to get angry, but she just seemed interested instead. It probably helped that the book didn't have saliva, so it was just a wad of dry shredded paper.

"Where is it storing the paper?" Kanderon said, and pried the book open. It struggled for a moment, but settled down when the sphinx glared at it.

Kanderon stared at it for a while, muttering to herself, then plunged a claw into the crystal spellbook. Hugh started, at first thinking that she was damaging it, but then realized that the claw seemed to disappear into space just inches above the book.

"Fascinating," Kanderon said, probing deeper. **"I had thought that the traces of stellar and planar mana I smelled on the book were merely from it draining those reservoirs to power its form-taking, but it appears that it actually fashioned itself some sort of internal pseudoplane. It's not a proper plane— it's fractured and twisting, and it only seems to want to accept written records, of all things, but it's definitely there."**

Kanderon glanced up at Hugh. **"It actually reminds me of a labyrinth, structurally. It seems to be a fairly safe bet that the stone crafted this space when it was attaching itself to the aether crystal. I had wanted you to avoid attuning the crystal anytime soon, because ideally you could have done so with a spell that tapped into all three of our affinities, but the stone at least prevented the**

planar affinity from being wasted. The stellar affinity, unfortunately, did go to waste, other than as raw power."

Hugh stared at her blankly.

Kanderon sighed and pulled her claw out of the book. **"You can magically store books, paper, and such in there, if you can get it to swallow them without chewing. And if you can get it to spit them back up. It's basically a portable library. On top of that, you should be able to write an almost unlimited amount in the book's crystal pages without running out of room. You've got your own personal library."**

Hugh smiled. He rather liked the sound of that.

"I'd be a little shocked if it didn't manifest other abilities. The internal pattern of an attuned aether crystal is extremely complex, and continues to slowly change for quite a long time. Though, there is one aspect of it you don't seem to have grasped yet. Do you remember how heavy your aether crystal was before you mastered the proprioceptive link?"

Hugh nodded.

"All that weight is still there, and the book is continuing to grow in density. The book, like my… the book is growing outwards into its little pseudoplane. It will continue to grow heavier and denser over time, though your link to it will let you carry it without noticing most of the time. It already weighs at least a third of what you do. By the time you've finished your apprenticeship, it will likely weigh what you do now. On top of that, it's unusually sturdy, even for an aether crystal— attuning it to construct a ward seems to have considerably reinforced its pattern."

"Meaning?…" Hugh asked.

"If you're somehow able to train the pesky thing, it should be able to guard you in battle, and cause quite a

bit of trouble. And even if something does damage it, it should be able to heal itself over time."

Hugh smiled widely.

"I thought you might enjoy that," Kanderon said. She removed her paw from the book, which immediately shot away from her and buried itself in the sand behind Hugh. She gave it another irritated look as it did so. **"I can still try and figure out a way to deal with that personality problem it has, if you'd like."**

Hugh shook his head. "It's growing on me, I think."

Kanderon snorted, swishing her tail through the air. **"Very well. We've got a lot more work to do, Hugh. I want to start you on pattern linking crystals other than quartz today."**

She wasn't exactly telling the truth. 'A lot more work' made it sound far easier than it ended up being. 'Bruising and exhausting labor' might have been a better choice of words.

CHAPTER EIGHT

Fatigue

By Fourthday on the second week of classes, Talia felt ready to explode. Either that, or sleep for a week.

Classes had hardly been easy last year, but two weeks into classes this year and she was already feeling overwhelmed, and her friends weren't doing much better.

If Talia's lessons were more interesting, it might have been going better, but they were far from it. She'd been excited when Alustin told her he'd arranged for a fire mage to tutor her, but finding that said fire mage was a street entertainer dampened her enthusiasm considerably.

She'd had a little success creating an illusion of fire using her dream affinity last year, but only a little bit. The fire tended to take on the fragmentary shapes of monsters, creatures, and buildings, and it just looked terrible in general.

Trying to craft illusions of anything else just failed entirely. So, Alustin's brilliant idea had been for Talia to try to use her malfunctioning dream affinity to mimic a flame affinity crafting the moving puppets and sculptures of a flame mage.

It was going miserably. Flame-based puppetry was crude at the best of times, and relied as much on the narration and acting abilities of the mage as anything else. There really weren't many ways to make a crudely fashioned six-inch-tall puppet made entirely of fire look much like any specific person.

Her tutor spent as much time instructing her on how to act out scenes as on helping her figure out increasingly convoluted methods for making dream-based illusions of flame resemble flame-based puppets.

Still, that was going better than her tutorship under her dream mentor, who was the most infuriating woman she'd ever met. The woman seemed convinced that Talia's failures were entirely in her head, not deriving from her tattoos, and that she could overcome them by sheer force of will or something.

The two of them having to go to the hospital wing to get burns treated after she tried to make Talia go through a standard dream training exercise had somewhat cured her of that, at least.

Talia had to admit that the woman actually knew what she was talking about when it came to dreamfire. They'd started working together on the more traditional uses of dreamfire— that of disrupting nightmares. Talia had thought it a frivolous use of the skill, but it was apparently often used to help warriors who had seen too much battle.

There were more than a few warriors who experienced that in Clan Castis. Some could spend years going on raid after raid and never suffer even the smallest loss of sleep, but that life could break something in others. The elders frequently stopped warriors and mages from the clan from going on too many raids in a row, and kept a close eye on them when they returned.

Her bone affinity studies were considerably less infuriating. They largely consisted of just causing countless explosions with different combinations of animal bones, levels of mana, rates of infusion, and any other variables Talia and Alustin could think of.

The test chamber had a built-in blast shield that hardly obscured her view at all, so she was having quite a lot of fun there.

And, it turned out, her abilities interacted in a very interesting way with dragon bone.

It wasn't any of these classes, or even combat training, however, which really bothered her the most.

Talia quite enjoyed combat training, in fact. Especially watching Hugh try to learn unarmed combat, something that he very much wasn't a natural at.

No, it was cryptography that was the worst.

It was taking up more time to do her cryptography homework than the rest of her homework combined. With math, at least, she could turn to Godrick to help her through it, but this was new material to all of them. The others seemed to be handling it well enough, but Talia was getting headaches almost daily from it.

She wasn't meant for subtlety; she was meant for battle.

Talia could handle all the extra classwork if not for everything else.

Sabae was off in her own head sulking and refusing to talk about things, which was ridiculous and counterproductive. Of course, Talia had to acknowledge— to herself, at least— that she'd refused to talk about problems before out of pride, so she couldn't blame Sabae too much for being ridiculous.

Hugh was being more talkative than usual, but the longer he was away from Avah, the more he talked about the Radhan girl. Talia didn't dislike Avah, but she had better things to do than talk about her. Or talk to her. There was only so much talk of imports and exports and trade patterns you could listen to.

Godrick, at least, was being his usual solid, dependable self.

Alustin was, of course, the biggest source of her problems right now. When wasn't he? She was grateful, even loyal, to him for making her into a worthwhile mage, but that hardly meant he couldn't be a pain.

Like now, for instance.

"Why aren't we just using fire for this?" Talia demanded through the handkerchief tied over her face.

Alustin sighed through his own. "Fire would hardly help us preserve the books, would it?"

Talia growled, then turned back to sprinkling foul-smelling powders on the books in front of her. Hunting the rogue pack of books last week had at least been interesting. This week, Alustin had taken them into the Grand Library simply to clean up an infestation of some sort of magical mold. Which, of course, smelled vile, and required even viler-smelling powders to clean.

Hugh yawned through his own handkerchief. There was a lump tied into it near his nose— a little enchanted glass sphere that absorbed odors, which had been a gift from Godrick.

Talia elbowed him in the side. To keep him awake, certainly not for any other reason. Certainly not because Hugh was suffering less than any of the others. Well, except for Godrick, who had a scent affinity, but that was fairer.

Hugh glared at her. "What was that for? I swear, your elbows are so sharp you don't need to carry daggers with you."

Talia snorted. "If I were a proper bone mage that might actually be true. I've been reading about them lately, and some bone mages grow their bones into spines and blades that protrude from their bodies. Elbow spikes are one of the most popular."

Hugh gave her a slightly queasy look.

Sabae snorted. "Can you imagine Talia as a dressmaker? The dress would weigh as much as a suit of armor from all the daggers and other weapons she'd hide in it."

"More weapons isn't always better," Talia said. "You're liable to trip yourself up. I heard of one fellow who tried to go into battle with three swords, an axe, several daggers, and a crossbow all strapped to him. He ended up…"

"You're missing the point of what Sabae said, ah think," Godrick said.

"Careful weapon choice is important!" Talia protested.

"You're going to get invited to a ball some day and bring a spiked flail," Sabae said.

"A flail would be a terrible choice of weapon for a ball," Talia said. "Dancing would set it to swinging all over the place, and it'd probably hit another dancer, which would be rude. You should only strike someone with a weapon when you intend to."

"Still missing the point," Sabae said. "Also, I think that striking anyone with a weapon at any point is rude."

That didn't sound quite right to Talia.

"Well, what would be a good choice of weapon to bring to a ball?" Hugh asked.

"That depends on a lot of different things, ranging from your age to the occasion," Talia said.

Sabae sighed. "I can't believe I'm going along with this, but what kind of weapon should a girl like you bring to a ball?"

"I'm not a girl, I'm a woman," Talia said.

Sabae gave her a dirty look over her handkerchief. "You're sixteen, unless you're using a really pastoral definition of when you become a woman."

"Remember that pirate ship I blew up this summer?" Talia asked. "Is that the action of a girl?"

"Are you using violence as the qualifier for being an adult?" Sabae asked.

"No, anyone can commit violence," Talia said. "I'm talking about blowing up a pirate ship here. Much more impressive."

Sabae raised her eyebrows. "You're saying that blowing up a pirate ship makes you a woman."

"Honestly," Alustin said, "it makes about as much sense as half the definitions of adulthood I've encountered."

Sabae glared at him. "Guess I need to go blow up a pirate ship," she muttered. "Then maybe I'd feel more prepared for…"

She cut off abruptly, and focused back on the mold, several tendrils of which were weakly trying to grab her hands.

Hugh gave Sabae an awkward look, then turned back to Talia. "You didn't answer the question, though. What weapons would you bring to a ball?"

Talia thought about it for a moment. There were a lot of tempting choices.

"I think…" she said. "I think it would have to depend on my dress. You wouldn't want them to clash."

Godrick and Hugh chuckled at that, and even Sabae gave an exasperated groan, but Talia would wager good coin that she was smiling under the handkerchief.

Talia didn't care about anyone claiming she was "too serious" or "terrifyingly bloody-minded", she could be funny when she felt like it. More importantly, the others seem to have perked up a little bit. Hugh hadn't mentioned Avah in at least ten minutes, and Sabae's shoulders seem to have relaxed a little bit.

Talia did have to admit that the topic was a little bit ridiculous, of course. It would be absurd to match your weapon to your dress.

It made so much more sense to match your dress to your weapon.

"So," Alustin said, holding three dense, almost book-thick folders in his hands. They were in another reading area in the Grand Library, this one on one of the floating islands in the center. Talia wasn't especially fond of being this exposed, but she did like the line of sight it provided her. "There were five council members attending the vote on your end of year test. Three of them voted against allowing you all to take it in a different labyrinth. Kanderon was there, of course. Anders vel Seraf, the Dean of Students, was the other who voted to allow the alternate test."

Talia had never heard of vel Seraf before, but Alustin continued before she could ask.

Alustin dropped the first folder on the table. "Headmaster Tarik voted against the alternate test."

Talia raised her eyebrows at that one. The grey-haired woman was one of the most powerful stone mages alive, and she had quite the reputation among the mountain clans. She'd singlehandedly built an entire castle in a week during one of the Havath Dominion's numerous wars of expansion, and had crushed countless clan raiding parties under avalanches while she helped defend the northern borders of Highvale.

If she was working with Bakori, they were all in trouble. Well, they were in trouble regardless of who was working with Bakori, but they'd be in more trouble.

Alustin dropped the second folder on the table. "Abyla Ceutas, the Chair of Admissions, voted against the alternate test."

Sabae's brow narrowed at that, but she didn't say anything.

Alustin dropped the final folder on the table. "Rutliss the Red, Skyhold's Bursar, voted against the alternate test."

Talia hadn't heard of Rutliss either.

No one said anything or went for the folders for a moment. All the talk of there being a traitor on the council hadn't seemed real until now, when they were actually being presented with suspects.

"You're missing a folder," Sabae said.

Alustin cocked an eyebrow at her.

"Anders vel Seraf," Sabae said.

"But he voted to allow the alternate test," Hugh said, pulling his spellbook away from Abyla's folder before it could start chewing on it.

Talia rather liked Hugh's new spellbook. It kept him on his toes.

"We don't actually know what Bakori's endgame is here. It seems probable that he's after Hugh, for revenge or whatever reason, but we can't assume that guarantees our suspect is among the three that voted against the alternative test," Sabae said. "The only safe assumption we can make is that it's not Kanderon working with Bakori— because if it is, we've already lost."

"She's right," Talia agreed. "In stories, the traitor's never one of the main suspects— it's always someone you overlook, because it's obviously not them, or it's so obviously one of this other group. In fact, maybe we should be looking at Kanderon, just because it seems so unlikely it would be her."

Sabae sighed, but just kept staring at Alustin. The paper mage returned her gaze for a long pause and then smiled. His arm tattoo lit up, and he pulled another folder from midair.

"Well spotted," he said. "I genuinely don't think it is Anders, both out of personal and professional inclination, but it would be foolish to ignore him."

He dropped the folder on the table. "We don't have a reliable way to test them directly for Bakori's influence, so we're going to have to try and find a paper trail. Someone's been leaking information about the inner workings of Skyhold for some time, and until now we haven't had a way to figure out who. There's thirteen members of the council at large, and most of the known leaked information could have come from any number of them. Hugh's contract with Kanderon was the first one that we could narrow down to a specific sub-council. It seems probable that the leak would be the one working with Bakori."

"Why?" Talia asked. "There might just be two traitors. Happens all the time in novels. Wouldn't it make more sense for Bakori to try and hide the fact he'd subverted a council member than to leak information?"

"I'll have to take your word for it, Talia," Alustin said. "I'm not a particularly well-read devotee of novels. I prefer non-fiction. In real life, it's rare to find multiple leaks in one organization when it's well run. Not unheard of, but rare. A poorly run organization will often have more leaks than hull, if you'll permit me to extend the metaphor, but Skyhold is assuredly not poorly run."

Alustin leaned forward. "In this case, however, it seems likely that rather than trying to cause leaks, Bakori chose a pre-existing leak to work with. Someone who was already willing to sell Skyhold's secrets would be much less likely to resist being gently pushed against Skyhold's interests."

"Take your time, and read through everything we've assembled on each of the suspects. We'll try and arrange opportunities for you to meet each of the council members as well. If it takes a little of the pressure off, this doesn't all rest on your shoulders— we have others looking as well. Each set of trustworthy eyes on the matter increases our chances of flushing out our prey," Alustin said, leaning back in his chair. "After you've spent a little time familiarizing yourselves with the contents, I'll take these to Hugh's room for you. It's the only reasonably secure, well-hidden location available and convenient for your purposes. Do not remove them, and do not let anyone else stumble across them."

No one spoke for a time as they perused the folders. Sabae, despite her interest in Anders vel Seraf, ended up taking Abyla Ceutas' folder, so Talia snagged Anders for herself. Godrick took Headmaster Tarik's folder— which was appropriate to Talia's mind, given that they were both stone mages. Hugh was left with Rutliss the Red's folder.

After about an hour of reading, Alustin called a halt and retrieved the folders. Before they left, he repeated all of his warnings again. Along with one other thing.

"I'll be leaving tomorrow on a mission. I know this is short notice, but I've made all the necessary arrangements you'll need to get by in the meantime."

"When will yeh be back?" Godrick asked.

"I wish I knew," Alustin said. "It could be a couple of weeks, or it could be much longer. Or I might not come back. Being a Librarian Errant is hardly a safe career choice."

Talia wanted to believe that he'd be back just fine, but she'd seen too many warriors of her clan fail to return from raids to delude herself. There was always a chance a warrior wouldn't come back. Skill at arms, cunning with magic, and even courage weren't always enough. Sometimes luck was just against you.

What really worried Talia wasn't Alustin's chances, however. For all the trouble he brought them, for all the risky situations he pushed them into, Talia couldn't help but feel that they were still much safer with him around.

CHAPTER NINE

An Unpleasant Surprise

Hugh carefully peeked around the corner. It had been a couple of weeks since Alustin had left, and things had been going fine at first.

At first.

The fact that there was a traitor in Skyhold working for Bakori had seemed to be a lot more manageable with Alustin here. He'd tried talking to Kanderon about it during one of his lessons, but as capable and intelligent as the sphinx was, she was far from being particularly comforting.

The overwhelming class-loads the four of them were facing weren't helping things much either.

They probably could have handled all of that a little better if Sabae was on her game— she usually did a great job of keeping the others focused and preventing them from being idiots. Sabae, unfortunately, was spending most of her time clearly stressing about the thing with her grandmother and refusing to talk to the rest of them about it.

To Hugh's great surprise, though, his biggest day-to-day bother had been his wardcrafting class. That student from Theras Tel had, apparently, been telling everyone else from the class all about Hugh's exploits over the summer, and now every time he showed up to class, unless there were attention wards hiding them from one another, he got beleaguered with questions about the storm ward he'd constructed around Theras Tel.

Or he got called Stormward, a title which he had decidedly mixed feelings about. Not that he particularly enjoyed being called Hugh of Emblin, of course, but it at least wasn't so grandiose as being called Stormward.

Plus, the Theran student seemed to be giving them a completely inaccurate image of what he'd done. He certainly hadn't battled one of Ataerg's dragons. Alustin might have pulled it off, but Hugh and the others were nowhere near being able to handle a dragon, even a young one.

Well, maybe Talia could, but she hadn't. Hugh thought she was actually a little irritated at that, because she tended to change the subject quickly when he brought up his complaints about him supposedly being a dragonslayer.

If their classes had been more typical lectures, he could have just slipped into the back and ignored everyone, but the instructor, Loarna of the Vault, still hadn't shown up to a single class. Each class was a series of escalating challenges involving wards— students had to pass, solve, and break countless different wards in order to turn in their homework, get their new assignments, and get the location of the next class.

Of course, if you failed, you still got the location of the next class delivered to you, but that, everyone was sure, counted against your grade fairly highly.

Hugh was sure that, if things were different, he would love this class. It was stretching his problem-solving abilities, his creativity, and even the way he thought about wards.

Unfortunately, the class also left considerable time for students to talk to one another. It seemed that group work was encouraged, save for a small portion of classes featuring attention wards.

So, Hugh often found himself lurking around corners to try and avoid the gossiping crowd.

It hadn't actually even been this bad in Theras Tel itself— he'd easily been able to lose himself in the crowd, so long as he didn't bring his spellbook with him. Which had been much easier at the time, as it had only just started waking up.

The book in question shifted contentedly. It had managed to get into a crate of old student papers meant for disposal, and had gorged itself on them until it could barely move. Hugh shook his head, and turned his attention back to the classroom.

This class, unfortunately, Hugh couldn't tell whether there were attention wards or not. He'd found a somewhat out of the way side hall to watch other students enter the hallway outside the classroom, but each time they did so, they vanished from sight. It didn't look like an attention ward, though— they were actually disappearing in a flash of light, not simply becoming impossible to consciously pay attention to.

Footsteps started echoing down the hall behind him. Hugh sighed, and prepared to head towards the class location rather than engage in another awkward conversation with one of his classmates.

"Hugh!"

Hugh tensed, and his stomach rose up into his throat. He knew that voice.

It was Rhodes.

Not even looking back, he darted into the wards shielding the classroom. He was momentarily blinded by the flash of light.

"Stormward!" a different voice called. Someone not Rhodes.

Hugh rubbed his eyes, and found himself in a quite average seeming classroom, save for the fact that there was only darkness behind him in the doorway. He ignored the other students for a moment, poking the darkness.

It felt slick as glass, and didn't yield in the slightest.

"We think we're supposed to try and figure out a way to escape the room," one of the other students called. "Any ideas?"

Hugh backed up into the crowd, his heart hammering in his chest. He could hear others talking to him, but he didn't pay attention.

His heart gradually slowed its pounding as the doorway stayed empty. No one passed through it, and he gradually let himself become convinced that Rhodes wasn't coming in. He'd never seen anyone outside the class in one of their testing areas before, so it wouldn't surprise him if Loarna had warded them out somehow.

Hugh sighed, then turned his attention back to his classmates and the challenge ahead of them.

"We should teach him a lesson," Talia said, panting.

"A lesson?" Hugh asked, just as out of breath.

"A very pointed one," Talia said, miming stabbing someone.

"Yeh ain't murderin' another student when yer under mah supervision," Artur said, jogging alongside the apprentices. He wasn't out of breath in the least, despite being decades older than them.

"Ah feel like murderin' Rhodes might just piss off his uncle," Godrick said. "And, yeh know, his uncle is still the king of Highvale and all that."

"We don't have to murder him all the way," Talia said. "Just, you know, enough to teach him a lesson."

Hugh sighed. Fantasizing about taking revenge on Rhodes for all the bullying he'd suffered at his hands did feel a little good, but for the most part, Hugh would be happiest just never seeing Rhodes again. They might attend the same school, but given that there were thousands of students, and that the school was a sprawling complex carved into a mountain, Hugh was quite happy giving avoiding Rhodes forever a good try.

Honestly, he'd be happy not even talking about Rhodes, but his friends had just kept coming back to it ever since he'd told them about the encounter the night before at dinner.

Rhodes had been gone by the time the class escaped the classroom, but Hugh had still been extremely nervous leaving— enough that he actually put up with the company of some of his classmates for part of his walk back towards the library.

His spellbook, from where it lay across the room, sent Hugh an image of it chewing on Rhodes' head. Hugh smiled a little at the thought. For all the trouble the book got into, it seemed quite fond of him, at least.

Sabae opened her mouth to respond to one of Talia's plans regarding Rhodes, then shut it again, an unhappy look going across her face.

"Sabae, what's?..." Hugh began, but Sabae just shook her head and sped up.

When they finished running laps around the stone training chamber, Hugh finally confronted Sabae. She'd looked more and more upset through the entire run, and Hugh was tired of Sabae sulking and refusing to talk to them about her emotions over the past few weeks.

"Everything's fine," Sabae said when he asked, cleaning off sweat with a cantrip.

"You spent half the run looking like you thought you were about to die," Hugh said.

"I'm fine, Hugh, don't worry about it," she said, glancing over towards the others for an escape. Godrick and Talia were a ways off talking with Artur, however.

"How am I supposed to not worry about it?" Hugh asked, glaring up at Sabae. She wasn't that much taller than him, but she could still look over his head without craning much. "You're my friend, me just not worrying about it really isn't an option."

Sabae sighed. "I appreciate it, Hugh, but I can handle my problems on my own."

"You're always telling me that talking about my worries will help," Hugh said, "and you're just about always right. More often than not, I'm just building up a situation in my head to ridiculous levels, and talking about it to someone helps show me that."

"Are you saying I'm just imagining my problems?" Sabae asked, looking irritated.

Hugh started to panic for a moment, thinking Sabae was angry at him, then frowned.

"You're doing that on purpose, aren't you?" he said. "Trying to put me on the back foot so you can escape the question."

Sabae opened her mouth to say something, but Hugh just plowed forward.

"You can't just expect me to share all of my fears and worries with all of you, but then just refuse to open yourself up to the rest of us. That's not alright, Sabae."

Sabae closed her mouth in surprise.

"I'm not saying you can't have secrets, or that you have to share absolutely everything with us, but you also can't just leave us to worry about you and not let us help," Hugh said.

"You really don't need to worry about me," Sabae protested weakly.

"Yes, we do," Hugh said. "You literally ran away when you received the letter from your grandmother, and you've been distracted and upset ever since. You've been talking about half as much as usual, and a good chunk of that is just snapping at people. You're definitely not fine, Sabae, and I'm worried. We all are."

Sabae opened and shut her mouth in surprise, vainly trying to find something to say. She eventually appeared to gather her thoughts and gave Hugh a weak smile.

"I've got to be honest, Hugh, you're really the last one I expected a speech like that from."

Hugh shrugged and rubbed the back of his head, suddenly uncomfortable. "It's easier to stand up for someone else than for myself, I guess. Even if the person I'm standing up for is also the person I'm standing up to."

Sabae's smile grew a little more genuine at that. "I know the feeling."

She walked over to the wall, then leaned against it and slid down. Hugh took a seat next to her.

"You're right," Sabae finally said. "I can't stop worrying about my grandmother's visit. She didn't mention arranged marriages at all in the letter, but I just really can't think what else could be driving her to travel that far away from Ras Andis. She never leaves."

Hugh didn't say anything, just waited for Sabae to continue. Of course, standing up to Sabae had been emotionally exhausting, so he was quite happy not saying anything for the moment.

"I just can't stop thinking about my own parents," Sabae finally continued. "My mom fled the family entirely rather than go through with her own arranged marriage. We marry to maintain our lineage as storm mages, but my mother chose a healer, instead, and look what it did to me. It turned me into a failure as a Kaen Das."

"You're not a failure," Hugh interrupted. "You're turning into a great mage!"

Sabae shook her head. "Maybe, but not a great member of the Kaen Das family. We're storm mages, and the heart of being a storm mage is working over great distances."

Sabae spun up a weak bit of storm armor around her wrist, staring at it bitterly. "I can only extend my magic a few inches from my body, other than the odd uncontrolled burst of wind. I'll never be a storm mage of any sort. I am, no matter what my other skills, a failure as a Kaen Das."

She let the bit of wind armor disperse harmlessly. "It broke my mother, you know. She was proud of her rebellion against the family. She never hated them, but she always felt that she did the right thing. She was always too fiercely independent to have ever tolerated living her life obedient to the needs of the family. Then father died, and we came crawling back to the family. If…"

Sabae was silent for a while, breathing a little irregularly.

"If I hadn't been a failure as a Kaen Das, or father hadn't died, or if she hadn't brought us back into the family fold, maybe things would have been different. Maybe she wouldn't have left. But it broke something in her when it turned out that her marriage, her rebellion, had ruined me as a Kaen Das. Her pride, maybe?"

Hugh felt like he should say something, but he made himself stay quiet.

"She could hardly look at me after that. She'd already been spending more and more time aboard seaborne merchant fleets, protecting them from storms, pirates, and monsters. When my… failings became clear, she barely spent more time than she had to ashore. I don't think she hates me, I think she hates herself, and I'm just a reminder of that. It still hurts, though."

Hugh reached out and squeezed her hand gently.

"When I was growing up, she always told me to marry for love, not for duty. After father died, and we moved back into the family compound, she told me that less often, but she didn't stop entirely. When I came into my magic early, though, and it turned out I couldn't be a storm mage… she stopped telling me that entirely. I actually started blaming her for my trouble— if she had married as she was supposed to, I never would have had these problems."

Sabae chuckled bitterly. "That didn't help our relationship any. I started telling myself that I would marry whoever grandmother chose for me without complaint. It's why I haven't dated until now, why I've avoided any romantic entanglements. Every time one of you comes to me for advice, I feel like a fraud giving it, because you've all had more romantic experience than me."

Hugh smiled at her. "You wouldn't know it from your advice, which, if you ask me, is all pretty great."

Sabae managed a weak grin in return. "That means a lot to hear, but it still felt a little ridiculous. I thought I genuinely was doing the right thing, though, until I got the letter from my grandmother. At the thought of an arranged marriage happening, something in me just... revolted. I guess I'm more my mother's daughter than I thought. But I'm not willing to just run away like she did. I still want to serve the needs of my family, and we lost too many in the Blue Plague for the family to be able to afford to lose me too."

Hugh leaned over and gave her a hug. "Whatever you do, you know we all have your back, right? If you end up needing to turn away from your family like your mother did, well... just remember that as far as I'm concerned, we're your family too, and we're definitely not planning any arranged marriages for you."

"Thank you," Sabae said, squeezing him hard. "That really means a lot to hear. And I think of you all as family too. And... thank you for listening, even if it wasn't very fun to talk about."

"You still have to tell the others all this," Hugh said as he pulled back from the hug.

"Couldn't you do it for me?" Sabae asked.

"Not a chance," Hugh said. "Think of it as your punishment for making us worry about you."

"Ugh, you're the worst," Sabae said with a smile. "It is a relief to hear that you're not arranging any marriages for me, though," Sabae said. "I'd dread the thought of who Talia might find for me."

They both laughed a little at that. Hugh looked over to see Talia lecturing Godrick and Artur about something. Each of them was around three times her size, but both somehow managed to look like children being chastised.

When he pointed that out to Sabae, they laughed quite a bit more.

"By the way," Hugh asked, still chuckling a little. "What was bothering you so much while we were running?"

Sabae looked a little embarrassed. "You were all talking about Rhodes, and then I had the thought that maybe my grandmother was trying to arrange a marriage for me with him to tie Ras Andis closer to Highvale. It's not impossible."

Hugh blinked. That was a truly awful thought. "Well, if that ends up being the case, I think we might need to have Talia dispense some of her pointed lessons."

CHAPTER TEN

The Hidden Valley

Alustin sighed, his breath fogging up in the cold alpine air. He tried to ignore the distant commotion behind him as he quickly sketched the valley below the cliff he sat atop. It was about the right size, but otherwise…

The valley was hidden away deep in the Skyreach Mountains. It was low enough in elevation that it wasn't frozen over like the mountains surrounding it, and in some ways quite strongly resembled one of the many alpine valleys that made up the kingdom of Highvale.

There was too much wrong with it, though. There were few rivers or streams leading down into the valley, and instead of being rich and verdant like the Highvale valleys, it was barren, with only scrub growing on the slopes. Even though it wasn't as far north as Highvale, it looked like something you'd find even farther north than that— maybe even past the clan territories Talia grew up in.

Maybe if the lack of water had been a recent development, it wouldn't have been an issue, but the valley curved to its flat bottom, rather than descending at a sharper angle, indicating it had been formed by glaciers, rather than rivers. Alustin doubted that there had ever been much in the way of water in the valley. And, without water, it was clearly not a good candidate.

It was, of course, better to be safe than sorry— there was just too much riding on this. The water problems were far from the only disqualifier, however.

For one thing, there was the valley's remoteness. It was clear that a good candidate site needed to have viable shipping routes in and out, and this one most certainly did not. Alustin had actually had to fly in a good chunk of the way.

Through a snowstorm, at that. Snow was hell on his paper wings, and he'd burned through an absurd chunk of his paper supply and mana reservoirs making it through. He'd also almost smashed into several mountainsides on the way thanks to low visibility. You'd think that a farseeing attunement would be considerably more effective during a blizzard, you really would.

Alustin tried to ignore the growing commotion behind him.

There was really no way that you could do any reasonable amount of shipping to or from this valley, so another check against it.

The cold was also a strong marker against the site. They could work with a fairly wide temperature range, but this seemed outside of plausibility.

Finally, there was the aether situation here. A viable candidate site needed to have a historically low aether density— possibly even to the point of being a mana desert— that had begun increasing recently.

This site certainly met the last criteria, at least. The aether density was so low here that he'd almost completely drained his mana reservoirs getting into the valley. It was, however, measurably higher than past reports indicated, and Alustin had measured further, if incremental, increases in the couple of days he'd been here.

Which, honestly, he really didn't need to have spent here. He'd known it wasn't a viable site since just a few hours into his visit, largely because of the labyrinth sitting smack-dab in the center of the valley. While the candidate sites needed to have a mana well, it had to be a lateral well, not a junction well. And it certainly couldn't have a labyrinth in it.

He'd been fairly sure that the valley hadn't been a viable candidate from the beginning, just from scrying it. Kanderon, of course, still insisted every location be checked out in person, and he'd had the poor luck of being assigned this particular mission.

Though, he had at least figured out the mystery of the valley's increasing aether density. Some idiot had decided to try and seal the labyrinth— it was, apparently, home to some fairly nasty inhabitants they didn't want getting out.

Sealing a labyrinth, however, was almost never a good idea. Capping it in a way that allowed the aether density currents to still escape was a much better one— it's what they practiced at Skyhold, at the gorgon capital, and at least a dozen other sites that Alustin knew of offhand. The downside to that, of course, was that capping a labyrinth required constant maintenance and observation, and these idiots hadn't wanted to do that— they just wanted to shut down what they saw as a major threat.

Alustin set down the illustration of the valley to give the ink a chance to dry, and began cleaning off his quill and putting away his supplies into his storage tattoo.

It had probably been a dragon that had sealed the labyrinth. Most of the major territories in the southern Skyreach range were dragon territories, with a few exceptions like Jaskolskus, the gorgons, a handful of human cities, Kanderon, and whatever it was that lived in the far south near the sea. He was fairly sure Kanderon knew what it was, but she wasn't talking. The borders of its territory had remained constant for centuries, at least, and Kanderon didn't think it would stir itself anytime soon.

Which would make it one of the only major powers not to be stirring right now. The dragons had been especially active lately, with Andas Thune's territorial expansions, the death of Ataerg, and… well, the distressing number of major powers who either knew what was happening, suspected it, or were at least aware that there was something going on. The last group was, in many ways, the most concerning— the powerful dislike being kept in the dark, and tend to behave dangerously and unpredictably when they realize it.

Of course, even if things weren't so tempestuous right now, he'd have no easy way to tell whose territory this valley had belonged to when the seal was built. Keeping track of the shifting territories this deep in the Skyreach range was a nightmare even in calmer times.

Alustin sighed again at the commotion, and picked up the drawing. He blew on it one last time, then stored it away in his tattoo.

So someone, most likely a dragon, had sealed the labyrinth in this valley, probably because it didn't want to deal with annoying labyrinth escapees. This kept the aether flows from escaping the mana well, which in turn drastically lowered the aether density around the valley.

But, just like what happened literally every time someone sealed a labyrinth, it would eventually rupture, leaving the region flooded with highly dense aether. It hadn't fully ruptured yet, but Alustin couldn't see the seal lasting more than a decade or so.

Of course, when a sealed labyrinth began to leak aether, it also began to release its inhabitants, which tended to do best in highly dense aether regions.

Or, to sum up Alustin's past couple of days in a nutshell, the valley was absolutely filled with monsters. Monsters that had flooded out into a region that was suddenly developing aether thick enough to sustain them, but that didn't have anything to eat save for each other.

And now, Alustin.

Alustin stood up and turned, drawing his saber from his tattoo as he did so. He slashed at the lead beast in the pack, cutting across its snout, though not killing it, unfortunately.

They were, of course, the same odd wolf-creatures that had been his biggest problem the whole time he'd been in this damn valley. They were around twice the weight of a normal wolf, had disturbingly elongated jaws, and had coats that appeared to be made of strands of dirty blue chitin, not fur. The chitin strands clattered together as the creatures moved, making a truly incredible amount of noise.

They didn't have eyes, either. Nor even a place where eye sockets would go— their skulls just descended straight from their spines to the tips of their snouts.

Alustin really didn't want to know what kind of environment they'd wandered into the labyrinth from.

He also doubted that they had been what had led to the sealing of the labyrinth— they were dangerous, but hardly enough to cause problems for anyone powerful enough to seal a labyrinth. Sealing a labyrinth was an almost prohibitively expensive endeavor, and the loss of aether density often crippled the value of a territory.

Besides, the ecosystem of a labyrinth was hardly likely to remain stable for anywhere near long enough for the seal to rupture, so whatever had provoked the sealing had likely died or moved back downwards into the labyrinth long ago.

He danced along the rim of the cliff, dodging the lunges of the wolf-things as his boots crunched on grit and sparse patches of snow. He'd really hoped that he'd get at least another hour before one of the packs of these creatures roaming the valley made their way up here. He could have easily refilled his mana reservoirs enough in that time to reform his wings and escape the valley.

Alustin cut through the neck of one of the wolf-things. There was little his saber couldn't cut through, and the creatures were being cautious enough fighting at the edge of the cliff that he didn't need to funnel mana into its primary enchantment.

Hmm. One of the creatures wasn't attacking him. It was just watching the whole ordeal from atop a nearby boulder. Well, not watching, but keeping track via however these things perceived the world.

Their leader, perhaps? No, more likely a lookout.

Dismissing the matter, he ducked another lunge and considered his options. His mana reservoirs weren't filled enough to attempt anything but the shortest flight, and he did not want to strand himself on the shoulders of one of the nearby mountains while they refilled. He was dressed for cold weather, but not sitting in the snow atop a mountain for hours and hours.

Flying elsewhere in the valley would only delay things for another showdown. This location had been the most secure he'd found yet in the valley, and he couldn't reasonably expect to find a better one.

He could demolish the pack easily enough with his magic, but that would likely just draw the attention of more packs. They seemed to be able to sense magic being used.

Fighting them seemed to be his best option, but he wasn't going to be able to handle the entire pack for much longer on just his personal combat skills.

Alustin sighed, and began funneling mana into his saber's activation spellforms. It would, at least, use a bit less mana than many of his spells, and if he got lucky, it wouldn't alert other packs of the wolf-creatures to his presence.

"This has been a thorough waste of my time," he told the creatures, as the spellforms of his saber began to glow.

They didn't have any response beyond snarling, but then good conversation was always hard to find.

CHAPTER ELEVEN

Motives

Godrick grunted as he squeezed behind the shelf that concealed Hugh's room. It had always been a tight fit, but Godrick was fairly confident that someone had pushed it closer to the wall over the summer, just to inconvenience him.

He knocked on the door hidden behind the overstuffed shelf. You'd hardly know it was back there, even if you had reason to be in this almost forgotten annex of the library stacks. Even, for that matter, if you could see past Hugh's wards, which made people's attention drift away from it.

"Come in!" Hugh called from inside.

Godrick eased the door open and slipped inside, sighing in relief as he did so.

Hugh was crouching under his window with a brush, doing something to the painted wards around his window.

A Traitor in Skyhold

"What are yeh workin' on?" Godrick asked.

"Remaking my wards," Hugh said, glancing back at Godrick. "They started decaying. Not badly, but they had started letting the night air in, and I'm not a fan of sleeping in a cold room. It probably should have been a ten minute fix, but once I got looking at them, I realized how much better of a job I could do these days, and it's been a couple of hours now."

"So they heat the air as it comes in the window? Tha' seems a little inefficient," Godrick said.

Hugh shook his head as he worked.

"No, the ward acts as an insulator, sort of. It lets air through, but it doesn't let the heat escape."

Godrick wasn't sure how exactly you could let the air move without the heat moving with it, but he hadn't come here to talk wards with Hugh, who was more than a little obsessed with the topic. Not that Godrick found it boring, but Hugh could get a bit overwhelming on the topic.

Godrick shook his head, focusing back on the reason he'd come. "Alustin's back," he said.

"It's about time," Hugh muttered. "Is he alright? When did he get back?"

Godrick shrugged. It had only been about a month, but given the whole situation with the demon and such, he could understand why Hugh wasn't too happy about things. "He just showed up this mornin', lookin' a bit tired. Meetin' with Talia right now, but he wants us ta meet him at his office afterwards. Yeh probably have plenty a' time ta finish yer ward."

"Meeting with Talia?" Hugh asked.

"Alustin brought her a bunch a' bones. Creepy skulls with no eyes in 'em. She immediately dragged him off ta her explosion room ta try them out, and show him a few things she'd been working on. I came to tell you instead, and Sabae apparently had to go look over some public Council voting records or something."

Hugh rolled his eyes, and Godrick shrugged in agreement. As much as they all enjoyed Talia's company, they had all grown thoroughly sick of Talia's testing room. There were only so many explosions you could really deal with watching in a day before you started getting a pretty severe headache.

Unless, of course, you were Talia.

"So," Alustin asked, "who's our traitor?"

The paper mage was sprawled out in the armchair behind his desk. He looked tired enough that Godrick was a little shocked he was even awake.

"No idea," Talia said.

Godrick shook his head.

"Sorry, sir," Hugh said.

Alustin frowned at Hugh. "Is this just always going to be an ongoing thing, where you listen to everything I say except when I tell you to call me by my name?"

Hugh opened his mouth to respond— Godrick would wager actual money that he was about to apologize to Alustin again and keep calling him sir— when Sabae interjected.

"We don't have enough data to tell," Sabae said.

Alustin raised an eyebrow at that.

"You personally told us that the traitor has been leaking information to other countries for some time, and mentioned several confirmed instances of it, yet you've provided useful details on almost none of them," Sabae said.

Alustin failed to contain a smile. "Well spotted. Unfortunately, we've shared everything that we are allowed to share with you. While Kanderon is influential enough to allow you in on the investigation to the degree she has, she does not have the ability to share actual Council secrets with you. If you're caught now, she can at least cover herself by pointing out that you were already involved to a certain degree. If she shared Council secrets with you, well... that could involve an unacceptable degree of damage to her political power, and Kanderon hasn't remained the last of Skyhold's founders still in power through might alone."

Godrick couldn't help but notice that Alustin was leaving open room for other founders to still be alive, which was somewhat alarming after centuries.

"So this really is just training and nothing more," Sabae said.

Alustin shook his head. "It is training, but we're not completely discounting your ability to find something we've missed. Even if you don't solve it, you might find something that contributes to the case against our traitor."

The gangly paper mage leaned forwards in his chair. "Alright, here's a better place to start— let's try and figure out who has the least legitimate motive for voting against the alternate test exercise."

"What about Anders vel Seraf?" Talia asked.

"In his case we'll consider the strength of his motive to vote for it," Alustin said. "Let's start with Headmaster Tarik."

Everyone looked at Godrick. It was a little exasperating that everyone had just immediately expected him to focus on Tarik, just because they were both stone mages.

It was even more exasperating that it actually had been his reason, but he wasn't going to mention that part.

"Tarik, no other names. People have tried givin' her others, she tends ta reject or ignore 'em, save for her title as Headmaster."

Hugh muttered something inaudible at that.

"Crazy powerful stone mage. Born and raised here in Skyhold. She's an incredibly rigid person, and tends ta' stick to the letter a' the law above all else," Godrick said. He glared at the rest of them challengingly. "Which ain't a trait a' stone mages in general, na matter what people say."

No one responded to that one, and Godrick continued. "And… that's it, really. She claimed in the record a' the meetin' ta have voted against it because it was against Academy policy. It might be absurd comin' from anyone else, but… it's nowhere near the oddest thing she's done in the name a' the rules. She also claimed to believe that we actually hadn't seen a demon, but were just scared and imagining things, but it seemed to be an afterthought for her."

"That still seems a little crazy," Talia said. "And she can go jump through winter ice for not believing us."

"Wouldn't it be harder for Bakori to manipulate someone that rigid?" Hugh asked.

Alustin shook his head. "We don't understand exactly how Bakori's abilities work— they're quite literally not of this world— but we don't believe so, based off the attunements we know that can manipulate people similarly, like dream attunements."

Talia coughed pointedly.

"Well, dream attunements other than Talia's," Alustin corrected. "Dream mages aren't usually nearly so destructive. But no, to answer your question, rigidity is not strength, and it in many ways is an advantage for manipulators when they are dealing with a rigid person. It limits the number of choices they can steer their targets down, but those choices are much easier to guide them down, and much harder to fix the manipulation."

"Yeh can't discount Tarik as a suspect, then," Godrick said.

Alustin shook his head. "If we could discount any of them as suspects, they wouldn't be on the list." He sighed. "Alright, suspect number two. Rutliss the Red, school bursar."

The others all turned to Hugh, who had spent the most time reading about Rutliss.

"Rutliss is a bureaucrat who got his name because he wears nothing but red," Hugh said. "He was also born and raised in Skyhold. He has a saltwater affinity, and is probably the least dangerous mage on the council. Not really a battlemage at all, so far as I can tell."

Alustin raised his eyebrows at that. "I'd warn against underestimating anyone on the Council."

Godrick frowned. That had been bugging him for a while now. "Why *are* all the Council members so powerful? It doesn't seem like yeh'd need that ta be effective administrators."

"Not now, perhaps, but Skyhold wasn't always as secure as it is today, and customs can be enduring things," Alustin said. He gestured at Hugh to continue.

"He, so far as I can tell, just about always votes against Kanderon. The dossier you gave us is a little short on speculation why, but it makes a point to note that he also continues to vote against any expansion of the miniscule quota of nonhuman students allowed at the Academy, so I'm guessing he's got some sort of problem with nonhumans in general. He also seems pretty rigid and rule-bound."

Godrick felt a little vindicated at that— it was clearly more of a bureaucrat trait than a stone mage trait.

Alustin grimaced. "He's definitely a human supremacist, I can tell you that much. I've had enough unfortunate conversations with him to be sure of that one. Especially during the debriefings from that whole thing with the gorgons. And, on top of that, his concern for the rules is strongest when it's to his advantage."

Godrick started to ask about the gorgon incident when Alustin interrupted him— like he always did to anyone who tried to ask about the gorgon incident. "So, what are your thoughts on the plausibility of his vote?"

"As unpleasant as his reasons are, they might be the most believable of the lot," Hugh said. "He essentially votes against everything Kanderon brings before the council, and even a lot of the things she simply votes for."

"Maybe Bakori got to him when he was a student here," Talia said, "and he's just had Rutliss voting like that to throw off the trail all this time."

"Disturbing, and not implausible, even if it would also seem a little petty on Bakori's part," Alustin said. "He could have done something similar to Tarik. Still, too much meddling is a major risk on Bakori's part, given the probability that Kanderon or one of the lesser archmages at Skyhold might detect it."

Godrick would have greatly preferred it if instead of using Hugh— and, by extension, himself and the girls— as bait to make Bakori reveal himself, Alustin and Kanderon hadn't made them go into the labyrinth blind, but that was water under the bridge at this point.

"Alright, suspect three. Abyla Ceutas of Yldive, Chair of Student Admissions."

Sabae took a moment to start. Godrick realized that she'd been unusually quiet this whole time.

"Abyla Ceutas is the youngest member of the Council, in her early forties. She has an incredibly powerful magma attunement, and is one of the most dangerous combatants on the Council— not just the Academy sub-Council, the whole thing."

Godrick wasn't really surprised by that. Even a new mage with a barely developing magma affinity was exceptionally dangerous, up there with glass, sound, or solar mages. Or Talia. A fully attuned magma mage?

He really, really hoped she wasn't the traitor.

"She gave no reason why she voted against the alternate test," Sabae said.

"That's not suspicious at all," Talia said sarcastically.

Sabae and Alustin seemed to be staring each other down. Finally, Alustin sighed. "I think we both suspect the same thing. You might as well tell the others."

Sabae didn't seem happy about that, but nodded. "She voted against the test because of me."

Godrick wasn't alone in giving her a confused look.

"Yldive has something of a rivalry with Ras Andis," Sabae finally continued.

"A rivalry that has broken out into open war more than once," Alustin mentioned.

Sabae just nodded at that, looking unhappy. "Before my family rose to prominence in Ras Andis, and before Indris made Theras Tel into a major port, Yldive was the dominant regional power of southwestern Ithos. They haven't forgiven or forgotten. The Ceutas family used to rule in Yldive, and they directly blame their decline and loss of power on us. Abyla Ceutas is trying to cause problems for you to get at my family. She's not Kanderon's ally, but she's not an outright enemy, either. If it wasn't for me, she probably would have voted to allow you to take the alternate test, and none of this would have been a problem."

It suddenly made a lot more sense to Godrick why Sabae had been so quiet. He leaned over and wrapped his arm around her shoulders. "No one blames yeh, Sabae. If Ceutas wants ta grossly abuse her power for a personal grudge, that's clearly on her shoulders."

Talia looked angry for a moment, then sighed. "I was going to say we should set her on fire or something, but I'm not quite crazy enough to think we can take her on. Or probably any of the council members, other than maybe Rutliss."

"Besides," Hugh said, "It's a bad idea to assume that her grudge isn't being exacerbated by Bakori to make her vote against you. That's how he works."

Hugh paused for a moment. "I intended that to sound more comforting than it actually did."

Sabae smiled weakly at that.

"As happy as it makes me that the four of you are so supportive of one another, we have one more candidate to discuss," Alustin said.

Talia leaned forward eagerly. "Anders vel Seraf, school Dean. He's a silk mage from Tsarnassus and one of the older members of the council. Kanderon's closest ally on the council, and her only reliable ally on the academic subcouncil, and therefore, the best positioned to betray her. I'm not really sure how a silk mage is supposed to be dangerous, but then, I didn't think a paper mage could be dangerous, either."

Alustin smiled at that. "Many of my combat techniques were, in fact, inspired by Anders. He wears voluminous silk robes, with countless dangling tassels and strips of silk— which he is usually vain enough to have floating around him. In battle, he tends to bind and blind foes with silk. What he's most famous for, however, is his use of glyphs in combat. His robes are filled with countless embroidered, interlocking spellforms— some that are garishly bright, and some in the same colors as the robes, but all of which are almost indecipherable to anyone but him. He can pump mana into any of them with ease and without mistake, giving him access to a truly massive array of cantrips and other glyph spells during battle."

Alustin looked a little nostalgic. "He helped me develop my personal combat style, and he was the one who recommended me to Kanderon as a Librarian Errant candidate. At the very least, he thought that it was too ironic that there weren't any paper mages among the ranks of active field agents. You'll almost certainly all get a chance to meet him soon enough— he was quite angry about the way the vote went."

Talia gave him a skeptical look. "Well, that certainly makes for good reasons for you to trust him, but that also gives him more room to betray you."

Sabae rolled her eyes. "We're definitely still investigating him, but I'm willing to bet quite a bit that he's not responsible. If Bakori gets his hands on Hugh, he gains a link to Kanderon that he might be able to use to attack her. Why would Bakori push against that?"

"I'll take that bet," Talia said. "We don't know how demons think. Who knows why he could be doing it? What are we going to wager on it?"

Alustin raised his hands to stop them. "Talia, Sabae, we are *not* betting on an active investigation. It promotes entirely the wrong mindset. You need to be open to all possibilities, not setting out to prove a specific idea. That's a fast way to ruin investigations."

Godrick was a little disappointed at that. Any stake that Talia and Sabae agreed on would have been entertaining, to say the least.

They spent another hour or so bandying about theories and plans for investigation. Eventually, Alustin called it to a halt, deciding they weren't going to make any more progress that day. He did have one quite welcome piece of news for them, however— the *Moonless Owl* was going to be docking at Skyhold in a few days.

Godrick was definitely excited to see Irrick again, but Hugh was… well, not bouncing off the walls. He was too reserved to display that much emotion, but it was clear that any thought of the investigation had fallen completely out of mind for him.

He was just shy of skipping. Godrick glanced back to see Talia rolling her eyes at Hugh's behavior.

"Are you as excited to see Irrick as I am to see Avah?" Hugh asked.

Godrick chuckled. "Irrick and me aren't that serious, Hugh. Ah'm excited, sure, but he's got an arranged marriage ta a girl on another ship next year that he's quite excited for."

Hugh seemed to deflate a little at that. "Really? I thought…"

Godrick grinned at Hugh, and gently elbowed his shoulder. "Ah knew about it going into things; it's fine."

Hugh looked a little doubtful at that, but nodded. Godrick sighed in relief internally. He'd been a little worried about how Hugh would react to that— Godrick was fairly sure that Hugh had been weirdly linking the success of their respective relationships, as though if Godrick and Irrick broke up he'd somehow never see Avah again.

Though, speaking of how people would take things…

"Could yeh all do me a favor?" Godrick asked. "Me da still doesn't really know about Irrick and me. Could yeh not mention it around him?"

"Does he have a problem with men loving other men?" Sabae asked. "I've heard some people from Lothal do."

Talia looked like she was about to offer to fight his da, which was entirely unnecessary.

Godrick shook his head. "He's fine with that, ah'm pretty sure. What he's not fine with are flings. He wants me ta settle down with someone and stay with them. Bit of a romantic. He's still never found anyone else after ma died, even though ah'm sure she would have wanted him to. Ah don't think he'd be mad at me, just… disappointed."

Sabac rolled her eyes at that, but Hugh and Talia both seemed to think it was romantic. And then started interrogating him about his parents' relationship.

CHAPTER TWELVE

The Owl Returns

Kanderon was, to say the least, not happy with Hugh being so distracted.

"Pay attention, Hugh," the sphinx growled, knocking him to the ground with a nudge of her paw.

"Sorry," Hugh said.

The two of them stood atop a wide, flat ledge near the base of Skyhold, where stone mages often came to train.

"Focus your affinity sense on the boulder," Kanderon said as Hugh picked himself up off the ground.

Hugh did so. He could feel the crystals making up most of the boulder, but they were… jumbled, malformed, and tiny. He relayed that information to Kanderon, who nodded.

"Now lift it."

Hugh stared at the boulder skeptically. "I don't think I'm strong enough."

Kanderon sighed. **"With your crystal affinity, Hugh."**

"Just… lift it? Like I would a crystal?" Hugh asked.

"It's made almost entirely of crystals, isn't it?" Kanderon asked. **"So lift it."**

Something about that felt weird to Hugh. It was like Kanderon was just casually asking Hugh to do stone magic. Still, he gave it a try. The boulder was too large for Hugh to lift it with a levitation cantrip, so he visualized a simple crystal levitation spellform— which really wasn't that different— then flooded it with mana from his crystal affinity reservoir.

The boulder lifted into the air and started spinning wildly, then rolled out of the spell.

"You've just encountered one of the fundamental limitations of crystal mages, Hugh. We operate best with larger, well-formed crystals. Our spells are designed to interact with the patterns that comprise those crystals. When we're forced to work with a jumble of different crystal patterns, such as in this boulder, spells tend to prove difficult for us to control. You might be able to magically affect stone, but don't expect to ever directly overpower a stone mage trying to affect the same stone."

"Can't we… pattern link it, to improve the crystals inside it?"

Kanderon raised an eyebrow at Hugh. **"We can, but pattern linking on that scale inside a solid object takes considerable amounts of time and mana— it's not overly suited towards battle. Fluid solutions containing the necessary ingredients are the best locations to grow crystals in, and many crystal mages possess sizable labs dedicated purely towards growing crystals to their required specifications."**

"You've never actually told me what you specialize in as a crystal mage," Hugh said.

"Aether crystal manipulation," Kanderon said. She shook her massive crystalline wings, which chimed almost musically as she did so. **"Over the centuries, I've bonded with my aether crystal until it feels even more like a part of me than my old wings did before I lost them."**

"You never did tell me how you lost your original wings," Hugh said.

"No, I didn't." Kanderon said.

Kanderon didn't seem angry— she seemed more sad than anything— but Hugh still thought it best not to inquire further there.

The two of them spent another couple of hours working on ways to deal with suboptimal crystals, and by the end Hugh was able to reliably lift the boulder.

"Good," Kanderon said, as Hugh slowly lowered the boulder one last time. **"Now, why were you so distracted at the beginning of the lesson?"**

"The *Moonless Owl* is arriving at Skyhold soon," Hugh said sheepishly.

"And?" Kanderon asked.

"I get to see Avah when it gets here!" Hugh said.

Kanderon looked distinctly uncomfortable. **"There has been something I've been meaning to discuss with you in regards to her since you returned to Skyhold, Hugh."**

That hardly sounded good.

"As your master, it's my responsibility to instruct you in the use of... well... certain cantrips that romantically involved humans need to know if they wish to prevent..."

Hugh felt his cheeks turn bright red, and realized that Kanderon was blushing too.

"You don't need to teach me those, Master, Alustin already did. It's fine, I know them already."

Alustin had, in fact, chosen to instruct him on contraceptive cantrips in front of his friends on the deck of the *Owl*, who had all decided Hugh's embarrassment was quite amusing. To make things worse, Avah, who seemed to have some sort of affinity sense for Hugh being embarrassed, had wandered up to them halfway through the lesson, and she had decided that Hugh's lap was exactly where she wanted to sit to enjoy his even further embarrassment.

Not that they'd actually needed to use said spells yet.

"Well then. That's… that's all for the best, then," Kanderon said awkwardly, still a little red. **"I, uh… I should be going. Good lesson, Hugh."**

The massive sphinx took off in a much less dignified manner than usual. As she did so, Hugh could hear her muttering to herself.

"...ridiculous humans with their constant mating and their..."

Hugh awkwardly drummed his hands on his hips, still a little red, then turned and headed back towards the nearest entrance into Skyhold.

Really no reason to share this story with his friends. Or Avah. Definitely not Avah.

Hugh was essentially useless the morning of the Fifthday the *Owl* was supposed to be arriving.

"Maybe we should head down to the docks now?" Hugh asked, pacing across his room.

Talia rolled her eyes from where she was sitting on Hugh's bed. "The ship's not supposed to be here for hours yet, Hugh."

"Da actually designed our armor based off a' illusion magic," Godrick was saying from where he sat on the floor. "Yeh remember how Captain Bandon had all those illusions? Well, in order for it ta work, he had ta anchor all of them to his own image. Da's armor works the same way, except, ah… what's the word he used… intaglio! The illusion anchors affect the shape a' the inside a' the armor, rather than the outside. Otherwise, it'll try an' smash yeh while yer wearin' it."

"You're right. That's nothing like how my armor works," Sabae said from Hugh's desk, where she was idly thumbing through one of the suspect files. "It doesn't seem that complex, though, so why haven't more people copied him?"

"What if Avah doesn't want to date me anymore?" Hugh asked, falling on his back onto his bed and clutching his face.

"Then she doesn't want to date you anymore," Talia said, rolling her eyes again. "You'll be sad for a while, then eventually get over it."

"What, no threats ta burn down the *Owl?*" Godrick joked.

Talia threw Hugh's pillow at Godrick. Hugh's spellbook poked out from under the bed at that, but soon slid back underneath.

"It's trickier than it sounds," Godrick said to Sabae. "Illusion magic was not intended fer use with stone. It took years fer Da ta' figure out. Plus, there's a bunch more ta the armor than just that— yeh got to deal with makin' sure yer joints move, makin' sure yeh can breathe and see without decreasin' yer protection too much, so on and so forth. It's not just a matter a' memorizin'…"

Hugh groaned loudly, and Godrick reached back and patted Hugh on the leg sympathetically. Sabae threw Hugh's pillow back to Talia, who began mock-smothering him with it.

"It's not just a matter a' memorizin' a few spellforms," Godrick continued. "Constructin' the armor is a whole ordeal every time. Plus yeh need ta practice mana layering ta move the armor properly, and ah'm nowhere near as good as yeh are at that."

"When do you think you'll be able to do the whole suit?" Talia asked, ignoring Hugh saying something about Avah beneath the pillow.

"Definitely by the time we've got ta enter the labyrinth," Godrick said.

Hugh groaned even louder at that one.

"Which hopefully we'll do in a different labyrinth," Sabae added. "Is the gorgon labyrinth still the one Alustin is talking about?"

"Yep," Godrick said.

"Anyone have any more clues about what the gorgon incident was?" Talia asked.

Everyone shook their heads at that one.

"Hugh, you need to seduce the truth about the gorgon incident out of Avah," Sabae said.

Hugh was silent for a moment beneath the pillow and then muttered something incomprehensible. Talia sighed and picked up the pillow. "What was that?"

"Avah wasn't on the *Owl* during the gorgon incident," Hugh said, then pulled the pillow back down onto his face.

"Well, Godrick, it looks like it's up to you then. You need to seduce the truth out of Irrick," Sabae said.

Godrick saluted her.

All of Hugh's worrying, thankfully, turned out to have been unnecessary. The *Owl* hadn't even come to a full halt before Avah vaulted off the side. Hugh frantically began a levitation spellform, but a thin ribbon of sand rose up and caught Avah, gently lowering her down to Hugh.

"That's new," Sabae said.

"Avah and Hugh being annoying in public?" Talia muttered.

Hugh made a rude gesture in Talia's direction, as talking was a bit difficult for him at the moment.

The gangplank had already been lowered by the time Hugh got a chance to catch a breath, and Irrick was striding down it.

"Show off," Irrick said to Avah. "She's been doing that nonstop since she learned how."

"What, kiss Hugh?" Avah said. "You're just jealous."

Irrick rolled his eyes. "No, the sand ribbon. No offense, Hugh, but I prefer a bit of height."

"None taken," Hugh said, still a little out of breath.

"I will take one page out of Avah's book, though," Irrick said as he reached Godrick.

It took a solid hour for them to get away— Irrick and Avah had to help prepare the ship for unloading, and Captain Solon, Deila, and many of the crew-members wanted to say hello to the students, but they eventually all managed to escape.

The six of them went to eat at one of the cafes near the dock that specialized in meat pastries. This led to the usual round of jokes about Hugh's obsession with baked goods, like whenever they visited.

Hugh was too busy eating a pastry to dignify that with a response.

"How did you know we were arriving today?" Irrick asked. "Were you just checking the lists every day to see? That's quite flattering."

"The lists?" Talia asked.

"Skyhold scryers monitor all approaching ships and post lists of their projected arrival times every day," Sabae said. She had her finger stuck in her mug of water, which was spinning rapidly. "It's standard practice at most large ports. And no, Alustin told us."

Irrick and Avah just nodded at that, as though nothing Alustin did would surprise them.

Which, honestly…

Hugh attempted a joke about that, but only managed to spray a few crumbs.

"Could someone elbow Hugh for me to remind him not to talk with his mouth full of pastry?" Talia asked.

Avah and Sabae, sitting on either side of Hugh, promptly both complied. Which in turn resulted in the spraying of considerably more pastry crumbs.

Hugh managed to swallow most of the mouthful by the time everyone else was done laughing.

"Hugh!" a voice called out from behind him.

Hugh froze. He literally could not think of a worse time to run into Rhodes than with Avah here. Normally, he'd be fine just running, but…

Without missing a beat, Sabae turned, pulling her hand out of her mug. The water came with it, rapidly spinning around her hand.

She blasted it straight behind Hugh.

No one spoke for a moment, though everyone but Hugh was looking behind him. Several people at nearby tables were giggling. Hugh could hear water dripping behind him.

"I just want to talk!" Rhodes called.

"Hugh doesn't want to talk to you," Sabae replied. She stuck her hand into Hugh's water mug.

"I…" Rhodes started.

Before he could finish, Sabae pulled the water out of Hugh's mug and sent it blasting towards Rhodes again.

Rhodes coughed and spat for several moments. The giggles around them had grown quite a bit louder.

"Fine, whatever!" Rhodes yelled. Hugh could hear him stomping off. And dripping.

Hugh slowly relaxed as the others turned away from Rhodes. He took another bite of his pastry so he wouldn't have to talk to anyone.

"An ex you haven't told me about yet, Hugh?" Avah asked.

Hugh spat out quite a few crumbs coughing at that.

"Definitely not," Talia said. "Enemy would be a much better description."

"Can we not talk about Rhodes right now?" Hugh asked.

The conversation switched to Sabae's water blasts after that. Sabae was progressing quicker with her study of water magic than she had with her wind magic, which was apparently quite common. Water, along with stone, was supposed to be one of the easiest affinities to learn and attune, at least at first.

Everyone else seemed to be having a good time, but Hugh couldn't quite shake off the mood that Rhodes had left him in.

CHAPTER THIRTEEN

Sand, Stone, and Crystal

The *Owl*, unfortunately, was only staying at Skyhold overnight— long enough to unload and load their cargos and replenish their supplies.

Captain Solon (or his mother Deila— Hugh had never entirely been sure who was actually in charge of the ship) had, at least, given Avah and Irrick leave from having to help.

The group spent a lot of their limited time wandering about Skyhold's harbor. Hugh had spent as much free time as possible exploring it, but he'd not even come close to seeing everything there. Sabae, Talia, and Godrick all knew it a lot better than he did, but then they hadn't been manipulated into spending literally all their time inside the mountain by a demon last year.

Avah found it surprising that Hugh knew so little about Skyhold's exports— while it was a major source of income for Skyhold, the Academy was a good ways down from being the biggest source. Skyhold, like Theras Tel, provided water for visiting ships via an almost identical water pumping system. The major difference, apparently, was that the granite of Skyhold left the water slightly toxic, so a large contingent of water mages remained on duty to purify it at all times.

Even more important than that were the exports from the labyrinth— rare magical reagents, materials, and living creatures that couldn't be found anywhere but in labyrinths. Hugh had known about the labyrinth's profitability, but he hadn't even come close to understanding exactly how profitable it was.

Avah actually seemed disappointed she couldn't visit the labyrinth, though even Irrick thought that was a little crazy.

Hugh grew more and more nervous as the day went on, thinking about Kanderon's well intentioned— if mutually embarrassing— discussion with him. At the end of the night, however, Avah merely kissed him goodnight and headed back towards the ship.

He couldn't help but feel irritated at his emotions, for not being able to make up their minds about whether he should feel relieved or disappointed.

The next morning, they all met up again at a dockside cafe for breakfast. Avah arrived looking singularly pleased.

"Guess what, Hugh!" she said, hugging him hard enough to make his ribs creak. She continued before he could hazard any guesses. "Grandmother and Alustin have made plans for me and Irrick to visit again! We're going to be here for a whole month."

Irrick looked somewhat pleased, but mostly just tired as he rolled his eyes at Avah. "For a month around Midwinter," he said. "We're not staying just yet."

They sat at a table right on the edge of the harbor, and Avah amused herself during breakfast by trying to control her silverware with a tendril of sand.

Hugh, of course, promptly got sand in his food.

With a little effort, he was able to devise a simple spell to pull out much of the sand— it was a fairly simple variant on a levitation spell, which was one of Hugh's specialties. He had to recast it several times, targeting a different type of crystal each time. Quartz first, followed by feldspar, followed by various types he couldn't name after that.

When he took a bite, however, he could still feel sand in his egg scramble.

Godrick yawned, then cast a spell— apparently intended to clean up rock dust— to remove the rest of the sand from Hugh's plate.

Hugh frowned at his plate thoughtfully.

After they saw the *Owl* off, a process that involved Avah delighting in embarrassing Hugh again, as well as Hugh's spellbook somehow sneaking into Captain Solon's cabin and trying to eat the ship's logs, they all hurried to meet Alustin for their morning training.

Alustin might be a harsh taskmaster, but he was fairly forgiving about them being late this time. Not entirely forgiving, however— today he took them outside Skyhold to run in the desert sand.

As usual, Alustin lectured them while they ran— today on mage tactics in large battles. Generally mages stood either in the back of the lines, firing spells at range, or spread through the ranks, helping maintain windshields or alternative defenses for the army. The trick was matching the drain on the aether by an army's mages with the density of the local aether— if you used too much, you were liable to leave the local aether and your mages mana reservoirs drained, with the opposing force's mana reservoirs still intact.

While the four of them were exhausted— Alustin had even forbidden Godrick to use his sand hardening spell while they ran— Alustin didn't even seem out of breath as he lectured. And he was jogging backward so he could face them, at that.

Hugh, however, was having trouble focusing on Alustin's instruction. He kept thinking back to the sand at breakfast.

Finally, to his own surprise, he interrupted Alustin. To Alustin's surprise as well, apparently, because the paper mage tripped and fell, though he was back on his feet almost immediately.

"Why can Avah, Godrick, and I all affect sand?" Hugh asked.

"What do you mean?" Alustin said, brushing sand off of himself, and gradually coming to a halt.

The apprentices stopped gratefully, and Talia immediately flopped down into the sand, despite her oft-proclaimed dislike of it.

Hugh related the story of the sand in his food. "One of the first things you get taught when you arrive is that the boundaries between affinities are blurry, and that mages in adjacent affinities will often be able to challenge one another for control of a material. This morning, though, it really started to bug me for the first time. Why are affinities so… blurry? Shouldn't they be better defined?"

Alustin smiled, sat down, and picked up a handful of sand. He slowly let it trickle between his fingers. Hugh, Godrick, and Sabae all took his lead and sat down as well, and Talia sat up.

"I was wondering when one of you would ask a question like that," Alustin said. "It is, it seems, time to let you in on a few truths about the nature of magic."

Hugh and the others exchanged confused glances.

"Can anyone tell me what sand is?" Alustin asked.

Everyone just stared at him, until Godrick finally ventured an answer. "It's just… bits a' rock?"

"Gravel's just bits of rock," Alustin said, "and you don't see that many gravel mages, do you?"

Hugh had never even heard of any gravel mages.

"It's… really small bits of rock?" Sabae guessed.

"Pick up a handful," Alustin said, "and really look at it closely. Feel it. Grains of sand are small, but they're not that small."

Hugh did so. He also extended his crystal affinity sense into the handful of sand, feeling all the different types of crystal in it. Lots of quartz, a bit of feldspar, a variety of other bits. A decent number of non-crystalline grains were scattered throughout as well.

"So… sand is just small bits of rock in a particular size range?" Hugh asked.

"Essentially," Alustin said, picking up another handful of sand.

They all waited for him to elaborate or explain, but Alustin seemed content to just wait.

"That's stupid," Talia finally said. "Why would there just be an affinity for rock bits of a particular size? There's got to be more to it than that."

"More to sand?" Alustin said. "I mean, there's lots more— figuring out where the grains eroded from, how they were transported to their location, whether they were weathered by wind or water…"

"You know what I mean," Talia interrupted, narrowing her eyes at Alustin. "There's got to be more to the nature of sand and sand affinities than that."

Alustin considered for a moment. "Do you mean something along the lines of a magical energy signature specific to sand, that people naturally gravitate towards and resonate with, resulting in them gaining sand affinities? Or perhaps some higher realm of reality where an ideal version of sand exists, with all actual sand and sand affinities all referring back to this ideal sand, along with ideal versions of everything else?"

"Exactly," Talia said.

"No," Alustin said.

Talia spluttered in frustration, while he just kept playing with sand.

"So it's just a variant of a stone affinity, then?" Sabae said. "Sand affinities just tap into that magical signature for stone, but something happens that makes them just affect stone bits of a particular size?"

Alustin idly threw a handful of sand in Sabae's direction, though it fell far short. "Not at all. Stone doesn't have any sort of magical energy signature identifying it as stone either, nor is there any ideal version of stone found in another realm. There is absolutely no material, so far as we can tell, that has anything of the sort. Not stone, not wood, not fire, not water, and not shadow."

"Then how do mah affinity senses know I'm lookin' at stone?" Godrick asked. "There's got ta be some way they identify it."

Alustin reclined back in the sand. "Now you're getting closer to the right question," he said. "Still not quite there, though. Recall how the aether is always unattuned mana? Storms increase aether density, but it's not wind mana. Volcanoes do it too, but it's not magma, stone, or fire mana. Any phenomena that releases large amounts of energy does it— earthquakes, forest fires, blizzards, and the like— yet none of them ever produce attuned mana. Mana is only attuned inside living things."

"Ship," Sabae said.

"What about enchanted items?" Godrick asked.

"Well, yes, some enchanted items do it as well, but those are built by living things, it doesn't happen naturally," Alustin said.

"There's a ship coming this way, we should probably move," Sabae said.

A couple minutes of undignified scrambling up a nearby dune later, they resumed the lecture, albeit while watching the sandship cruise towards the port.

Hugh used this opportunity to take his spellbook off. Even with the proprioceptive link, it was quite heavy.

"So are you trying to tell us that affinities are just nonsense people make up?" Talia asked, looking dubious.

Alustin shook his head. "Not at all. It's somewhat tricky to explain, but if you'll permit me to tell you a story, it might help."

"Better a story than more running in sand," Talia muttered.

Alustin ignored that and continued. "Around six hundred years ago, the Ithonian Emperor Dulius grew interested in the question of how people gained their affinities. He funded a grand research program employing hundreds of mages and scholars. Many were frauds seeking wealth, but Dulius was no fool, and he quickly weeded them out. He was also far from kind, so the example he set of them was, by all accounts, quite effective at deterring others from trying to fool him."

"After ten years, the effort had come up with only two solid conclusions. First, what I've just told you— that materials did not seem to possess any sort of unique magical essence, signal, resonance, or anything else that led to attunement. That conclusion caused significant, and sometimes even bloody, dissent among the researchers."

"The second conclusion was viewed as something of a curiosity at first, but it quickly grew to be the primary focus when efforts to disprove the first conclusion failed. Essentially, some of the researchers had found that affinity distribution by population varied wildly across the known world. One region would tend to have a whole different proportion of, say, fire mages to wood mages, while another might have almost none of either and a preponderance of gravity mages."

Alustin's expression had lost its humor at this point. "This was the beginning of the nastiest period of Ithonian history, leading up to their fall. Their findings led to many in the empire claiming that this difference in affinity distribution between regions was an indicator of how worthy the civilizations residing in them were. Unsurprisingly, they began to declare that this proved that the Ithonians were truly the worthiest civilization and people."

Hugh tried to ignore his spellbook happily burrowing into the sand next to him.

"They'd already conquered much of the continent at this point, but their expansion accelerated rapidly after that, using their findings as a justification."

"Emperor Dulius was many things— cruel, ambitious, and paranoid— but he was no fool. There was little that he distrusted more than flattery, and he immediately recognized the rhetoric the program had spawned to be such. He also recognized its value as propaganda, of course, but he never bought into it himself. He kept the research program under his strict control."

"It found some strikingly unusual results. Most significantly, they found that changes in affinity distributions weren't actually caused by their conquests of regions, but by the use of the tongue eater. The Ithonian Empire kept painstaking records throughout their entire history, and they were able to find that affinity distributions were most strongly affected by language, not by who ruled a region."

"Much of the reputation for cruelty that Dulius and his successors gained came from the experiments that followed. They raised thousands of children with no exposure to language, to see whether they would develop affinities. They created artificial languages intended to try and create specific affinity distributions, then forced entire populations to speak them. They taught other artificial languages to children who knew no other languages, taught them magic, and then used the tongue eater on them. There were plenty of horrific experimental spells, vivisections, and other senseless experiments performed as well. Tens of thousands were killed, driven insane, or tortured and traumatized in these experiments over the next century."

Alustin picked up another handful of sand, letting it trickle from his fingers again.

"For all of the horrific nature of the experiments, and the senseless extremes they took them to, they got results. They figured out quite a number of key details about how affinities work. On the distribution side of things, they figured out that three things were most responsible for determining what natural affinities a person would gain. First was language. Second was locale— if you lived in the Endless Erg, you saw much less in the way of saltwater affinities. Third seemed to be simple heredity, though it was much less significant than most people would guess. Cases like Talia's, where the child of mages has a radically different set of affinities than their parents, are more common than people realize, though we still don't understand exactly what causes them."

"There were a couple of relevant tangential findings from this time I should mention now. First, they found that only creatures with language have affinities that vary between members of the species. Organisms without language can utilize mana, but individual members all have the same affinities. Second, this was also when they figured out the exact percent of the population that can't use magic. It turns out to be around one in every fifty people that can't learn magic. The only thing they have in common is an inability to picture things in their mind. If you were to ask them to visualize a forest, they would know what a forest is, but no image would appear in their mind."

"But I've heard stories of blind mages before," Talia said. Unlike Hugh interrupting, Alustin seemed entirely unsurprised by Talia's interjection.

"Blindness and mind blindness, as the Ithonians called it, are two entirely different things. There are plenty of blind mages— they have a bunch of obvious disadvantages, but they also tend to have much more powerful affinity senses."

"If almost everyone can learn magic, why are there so few mages?" Hugh asked. He always felt better about asking questions when someone else started first.

"Well, among other things, the aether wouldn't be able to sustain a population where everyone was a mage. It'd be tapped dry all the time, and people would be fighting over mana. For another, training a mage is a lot of work, and most people don't actually make good mages."

That seemed obvious in retrospect to Hugh.

"Back on topic…" Alustin shifted irritably, and Hugh could see something moving through the sand below him. To Hugh's embarrassment, he saw a brief flash of green.

"Back on topic," Alustin continued, "the Ithonian Empire also began to realize that the actual range of affinities changed from language to language. That is, the range of materials, substances, energy, or organisms a single affinity affects. In one language, for instance, there might be no difference between dirt and sand affinities. In another, you might have affinities for every variety of tree in their region, while another might just have a single catch-all affinity for plants in general."

"The first theory that presided was that affinities were entirely based off of human ideas. The Ithonians promptly developed an artificial language that contained a number of absolutely nonsensical concepts, in order to try and create brand new affinities no one had ever seen before. They taught it solely to children who spoke no other languages. The effort failed miserably— like all artificial languages, the affinities developed by its speakers were fewer and weaker in number, and none of the hoped for new affinities manifested."

Hugh, not wanting to be further distracted from the lecture, tried to will his spellbook to stop digging around underneath people.

The spellbook just sent Hugh a feeling of innocent confusion and promptly started burrowing underneath Godrick.

"The Ithonians eventually gave up the effort as impossible, but that hardly ended the research. They came to the conclusion that affinities had to correspond to existing, real-world substances, energies, or entities."

"Like dreams?" Talia asked, seeming a little sarcastic.

Alustin smiled at that. "Some affinities correspond to slightly less concrete substances, but I've never met anyone who claimed seriously that people don't dream."

"The exact borders of an affinity aren't static, however. They not only vary from language to language, they frequently overlap with other affinities, as is the case with sand, crystal, and stone affinities. Their specific interactions with the substances they're overlapping with often behave wildly differently."

"The Ithonian Empire started to go down some very strange paths after that. They believed that it was possible to extend the range of affinities, linking more and more of them together, until they fashioned some sort of omni-affinity. Most scholars seem to think that it was a fruitless effort, since the less specific an affinity is, the less powerful it tends to be, as in the case of a steel affinity being stronger than an iron affinity. They were also, however, pursuing creating the most specific affinities they possibly could, which would likely have been far more effective paths to power. Thankfully, the Ithonian Empire was overthrown before they could travel too far down those paths."

Alustin went silent after that, and Hugh took a moment to process everything he'd just heard. It was all… somewhat terrifying, to be honest. He'd just had the foundations of his understanding of magic shaken severely. Especially…

Hugh realized that Alustin had begun speaking again, and turned his attention back. The spellbook had surfaced again, and was shifting its attention between Hugh and Alustin, seeming confused and uncertain. Hugh frowned at it briefly.

"Most of the extensive records of the Ithonian Empire were lost in its fall, since most of them were stored in Imperial Ithos proper, so we've had to puzzle most of this out from letters sent by the researchers to their colleagues in various regional garrisons and provincial outposts," Alustin continued. "The wide use of thc tongue eater, and the resulting linguistic monotony of the continent of Ithos, do explain why, at least, affinities tend to be so much more predictable than across other continents."

"Hold on a moment," Sabae interrupted. "If language determines affinity…"

"Linguistic concepts that correspond to things in the real world determine affinity," Alustin interrupted. "A fine distinction, but an important one.

"Regardless," Sabae said. "Doesn't that say some pretty terrifying things about the fact that the Ithonians developed a language affinity and the tongue eater? What could someone with today's understanding of magic do if they got their hands on them?"

The paper mage gave them all a serious look. "It's a question I've spent a lot of time considering. I wouldn't recommend following in my footsteps there."

Hugh sighed. Right, because telling someone not to think about something really ever worked.

CHAPTER FOURTEEN

Shield

Alustin left on another mission a couple weeks after the *Owl* visited, telling them that he'd be back before Midwinter. Before he left, however, he let them know that he'd arranged opportunities for them to meet the members of the Council while he was away.

They would each have a plausible, if flimsy, cover story— one that was supposed to be seen through with little effort. Below that was another cover story— these meetings were chances for the students to personally try and persuade at least one council member to change their vote.

The fact that this was a genuine goal made the second level of cover stories much more believable. Sabae's grandmother had always taught her that the best lies are the closest to the truth.

"What do you mean, nothing?" Talia demanded.

Godrick shrugged. "Tarik wouldn't talk about the Council vote at all, she just told me that Council business was none a' my affair."

"But the vote was literally about you! And us, but it's still entirely your affair!" Talia yelled.

Sabae watched Hugh flinch a bit at the yelling, but he didn't turn away from his desk, where he was working on his new set of warded slingstones. He was growing these ones out of crystal from scratch, converting piles of sand into thin-shelled quartz spheres engraved with his ward designs— which, apparently, was not a shape quartz liked to take.

Sabae wasn't sure how a crystal could have preferences, but she had enough to worry about for now, between her classes, the investigation, and her grandmother's impending visit.

"What would she talk about?" Sabae asked as she took notes on what Godrick had to say. Godrick's training session with Headmaster Tarik had been the first of the planned meetings with the council members.

"She was willin' ta train me, and nothin' else," Godrick said. "Ah learned a good bit about stone magic, but nothin' for the investigation."

"What did you learn about stone magic?" Hugh asked.

"And her combat capabilities?" Talia added.

Godrick shrugged. "She's got larger mana reservoirs than any four other human mages ah've ever met. Makes it pretty easy ta accomplish great feats then. On top a' that, she takes every possible route ta increase her mana efficiency and decrease loss. Half her study was filled with tomes and manuals meant for mages whose mana reservoirs are way too small."

"That's ridiculous," Talia said. "And don't most of those tricks for weak mages actually lower the power of your spells?"

"A lot of them," Hugh interjected, not looking up from his desk, "but not all of them. Some just require the use of much more complex spellforms, or are techniques to focus the mind's eye so distractions don't interfere, and so on and so forth. We learned a little about them in my spellform lecture."

Godrick just shrugged at that. "That's basically what Tarik told me too. Apparently her favorite combat strategy is just levitatin' house sized boulders and dropping them on her foes, so... not too much practical utility for me, though I did pick up a few tricks."

Sabae couldn't help but be a little impressed at that. It wasn't on the same scale as what her grandmother, Kanderon, or Indris could do, but it wasn't anything to laugh at. It seemed unlikely that any but the mightiest magical defenses could do anything at all against having a giant boulder dropped on them.

She shook her head and focused. "Well, even if she wouldn't talk about anything else, there might have still been something relevant. What was her attitude towards you like?"

Godrick shrugged. "She might have scowled a little bit when I tried ta get her ta talk about the vote, but she was otherwise all business."

"Maybe you'll get more chances in the future?" Talia said.

Godrick shook his head. "Tarik's one of the busiest mages in Skyhold, ah'm surprised Alustin and me da even managed ta arrange this one. Ah just hate the fact that it was a waste."

Sabae sighed. "It still might not be. What did you see on her desk?"

Sabae spent a solid two hours dragging every possible detail out of Godrick about the short meeting with Tarik. By the end, even he seemed frustrated and impatient, and Sabae could count the number of times she'd seen Godrick irritated on the fingers of one hand.

Eventually, though, Sabae had to admit to herself that they probably weren't going to get anything out of the lesson with Tarik. She certainly couldn't blame Godrick, because she doubted she could have gotten any more out of the headmaster.

Tarik really did confirm a lot of stereotypes about stone mage personalities.

Sabae's upcoming appointment in the enchanting labs did cheer everyone up quite a bit, however.

The four of them, unfortunately, were left to wait impatiently for nearly an hour before they were allowed into the enchanting labs.

Finally, a frazzled-looking journeyman enchanter came out to fetch them. Her hair had been cut short, but it still managed to be a complete mess, complete with several burnt patches. Most enchanters Sabae had met eventually just started shaving their heads.

It was something of a tossup whether alchemy or enchanting was more dangerous. Regardless, Sabae had no interest in learning either.

Sabae liked to tell herself that she wasn't a particularly vain person, but she was still entirely too attached to her hair to sacrifice it to her profession. Her long, gold-bordering-on-white hair barely even needed brushing in the morning, let alone any real attention.

The enchanter led them past a series of heavily reinforced windows looking in on various labs.

One held what looked like a miniature forest behind it, with trees growing in the shapes of bowstaves, shields, armor, and even a few swords.

The next appeared to be a glassblowing shop, save for the fact that the room itself had apparently been enchanted to nullify gravity— the enchanters inside, the tools, and the glass itself all floated in midair. Most of the items they were working on were eyetwisting shapes that didn't look like they should actually be possible, though Sabae spotted a few more familiar shapes— goblets, lenses, and the like.

Sabae moved past that one quickly. Glass mages were terrifying, even the non-combat ones. They were part of a select list of affinities you wanted to avoid at all costs. Affinities were far from equal when it came to danger, and glass was right near the top. She'd heard plenty of stories of mages who thought they'd survived battles with glass mages, only to die days or weeks later from inhaling too many tiny shards of glass.

The next room seemed to be an entirely normal blacksmithing shop, save for the fact that the smith was forging an inordinate number of wires of different metals into the sword he was working on. Well, that and the fact that Sabae was pretty sure she saw something staring at her from inside the forge fire.

The enchanter must have led them past a solid dozen labs, not to mention several hallways containing more. Sabae practically had to drag Talia away from a room filled with bones, where enchanters were carefully inlaying a bone staff with spellforms carved from the bones of other animals.

Finally, the enchanter led them down a slightly dingier hallway, where the labs tended to be filled with accumulated junk, miniature forges, lathes, and all sorts of other tools. She explained that these were the restoration labs, where old enchantments were repaired, altered, or decommissioned safely. Only half of them were full.

The lab the four of them were led into was near the end of that hall, but Sabae was impatient enough that she paid little attention to the activity in the other restoration labs.

As they reached the last lab in the hall, she leaned up against the glass, smiling. There, sitting clamped in vices on the counter, lay her buckler.

Hugh had found the little round metal shield for her while they were trapped down in the labyrinth last year, but it had been too badly damaged to work at the time. Alustin had left it in the care of Skyhold's enchanters, and it had taken them months to repair it.

Which was a bit unfair, to Sabae's mind, considering how much less time it had taken for Indris' enchanters to build Godrick's hammer, but then, having a two hundred foot dragon ordering you around was likely a pretty good motivator.

"This shield was a bit of a nightmare to work on," the journeyman enchanter said, as she let them into the lab. "Don't touch anything, by the way, unless you enjoy melting. Anyhow, there was an entire missing front plate to the shield that we had to reconstruct from scratch. As it was, the first decent hit against it would have broken the spellforms and made the whole thing explode, most likely."

The buckler was considerably thicker than the last time Sabae had seen it, and the front of the little round shield curved gently, instead of just being flat.

The enchanter pulled out a series of sketches of the spellforms inside the shield, pointing to various parts as she talked. "Since the front plate was completely missing, we ended up having to devise entirely new spellforms for the front plate— thankfully, most of the core functionality of the shield was on the back plate. The missing spellform links were easy enough to figure out, and we added spellforms to reinforce the shield and to reduce the impact from blows to the front. Pretty standard stuff on a shield."

The enchanter started freeing the shield from the vices.

"So… what does it actually do?" Sabae asked.

The enchanter gave her an incredulous look. "What?"

Sabae shrugged. "Our master likes to surprise us. He refused to tell me what the enchantment does."

The enchanter just sighed at that. "One of those, huh? My master was the same way." A sudden grin crossed her face as she finished freeing the shield, then set it on the counter. "So I suppose in that spirit, I should show you what it does, rather than just telling you. Pick it up."

Sabae traded excited looks with the others, then she reached out to lift the shield.

It wouldn't budge in the slightest.

Sabae grunted and pulled for a while, then glanced over at Godrick. "Want to give it a try?"

Godrick cracked his knuckles and smiled. "It would be mah pleasure."

The massive apprentice grasped the shield firmly with both hands, then heaved. Sabae could see his face begin to darken with the effort, and she could see the stone counter actually begin to shake before Godrick gave up, gasping for breath.

The enchanter laughed, then almost casually reached out and picked it up, handing it to Sabae.

"How…?" Sabae started, turning over the buckler in her hands to inspect it. She noticed that there weren't any straps on the back, or even places to put them.

"When you channel mana into the shield, you can make it stick to things," the enchanter said. "It only sticks to what you want it to stick to, and it's incredibly mana efficient— I was able to keep it stuck to the counter even with as much force as your friend there was putting into it. Honestly, if he'd put much more effort into it, he probably would have torn off the surface of the counter before the enchantment broke."

"How am I supposed to carry it without straps?" Sabae asked.

"Same thing," the enchanter said. "Just stick it to your arm. The enchantment has a function built into it to keep from sticking too hard in the wrong places and tearing your skin, which the impact dampening enchantment in the front should help with too. When you're not using it, just stick it to your back."

A Traitor in Skyhold

Sabae did so, and found that the shield would adhere and come loose perfectly, so that it wasn't uncomfortable or difficult to flex her back, twist, or even bend over.

"You can selectively stick to whatever you want, and let things go from the shield without releasing everything else," the enchanter said. "It's got a surprisingly far range for channeling mana into it— a good couple of hundred feet, though control of it gets worse with distance— and other mages can't channel mana into it while you are. That last is pretty standard for most magical items, but this one actually takes it a step further— after you use it regularly for at least a couple of months, it should begin to attune to you, to the point where other mages won't be able to use it at all. Once it's attuned to you, it can probably go a solid year or two before anyone else will be able to use it. It's a handy little enchantment, though it's not often used, thanks to its complexity."

Sabae could feel a wide smile working across her face.

"Let's see if I'm missing anything…" the enchanter muttered, poring over the spellform diagrams. "Oh, right! It's got its own small built-in mana reservoir, so you can leave it stuck to something, and it will stay there for quite some time. Magic items with their own mana reservoirs are extremely rare, you're lucky to have it. And it's all quite intuitive to use. It shouldn't take too much practice to get used to it."

"It'll be pretty handy for binding up your enemies' weapons when they attack you with them, at least," Talia said. Sabae could tell the tattooed redhead was trying to sound casual, but the envious look on her face was pretty obvious.

Sabae smiled at her buckler. "Oh, I can think of much more interesting uses for it than that already."

CHAPTER FIFTEEN

Dragon Bones

Talia glared at the shard of dragon bone lying on the stone slab she used as a table.

When she'd started working with the dragon bone, she was expecting it to give her much larger explosions.

She hadn't gotten them.

Instead, Ataerg's bones were actually proving resistant to her magic.

Talia had spent quite some time poring through the books on bone magic that Alustin had provided for her, and they did seem to have a reputation as being among the most difficult bones to work with, so they weren't particularly favored for ammunition or other combat uses by bone mages.

They were, however, highly favored for more long-term use. Bone mages lucky enough (or dangerous enough) to get their hands on dragon bone regularly fashioned it into weapons and armor. It was particularly notorious for holding enchantments well.

Thankfully, dragons didn't, for the most part, tend to take offense at humans using dragon bones like this— they liked to keep the bones of their rivals as trophies, and viewed using dragon bones to craft with as a fairly natural extension of that.

Most of the books still agreed that it was best not to flaunt that you were using dragon bones, however. Better safe than sorry.

Talia just kept glaring at the shard of Ataerg's bones. Even the legendary strength of dragon bone hadn't held up to the impact that killed the ancient wyrm, but that actually made it quite a bit easier for Talia— otherwise, few of the pieces would have been small enough for Talia to carry, let alone work with.

She picked up the forearm sized shard, looking it over for the twentieth time. About half its thickness was from the surface of the bone— a smooth, thick, opalescent white layer that was almost impregnable. The inner part of the bone was spongy and porous, which Talia imagined helped cut down on weight, though it was already extremely light.

The inner part looked quite fragile, but she'd earned enough cuts from it to prove otherwise. She'd barely been able to chip it with a hammer, and even Godrick and his sledgehammer had trouble with it.

A big part of that was likely thanks to Ataerg's age— dragon bones grew steadily stronger as dragons aged and grew. It slowed over time, but never stopped entirely.

She shook her head. No point staring at the damn thing all day, might as well try another test.

Talia retreated from the slab, climbing into the little bunker just across the chamber. There was a thick slab of enchanted glass facing the slab, so she could get a good look at the explosions she was creating without concern. The bunker also had a number of sound dampening enchantments to protect her ears from the noise.

Talia shook her hair out of her face, then focused on the dragon bone. She visualized the mana channeling spellform, and then began pumping mana into the shard.

The bone promptly began glowing, but there wasn't even a hint of growth. She waited a few seconds to be sure, but nothing happened. Talia sighed and began pumping more mana in.

Finally, the bone shard reached its limit. Dragon bone seemed to have a very strict tolerance for how much of her mana it would accept. And when it reached that limit, it started expelling that heat. Violently.

Jets of fire gouted out of the bone for a moment, then fizzled out just as quickly.

It would seem useful, save for the fact that it was largely uncontrollable. And, while Talia had finally found a way to magically produce actual fire, uncontrollably doing so was worse than not doing so at all.

Fire really wasn't the sort of thing you wanted uncontrolled.

Talia sighed and went to go check the bone, just in case anything was different this time.

Nothing.

She trudged back to the bunker, then started to pump mana into the bone again. She was currently trying to determine the exact mana capacity of dragon bone, which required pumping mana in slow increments.

She'd tried a few different ways of channeling mana into bones so far. The first time she'd succeeded at using her bone affinity— well, managed to blow a giant crab up with it— she'd accomplished it via just flooding the mana through her spellform tattoos. It had worked, but it had been really messy.

It had also been incredibly painful.

No one had figured out exactly what part of her tattoos was causing many of the strange interactions with her bone affinity— her tattoos had literally dozens of functions, ranging from enhancing the power of her fire spells, to increasing her control, to even boosting the range of her affinity senses.

If she had actually had a fire affinity, she would have been truly terrifying. All of her brothers had fire affinities, as did both of her parents, so she should have been a safe bet as well.

She hadn't been.

Still, if she had, she never would have come to Skyhold, or met Sabae, Godrick, and Hugh, or gotten the opportunities to blow up a pirate ship or kill a...

Talia shook her head. It was best not to obsess too much about secrets, unless you wanted to accidentally expose them.

One of the planned functions of her tattoos had been to let her cast a limited number of fire spells without spellforms— Alustin was fairly sure that was how she'd managed to charge the bones with mana in the first place. It was an unintended use, but it worked, unlike almost every actual bone spellform she'd tried. They usually just collapsed, uncontrollably starting fires.

It really needed to be reiterated that successful fire mages were *not* fans of anything uncontrolled or chaotic. They were fans of things that were explosive and destructive, certainly, but doing anything uncontrolled was a great way to maim or kill yourself when it came to fire magic.

Based off the way Alustin had explained it to her, when the body converted raw mana from the aether into attuned mana, it fundamentally altered the properties of the mana. It still behaved like a liquid for every known affinity, but there were major changes to mana's analogues to density, viscosity, and the like, based off what affinity the mana had been attuned to.

That didn't even go into all the properties mana had that didn't correspond to any natural fluid whatsoever, but no one had ever come up with a better analogy for mana's behavior.

After the mana was converted, the body could store it for quite some time, though it would leak away eventually. In order to cast spells, the mana had to be forced into certain patterns of flow, which caused the attuned mana to react, converting to energy in the form of spells. Spellforms did this explicitly and reliably. Formless casting was the art of forcing the mana to move in the necessary patterns with your will alone— it could be done, but it required singular focus and strength of will, and it was still usually less precise and controllable. The speed of casting and raw power you got in return was usually considered worth it, however.

Her tattoos were trying to help her body convert the aether into fire mana— but since her body wasn't actually converting aether into fire mana, it forced a number of non-standard properties onto her bone and dream mana. Spellforms for a particular attunement were usually built to work with the quirks of that type of mana— forcing the wrong type of mana into it usually forced it to fail. And, since her mana didn't match any other known type, her spellforms tended to fail quite badly, especially with her bone mana.

Her altered dream mana wasn't nearly so much of a problem— dream mana was capable of replicating the behavior of quite a few other types of mana, so its spellforms tended towards the robust. Talia was much less versatile than most dream mages, but she definitely wasn't complaining, since she could produce dreamfire more easily and in much larger quantities than other dream mages.

Her bone mana, though… no one had ever run into anything like it. None of the bone mages at Skyhold had been the slightest bit of use in figuring it out, and they'd repeatedly taken that out on her, claiming it was just her failing as a student. The others might think it odd that Alustin wasn't turning to any bone mages to help her, but Talia was actually glad of it.

It was still a challenge, though. She'd found a couple of very basic mana channeling spells that worked for charging bones, but any spellforms more complex were beyond her. Spellform improvisation and construction like Hugh did wasn't much use, either— the ability to construct spellforms was based off understanding the specific properties of the mana type in question and adapting the spellform to work with it. Formless casting didn't work around that— it actually required a much greater understanding of the properties of the mana in question, since you could do magic via spellform using simple rote memorization, or even just carrying pictures of spellforms in a spellbook. Most affinities had histories going back centuries or millennia, so their properties were well understood.

Talia had none of that. Her weird bone affinity had no history, no tradition to draw from, nothing. Any understanding about the properties of its mana, any spells— she'd most likely have to figure them out herself, and then record them in case anyone else developed something like her attunement.

Which was unlikely. Unique attunements like hers were extremely rare, but they did happen— and then usually never happened again.

If there had been someone else, maybe they'd know a way to make using her affinity stop hurting. Using the spellforms worked better than forcing it through her tattoos, but using her bone affinity more than a handful of times in a day began getting painful quickly. Not enough to stop her, or even slow her down, but it certainly wasn't pleasant.

She wasn't going to complain to anyone— not about the pain and not about the fact that she didn't really have anyone to turn to for help. She could handle it without anyone's help. But sometimes…

Talia shook herself out of her fugue. She'd run around that mental bush more times than she could count, and any answers she thought she was chasing around it had long since fled. She needed to finish this round of experiments before dinner.

She blinked in surprise. She'd spaced off for at least a couple of minutes, and the bone was still glowing— it hadn't expelled the heat at all.

Now *that* was interesting.

Talia quickly donned the thick flame-resistant suit that hung in the bunker. The glass facemask was enchanted the same way the bunker window was, and spellforms were sewn into the thick leather of the suit. It was hot, uncomfortable, and smelly, but if there was one thing Talia respected, it was fire.

She had worried that the bone shard might expel its heat while she was putting the suit on, but it was still glowing strong by the time she finished.

Talia approached it carefully, in case it was about to jet flame like in the past tests. It... seemed stable, though.

She carefully pulled off one glove and reached out. She could feel the heat rolling off the shard even from a foot away. Much closer and it actually got painful just having her hand there.

Talia retreated back to the bunker and cast a simple temperature gauge cantrip on the bone shard. The cantrip didn't actually directly measure the bone's temperature— it instead tried to match the temperature of a shielded thermometer in the bunker to the temperature of whatever she cast the cantrip on.

The readings were always a bit off, since her tattoo messed up cantrips as well— they were prone to setting things on fire, or at least heating them up, but Alustin had helped her precisely calibrate how much her cantrip increased the temperature reading by, so she could account for that easily enough.

A smile threatened to split her face in half. She considered running to find the others in order to tell them about her discovery, but decided against it. Hugh was getting ridiculous again as Midwinter and Avah's next visit drew closer. He spent half his time moping and worrying that Avah was going to suddenly decide she wasn't interested anymore, and the other half being unbearably excited and cheerful about the upcoming visit.

Either way, he hardly talked about anything else.

Talia didn't dislike Avah, she just didn't think she was right for Hugh.

She shook her hair out of her eyes again. Besides, there was an excellent reason not to tell her friends about her discovery just yet— surprising people with new ways to destroy things was even more entertaining than destroying things.

Well, no, that was a lie. Destroying things was definitely more fun. The surprise thing was a close second, though.

CHAPTER SIXTEEN

Obsidian

Hugh had been surprised to find out that he was not going to be the one meeting Rutliss the Red— instead, he'd been scheduled to meet Abyla Ceutas.

Sabae had been pleased by the idea, though.

"We'd be deliberately running our ship onto the rocks if you met with Rutliss and I met with Abyla," Sabae had told him. "She hates my family, and Rutliss hates Kanderon. Either way, it doesn't seem plausible that we're trying to convince them to change their votes if we're antagonizing them."

"But we've been mainly focusing on…" Hugh had started.

"You've read all of the suspect dossiers, haven't you?" Sabae interrupted. "It will be fine."

Judging by Abyla's office alone, her family was the kind of wealthy that loved to rub their wealth in your face, yet abhorred ostentation. There was nothing in the way of gaudy ornamentation or obvious displays of wealth. Instead, it came out in the quality of her desk and chairs and the elegance of the wall-hangings.

That was the third thing you noticed when you walked into Abyla's office.

The second thing you noticed was the back wall. Or, rather, the lack of a back wall. Abyla's office had a waist high retaining wall, but above that, it was simply open to the Endless Erg behind her. From this high up the mountain, the view stretched on seemingly forever. Hugh could spot at least a dozen ships sailing the desert, looking like insects from this high up and far away.

Another might not have paid them attention, but there was a fairly intricate ward along the top of the retaining wall, though Hugh couldn't quite make out what it did from here.

The first thing you noticed were the floor, walls, and ceiling of Abyla's office. She'd fused them all into solid obsidian. The obsidian seemed to glow from within as the desert sun hit it, giving the office a strange, jewel-like shimmer. Even the retaining wall was crafted out of pure obsidian.

Hugh didn't feel ashamed in the slightest to admit he was intimidated by the office. The dossier had even warned him about the obsidian— she'd crafted the room herself using her magma affinity.

The last thing you saw was Abyla. By the time you finished taking in the sights, she'd had plenty of time to take your measure.

Abyla was a stern woman in early middle age. She made no effort to dye or conceal her white hairs, and she sat rigidly in a plain— though clearly expensive— wooden chair. She held a quill in hand, staring at Hugh as though he were interrupting her.

Hugh had an appointment, but part of him still felt like he should leave and stop wasting her time.

"I'm here to…" Hugh started.

"No," Abyla said, "you're not. Despite what I'm sure is a very convincing cover story, you're here to try and persuade me that I should allow you and your friends to violate both Skyhold policy and centuries of tradition, because you claim to have a demon after you. While I understand that getting stranded in the depths of the labyrinth was traumatic for you and your friends, I unfortunately have to doubt your claims of running into the demon Bakori, given how public and complete his destruction by Kanderon was two centuries ago. And even if he did somehow survive, our security measures should be more than enough to keep you safe during the test. I'm sympathetic to your fears, but you'll need to face them to get over them. I won't be changing my vote."

Abyla turned back to her desk and resumed writing.

Hugh just gaped at her. They'd expected the first level of cover story to be seen through, but they hadn't expected anything quite like this.

"You may go now," Abyla said, not looking up at Hugh.

Hugh found himself turning to leave almost without thinking, then stopped.

He couldn't just leave with nothing. Maybe they should have just had Sabae come instead, if…

Hugh gulped, then turned around.

"You're lying," he said, his voice quavering.

Abyla stopped writing, set down her quill, and stared at him.

"Excuse me?" she asked, her voice flat.

"You didn't vote against us because you don't believe us, or because you care that much about tradition," Hugh said, shaking a little out of fear. A large part of him couldn't believe what he had just said, and was telling him to apologize and run away right this instant. He somehow ignored it and pushed on. "You voted against us because of Sabae, because you have a grudge against the Kaen Das family. You're abusing your power to get petty revenge."

Abyla stood up, furious. "How dare you speak to a council member this way!" she yelled. "Do you know what I could do to you…"

"Nothing," Hugh interrupted. "One mage can't punish another's apprentice without taking them before the council. And when a councilor is involved, it has to be before the entire council, not just the academic council. And from what Sabae tells me, Kanderon has a lot more allies on the full council than you do."

Hugh had, during the height of Rhodes' bullying last year, spent quite some time looking through Skyhold's disciplinary rules. He hadn't found anything to help stop Rhodes, but he knew exactly the grounds he stood on here.

Abyla glared at him, turning red in the face. Hugh realized that the room was getting quite a bit hotter, and there was a glow coming from the obsidian surfaces in the room that was *not* reflected daylight.

"You little brat!" Abyla spat out. "Do you have any idea…"

She caught her breath, then laughed. There wasn't any humor to it.

"You know what? You're right," Abyla said. "I did vote against the alternate test because of the Kaen Das chit. Her family is a blight, and if she gets killed down in the labyrinth, well, I wouldn't complain. I don't expect it to happen, however— what I expect to happen is that her damn grandmother will withdraw her from Skyhold first, or that she'd willingly leave the Academy herself. I had intended to change my vote after that happened to allow you to take the alternate test, but I think you've successfully taken that off the table."

Abyla smiled widely. "You can leave now. Enjoy getting eaten by a demon— unless, of course, you want to withdraw from Skyhold. Oh, and I'm not sure if you're aware, but mages affiliated with Skyhold can't teach or aid dropouts in their education. Which includes Alustin and Kanderon."

She sat back down and started writing again, ignoring Hugh. The heat from the obsidian had only grown stronger, and it was glowing a dull red now.

Hugh left.

Sabae and Talia just stared at Hugh in shock after he finished telling them about his meeting with Abyla.

"Talia has been a truly awful influence on you," Sabae finally said.

Talia jabbed her in the side with a finger.

"I like confident Hugh," Talia said.

"You mean insane Hugh, right?" Sabae asked.

Hugh snorted at that, sitting back down on his bed. "I found a convenient corner to have a panic attack in for a solid hour after the meeting. I don't think confident is the right word here, but I wasn't being crazy, either."

"You threw away our chance of changing the vote," Sabae said.

Hugh shook his head. "She was only going to change her vote if you left or were withdrawn, Sabae. That's not good enough. Besides, our first priority isn't changing the vote, it's finding the traitor."

Sabae frowned at that. "There are plenty of other agents working to try and figure that out, Hugh. We need to balance our goals here. Seriously, how likely is it that four apprentices will solve the problem?"

"Probably not very," Hugh admitted. "But we just got our first piece of solid evidence in the case. I got Abyla to admit that she voted against the alternate test because of you."

"We already basically knew that," Sabae said, frowning.

Talia poked her in the side again. "If it were literally any other guess about the case you'd demand evidence of some sort."

Sabae glared at Talia— she was the least tolerant of being poked and elbowed by the redhead of anyone in the group— but it was fairly halfhearted.

"You're right, I guess," Sabae muttered.

"And?" Talia said.

"And what?" Sabae asked.

"Thank Hugh for having your back and refusing to throw you under the wagon wheels?"

"I didn't actually find out that she was planning to…" Hugh started.

"Hugh, quit trying to diminish your victories," Talia said. "You deliberately provoked Abyla in defense of Sabae."

Hugh opened his mouth to respond, but Sabae beat him to it. "Hugh never would have needed to stand up to her if it wasn't for me. It's my fault…"

Hugh threw his pillow at her. "We had that conversation already, quit that. It's not your fault Abyla is a raging jerk."

Sabae caught the pillow in midair and sighed. "Sorry. I'm supposed to be the one reminding you all not to be idiots, not the other way around. And... thank you."

A knock came at the door. Talia got up and opened it, letting Godrick in— who was carrying a cake.

"Happy birthday!" Hugh, Talia, and Godrick chorused.

Sabae just stared at them. "It's not my birth..."

She stopped and did some mental math in her head.

"It is my birthday, isn't it?"

The others burst out laughing.

Sabae sighed. "I think I might have too much on my plate right now."

"You're seventeen now, by the way," Talia said. "Just in case you'd forgotten."

Sabae made a rude gesture at her.

They pulled Sabae's gifts out from under Hugh's bed while they dug into the cake.

Godrick had gotten Sabae an enchanted blacksmith puzzle— interlocked metal shapes that had to be solved by rotating, shifting, and sliding them apart. They were deceptively complex, and each time this one got solved it reshaped itself into a whole new puzzle.

Talia had painstakingly carved Sabae a pair of hairsticks out of the opalescent white outer layer of dragonbone. She'd even gone to the trouble of carving the traditional flames of Clan Castis into them— something done only for good friends of the clan. She'd also given Hugh a Clan Castis dagger for his last birthday.

Hugh had spent ages trying to figure out what to get Sabae for her birthday. He'd known that he wanted to craft her something himself— partially because his modest allowance he received from Alustin didn't go that far, but mostly because he just really enjoyed making things for his friends.

For her birthday, he'd made Talia a protective ward circle on a strip of leather that could be unrolled anywhere. He'd briefly considered making the same thing for Sabae, but he dismissed the idea. As useful as a portable ward was, he didn't think they needed multiple of them in the group, and he wanted to be a little more creative with his gifts.

The problem was, of course, that wards weren't generally the best choice for gifts. Since wards were designed to apply to specific spatial locations, taking into account the movement of the planet, they didn't tend to travel well. Hugh could pull it off better than most, since he could imbue his will into his wards, but that only worked while he was the one powering them. That had, in fact, likely been the only reason his old ward slingstones hadn't exploded while he was carrying them around.

You could build a ward to handle travel better, which he was doing with his current ward slingstones, but it was tricky. Plus, it was tough finding a way to craft a personal ward-based item that worked as well as a comparable enchanted item.

Eventually, though, he'd settled on something. He'd bought Sabae a travel pack, then sewn a series of wards into the mouth of the pack— wards that excluded dirt, grease, and various pests from passing. Putting an item of clothing (or anything) into the pack would actually clean it. Not as well as actually washing it, of course, but it was better than nothing, especially while traveling.

Hugh had been pretty rusty at sewing— he'd needed to repair his own clothes often enough back in Emblin, though he hadn't needed to since he arrived at Skyhold. He'd pricked his fingers countless times while working on it, and he'd needed to pick away the ward thread more times than he could count and restart, but he'd finally gotten it.

He'd had some difficulty deciding whether to have it powered by the user or by tapping into the local aether—wards, unlike enchantments, generally didn't drain the surrounding aether to any noticeable degree, but if he did that, then it would be active all the time, and dirt would start getting trapped inside the ward as well.

Which he found out the hard way.

Eventually, he'd managed to rig the ward to be one directional, which had taken quite a bit more time.

His homework had definitely suffered for a while there, between that and crafting Godrick's present, since his birthday was a couple of days before Midwinter.

Hugh didn't mention any of that to Sabae, though. As much as he enjoyed monologuing about his wards, Sabae's birthday was perhaps not the best time for that.

Sabae, thankfully, relaxed quite a bit over the course of the afternoon— by the time they'd finished giving the gifts, she was laughing and joking almost like normal again.

Hugh's spellbook, unfortunately, decided that now was the best time to try and steal a piece of cake, which… didn't go exceptionally well, especially for the spellbook.

CHAPTER SEVENTEEN

Arrivals

Alustin and the *Moonless Owl* both returned to Skyhold within a week of one another.

Alustin arrived first, riding in on another Radhan vessel. Radhan traders made up a relatively small percent of the sandships travelling the Endless Erg (or on any sea, for that matter), but according to Alustin, they were not only the most reliable, but also the friendliest option.

He also returned with a broken arm and cryptic complaints about treasure hunters and unreliable treasure maps.

Hugh was certainly happy to see him— not least because he was ready for Alustin to take over their lessons in the Library again. The librarian that had been covering for him— a copper mage always surrounded in floating, intricate patterns of wire, which she could redistribute heat through rapidly, or use to ensnare recalcitrant books— was interesting to listen to lecture about the ecosystem of books in the library, but she was no Librarian Errant.

Hugh was definitely getting rather attached to the idea of joining the Librarians Errant.

Alustin's reaction in regards to the news from Hugh's visit with Abyla was somewhat mixed— he was certainly pleased at the confirmation of his hypothesis in regards to her motives, but he thought Hugh had taken too much of a risk. Even with a patron as powerful as Kanderon, there was still plenty of trouble Abyla could cause him.

Hugh and his friends spent the afternoon of the *Owl's* arrival waiting for it at a harborside teashop. Alustin had informed them fairly precisely when the sandship was due in to port, but Hugh was feeling too antsy to get anything serious done.

Alustin joined them about a half-hour before the ship arrived. Skyhold's healers had fixed up his arm easily enough, but he was still favoring it quite a bit. Healing might be magic, but it wasn't by any means perfect or instantaneous.

Hugh wasn't really paying attention to the conversation, spending most of his time watching the horizon. He'd already mistaken several other sandships for the *Owl* already. Even when he didn't say anything to anyone else, it was still fairly embarrassing— the *Owl* was highly distinctive. It was fairly low and wide as far as sandships went, and instead of traveling on runners, it slid along its broad, sled-like hull instead.

Hugh caught a glimpse of red hair in the crowd on the docks and frowned. He could have sworn that was Captain Bandon from Theras Tel, but…

He shook his head and turned his attention back to the conversation at hand.

"There's a reason most mages don't carry that many enchanted items with them, Talia," Alustin was saying. "Either you have to supply mana to them yourself or they tap into the local aether, which can interfere with your own ability to refill your mana reservoirs, even in a place as aether-rich as Skyhold. I really don't recommend carrying more than two or three at a time."

"And what if you're only planning to use the ones you're powering yourself, and only for very specific situations?" Talia said. "It could greatly improve your versatility, couldn't it? And some enchantments even have their own mana reservoirs built in."

Alustin sighed. "Yes, but that's the sort of thing you're usually better just developing your own magic to help you do. Most affinities are far more versatile than you'd think. Also, Skyhold only produces a handful of enchanted items with their own mana reservoirs each year. They're hellishly difficult to make, and there's an enormous waiting list for them. I'd feel far more comfortable about all this if you'd tell me exactly what sorts of enchanted items you'd commissioned."

Talia considered. "I'd really rather it be a surprise, honestly."

"How can you afford that many commissions, anyhow?" Godrick asked.

"You know I can just go over your head and get the information from the enchanters directly, right?" Alustin asked.

"My clan's been raiding and pillaging for ages, and it's not like we have that much to spend it on. We live way up in the mountains, and we're pretty self-sufficient. We have a huge hoard that's just been sitting there for generations. How do you think my family could afford to send me halfway across the continent to a school as expensive as Skyhold?" Talia said to Godrick, then turned back to Alustin. "And you could do that, but that would be a hassle involving lots of paperwork for you, and it'd also ruin the surprise."

Hugh just felt bemused at all of this. Talia had been dropping hints about her commissions for days now. She might intend it to be a surprise, but whenever she did show them her new enchanted items, he was fairly sure they were going to be a bit of a letdown after all this.

144

The *Owl's* arrival went about the same as the last time— Avah was nothing if not quite public about her affection, and the crew of the *Owl* were, as usual, endlessly entertained by Hugh's embarrassment.

So were his traitor friends, too. Hugh felt a moment of gratitude towards Talia, who at least was pretending like she wasn't seeing anything to give Hugh a little privacy.

Hugh was thankful he wasn't in Alustin's shoes right now, though. He'd rather deal with a little public embarrassment— which did have its upsides— than with the lecture Alustin was receiving from Deila about keeping Avah and Irrick safe while they were staying here.

Irrick and Avah had packed surprisingly lightly, bringing only a single small bag apiece. Or maybe not so surprisingly, considering that they lived on a cramped ship year-round.

Godrick, of course, immediately picked up both bags and refused to let anyone else help. He was, as always, essentially incapable of not helping people when they had something to carry.

Hugh, partially to be helpful and partially to get back at Godrick for enjoying his earlier embarrassment, promptly cast a levitation cantrip on the bags to lighten them— not enough that anyone else would see, but enough that Godrick noticed immediately.

Alustin led the group up through the passages and stairwells of Skyhold to the student dormitories where Talia, Godrick, and Sabae slept, and where Avah and Irrick would be staying as well. The rooms were all individual ones, and there were always extra unused rooms— Skyhold's population was higher than ever, according to Kanderon, but it seemed to never run out of empty hallways, classrooms, dorms, or passages.

There were supposed to be secret rooms and passages all over the place, too, but Hugh and the others hadn't really found any, beyond his room and a hidden entrance into the Grand Library.

The rooms set aside for Avah and Irrick passed Deila's inspection— barely. Avah's grandmother reminded them to come say goodbye before the *Owl* left harbor, then she dragged Alustin away to inspect the dining halls.

"So where are your rooms?" Avah asked. Their tour hadn't made it up here on the last visit.

"Right this way," Sabae said.

Hugh struggled to hold back a smirk.

"Alustin and Godrick's dad decided it would be most convenient to move us all into adjacent rooms," Sabae said, leading them the short distance from the guest dorms to their hallway.

"This is my room," Sabae said, opening her door. The wards Hugh had installed for the others on their rooms were more subtle than the ones on his room, but they were powerful nonetheless, and wouldn't let anyone outside of their group open their doors. That didn't even mention the sturdy, conventional locks on the doors.

Sabae's walls were covered in thick, embroidered wall hangings and tapestries from Ras Andis, and she had a thick patterned rug softening the stone floor. She'd covered all the glowcrystals in the room, save the one above her desk, with thin fabric coverings to soften the light. The whole room was a wash of color. All of her books, homework, clothes, and other items were neatly put away, and her bed was precisely made without a wrinkle— it was rare for Sabae's room to be anything but spotless. There weren't any windows, but then, none of the dorm rooms had windows.

Avah promptly had to inspect all of Sabae's decorations in detail, of course.

"This is part of how you can tell that Avah plans on captaining her own ship someday," Irrick confided to the others. "You can't take her anywhere near anything that even vaguely resembles trade goods without having her inspect them."

Hugh imagined himself living on a ship full time—Librarians Errant traveled all the time, so it wouldn't be impossible. Alustin actually spent far more time at Skyhold than most of his order since he'd taken on apprentices.

Eventually, Irrick dragged Avah out so they could continue the tour.

Talia's room was almost the exact opposite of Sabae's. The room was almost entirely filled with clutter. Weapons and animal bones of all sorts hung on her walls or were propped up in the corners. Her desk was covered with jumbled papers and stacks of novels, and more heaps of books and bones turned the floor into a maze. At least one of her glowcrystals had been shattered somehow, and there were quite a few suspicious looking burn marks on the walls. Talia's bed was a tangled heap of blankets, pillows, and at least one wolf pelt.

"I feel like I'd trip on a pile of books and disembowel myself on a battleaxe if I tried to walk through here," Irrick said.

Talia gave him an affronted look. "I keep all of my weapons properly put away, thank you very much."

"Is that a spiked flail underneath your bed?" Avah asked.

Hugh peered under the bed as best as he could from this angle. Sure enough, there was a flail lying underneath the bed.

"When did you get that?" he said. "I thought you weren't planning on taking flails to any of the Midwinter balls."

Talia gave him a dirty look, but Avah interrupted first, grabbing Hugh's arm. "Midwinter ball? As in dancing and such?"

"Yeah," Hugh said. "There's a few of them on Midwinter night."

"And you weren't going to take me?" Avah asked.

"Of course I was," Hugh said.

Honestly, he hadn't really thought about it that much— he hadn't attended any of the festivities last Midwinter night. At the time, he'd only just met Talia and Sabae, and he preferred to spend every moment he could avoiding other people.

"I'm going to need to fetch a few more things from the ship before it leaves, then," Avah said, smiling.

"Fetching later, more tours now!" Irrick said.

They probably should have started with Godrick's room, Hugh thought. Compared to the other stops on the tour, it was almost disappointingly normal. There were a few books and papers scattered around, but Hugh wouldn't call it messy, by any means, just a little untidy. The only things of note were Godrick's enchanted warhammer propped up in one corner and his oversized bed.

Irrick, of course, immediately strode into the room and flopped right down onto the bed. He shifted a bit, testing it out, then sat up and smiled. "Roomy," he said, waggling his eyebrows at Godrick.

It was Hugh's turn to get to enjoy one of his friends being embarrassed now, and he savored every moment of it.

It did honestly feel a little strange to Hugh that embarrassment might not always be unpleasant. Before he'd gotten to know his friends, it had always been miserable for him, but it was somehow… comfortable now. He knew that there was no cruelty to his or his friends' enjoyment, which made a world of difference.

"Please, like you didn't see this room last time we were here," Avah said, sticking her tongue out at Irrick.

Godrick looked a little more uncomfortable now, so Hugh quickly spoke up. "Who wants to see my room?"

He could tell his friends were struggling to contain their laughter at that.

They went down the hall to the next door down, Avah and Irrick bickering cheerfully the whole way.

Avah pushed right up to the front next to Hugh as he opened the door…

To an empty room, save for a single thin blanket and small pillow on the floor.

Avah and Irrick just stared at the room, dumbfounded. "Is that…" Avah said, "is that really your room? You're messing with me, right?"

Hugh opened his mouth to respond, but simply burst out laughing instead. His friends all started laughing as well.

"Yeh ruined it, Hugh," Godrick said when he caught his breath.

"We were going to see how long we could get you to believe this was Hugh's actual room for." Sabae said, "If, you know, Hugh could keep a straight face."

This room actually sort of was Hugh's room— Alustin doubted the Academy would be overly fond of him sleeping in the library, so he'd set up a fake dorm room for Hugh. He never used it, but it was there. They'd just moved all the furniture to a nearby empty room for the prank.

"He really would be the best kind of opponent to play in cards," Irrick mused.

"Oh?" Hugh asked.

"The kind yeh can always beat," Godrick said.

Everyone burst out laughing, including Hugh.

"Come on," Hugh said, "let's show you my actual room."

Midwinter came quickly after that. Their classes had already started to wind down, and even Alustin seemed ready to give them a break— according to him, he wanted to make them into great mages, not break them, and a little downtime was important.

Godrick's father hosted Godrick's seventeenth birthday gathering, since none of their rooms were big enough to comfortably fit everyone. Artur's rooms were enormous— all of their rooms could probably fit inside. Artur even had his own kitchen— and, to everyone's delight, was an excellent chef.

He'd also magically shaped all his own furniture out of stone, except for the cushions, which definitely gave his apartment a distinctive feel.

Given how many people were there, Godrick had a fairly large pile of presents.

Talia had commissioned an enchanted shaving razor for Godrick— nothing fancy, it just never needed to be sharpened. She'd also had the Clan Castis flames added to it, so that Hugh, Sabae, and Godrick all had Clan Castis marked gifts.

Hugh was jealous— not of the razor, but of the fact that Godrick needed to shave more than once a week. Actually, he was a little jealous of the razor— he was pretty terrible at shaving, and there were, unfortunately, no shaving cantrips he'd been able to find so far.

Sabae had gotten Godrick a scent magic spellbook— an impressive find, given how rare scent mages were.

Hugh was particularly proud of his present for Godrick. He'd fashioned him a thick, T-shaped quartz faceplate for his stone armor— now that Godrick could fashion a helmet as well, his eye and mouth holes were among his few points of vulnerability. The faceplate he'd fashioned probably wouldn't stop a direct hit with a spell or weapon, but it would certainly turn glancing blows and keep debris out of his eyes better than the empty holes he had now.

Hugh had also fashioned it with several breathing holes surrounded by wards that would prevent dust, smoke, and various toxins from moving through them. This was a fairly common ward, so Hugh had only needed to modify it for moving around on a helmet.

Avah and Irrick had gotten Godrick a box full of all sorts of hammers, ranging from a tuning hammer smaller than Hugh's pinkie to a mallet half the size of Godrick's sledgehammer. Godrick, of course, thought it was hilarious.

Artur seemed a little embarrassed at his gift— he'd just bought Godrick a new set of formal wear. His self-deprecation had promptly been shouted down by the group, however, who had all happily gorged themselves on his cooking.

Plus everyone agreed that Godrick looked excellent in it.

CHAPTER EIGHTEEN

Midwinter

The Midwinter ball they'd chosen to attend was being held in a ballroom built into an outcrop that jutted out of the side of Skyhold towards the Skyreach Mountains. Three walls of the ballroom were open to the night, with only rows of— admittedly massive— columns holding up the outcrop above them.

The ballroom was lit by a series of massive floating glow crystals that hovered just below the ceiling, orbiting one another in a stately, intricate waltz.

Hugh, Godrick, and Sabae were waiting a little ways from the entrance for the others. Godrick was wearing his new formalwear, and Hugh and Sabae were just wearing their formal school uniforms.

Hugh was sorely tempted to sneak over to the wards inlaid into the floor between the columns. He was guessing their main function was keeping wind and temperature extremes out. The Endless Erg and the Skyreach Range bordering it had cooled off quite a bit as Midwinter approached, but Hugh wouldn't label it as anything like an actual winter. Still, nights in the desert were always chilly.

Sabae nudged Hugh. "Talia's here, and she's got a date!" she said.

Hugh turned around promptly at that. Talia hadn't said a word about having a date.

She also hadn't said a word about her outfit.

Talia was wearing an elegant, slim blue dress that perfectly matched the color of her spellform tattoos. The dress left her arms and shoulders exposed, but she wore matching gloves reaching up most of the way to her elbows. Both the gloves and dress bore intricate embroidered red spellforms that exactly matched the shade of her hair— which was done up in one of those deceptively simple looking hairstyles that must have taken her hours to pull off, especially considering how difficult her hair was to manage most of the time. She also had a large necklace dangling around her neck. She was even wearing an elegant pair of sandals that laced up her calves, instead of her usual heavy boots.

As Talia and her date drew closer, Hugh turned his attention to her date. To his surprise, he recognized him from their cryptography class. He was tall— taller than Sabae, though not anywhere near as tall as Godrick— good looking, and had the copper skin of a resident of southeastern Ithos.

Hugh was pretty sure his name was... Ussif? Uldan? Definitely something like that.

"Everyone," Talia said as they approached, "you remember Phusan from cryptography?"

Close enough.

Everyone nodded and said hello, though Sabae sighed theatrically. "I thought you weren't bringing a date," she said with a smile. "Now I'm the only one of us without one tonight. I'll have to pine tragically by the snack table, all alone while you all dance."

"And ah thought yeh were bringin' a spiked flail ta the ball," Godrick said. "And ah certainly didn't expect yeh ta come unarmed."

Talia scowled at him. "I told you I wasn't bringing a flail— that's a terrible choice for a dance. And I'm not unarmed."

Phusan gave her a slightly confused look at that.

"You definitely look unarmed," Hugh said.

Talia rolled her eyes, and pulled her dress up her right calf, revealing a sheathed dagger strapped to her tattooed calf. "Magic dagger from the labyrinth," she said.

She dropped the dress on that side and revealed a dagger strapped to her other calf. "My newest toy," she said fondly.

Something looked a bit odd about it to Hugh, but he didn't know enough about daggers to tell what— though it also bore enchantment spellforms.

Talia dropped her dress and reached into the top of her right glove, pulling out a short, thin, and flat throwing knife. "Throwing knife sheathes built into my gloves," she said, pulling yet another out of the top of her right glove, then tucking both away with a flourish.

Talia reached into the back of her dress, pulling out a thin coiled wire. "Garrote," she said, looking proud as could be.

Hugh was genuinely nervous that one of the faculty might see Talia showing off her weapons and kick them out of the ball, but Sabae and Godrick were struggling to contain their laughter.

Phusan was definitely looking a little uncomfortable.

Talia tucked away the garrote again and pointed to her hair. "They're not strictly weapons, but I have six of the lock pick hairpins Godrick gave me for my birthday in my hair."

Godrick chuckled. "Yeh certainly came prepared, ah'll give yeh that much. How long did…"

Talia interrupted him. "I'm not done yet!" She reached down to her sandal, pulling on a blue bead stuck to the back of her right sandal's heel. It came right out, revealing a thin needle engraved with intricate spellforms. "Tracking pin—tuck it into someone's clothes, you can *pinpoint* what direction they're in with a simple cantrip."

"That pun was the most painful weapon yet," Sabae muttered.

Talia stuck her tongue out at Sabae as she inserted the tracking pin back into her sandal. She then pulled a matching pin from her left sandal. "And this one's got a sobriety enchantment on it. Jab it into someone and pump mana into it, they'll sober up in minutes. It'll be really messy, though. Would be kind of fun to use this on a handsy drunk."

Talia paused. "At least, I think the tracking pin is on the right and the sobriety pin is on the left. I really should have gotten them with different color heads."

"Couldn't you just use the tracking cantrip to tell?" Sabae asked.

"Oh yeah!" Talia said.

She closed her eyes and concentrated for a few seconds, then frowned. "Huh. I guess I left the tracking pin in my room. So which one did I bring instead?"

Talia looked concerned for a minute, then just shrugged. "And then I've got this," she said, pointing to her necklace.

Hugh focused on it, then sighed. It was a sturdy silver chain bearing a series of bone beads, with a series of long, thick bone needles dangling down from it. They were clasped onto the necklace with thin loops attached to their blunt ends.

"I can tear all of these off individually without breaking the necklace," Talia said. "This one right here is carved from a chunk of whale bone— when I do my stuff with it, it sends drops of burning oil everywhere. I got the idea from a novel I read, where a ship's crew is stranded on an island in the far north, and has to burn whale bones to stay warm. They're full of oil and quite flammable."

"We need a proper name for the way you explode bones," Sabae said. "You guys name all of my techniques, so it's only fair."

"Bonefire," Hugh said idly.

"That's way ta obvious," Godrick said. "And what, are we goin' ta call it bonefirin' when Talia actually starts the process?"

"It's obvious, sure, but it's still the best name for it," Hugh said. "And no, we'll just call the process of actually doing it igniting it."

Talia cleared her throat pointedly. "I wasn't done yet," she said, then pointed to the next needle. "This one's made from birdbone— a hawk of some sort, I think. Barely had to carve it into shape. Birdbones grow and detonate much faster, thanks to being hollow and light, I think, but they don't explode as hard."

Phusan was looking a bit overwhelmed at this point.

155

"This one's carved from a cuttlebone," Talia said. "Cuttlefish use them to help control their buoyancy by altering the mix of gas and fluid in them. When I ignite them— thank you, Hugh— the explosion is mostly just a blast of superheated air."

"And this one is a squid pen," Talia said, pointing to the next one down the necklace. "Only bone squids have in their body. Barely had to carve it at all. It blasts out choking black smoke when it explodes, I think because... Are you all even still paying attention? I have quite a few to go."

Hugh was, in fact, not paying attention any longer. Avah had just walked in the room alongside Irrick, and he was having trouble paying attention to anything else at the moment.

Godrick would have normally been quite amused by Talia's frustration, her date's uncomfortable expression, or the fact that Hugh was staring so hard at Avah that his jaw had literally dropped open— Godrick had thought that was just a figure of speech, he'd never actually seen it happen before.

He was barely paying attention to that, however. Godrick was fairly sure he looked as silly staring at Irrick as Hugh did at Avah.

Irrick was wearing a sleek, well-fit suit that reminded Godrick of nothing more than sand being hit by midday sun. He'd had his usually messy hair cut down almost to the scalp on the sides and back, and a little longer on top. He'd even found an elegant little yellow flower to tuck behind one ear.

Godrick gulped, trying to regain his composure— or at least try not to stare at how Irrick's calves looked in his suit.

Irrick smiled at Godrick as he sauntered up to him, gently running a finger down Godrick's chest. Godrick realized that all the spit in his mouth had mysteriously vanished, leaving it bone dry.

Someone had definitely perfected some sort of mouth drying cantrip. Yep. That was it.

"Ah…, uh… ah like yer suit," Godrick finally managed. "Yeh look really pretty."

"I was going more for handsome," Irrick said, "but I can live with pretty. You're quite pretty yourself tonight."

"Do you like my suit?" Godrick said.

"I've seen it before," Irrick said, laughing, "but yes, I do. Your hair looks fantastic as well."

Godrick certainly hoped so, he'd spent over an hour tidying his curls with his da's help. Not for the first time, he felt a little envy for Sabae and Hugh— her for having perfect hair that never seemed to need any work, him for just having short hair. Not that Godrick would willingly give up his curls if he had a choice about it, but…

"You don't need to be nervous, Godrick," Avah said, laughing. "Irrick has spent the last three hours in a near constant state of panic, trying to make sure he looked perfect, convinced that you would hate it."

Irrick's face turned bright red. "You are literally the worst cousin ever!" he said.

Avah laughed even harder. "Well, next time I won't cut your hair for you, then."

Irrick swelled up with a response, but Godrick spoke first. "She did a really good job on yer hair," he said. "Ah like it this short."

Irrick turned even redder.

"Irrick tries to play it like he's all suave and sophisticated," Avah said to the others, "but he's not at all. Good at hiding it if you don't know him well, though."

Godrick managed to drag his eyes away from Irrick long enough to look at Avah's outfit. Hugh was still trying to catch his breath from Avah's customary enthusiastic greeting kiss.

Her dress was a strong but not lurid yellow, and she'd woven matching yellow flowers into her long, wavy, dark hair. The desert wasn't exactly renowned for its flowers, but she'd almost certainly gotten them from Skyhold's greenhouses on its southern face. The plant mages there could grow flowers to order in mere days— less, if you were willing to pay quite a bit. Godrick couldn't imagine they'd been cheap, but he'd seen Avah haggle before in Theras Tel— he almost felt sorry for the Skyhold plant mages. There was no way they'd gotten a good price out of her.

That also explained where Irrick's flower had come from.

Avah's dress was also very revealing, so poor Hugh was having a lot of trouble deciding where to look.

"The dancing probably won't start for a little bit." Sabae said, "Anyone want to join me in a raid on the snack and drink tables?"

"Are we actually going to plan it out, or just try and do as much damage as possible?" Talia asked.

"Ah say we lay waste ta them," Godrick said. He was feeling extremely hungry— he'd been too nervous most of the day to eat.

After they'd worked their way through the crowd and gotten their food and drinks, they all sat at one of the large empty tables near the dance floor. Godrick had piled up his plate with finger foods— there were more substantial offerings available, but he really liked finger foods.

Talia finally finished listing off all dozen or so different types of bone hanging from her necklace as the musicians finished setting up to play.

"They seem to be pretty disproportionately from sea creatures," Hugh said.

"I think there's just more variety when it comes to animal body structure in the ocean," Talia said. "There's not much difference between the way wolf and cow bones ignite, for instance, though there's more of a difference between them and birds."

"Your dad and Alustin are here," Sabae said, nudging Godrick.

Godrick glanced over. Sure enough, his da and Alustin had just entered, laughing about something. Alustin had, to Godrick's mild surprise, a date— he vaguely recognized her from somewhere, though he couldn't quite place her. She was definitely drawing a lot of eyes, though.

Sabae laughed. "That's the Alikean ambassador's secretary," she said. "How did Alustin get a date with her?"

"Isn't she…" Godrick started, then stopped. Alustin had mentioned that the Alikean ambassador's secretary was a suspected spy, but it was probably best not to mention that in public.

"And since when does Alustin go on dates at all?" Talia asked.

Godrick glanced over at Irrick, and to his surprise saw him frowning. "What's wrong?"

"Guess we won't be doing any dancing tonight," Irrick said, nodding at Artur.

Godrick's heart sank a little. There were at least three or four different balls at Skyhold tonight, he'd somehow expected not to have to worry about this. He still hadn't told his da that Irrick was anything more than a friend. It's not that he would get angry at Godrick— Godrick could count the number of times that had ever really happened on his fingers, and they'd all been for good reason— but Godrick had never heard him have anything good to say about people who dated around a lot. Which Godrick really hadn't, but he was fairly sure that his da wouldn't think too highly of dating someone when you knew there wasn't a future in it.

"Ah'm an idiot who needs ta stop overthinkin' everythin'," Godrick muttered under his breath.

He stood up and offered a hand to Irrick. "Ah thought the whole point a' tonight was the dancin'."

Sabae smirked as Avah dragged Hugh out onto the dance floor after Godrick and Irrick. Hugh was definitely in over his head with that one, but if he'd fallen for a girl who wasn't willing to take the lead, she was fairly sure nothing would ever happen.

Though Sabae definitely claimed some of the credit for herself. Avah wouldn't have even gotten the chance to get to know Hugh if Sabae hadn't hauled him out of his hiding spot.

She turned back to Talia and Phusan. "You two should go dance too! Don't let me hold you back!"

"Are you sure?" Talia asked. "I don't want to just leave you here by yourself."

"It's fine," Sabae said, waving her away. "I'll probably go annoy Artur and Alustin or something."

Sabae spent a couple of minutes just watching her friends dance and drinking the aggressively mediocre wine Skyhold had provided. Skyhold might be incredibly wealthy as an institution, but no one ever spent more than they had to on students.

She couldn't help but wonder what it would be like if she let herself date like her friends. Irrick even had an arranged marriage, and he was still dating Godrick. Maybe she could do the same?

No. She'd seen up close how it had gone for her family, she knew better.

Sabae stood up and headed for Artur, Alustin, and Alustin's date. She had no idea why Alustin had brought a known spy to the dance— it sometimes felt like he wanted to get caught. His behavior violated countless rules of espionage, at least according to everything her grandmother had taught her. Spies were supposed to be forgettable, boring, and bland to a fault.

According to Alustin, the Alikean ambassador's secretary was apparently here to spy on the trade delegations from Sica and Tsarnassus, rather than on Skyhold. Given that all three nations were from the Eastern half of Ithos, it amused Sabae that they were negotiating a trade deal on the western side of the Skyreach Range, but then again, she definitely understood why they wouldn't want to meet in the middle— that would put them right in Havathi territory.

She doubted that Alikea cared too much about Sica— Sica was in the far southeast of the continent, while Alikea was in the northeast— but they certainly cared about Tsarnassus, given that they were neighbors, and had fought more than a few wars in the past. They had a truce against Havath, but it was far from a comfortable relationship.

Alustin and his date headed towards the dance floor as Sabae approached. Alustin winked at her over his shoulder as they did so, and Sabae rolled her eyes.

"Ah think Alustin and his date were particularly happy yeh arrived, lass," Artur said. He chuckled. "They didna want ta leave me here on my lonesome while they danced."

"I know the feeling," Sabae said.

"It looks like Godrick finally feels comfortable not hidin' his boyfriend from me," Artur said with a smile.

"You knew?" Sabae said, surprised.

"Course ah did," Artur said. "Yeh'd have ta be blind not ta spot that. Ah wish he had been more comfortable tellin' me, but ah wanted ta respect his privacy."

Sabae considered that for a moment, then shook her head. "He was worried you wouldn't approve."

The big stone mage gave her an affronted look. "Why wouldn't ah approve? Irrick seems like a good sort."

"Their relationship also isn't going anywhere," Sabae said. "Irrick has an arranged marriage in the summer. Godrick was worried you wouldn't approve because you don't approve of flings."

Artur stared at her for a moment, then groaned. "Ah'm not a fan a' them, but ah wouldn't be angry at Godrick or anythin'. Stones, ah'm friends with Alustin, and ah'm not sure that man is physically capable a' settlin' down with anyone. He's got a different lad or lassie on his arm nearly every week, ah swear."

Artur stopped, then shot her a sharp look. "Not that ah'm not grateful yeh told me, but shouldn't yeh have let Godrick tell me?"

Sabae shrugged. "I love Godrick, but he's almost as bad as Hugh when it comes to overthinking things. Talia too, for all she likes to pretend she's made of fire and battle. Sometimes I feel like my friends would never get anything done without a push."

Artur rubbed his beard. "Ah've had plenty a' friends like that, but ah'm not sure yer actually doin' them a favor there. They won't always have yeh to help them, and if they never learn ta act on their own…"

"There are plenty of people who never get comfortable taking those sorts of risks," Sabae said. "I'd rather my friends be happy now than waste their youth in service of the future."

Artur gave Sabae a thoughtful look. "Ah'm not sure yer just talkin' about yer friends anymore. Yeh sounded a little bitter about somethin' there."

Sabae started to deny it automatically, but something about the knowing look in Artur's eyes stopped her. Godrick's father liked to pretend he was just a friendly but not too bright giant, but it was hard to spend much time around him and not see how intelligent he was.

Finally, she sighed. "I guess I was talking about myself as well."

"Would yeh like ta talk about it?" Artur asked.

Sabae was torn. She already felt weird about her friends knowing about her worries, and she didn't know if she was comfortable talking to others about it as well. On the other hand… maybe it would help. At worst, talking it out a bit more might help her make up her own mind about things.

Artur didn't say anything while she argued with herself; he just waited patiently. In the end, that was what decided the matter for her— if he was willing to be that patient while she thought about it, she was pretty sure he'd be a safe audience to talk about things to.

So she told him all about her fears in regards to her grandmother's visit. Her family history, her fears about an arranged marriage, all of it.

Artur was quiet for a moment when she finished. "That's a tough un, lass. Ah wish ah had some sort a' easy answer fer yeh. If ah were a character in a novel, ah might tell yeh ta just follow yer heart and live yer life as yeh will. That can be a selfish way ta live, though. Yer right ta worry about yer duty ta yer family as well. In the end, yeh need ta find a way ta balance them out."

He sighed. "If ah knew yer grandmother at all, ah might have better answers for yeh. All ah know about her are the stories everyone knows— fleets sunk, storms quelled, sea monsters slain. Ah think all yeh can do is wait until she arrives an' talk to her. Ah wish ah had better advice— waitin's about the most miserable thing yeh can do when yeh've got a problem. Yeh have a good head on yer shoulders, though, and friends that really care about yeh. Yeh'll get through just fine. Just remember that yer friends aren't the only ones ta overthink everythin'."

Sabae smiled, then wrapped her arms around Artur. Or at least tried to— she couldn't even wrap her arms all the way around Godrick, and Godrick hadn't even matched his father's bulk yet.

"Thanks," she said quietly.

Artur patted her gently on the back. "Yeh've had mah boy's back through thick and thin, lass. He might not have made it out a' the labyrinth last year if it weren't for yeh, Hugh, or Talia. Yer all as good as family, as far as ah'm concerned, and if any a' yeh ever need anything, all yeh have ta do is ask."

Sabae squeezed Artur harder for a moment, then let go, surreptitiously wiping at her eyes.

"So you mentioned something about Alustin's dating life earlier," she said. "How come he didn't date anyone last year?"

Artur smiled. "Oh, he did lass. He most certainly did. He just felt it wouldn't be appropriate ta gossip ta his students about his love life."

Sabae gave Artur a wide smile. "Any chance you could tell me anything about it?"

Artur burst out laughing. "Oh, have ah got some stories for yeh."

As Artur started telling a story about Alustin, a visiting merchant's husband, and a leaking alchemist's lab, Sabae's smile wasn't just for the story. Artur might not have had a solution for her, but she felt like some of the weight on her shoulders had been lifted. Not all of it, but… enough.

In novels, whenever a character was dancing with someone at a ball, they always glared at their enemies over their dance partner's shoulders.

Talia, unfortunately, was entirely too short to even see up to Phusan's shoulder, let alone over it, so she could only glare at Avah during the moments that she could see her and Hugh to the side.

Not that Avah was her enemy. Talia was just convinced that the Radhan girl was bad for Hugh, and that she was going to end up breaking his heart. She'd never even paid Hugh a lick of attention until he showed off his magical abilities by saving the *Moonless Owl* from a sandstorm.

Not to mention the way Avah was constantly embarrassing Hugh in public. It clearly made him really uncomfortable, but Hugh was too infatuated with Avah to stand up for himself, and she clearly didn't care enough to notice.

"Talia?" Phusan said.

Talia realized she'd missed something he'd said. "Sorry, I was leagues away."

Phusan chuckled. "No worries, I was just wondering if you wanted to take a break? My feet are killing me."

"I suppose I can make allowances for your weakness," Talia said, jabbing Phusan with her finger. She made sure to smile at him so he knew she was joking.

Mostly.

They stopped by the banquet tables to grab food and drinks, then headed over to where Artur, Godrick, Sabae, and Irrick were all sitting. They all seemed to be having a great time, which relieved Talia a bit— she hadn't really thought about how bringing a date might affect Sabae, since she didn't have one.

Artur groaned as they approached the table and pulled a coin out of his pocket, sliding it over to Sabae.

"Yeh just cost me our bet," the massive stone mage complained.

"We were betting on who would stay on the dance floor the longest," Sabae explained with a smug look. "I bet on Hugh and Avah."

"Ah'm still offended me own da wouldn't bet on me," Godrick complained.

"Ah was right not ta. Yeh were the first ones off the floor by a long shot," Artur laughed.

"I'm going to grab us drinks," Phusan said. "Want me to grab any food too?"

Talia shook her head and sat down next to Sabae. The taller girl stuck her finger in her wineglass, and a globule of wine began spinning up her finger. It rotated around her hand and up her arm, and then went around her neck and began orbiting her head. Sabae finally caught it in her mouth, looking even smugger.

"How long have you been working on that one?" Talia asked. "And how often did you get yourself soaking wet while working on it?"

"Oh, ages," Sabae said. "You wouldn't believe how many times I got water up my nose before I mastered it."

After they finished laughing about that, Sabae gave Talia a serious look and lowered her voice. "So did you really get those pins in your sandals mixed up? Because it's really not like you to take that little care with weapons, or anything even remotely useful for combat."

Talia shifted uncomfortably. Sabae was really too perceptive for her own good. Or, well, really too perceptive for Talia's own good.

"No," Talia said. "I just thought it would be funny to claim I did. They're where I first said they were."

Sabae's expression turned a little skeptical.

A Traitor in Skyhold

"Did you think it would be funny, or were you trying to make yourself more comfortable by presenting yourself as a battle-crazed barbarian?"

Sabae paused, then corrected herself. "*More* of a battle-crazed barbarian."

"I wouldn't…" Talia started, but it sounded unconvincing even to herself.

Sabae pulled another globule of wine out of her glass, but kept it orbiting her head while she spoke.

"I'm not trying to call you out or anything," Sabae said. "I've just noticed you tend to act a little more ridiculous when you're uncomfortable— more talk of battle than usual, more folksy sayings, that sort of thing. You know if you're ever uncomfortable, you can always let me know, and I'll try to help with whatever, right?"

Talia realized she was nervously fidgeting with one of her knives. She quickly rested her hands atop the table. "I know, but can we talk about something else right now?"

Sabae let the globule of wine fly into her mouth, then nodded.

"So when did Phusan ask you to the dance?" she said.

Talia smiled at that. "I asked him, actually! And I encrypted the note I passed him to do it, since we were in Cryptography."

It wasn't until much later that Talia thought to wonder whether there was anything else behind Sabae changing the subject to Phusan.

A part of Hugh was still genuinely surprised whenever he turned out to be good at something. At some point in the last year, however, he'd finally let himself become convinced that he wasn't worthless after all.

Still, he was a little surprised that dancing had come to him so easily, or that he'd enjoy it as much as he did.

It was a fairly sedate song at the moment, so Hugh had a moment to think as he and Avah slowly spun to the music.

Today was the one year anniversary of Alustin picking Hugh as a student. It somehow felt simultaneously much longer and shorter than that to Hugh. He wasn't exactly sure how he'd explain it to someone else, but it felt like this was his new normal now— friends who he actually felt safe and confident around, an amazing girlfriend, and opportunities to actually make something of himself.

Hugh actually wanted something more from his future than just being left alone now, and he wasn't entirely sure when that had become true. He was sure when it had started, however— the day when he first encountered Alustin, when the paper mage had rescued him from Rhodes and his cronies.

He couldn't help but frown a little at the thought of Rhodes. Why was Rhodes trying to talk to him? During their encounters, Hugh had automatically tensed up, expecting the worst, but in retrospect… Rhodes hadn't sounded angry, or like he was looking to entertain himself at Hugh's expense.

There wasn't a lot of chance he'd be able to be this rational next time he encountered Rhodes, though. As much as he hated it, Hugh would probably feel just as much fear then as he had every time before.

Hugh forced himself to stop thinking about Rhodes, tonight of all nights.

The song came to an end, and Avah slowly unwrapped her arms from around Hugh.

"We've been dancing for hours," she said. "I need a break."

"It hasn't been…" Hugh glanced around him, noticing that the dance floor was significantly emptier, and that the wine he'd drank earlier had mostly worn off. "Has it really been that long since our last break?"

Avah smiled at him. "I'm going to go get some air on the balcony, would you mind grabbing us drinks?"

"Of course!" Hugh said. "No, wait, I mean of course I would be happy to grab us drinks, not of course to me minding grabbing drinks…"

Avah giggled at that, then headed over to where some of the others were sitting.

Hugh sighed. For all the ways in which he'd gotten better, he still couldn't go very long between bouts of being a nervous idiot.

As Hugh wandered over to get more wine, he tripped on something heavy lying on the ground. He managed to catch himself before tripping, and turned to see what he'd tripped over.

It was his spellbook.

Hugh glared at the book. Its green crystal cover seemed to be projecting an image of innocence and confusion.

"I know for a fact I left you in my room. My locked room. How did you…?" Hugh asked it.

The spellbook excitedly sent him an image of it flying out the window, followed by several of it chasing sand drakes and stealing someone's hat.

Hugh folded his arms. "No more stealing from people. Even if their hats look tasty. How do you even taste things, anyhow?"

The spellbook gave him a sullen look, then spat out a chewed-up hat. Hugh felt relief for the hundredth time that the book didn't have spit glands.

"I expect to see you in my room when I get back," Hugh said as sternly as he could manage.

The book flipped over sullenly, then took off flapping into the air. He knew it didn't need to do that to get around, but it had picked up the habit from the books in the Grand Library.

Hugh shook his head wryly, then noticed that quite a few people were giving him weird looks. He blushed, then hurried to get the wine.

Hugh found Avah leaning against the balcony balustrade, staring out into the Skyreach Range. The balcony was only lit by the stars and the surprisingly small amount of light that leaked from the ballroom, so it took a moment for Hugh's eyes to adjust. Once they did, however, he could see for miles and miles. He was fairly sure that many of the larger peaks he could spot in the distance had their bases well past the horizon.

The night air was cold, but it felt good to cool off after hours of dancing.

Avah smiled as he handed her a glass of wine and gave him a quick kiss. They didn't say anything for a few minutes, just stared out into the mountains.

He was starting to feel the need to say something when Avah shivered and rested her head against his shoulder. He smiled and wrapped his arm around her.

He wasn't sure how long they stayed like that before a group of journeymen who had clearly had too much to drink wandered past them. Avah turned to look at them, giggling slightly at their antics. Hugh sighed quietly, wishing they had chosen to wander somewhere else, even though he'd started to feel cold. As he turned, he noticed another couple making out against a pillar a good ways down the balcony.

"Is that Talia and Phusan making out down there?" he asked.

"Where?" Avah said.

Hugh pointed.

Avah grunted. "I can barely tell there's anyone down there. How good is your night vision?"

"Better than I thought, apparently," Hugh said.

Avah chuckled, then took another sip of her wine. "Good on them," she said.

She took another sip, then set her glass down on the balustrade. "I think I'm about ready to head out," she said. "I've had more than enough dancing for the night."

Hugh's heart sank a little, but he forced a smile onto his face. "I'm glad you came, I had a lot of fun tonight! Do you want to meet up sometime tomorrow? I…"

Avah rolled her eyes. "I didn't mean by myself, dummy."

Hugh's brain took a second to catch up, then promptly stopped working. He managed to stammer out something incoherent, to which Avah only laughed and began leading him back through the ballroom by the hand.

They passed by Godrick, Irrick, Sabae, and Artur's table on the way out. All four looked like they'd had a bit too much to drink— which for Artur and Godrick, was truly an astonishing amount.

"Hugh, you remember your cantrip lessons, right?" Sabae called out, then the whole group burst into laughter.

Hugh turned bright red, which made them laugh even harder. He also caught Irrick winking at Avah, who seemed to be enjoying the whole scene immensely.

Hugh realized he was still carrying his wine glass, and downed the rest of his wine in a single gulp.

As it turned out, not only was his spellbook not in his room, but it had left him a pile of chewed-up hats on the floor.

He didn't really care much at the time, though.

CHAPTER NINETEEN

Narrowing the Field

If Godrick had thought second year was difficult before Midwinter, he'd been sorely mistaken. The four of them—well, except for Sabae— started off the second half of their school year behind already— Hugh and Godrick had been spending as much time with Avah and Irrick as possible before they left, and Talia had gotten caught up in her thing with Phusan, leaving all of them much less time to study than they really needed.

Sabae was willing to cover for them somewhat, but she couldn't maintain all of her friends' grades on top of her own.

Avah and Irrick left a few weeks after Midwinter, and Hugh and Godrick started to catch up on their studies. Talia and Phusan broke up about a week after that.

Godrick couldn't say he honestly minded. Phusan might have been gorgeous, but he was a bit boring. Godrick definitely did mind having to repair the stone of the walls and ceiling in their hallway a few hours after the breakup, but thankfully no one other than Godrick, Sabae, Hugh, and Hugh's spellbook had seen the damage Talia did to it.

The spellbook hid whenever Talia was around for a solid week afterward.

Once catching up on their studies began in earnest, they hardly had time to sleep, let alone pursue their investigation. Complaints to Alustin only received blithe assurances that he had complete faith in them.

So, of course, it ended up being sleep that they were missing out on.

Sabae wasn't doing much better than the rest of them, unfortunately. As her grandmother's visit grew closer and closer, she spent more and more time on the investigation, spending hours at a time poring over dusty council minutes dating back years.

One of the reasons they were missing out on so much sleep was something of a mixed blessing— Alustin had added an entire additional class onto their workload. It was a weekly seminar on battle tactics for just the four of them. They weren't learning any new spells or combat tricks, but were instead being taught to apply their current capabilities more effectively and creatively in battle, both individually and as a unit.

It was certainly an interesting class, but that wasn't enough on its own to move it from the curse category to the blessing one— the extra workload was far too exhausting for that.

No, what moved it into the blessing category was the fact that it was being taught by Anders vel Siraf, Dean of Skyhold and one of the suspects for the council traitor. It gave the four of them an excellent opportunity to get to know Anders and try to determine his guilt or innocence.

That was what moved it into the blessing category. Though, to be honest, Godrick was definitely considering moving it back into the curse category at the moment.

He had his back pressed to a stone pillar that barely hid him, and he was cautiously peering out into the mist that filled the training hall. He clutched the enchanted rod in his right hand a little tighter, took a deep breath, and dashed out of cover, towards where he knew the next row of columns would be.

He was sure he felt something fly past him in the thick mist, but he couldn't see anything more than a couple feet in front of his face. He could only tell where the stone columns were thanks to his affinity sense.

Godrick and the others were supposed to be hunting Anders through the mist and columns, but Godrick's affinity sense wasn't proving much use at the moment. Anders wasn't carrying anything steel that he could detect, and while some stone mages could detect footsteps and other vibrations in stone, Godrick hadn't put in the years of training that skill required.

Maybe, though…

Godrick tapped into his scent affinity. He used it far less than his other two— it was a lot less powerful than they were, for one thing, and he couldn't do much before he exhausted his scent mana reservoir. He also simply had much less training with it. Until they could find him a teacher, they'd have to puzzle out his scent magic from books.

Which left him with a few scent spells of somewhat questionable utility that did things like make food taste better, and a single stink bomb spell that completely drained his scent mana reservoir with a single casting.

The biggest advantage that he got from his scent affinity, however, was his associated affinity sense. It… well, it basically just made his regular sense of smell much, much more powerful.

One of the few spells he knew was quite powerful in combination with it— it made the direction of smells he encountered much more apparent. It wouldn't last more than a minute or two, but…

Godrick envisioned the spellform and powered it, then breathed in deeply through his nose.

He could smell Sabae and Hugh to his right, while Talia was some distance straight ahead of him. They were all staying quiet in the mist, trying to sneak up on Anders.

Anders himself, though... Godrick frowned in confusion and brushed one of his curls out of his face. He could smell Anders, but he wasn't quite sure where...

Godrick looked up and smiled. He stopped visualizing the scent spellform, tucked the enchanted rod in his pocket, and constructed an old favorite of his in his mind's eye— the basic stone sculpting spell he'd used back in the labyrinth last year.

He focused the spellform on the stone column, then started envisioning the shapes he wanted the stone to take. These sorts of sculpting spellforms were incredibly versatile, but were also slow and required a significant degree of focus to pull off. Crafting the ladder in the labyrinth had been absolutely exhausting last year, and he'd barely pulled it off.

This time, though, he'd constructed his ladder and ascended it to near the top of the room in under a minute. Part of it was just the growth in his mana reservoirs— they had to be well over twice the volume they'd been last spring. The rest, however, was all just practice and improving his skills.

Once he'd gotten high enough, he pulled the rod back out of his pocket and re-envisioned the scent direction spellform. He still couldn't see farther than a few feet— he could barely make out the nearest couple of columns through the swirling mist.

Godrick took a deep breath through his nose, seeking out Anders' scent again. He picked it up, but from the other side of the column he was on.

The back of Godrick's neck felt oddly warm, but that was probably just from the climb.

He tucked away the rod yet again, dismissed the scent spell, and began crafting handholds to move to the next side of the column.

Once there, he readied himself again. Rod out and pointing in Anders' general direction, he waited cautiously for the silk mage to draw closer.

At first he thought he was just seeing the mist shift, but then he realized what he was seeing— a long, thin ribbon of silk reaching out and wrapping about a column. Several more followed, with even more striking another visible column. They all pulled, and Anders drifted into sight.

The distinguished, grey-haired mage was suspended between the columns by countless ribbon of silk— he almost resembled a spider contentedly sitting in their own mobile web. More ribbons and threads dangled towards the ground, all converging with Anders' voluminous robes.

Unfortunately for the metaphorical spider in question, he was below Godrick, and too busy looking downwards for apprentices to wrap up in his web to look up.

Godrick slowly, quietly adjusted his aim and prepared to channel mana into the rod. The back of his neck felt uncomfortably warm now, but Godrick ignored it as he began to channel mana into the rod, which began to glow a faint pink.

Before Godrick could fire, though, a burst of pink light hammered into him from below. His limbs and body went limp, and Godrick plummeted from the side of the column. Above him, he heard Anders yell out in triumph.

Right before Godrick hit the floor, the training hall's safety enchantments kicked in, slowing his fall to almost nothing before he hit the ground.

He lay there limply for a few seconds, but the mist was already fading, and he could feel control over his body returning.

Godrick sat up and groaned.

"Well done, apprentices!" Anders called. "Two of you almost had me that time!"

Anders' ribbons carried the bound forms of Talia, Sabae, and Hugh over to Godrick, then released them. They all sat up, groaning.

"Godrick especially impressed me. I didn't even notice he was above me until after he fell!" Anders called. He came back into sight through the last of the mist. Unobscured, his robes were a brilliant cascade of color. He had dozens of different shades of silk sewn in, with even more colors of thread embroidered throughout. On anyone else it might have been garish, but on Anders, with the way swatches of silk were always orbiting him, plastering themselves to his robes, and sliding about, it went from garish to utter and complete visual chaos.

Looking at him actually hurt the eyes a little.

"How'd yeh get me if yeh couldn't see me, then?" Godrick asked.

"I didn't!" Anders called back cheerfully as his silk ribbons lowered him to the floor. "Talia did!"

Godrick gave Talia a confused look. It made sense— the spell effect that had hit him was what the training rods did— but what were the odds that Talia would randomly hit him as he was about to hit Anders?

Anders laughed at Godrick's visible confusion, then strode over to Godrick. He reached behind him and pulled something from out of the back of Godrick's collar

It was a pin with a blue bead on the end and tiny, intricate little spellforms all over the needle.

"Talia planted this on me before the exercise started," Anders said. "It was certainly clever, but my affinity senses gave her away the instant the needle was stuck in my silk. I transferred it over to you before the exercise started as well.

Talia was spending the entire exercise hunting you using the tracking pin, and I was lucky that she got you just in time to save me from a loss."

A big part of Godrick highly doubted that they would have won even if Talia hadn't shot him off the column. Anders always had another trick tucked away in his robes. He probably had some kind of glyph embroidered into his robes that would have just disrupted the rod's shot entirely, or something of the sort.

Anders chuckled and handed the pin back to Talia, who tucked it away in her clothes, grumbling to herself.

"There's definitely such a thing as being too clever, Talia," Anders said.

"That's why I prefer just destroying things," Talia snapped.

"Honestly, that's a fairly viable strategy in a lot of limited visibility situations," Anders said, "so long as you don't have to worry about hitting any allies."

Godrick sat down against a nearby column to listen to Anders lecture them on low visibility combat. Even if they weren't getting any clues for the investigation, the silk mage was an absolute treasure horde of useful advice and lessons on combat. He specialized in mage to mage combat, and he had seen more of it than nearly any other mage Godrick had ever met. He learned more in a single lesson with Anders than he did in half a dozen with most teachers.

On top of that, Godrick had never seen Anders in anything but the best of moods. He was always cracking jokes, insisting that others call him by his name and not his title, and always seemed genuinely curious about how the apprentices were doing when he saw them.

A big part of Godrick really hoped that Anders wasn't the traitor, and he definitely understood why Alustin was so vocal about feeling the same.

"So just because Anders is nice, he's the traitor?" Hugh asked.

"Yes! Well, no, but also yes," Talia said.

Godrick gave her an exasperated look. "That was real clear," he said. "Yeh really couldn't have explained that better."

The four of them were hypothetically supposed to be studying, but it was taking the form of them sitting around Hugh's room wasting time instead.

Well, three of them, anyhow. Sabae was ignoring them and poring through a massive stack of attendance reports and meetings for the Council on Hugh's desk, muttering to herself and taking notes.

Hugh's spellbook was napping in the windowsill after hours spent harassing sand drakes above the harbor.

"Look, when there's a traitor in a novel, if the writer is any good, they make sure to trick the reader into thinking that the actual traitor is the last possible suspect it could possibly be," Talia said. "They make the traitor boring and forgettable by making them a scribe or clerk to a more likely traitor; or they make them seem weak and ridiculous by making them nervous and giving them a stutter; or they make them so egregiously obvious as a traitor by having them sleep with the protagonist's wife or something, so the reader would never believe it was actually them, or they just make them way too nice."

Godrick sighed. "This isn't one a' yer novels, though, and yeh've been convinced Anders was the culprit from day one."

"I know it's not a novel," Talia said. "But the writer of one of those novels is trying to conceal the identity of the traitor, and there's only so many realistic ways to do that.

179

There's no spell that just conceals or reveals traitors, just like there's no such thing as a truth spell."

Hugh raised his hand. "I ran into a truth spell once, in the book of forbidden magic I found in the Library last year."

Godrick shook his head. "I attended a lecture on truth spells a while back. Every single one of them anyone's ever encountered is either a fraud, a scrying spell that doesn't actually detect truth, or does something like detects when someone says something the caster doesn't believe. That last one is probably the biggest reason most cities ban them. Which is probably why it was in a book of forbidden magic."

"This one also burned lies onto their speaker's skin," Hugh said with vaguely nauseous look. "That probably had something to do with it too."

"Gross," Godrick said.

"Anyhow," Talia interjected, "as I was saying. A traitor's first line of defense, in real life or in fiction, is simply going to be keeping people's attention off them. There's only so many ways to do that, so there's going to be a certain amount of overlap."

"Sure, but when yeh got a traitor hidin' themselves in fiction, it's goin' ta be in a more narratively satisfyin' way, more often than not. It's predisposin' yeh towards that sort a' answer," Godrick said. "Yeh really don't have any good reason ta think it's more likely ta be Anders other than the fact it's narratively satisfyin'."

"You were wrong about Eudaxus being responsible for the conspiracy in Theras Tel just because he was Indris' High Priest, and it's always the High Priest behind everything in books," Hugh said.

Talia stuck her tongue out at Hugh.

"Look, it's just as likely ta be Abyla, or Rutliss, or Headmaster Tarik," Godrick said.

"It's not Tarik," Sabae said.

Godrick started to continue, then he realized what Sabae had just said.

"What do yeh mean, it's not Tarik?" he asked.

"I mean, Tarik wasn't the traitor," Sabae said.

"We get that," Talia said. "How do you know it's not her?"

Sabae gestured at the pile of paperwork. "I've spent literally weeks poring over years of council attendance records and minutes and comparing them to the information that…"

"Stop!" Hugh yelled.

Everyone froze and stared at him.

"Someone's trying to get past my wards to scry on us," Hugh hissed. "Act natural, quick."

Hugh promptly sat down and grabbed the nearest book, pretending to be reading. Godrick scooted back over to his homework and pretended to be studying. Talia went and started staring out the window.

Godrick would be shocked if someone watching them couldn't tell how tense they all were. Godrick could feel the sweat rolling down his forehead.

A couple minutes of tense waiting later, Talia stepped away from Hugh's window nervously.

"Uh, Hugh? Your spellbook's doing something weird," she said.

The spellbook was standing up, looking intently around the room. Godrick had no idea how he could tell the spellbook was looking around, it was just sitting there motionlessly, but he could.

Seeming dissatisfied, the orange labyrinth stone set into the spellbook's front cover began to glow. The labyrinth pattern on the stone began spreading outwards through the green crystal.

Then, just as abruptly as it had started, the glow vanished, and Hugh sighed.

"I don't know how it did it, but it halted the scrying attempt," he said.

"What a good little book," Talia said. She reached out and scratched the book's spine, and Godrick could have sworn it looked pleased at the attention.

"Who do yeh think was spyin' on us?" Godrick asked.

"Probably Alustin testing Hugh's wards," Sabae said. "Now as I was saying…"

"What if it was Bakori?" Hugh said, visibly worried. "We know he's capable of scrying. What if he's onto our search for the traitor?"

"Then there's nothing we can do about it," Sabae said, "and we should just keep worrying about the investigation. Besides, it looks like your spellbook can protect us from that now. So as I was saying…"

Someone knocked on the door.

"Don't open it!" Hugh whispered. "What if it's the traitor?"

Sabae rolled her eyes, stood up, and went to open the door.

Godrick tensed up, but it was only Alustin on the other side of the door.

"How did you block my scrying attempt?" the paper mage asked excitedly.

Sabae rolled her eyes again.

After they explained what had happened on their end to Alustin, he spent several minutes examining the spellbook.

"It felt just like trying to scry into a labyrinth," Alustin said. "It's got to be a property of the labyrinth stone, not the aether crystal. Not that there's much difference now, but…"

Sabae coughed pointedly.

"Right, you were saying why you thought Headmaster Tarik was innocent," Alustin said. He sat down next to Godrick on Hugh's bed. Godrick scooted over to give him a little more room.

Sabae rolled her eyes again. Godrick was fairly sure she was going to sprain them at this rate.

"I've spent the last few weeks painstakingly going over attendance lists and minutes for every leaked secret you all know about that you were willing to share with us," Sabae said. "This all, by the way, would have been much, much easier if you'd been willing to share a little more."

Alustin opened his mouth to say something, but Sabae held up her hand to forestall him. "I know, I know, we're not cleared for that sort of thing as apprentices."

"Anyhow," she continued. "I just created a chart of how frequently councilors attended meetings where these secrets were discussed, and what I found was that Headmaster Tarik's attendance was far, far less frequent than any of the others at these meetings. I wasn't able to conclusively show that she missed any of the secrets entirely, but many of the meetings in questions had only the most rudimentary mentions of the leaked information. So I suppose I don't have absolute confirmation it wasn't her, but it's pretty telling."

Alustin got off the bed and walked over to her. "May I see your results?"

He spent several minutes reading through her notes and examining her charts, and then nodded. "You did a good job on this. You even spotted a handful of significant meetings we missed. Good work."

Sabae stared at him for a moment, then narrowed her eyes. "You knew," she said. "You've known all along that it wasn't Tarik and you didn't tell us. So much for our contributions mattering, then."

"We only figured it out a couple months ago," Alustin protested. "And while I've hardly kept it a secret that I consider this a training exercise for you, I also consider you part of a legitimate operation here. You're not the only investigators on the case we haven't told— we actually have quite a few people still looking into Tarik."

"That seems like a waste," Talia said.

"Better safe than sorry," Alustin countered. "We can't risk being wrong about a suspect when the stakes are this high. It would take remarkably little to pull her back into being a suspect again."

"Isn't it risky having this many people in on the investigation?" Sabae asked. "Even if there's only one traitor on the Council…"

Alustin nodded. "There almost certainly are other traitors in Skyhold as well. Bakori's magic can't penetrate into the Grand Library, though, and Kanderon has personally inspected most of the librarians for his influence. We think our security is good enough to look for more conventional traitors."

"Wait, if Kanderon can detect his influence like that, why is this investigation even necessary?" Hugh asked.

Alustin looked a little awkward at that. "Because the examination is long, unpleasant, and undignified. Even if Kanderon wanted to risk tipping her hand…"

"Paw, you mean?" Talia interrupted.

"The phrase refers to a hand of cards, not an actual hand," Alustin said. "And even if she wanted to risk tipping her hand, she'd have to convince the full Council to authorize it against another Council member, and she'd need to explain the whole story to them— which would include revealing the fact that you'd pacted to Kanderon, rather than just being the first crystal mage to come through Skyhold in decades, as well as being the student of her student."

Alustin answered a few more questions about the investigation before he got up to leave. As he put his hand on the door, however, Sabae spoke up again.

"I think we need to talk about what happens if we do end up having to enter Skyhold's labyrinth at Midsummer."

CHAPTER TWENTY

Long Overdue Explanations

Alustin pulled his hand off the door. "I remain confident that we'll be able to finish the investigation in enough time to prevent that," he said.

Sabae folded her arms. "It's already getting close to the spring equinox, and we've only eliminated a single suspect. Whether you're confident or not, it seems reasonable to assume the risk is there, and we should be prepared for it. We need to know what, exactly, we need to worry about from Bakori if we enter the labyrinth with him still inside."

Hugh watched the two of them anxiously. He knew Sabae was right, that they needed to be prepared just in case, but his stomach felt like it wanted to claw its way out of him thinking about the possibility.

Alustin sighed, then took his hand off the door. "Alright, but it's a long conversation, so get yourselves situated."

The paper mage actually pulled out a battered, overstuffed armchair from his storage tattoo, settling it under Hugh's window.

"Do you remember the lecture I gave you all on the nature of the aether, and how it's born from the slow decay of the universe?" Alustin asked.

Everyone except Godrick nodded. Hugh felt vaguely surprised at recalling that Godrick had only joined their group a good ways into the spring— actually, almost a year ago now.

"You've had that lecture, though, right?" Alustin asked Godrick, who nodded. "Good. So eventually, our universe will run down completely. The stars will go out and the planet will grow cold and… some nastier things will sometimes happen. Our universe is hardly the only one out there, though, and that's not the only way a universe can die. The other way is much, much faster."

Alustin pulled two sheets of paper off Sabae's research pile and made them hover in mid-air.

"Say these two sheets of paper are different universes. They're just doing their own thing, not worrying about anything outside themselves, right? It's not an overly accurate depiction— universes frequently intersect entirely without interacting— there are probably thousands of universes intersecting us right now, if not more, and we'd never know it."

Alustin brought the two sheets of paper together in midair.

"Sometimes, though, those intersecting universes start interacting more strongly. They start rubbing up against one another, and a hole starts to form. One of the first, and most important, consequences of this hole forming is a rapid increase in the density of the aether around it."

"Because it's leaking through from the other universe?" Talia asked.

Alustin shook his head. "No. Every universe has its own aether, but it doesn't leak through the holes. Rather, the universes rubbing together produces what might be called friction, which generates more aether on both sides. It's likely for the best, since from what we know, the nature of aether tends to vary wildly from universe to universe."

The two sheets of paper floating in the air began to rub together even more vigorously, and Hugh spotted a little smoke coming from the point of contact.

"These points of friction are known as mana wells. There are a couple different types of these. A mana well that only connects a couple of universes is known as a lateral well, while one that connects more than that is known as a junction well."

Several more sheets of paper joined in.

"Despite me describing them as holes, it takes a while before they're actually permeable. The membranes separating universes tend to be both thick and strong, so it can take quite some time for the friction to wear a hole anything can pass through. Many lateral wells never last long enough to form an actual hole. Junction wells, on the other hand, can form holes much more quickly, as well as producing far more aether density around them."

"This is interesting," Talia said, "but it relates to Bakori how?"

"I'm getting there," Alustin said. "When enough mana wells form in a universe, it starts to increase its aether density to a far greater level than would be naturally possible. When this happens, it starts to... change things. More and more creatures start to tap into the aether as part of their natural life cycle, and life starts to run riot. Eventually, aether densities will get so high that natural law itself will start to distort, and reality itself will start to break down. It wouldn't even be possible for us to even breathe the air there, I would imagine. We call this going aether critical."

A visible hole with charred edges had appeared where the group of papers were rubbing together.

"These are the universes where demons are spawned. They're lifeforms adapted for extreme aether densities, and they're constantly living on the edge of destruction. Most can only live in their own universe for a certain amount of time before aether densities grow great enough that they either die or are forced to abandon it to later generations better adapted, and so on and so forth. When they can escape, they put disproportionate demands on the aether of the worlds they invade— and if the aether can't sustain them, they die."

The hole in the paper was significantly larger now, and actual embers were visible.

"Eventually, aether densities in these universes grow so high that reality breaks down entirely, and they collapse. Thankfully, by that point most of the inhabitants can't survive other universes at all."

"So… Bakori is trying to get out of the labyrinth so he can colonize our world?" Hugh asked. "And how'd he get into the labyrinth in the first place?"

Alustin smiled excitedly. "I'm getting there! Labyrinths are the next piece of the puzzle. They only form on mana wells, and generally only junction wells. So far as we can tell, whoever designed labyrinths designed them to slow down this process, to prevent universes from going aether critical. They act as brakes on the amount of aether being generated by mana wells. We're fairly sure the wells can't be plugged, but the labyrinths seem to do an effective job at slowing down the process of universes dying this way— once they've arrived in a universe, they tend to reproduce and plant themselves in mana wells quickly. There's little we actually understand about how they grow or how they work, and even less about their creators, but trying to understand that is one of Skyhold's main reasons to exist."

Alustin raised a finger. "They also tend to overlay onto quite a few other worlds temporarily— many of the creatures in the labyrinth are drawn in during these brief periods, then they get stuck there when the overlay ends.

The papers were burning merrily now, but Hugh was fairly sure that Alustin had forgotten about his little demonstration.

"Skyhold's labyrinth bars the entrance to the largest junction mana well on the continent of Ithos, and one of the largest on all of Anastis. Bakori wandered into our labyrinth from his own universe, which was going aether critical. His own universe is too aether dense for him to survive in any longer, so he can't flee back there."

"So that's why he wants into ours," Hugh said.

Alustin shook his head. "If he wanted out, he likely could have escaped decades, even centuries ago. So far as we can tell, he'd been down there at least half a century before his battle with Kanderon two hundred years ago. No, we suspect that our universe is too aether poor for him to settle in long-term. We think, rather, that his goal is to shatter the labyrinth."

Alustin gestured for them to wait before they could burst into questions.

"Shattering the labyrinth would massively increase the aether density around Skyhold, giving him a broad territory he could inhabit for quite a long time. Thankfully, we're fairly sure he currently lacks the means, and that the shattering must be done from outside the labyrinth. So long as this is Kanderon's territory, he won't dare act. He's powerful, but by no means her match in a direct confrontation— as he learned before."

"What are his actual capabilities, though?" Talia asked.

Alustin started to answer, then noticed the burning scraps of paper in the air. He frowned, and the flames abruptly went out.

Hugh supposed a spell to put out fires would be quite handy for a paper mage.

As Alustin turned back towards them, Hugh's spellbook took its opportunity to dart over and devour the scraps of paper.

"We only have a partially complete picture," he said, "but it's pretty terrifying. First off, Bakori is freakishly strong, even more so than you might expect from a creature fifteen feet tall. He could probably tear apart a small dragon with his bare hands. If that wasn't bad enough, his claws can cut through most stone or metal fairly easily. The venom his tail stinger produces is toxic enough to kill most creatures smaller than him in minutes, and it even poses a not-insignificant danger to creatures Kanderon's size."

Hugh swallowed.

"He's capable of manipulating the minds of others to a small degree over the long term, as Hugh knows from experience, but it thankfully doesn't have a ton of use in combat, so far as we can tell."

"What about killing him?" Talia asked.

"That's a tough one," Alustin said. "First off, he's almost always surrounded by swarms of his imps. He spawns hundreds and hundreds of the awful things— you encountered a few on the first floor of the labyrinth. They're not much danger on their own, or even in packs, but in a truly large swarm they're a force to be reckoned with. Even if you can fight your way to him, any damage you do to him will be healed in moments— he drains the life-force out of his imps to do so. It took something like three seconds for him to regrow an arm that Kanderon tore off him in battle."

Even Talia was looking a little intimidated now.

"None of that is the worst part of confronting him, however. He comes from a different world, recall, and has an entirely different way of interacting with magic. Spellforms... decay around him. The longer you channel mana through a spellform, the more it decays, and the less stable it grows. After enough uses or time of a spellform near him, it's no longer stable in his presence— you become unable to cast any spell more than a few times on him, effectively."

Alustin leaned forward and looked at them all seriously. "What I suggest you do if you encounter Bakori again? Run."

No one spoke for a moment, until Alustin relaxed back into his armchair. "So, any questions?"

They, of course, had questions. Dozens of questions.

"Have you ever been to another world?" Talia demanded.

"No," Alustin said.

"Do yeh know anyone else who has?" Godrick interrupted.

"I suspect quite a few mages adventuring into the lower levels of the labyrinth have, but it is apparently a lot easier to get to another world than to return," Alustin said. "We're all descended from multiversal travelers, though— Anastis' absurd ecosystems are thanks to the fact that almost all the living things on the planet are descended from migrants through the portals. The sunlings and sunmaws are among the only life-forms that are suspected to actually be native to our world."

"Do you personally know any world travelers, though?" Talia said.

"Galvachren's the only one I know of," Alustin said. "I'm fairly confident Kanderon knows of a few more."

"Galvachren, as in Galvachren's Bestiary?" Hugh said, pointing to the massive tome under his desk.

"The very same," Alustin said. "He apparently just wanders from world to world writing guides on various topics. Bestiaries, mostly. He's been active here for a few decades now."

"Is this why you were asking me about the ecology of the labyrinth last summer?" Hugh asked.

Alustin nodded.

"Is there any risk of our universe going aether critical?" Sabae asked.

"Our world seems to have a disproportionate number of labyrinths— according to Kanderon, if it wasn't for them, we would have long since gone aether critical. But no, we should be fine, as long as no-one starts going around and wrecking a bunch of labyrinths."

It was over an hour's worth of questioning before Alustin finally took his leave. They bombarded him with questions ranging from what other demons were like to questions about how long ago humans had arrived on Anastis. Hugh was thinking over everything they'd learned from Alustin when he caught a sharp sense of puzzlement from his spellbook, which was alternating its gaze between the apprentices and Alustin, who had paused by the door.

Then Alustin left, and the moment passed.

"Is anyone else startin' ta see what kind a' mood that book's in?" Godrick asked. "Because it's kinda weird."

"It was definitely just giving us a confused look," Talia said.

Everyone turned to look at Hugh. "I've been able to tell its mood for a while now," he said. "It sometimes sends me images when it wants to tell me something more than that. This isn't the first time it's given Alustin weird looks, though. I have no idea what that's about."

"That is weird," Sabae said, "but I think that little lesson about Bakori provides a very good reason for us to batten down the hatches and get to work on this little investigation."

Hugh could hardly count himself excited about it, but Sabae was right— he was certainly well-motivated to not have to go into Skyhold's labyrinth again. Not that the idea had ever particularly appealed to him.

CHAPTER TWENTY-ONE

Starfire

Hugh wiped the sweat from his eyes as he focused his affinity senses on the boulder in front of him. The boulder was slowly crumbling as he shifted its feldspar crystals into alignment with one another.

It took almost an hour to finish, and his crystal mana reservoir was almost entirely tapped out by the end, but he'd successfully extracted all of the feldspar crystals and formed them into their own smaller boulder.

Kanderon looked up from her book.

"About time, Hugh. By Midsummer, I expect you to be able to do that in ten minutes or less," the sphinx said.

Hugh couldn't help but groan internally at that, though he tried to keep his face blank.

They were having today's lesson down in Kanderon's lair— a massive series of floating blue crystal platforms deep in the bowels of the Grand Library. Below them was only a mist-filled void, and above them was the intricate crystal machinery of the Index. Hugh seldom came down here— Kanderon usually preferred to have their lessons on the flanks of the mountain or out in the Endless Erg.

The first time he'd been down here, he hadn't realized that the platforms, and the index above, were actually made of the same blue aether crystal as Kanderon's wings. Now that he understood the sheer magical power needed to keep them afloat like this, they'd grown even more impressive to Hugh.

"Is that all for today, Master?" Hugh inquired. The lesson had already gone on considerably longer than most of his lessons with Kanderon.

"No, Hugh. Today I have something rather special planned— I'm going to be starting your instruction with our stellar affinity," Kanderon said.

Hugh's eyes widened in surprise and excitement. Though his pact with Kanderon gave him access to three different attunements, he'd only ever practiced with his crystal affinity. He'd used his stellar affinity only once, and that had been instinctive and uncontrolled in the depths of the labyrinth. It had left him unconscious for some time as well.

"The first thing to always keep in mind is that stellar affinity spells are gluttons for mana. You can expect to use far more mana on a single spell than for those of nearly any other affinity. Stellar affinities don't lend themselves to subtlety or caution. In compensation, stellar spells hit exceptionally hard— among your friends, only Talia is going to be able to do a comparable amount of damage with her spells as you."

Hugh was having quite a bit of trouble containing his excitement. The events of the summer had helped convince him up to a point that he wasn't a burden on his friends in battle, but he was still by far the least effective combat mage in his group. It would feel really good to be able to…

"Don't, however, assume that you're going to suddenly become a front line combatant on the level of your friends," Kanderon said.

Of course.

"You're capable of doing an immense amount of damage with your spells, but they're grossly inefficient. You'll only be able to use a few before your stellar reservoir dries up. They're best saved for emergencies."

Kanderon delicately pulled her bookmark out of her book, and slid it over to Hugh. On it was a complex spellform.

"This is one of the most basic stellar attack spells. Go ahead and memorize it, then draw it for me a few times so I know you have it down. And do *NOT* try to alter the spellform."

Hugh took a little extra time to examine the spellform. It really was shockingly complex for a basic attack spell— more than half of it seemed intended for containment purposes. As he worked, Kanderon let him know that the containment part of the spell was the only way to control starfire, or to keep it from immediately detonating. The targeting component seemed attached to the containment part of the spell, and it was just a fairly basic unguided straight-line movement in the chosen direction. The rest of the spell just seemed intended to fill the containment area with… something that wasn't light, as he'd expected from a stellar spell.

Once Kanderon was convinced that Hugh had the spellform adequately memorized, she raised a new crystal platform into position. A large boulder rested atop it.

"Give it a try," Kanderon said.

Hugh felt a little nervous about trying a new spell with this little preparation, but he knew better than to question Kanderon.

He glanced at the spellform on the paper one last time, then focused on the boulder. It had to be at least as tall as he was, and twice as wide. Both its appearance and his crystal affinity senses let him know it was a fairly standard chunk of granite like you'd find almost anywhere in the mountain.

Hugh extended his hand towards the boulder, carefully envisioned the spellform in his mind's eye, took a deep breath, and channeled mana into it.

The instant his mana touched the spellform, he could feel it *pull* at his mana reservoir. The pull wasn't on the same scale as when he'd built the stormward around Theras Tel, but it was more intense than any other spell he'd ever cast— not to mention it was coming out of his stellar mana reservoir, which was a good bit smaller than his crystal mana reservoir. It was still growing over time, but using and exercising his crystal mana reservoir was speeding its growth considerably more.

Hugh could feel the containment part of the spell forming first. A faintly visible sphere of ripples appeared in the air in front of his hand. It took two or three seconds to fully form.

The instant the sphere was complete, it filled with... something, then blasted forward out of his hand. He honestly couldn't understand what his affinity senses were telling him about the contents of the sphere. It was blue-white in color, and glowed bright enough to hurt his eyes, but Hugh could tell that the sphere actually dampened the glow.

While the construction of the sphere took much longer than the casting of most other ranged combat spells Hugh had seen— most of those could be cast in a fraction of a second— the sphere blasted forwards almost faster than he could follow.

The sphere slammed into the granite boulder and exploded in a glare of light.

It took most of a minute for Hugh's vision to clear and for him to focus back on the boulder. His stellar mana reservoir had been depleted by almost two-thirds by the spell.

The results were… somewhat underwhelming.

The boulder had a small crater in the front of it, and the rock around the crater had visibly melted a bit, but for the most part, the boulder was undamaged.

"That's it?" Hugh asked.

Kanderon, to his surprise, chuckled.

"That starbolt," the sphinx explained, **"would have been more than enough to kill a human. Cook them, really. Granite's melting point is almost as high as steel, Hugh, and it doesn't conduct heat nearly as well. It would take far more power than you have to melt that whole thing."**

"Talia could do it," Hugh said.

"Talia is a special case," Kanderon said. **She's already far more dangerous than the average battlemage, and she's only going to grow more dangerous over time. Be glad she's on your side, Hugh."**

"What exactly was in that sphere?" Hugh asked.

"That, Hugh, was starfire," Kanderon said. **"That was the very thing the stars in the sky are made of. If it hadn't been contained, it would have exploded and cooked you the instant you generated it. The containment shields necessary to control starfire are a major component of why stellar spells are so mana-hungry. That, and the sheer expense of producing starfire."**

Hugh was starting to feel a little more impressed at his affinity.

"For all the unusual size of your mana reservoirs for your age," Kanderon said, **"you're barely above the minimum needed to be able to use your stellar affinity.**

As your mana reservoirs grow, you'll find your stellar affinity to be more and more useful. It belongs to a category of affinities that are disproportionately more effective for powerful mages than weak ones."

For a moment Hugh's brain automatically dismissed that— Hugh clearly wasn't ever going to be that powerful, so what was the point?

Then he recalled the way all the students from Theras Tel— and quite a few others they'd told the story to, like his wards class— referred to him as Stormward, and frowned.

Kanderon gave him several new spellforms to practice before he left. One was a cantrip that shielded his eyes from the starfire, so he wasn't left blinded whenever he cast a spell. He was supposed to share that one with his friends— but only after they saw the results of the starbolt for themselves.

Kanderon was firmly convinced that humans needed a good reason to learn something, or they wouldn't bother.

The other two spells Kanderon showed him were stellar affinity spells as well.

One generated a narrow stream of starfire that extended out from a bottle shaped containment shield. The stream only extended out a few inches, but Hugh could use it to cut through metal with relative ease— though it was too unstable to use quickly or in combat. It used considerably less mana than the starbolt, however. He could think of quite a few uses for a cutting spell that powerful.

The last spell resembled a starbolt structurally, but it had a completely different function— it actually amplified the light from the starfire, instead of dampening it. It was designed to temporarily blind any nearby foes rather than injuring them.

Before Hugh left, he asked Kanderon about the difference between solar and stellar affinities. He was inspired to do so by his memories of all the time he'd spent searching through Galvachren's Bestiary for a potential warlock contract partner. Heliothrax had been his dream partner for much of that time, even if it was improbable that he'd get that chance. She was an elder dragon comparable in size to Indris, and she possessed a powerful solar affinity. Thankfully, she was a long standing ally of humanity, and had defended quite a few kingdoms from other dragons and encroaching monsters over the centuries.

Kanderon had given him a serious look before responding. **"A solar affinity is to a stellar affinity what a steel affinity is to an iron affinity."**

CHAPTER TWENTY-TWO

Thrones

The Council's meeting chamber was far from what Sabae had expected. She'd expected… a great semicircle of raised seats where the councilors could look down upon supplicants, perhaps, or a grand columned chamber where the councilors met, or perhaps a great table that they sat around.

The Council chamber was grand, certainly, but what Sabae hadn't expected was for it to be so… exposed.

The Council met at the very top of Skyhold, where the highest point of the highest peak had been shorn entirely off. There were no walls or ceiling to the council chamber—merely seats for the thirteen councilors, arranged in a great

199

circle. Each of the seats resembled a throne more than anything, and each was decorated to represent its occupant.

Abyla Ceutas' throne was made of solid obsidian. Anders Vel Siraf's seat was draped in fine silks. Headmaster Tarik's seat was undressed rough stone. Rutliss the Red's seat was— unsurprisingly— red, and it was set at the center of a saltwater pool, with a set of stepping stones leading to its base. Sabae spotted one throne that appeared to be made out of liquid water with fish living in it; one that appeared to be a living tree grown in the shape of a throne; another that seemed to be made entirely of shifting, roiling sand; while yet another was hollow glass filled with unpleasant-looking green mists.

There was an empty space along one side of the circle of seats, and that space impressed Sabae more than all the thrones combined. It was empty and unadorned, with no throne or decorations.

Kanderon didn't need either.

The only thing of note about the spot was that a huge, shallow bowl had been worn into the stone from centuries of Kanderon laying there. That was the kind of quiet statement of power that was really terrifying. It wasn't a bold monument to her power, like some of the thrones the councilors had built or commissioned for themselves. No, it was a quiet statement. It let you know that Kanderon had been attending meetings here for centuries, long enough to wear away a bowl in the stone just by lying on it. It let you know that no matter how powerful you were or how grand your plans were, Kanderon wouldn't be impressed.

She'd been there for half a millennium, after all, and there was no reason to believe she wouldn't remain there for centuries more to come.

Sabae finally tore her gaze away from the shallow bowl worn into the stone.

In the center of the circle of thrones was a massive, round metal seal embedded into the granite of the peak. It was covered in spellforms so intricate that she doubted that Hugh would even have a chance at figuring them out.

There were only three things outside the circle of thrones— the stairwell down into the mountain, a ring of massive, detailed wards inlaid into the stone, and the edge of the mountaintop.

Sabae raised her eyes out past the edge. The Skyreach Range stretched as far as the eye could see to the east, north, and south. It was the largest mountain range on Anastis— it stretched from the icy north shore of the Ithonian continent to the tropical south. Skyhold was carved into one of the largest mountains on the edge of the range bordering the Endless Erg, but there were some truly enormous peaks deeper into the range— peaks so high that even dragons struggled to reach their summits.

There were no foothills on this side of the Skyreach Range. On the eastern face of the range there were, but the western face was just a series of peaks jutting straight out of the ground. As Sabae slowly turned to take in the view, it reminded her of nothing so much as an impossibly huge wall holding back the Endless Erg.

To the west the Endless Erg stretched farther than the eye could see. Sandships looked like insects from this height, and Sabae spent a few minutes watching them skid about the desert.

In just a few days, one of them was going to arrive carrying her grandmother, and it would most likely mean that Sabae's life was about to change drastically.

She could only hope it would be for the best.

"Impressive, isn't it?" someone said.

Sabae tried not to jump in surprise. She'd been staring out into the Endless Erg for who knows how long and not paying attention.

She turned to see Rutliss the Red standing behind her. He was in his early sixties, and his bulk definitely wasn't muscle. He wasn't obese by any means, but no one would ever call him skinny.

"I still remember the first time I came up here like it was yesterday," Rutliss said. "I couldn't have been more than ten or eleven— my father had asked me to deliver a message to a councilor at the time. Innith Isleborne, her name was. She had a throne of sky that showed the night during the day and the day in the night. I was terrified that I would get in trouble for interrupting a council meeting, but it was just a few councilors taking care of minor procedural issues. They pretended not to notice me gawking as I took my time going back down into Skyhold."

For all that Sabae had come into the situation expecting to dislike the man on sight, he was fairly inoffensive looking. He was well-groomed and a little fussy looking, but mostly he just looked like a middle-aged man reminiscing about his childhood. He wasn't oily, or greasy, or shrewish, or anything else Sabae had expected from him.

Though, admittedly, those expectations were probably being influenced by Talia's novels, and her persistent ideas that the world should work the way they did.

They were definitely entertaining novels, at the very least, and Talia always seemed to know the best ones to recommend— not that Sabae had had many opportunities to read for pleasure this year.

The one part of Rutliss that did meet her expectations were his clothes— all entirely red. Even the leather satchel slung over his shoulder was dyed red.

"Councilor Rutliss?" Sabae said.

"You must be Sabae Kaen Das," Rutliss said, extending his hand to shake. His voice seemed to linger a bit on her family name. "I believe your master sent you with the proposed budget for your grandmother's visit?"

Sabae nodded, and handed over the folder Alustin had sent her with.

"If you'll give me a minute to look it over," Rutliss said, already engrossed in the contents.

Sabae turned her attention back to the view.

After a few minutes, she heard a polite cough from Rutliss.

"This all looks more than acceptable," he said. "Frankly, I wouldn't have blinked twice at a budget several times this size. Nor, in fact, was scheduling this meeting even necessary. This could have been sent to me via paper golem quite easily."

Sabae gave him a wry look. "A larger budget won't be necessary. My grandmother will be bringing just about everything she needs herself."

She turned her attention back towards the view.

"It's a claim to power," Rutliss finally said. "We're saying that we have so little to worry about from our enemies that we can just meet out in the open without a care."

Rutliss sighed. "It's not entirely true, though. This is probably the single safest, heavily defended part of Skyhold. It has some of the best constructed wards on the continent, along with plenty of other magical defenses. Even if someone were to attack, the council is comprised of some of the most powerful mages on the continent. Do you know what its greatest defense is, though?"

Sabae just waited.

"It's a little something Kanderon set up. If you were to head down the mountain, you'd be able to go down just fine— assuming you were a good climber. To traverse the same distance towards the top, however, would take you days or weeks. Kanderon did something to the space around this peak centuries ago— she altered it so that distance works differently depending on what direction you're traveling. The only reasonable way to get to the top is taking the stairs up."

Rutliss frowned, and tucked the budget proposal into his satchel. "Unless, of course, you're Kanderon. Every meeting, she flies right in, ignoring all the defenses like they're not even there."

He gestured around them.

"The Council Chamber is unquestionably a show of strength, but it's directed at the other council members most of all. Kanderon wants it to be very clear that we lowly humans could never defend Skyhold without her. That we're not fit to rule ourselves."

Rutliss' frown shifted into a smile. "Your family, though... you stand against all of that. Your grandmother is living proof that humans don't need a patron to get by in the world. We don't need a Kanderon, an Indris, or a Dorsas Ine to make us part of one of their territories."

"Neither do Highvale, Tsarnassus, or Havath," Sabae pointed out. "I think only around a third of the human population of Ithos lives under nonhuman rule."

"It's closer to half," Rutliss said, "but it shouldn't be any of us. Humans should rule ourselves, not be the playthings of those larger than us. And many of those states under human rule face far more frequent attacks on their sovereignty than states like Theras Tel or Ras Andis."

This wasn't, Sabae knew, entirely true. Large-scale warfare might be relatively rare on Ithos, but raids and attempts at conquest by duels between great powers were fairly common. Ataerg's attempted coup in Theras Tel, for instance— there wasn't much point to a protracted siege of the city, so he'd attempted to poison and replace Indris. In those states that lacked a great power like Indris or Kanderon protecting it, it was often actually more difficult for another to simply step in as a replacement. That wasn't to say they weren't at threat by the great powers, of course.

Besides, Sabae knew that attempts on Ras Andis were far, far more common than most people realized. Her family, however, specialized in information gathering and working storm magic at great distances— many attempts on the city were ended almost as soon as they had started.

Her grandmother, Sabae was fairly sure, was currently the single greatest cause of shipwrecks on the continent.

Still, there was always some dragon, sphinx, or deranged archmage convinced they could conquer a state that lacked a great power, so Rutliss wasn't entirely wrong.

Of course, there was often a reason why a state lacked a great power. Most commonly it was just due to low aether density in the region. Sabae had never even heard of a great power entering a mana desert like Emblin.

On the other hand, Rutliss had told her something important— so far as he was concerned, she was just another apprentice who didn't understand politics or power.

When Sabae was younger it had infuriated her when people underestimated her. Now, though, there was little that pleased her more.

"I know the real reason Alustin sent you to meet with me," Rutliss said. "He wanted you to try and convince me that you could get your grandmother to do something to make it worth my while to change my vote on the alternate test."

He paused for confirmation, but Sabae said nothing, merely looked at him.

"He thinks I'm a fool," Rutliss said. Sabae could tell his voice was supposed to sound disappointed, but she could hear the anger. "He thinks that I don't understand Kanderon's game. She doesn't need to win that many battles to stay in power. She only needs a few victories that will pay out in the long run. This is how she's stayed in power longer than anyone else on the continent— by focusing all her efforts on the long term, and by planning decades, even centuries, in advance. She's broken far too many rules in Hugh's situation already."

Rutliss put on a regretful look. "It's not that I wouldn't be tempted by some sort of favor from Ilinia Kaen Das. I'd be a fool not to be. Ultimately, however, I must hold myself to higher ideals. I've been given a chance to work for the betterment of humanity itself, and I cannot put myself first."

Sabae struggled not to sigh. What a petty, grubbing little attempt to try to raise the price on a bribe.

Rutliss reached into his satchel and pulled out a sealed letter. The spellform-imprinted seal, of course, was red.

Something else fell out of the satchel when he removed the letter. Sabae ignored the letter for the moment, and reached down for the other object.

It was a little green pill.

Rutliss groaned in irritation. "I swear, I'll never be rid of those things."

Sabae shot him a curious look as she finally took the letter.

"My predecessor as Bursar was more than a little unhinged," Rutliss explained. "He took these for his nerves, but I'm fairly sure they only made things worse. I've been finding them all over my office for years, and no matter how many times I think I've finally seen the last of them, more just keep showing up."

Sabae raised her eyebrow at that, but she didn't respond as she took the letter. She stared at it silently for a moment, then looked back at Rutliss.

"Your motives are, it seems, quite high-minded," Sabae finally said.

Rutliss smiled and opened his mouth, presumably to thank her or offer false self-deprecation.

"My family," Sabae continued, "is not, however, known for its high-mindedness. We're not known for our adherence to any sort of ideology. We're known for being powerful, and we're known for being good at holding onto that power. In voting against the alternate test, it's not just Kanderon you're crossing— it's my family."

Rutliss' face had taken on a vaguely fish-like look of shock.

"It's one of life's lovely little ironies that Kanderon is the one sheltering you from our irritation, isn't it?" Sabae said.

She smirked, then tapped the letter against her palm. "I'm sure grandmother will be most interested to read your letter."

Sabae strode to the stairs back down without sparing Rutliss another glance.

CHAPTER TWENTY-THREE

Ilinia Kaen Das

"How is it okay for you to threaten Rutliss, but not for me to get angry at Abyla?" Hugh whispered to Sabae, adjusting his spellbook's strap.

"Because I went in intending to threaten him," Sabae said. "I was baiting the hook for my grandmother to seal the deal."

"This is really not the time or place to be discussing that," Alustin interjected quietly.

Sabae frowned, rocking back and forth on her heels and clutching the package in her hands even tighter. Sabae hadn't wanted to talk about the package much, but she had let it slip that it held the Kaen Das book she'd claimed from the library last year, as well as the amulet she'd gotten from Indris, and that she was planning to give it to her grandmother.

He suspected that Sabae might be subconsciously trying to bribe her way out of an arranged marriage. At the least, she was definitely trying to prove that she wasn't a failure as a Kaen Das, despite her inability to become a traditional storm mage.

Hugh suppressed his grimace— he'd been trying to do his best to keep Sabae's mind off her grandmother's impending arrival, but somehow every topic kept wandering back that direction.

Though in fairness, Hugh was trying to keep his own mind off things as well. The docks were packed with people waiting for Ilinia Kaen Das' arrival— both the official greeting party and countless gawkers. Quite a few mages hovered in the air around the docks as well. Sabae's grandmother was one of the most powerful mages on the continent, and everyone wanted a glimpse of her.

And, to Hugh's displeasure, he and his friends, along with Alustin, were front and center.

From the looks they were getting from some of the Skyhold Councilors behind them, they weren't particularly pleased about having apprentices front and center either, but since Ilinia Kaen Das' expressed purpose for her visit was visiting her granddaughter, well…

Skyhold's harbor scryers hadn't listed Ilinia's ship on this morning's schedule, but soon after they were posted, the windtalker on duty had apparently collapsed, clutching their head in pain. They'd waved off any talk of healers, however— they knew exactly the cause of their abrupt headache. Ilinia had informed them of her impending arrival, and she hadn't bothered keeping it quiet.

After a truly uncomfortable wait, the murmuring of the crowd changed in pitch. Someone up on the balconies had spotted something, apparently.

"Here she comes," Alustin said. He was wearing the look that Hugh had, with experience, come to recognize as the one he wore when he was using his farseeing attunement to scry with.

On the horizon, a sand dune exploded.

It was a peculiar sort of explosion— as though a giant, invisible sword had cut down the middle, and then shoved the two halves aside.

A few seconds later, another dune did the same. This dune was much, much closer to Skyhold. Hugh could feel something actively draining the aether around Skyhold, which he never had before, even with thousands of practicing mages living on and in the mountain.

"Grandmother doesn't hold with going around or over dunes," Sabae said, looking a little embarrassed.

Hugh's eyes widened as he did a little bit of mental calculation. The sheer amount of power required to blast an entire sand dune apart with wind…

There must be a track of drained aether stretching all the way across the Endless Erg.

Another sand dune exploded, and Hugh finally caught a glimpse of Ilinia's ship.

It looked like no other sandship Hugh had ever seen.

Sabae had told them a lot about *That Old Pile of Junk*. It had been constructed especially for her grandmother as a gift by a past Prince of Ras Andis— she'd lived through three of their reigns so far, and since the Kaen Das family essentially propped up their rule, the ruling family was very attentive to her needs. They'd spent a truly mind-boggling sum on the ship.

That Old Pile of Junk was absurdly over-built for a sandship. The masts were not only much thicker than normal, but they also had massive braces running towards the fore of the ship, as well as cable stays running all the way to its aft. They were also covered in spellforms to help reinforce them and prevent them from breaking. (Sabae had, finally fed up with her friends getting nautical terms wrong, spent hours and hours over the summer drilling them on the correct terminology, with Avah and Irrick's amused help. Sabae only winced every third or fourth time they talked about ships now.)

That Old Pile of Junk had neither runners nor a sled-like bottom. Instead, the ship narrowed to a keel, giving it an absurd, top heavy appearance, like it would fall over at any moment. The bottom of the ship was apparently weighted pretty heavily to compensate, and the sheer speed it moved at increased its stability, but it was still pretty alarming watching it move without toppling.

That Old Pile of Junk, though, was built for speeds unmatched by any other ship in the desert. With Sabae's grandmother raising winds to propel it forward, it could traverse the Endless Erg faster than a sandstorm or most dragons. The reinforced construction, the enchantments, and the unusual keel— they were all designed to help it survive Ilinia's winds.

Even the huge metal weights inside the bottom of the hold were there more to keep the ship from getting lifted off the ground than anything.

The ship had apparently started life with the name *Pride of Ras Andis*, but Sabae's grandmother had decided she didn't like it, and the Prince of Ras Andis certainly wasn't going to argue with her.

As *That Old Pile of Junk* drew closer, Hugh could actually see the massive wind currents smoothing out the desert in front of the ship. Despite the gouting blasts of sand, not a grain of it landed on the ship, and Hugh could see a perfectly flat, even road extending past the horizon, with only a narrow gouge in the middle where the ship had sailed past.

He almost nervously took a few steps back as the ship approached— it was slowing down, but still going far faster than he'd ever seen any ship approach the harbor. Sabae wasn't moving, though, so he took his cue from her.

Quite a few people in the crowd were shuffling backward, though.

That Old Pile of Junk drew to a precise halt in a cloud of gusting sand— none of which, Hugh noted, landed on the ship or them, though plenty landed on the councilors immediately behind them.

As the ship came to a halt, several long metal rods were dropped along its sides. Hugh realized after a moment that they were there to keep the ship from falling over while docked.

No one on the ship moved for a minute, until an obviously distressed sailor staggered up to the ship's railing and vomited onto the sand.

Hugh glanced at Talia, who had a look of nauseous sympathy on her face.

A quiet refrain of muttering became audible from the ship, and then Ilinia Kaen Das came into view.

He'd been expecting a tall, regal looking older version of Sabae, honestly. Probably dressed in fine robes and jewelry.

Instead, a short, stooped, irritable, and wrinkled old woman stepped up to the railing, a large battered travel chest floating in the air beside her. Her dress was frayed and stained, her hair messy, and her only jewelry was a rather ugly looking necklace with chunky coral beads. Her muttering seemed to be entirely curses and complaints about the competence of the ship's crew.

So far as Hugh could tell, the only thing about her that resembled a legendary archmage was her cane, which appeared to be clouds trapped in glass and covered in spellforms.

She did look like Sabae, at least.

Hugh checked on Sabae again. She looked more nervous than ever.

Ilinia Kaen Das floated up off the ship, then gently sank down to the docks.

Sabae stepped forwards to greet her grandmother, visibly nervous. Hugh couldn't help but feel nervous himself as the old woman approached.

Sabae opened her mouth to say something, but her grandmother beat her to the punch.

"Quit looking so nervous, girl, I'm not going to eat you," Ilinia snapped. "Let me take a look at you."

The old woman reached up and grabbed Sabae by the ear, pulling her down towards her. She ignored Sabae's yelp and spent several seconds inspecting her, making thoughtful noises.

"You got taller," Ilinia complained. "I'm going to sprain my neck looking up at you."

"Sorry, ma'am," Sabae said.

"Don't apologize for what you can't control," Ilinia said, "it makes you look weak. And don't call me ma'am. I'm your granny, not some foreign ambassador."

"Sorry, m… Grandmother," Sabae said.

Ilinia sighed, then let go of Sabae's ear. "So formal."

Her eyes fixed on Hugh and the others, and a smile spread across her face. It was not a particularly comforting smile.

She stepped around Sabae and towards them, pulling out a flask from her sleeve. She sipped it as she stalked towards them, and Hugh winced— it smelled like cheap, nasty grain alcohol.

Somewhat to his surprise, he realized that Ilinia was actually shorter than him. Sabae was taller than a lot of men, and towered over Hugh's modest height, so he'd expected Ilinia to tower over him as well.

His musings were abruptly interrupted by Ilinia grabbing his ear. "You must be Hugh," she said, turning his head about to inspect him carefully.

"Ow," Hugh managed.

His spellbook yanked on its strap around Hugh's shoulder, nervously edging its way behind his back.

"I hear they're calling you the Stormward," Ilinia said. "My mother was the last one to bear that title, you know. It's her notebook I sent Sabae a copy of for you. I'm glad to see someone's putting my mother's wards to good use. No one in the family right now has the natural fussiness necessary to be a decent wardcrafter."

"Ow," Hugh replied.

"I quite enjoyed watching you work in Theras Tel," Ilinia said.

Watching him work? Ras Andis was as far away from Theras Tel as Theras Tel was from Skyhold. How could Ilinia have watched him build the stormward from hundreds of leagues away? Even Alustin's farseeing attunement didn't reach that far.

"Ow?" Hugh asked.

"Of course Kanderon had to go and make sure to claim you for herself, didn't she?" Ilinia said with a grim smile. "Pity. If you ever change your mind about working for her, you're always welcome in Ras Andis."

"Ow," Hugh said.

Ilinia released Hugh's ear and stepped over to Godrick, who edged back nervously. Before he could say anything, Ilinia levitated up into the air and snagged Godrick's ear.

"You're entirely too tall, young man. It's rude."

"Ow, I mean, sorry, ma'am," Godrick managed. "Ow."

Hugh was a little amazed Godrick was actually managing to get words out— Ilinia pinched *hard*.

"You're Godrick, I assume," Ilinia said, dragging Godrick's head around to different angles to get a better view. "Sabae had plenty to say about you in her letters as well. She mentioned that you were tall, but not that you were this unnecessarily tall. You must eat your family out of house and home."

Hugh noticed that Ilinia was slowly drifting back towards the ground, forcing Godrick to bend down. He heard a chuckle from behind the councilors, where Artur was standing.

Ilinia finally released Godrick and strode over to Talia.

"I will bite you," Talia said before Ilinia could grab her.

Hugh could feel the crowd tense up behind him.

Ilinia gave Talia a flat look, then cackled. "I like this one," she said.

Talia just folded her arms and glared.

One of the council members— Hugh couldn't recall his name— strode up to greet Ilinia, evidently wanting to get a jump on the others, who Hugh could see glaring.

"I'd like to formally welcome you to Skyhold," the councilor said.

"Take this to my room, would you?" Ilinia interrupted, levitating her travel chest into the councilor's arms.

Before the shocked councilor could say anything, Ilinia had grabbed Sabae and gone marching through the crowds.

"We have a lot of catching up to do, dearie," Ilinia told Sabae. "And I'm quite eager to see if your education is worth the fortune I'm spending on it."

Sabae, still clutching her package, just shot Hugh a helpless look.

A Traitor in Skyhold

CHAPTER TWENTY-FOUR

Setting the Stage

Avah arrived on the *Moonless Owl* two days after
Ilinia's arrival. Hugh, Talia, and Godrick met it at the docks,
which were thankfully back to their usual packed,
overwhelming bustle, rather than the gargantuan crowd that
had greeted *That Old Pile of Junk.*

They hadn't seen Sabae outside of class since Ilinia had
arrived, and she'd missed over half of that, caught up in the
wild swirl of politics and high level negotiations surrounding
her grandmother.

Hugh couldn't help but notice that a meeting between
Ilinia and Kanderon had still conspicuously not taken place
yet. When he'd asked Kanderon about that, the massive
sphinx had just stared at him cryptically until he changed the
subject.

There were two major differences to the *Owl* this time.
First, the ship was in bad shape— the decks and hull were
battered and splintered, and half the sails were torn.

When Hugh asked Avah about it, she sheepishly
admitted that they'd been maintaining the ward Hugh had
crafted to help them through the sandstorm last summer,
using it to pass through storms and cut time off their routes.
This most recent trip, however, something had gone wrong,
and the ward had barely made it through the storm.

Hugh promptly dragged everyone back on the ship to
inspect the ward.

Lecturing Captain Solon, and, more terrifyingly, Deila,
was a novel experience for Hugh. Having them listen to him,
and not only looking abashed, but actually apologizing to
him, was… well, eye-opening. Hugh really wasn't used to

thinking of himself as someone worth listening to even for other teenagers, let alone adults.

Hugh had Avah and one of the other Radhan sand mages haul sand on the deck for him, and he began pattern-linking the quartz in the sand into a new ward. He actually embedded the new crystal ward into the deck. A few Radhan wood mages followed behind him, doing something to the deck behind him— the deck apparently flexed a bit when the ship traveled, so they were doing something to limit damage to the ward.

The other difference was the absence of Irrick. They'd already known he wouldn't be there— his arranged marriage was this summer, and he'd transferred to his betrothed's ship a few weeks ago.

He'd left a letter for Godrick, though, which the big stone mage tucked away carefully for later reading.

To Hugh's great relief, Alustin had lowered their workload as Midsummer drew nearer. Hugh could spend time with Avah and his friends with considerably less guilt and avoiding homework than before, which was a pleasant relief.

It was, unfortunately, one of the only things going well at the moment.

Alustin— and nearly all of the other Librarians Errant— had vanished again on another mission for Kanderon, this time with only an hour's notice. Artur was distracted with preparations for the labyrinth final— helping with them was one of his major duties each year at Skyhold, at least when he wasn't being hired as a mercenary mage.

Kanderon had less time for Hugh than ever, and what lessons they did have were kept focused and to the point.

The worst part, though, was the fact that the investigation seemed to have stalled entirely. There were no further clues rearing up their heads, and nobody seemed to be available to talk to them about the investigation.

Ironically, the adult most closely associated with the investigation that had time for them was Anders Vel Siraf, who was still teaching them battle tactics regularly. Avah started sitting in on the sessions— she seemed endlessly entertained with watching Anders wipe the floor with the four of them again and again. Or at least the three of them, half the time— Sabae was still missing tons of classes.

The investigation was being further hindered by the fact that Avah wasn't using her own guest room, and so they could only safely discuss it when she was off doing something else on her own.

It was, to everyone but Talia's distress, looking like they were going to have to make a decision soon— either enter the labyrinth again, or be forced out of Skyhold.

Hugh was fairly sure that Talia's confidence about the labyrinth was mostly bluster, at that. Even though she was easily the most dangerous and combat-ready of the four of them, Bakori was a threat far out of her league. Talia couldn't stand looking vulnerable or weak, however, even in front of her friends.

If it wasn't for Avah distracting him, Hugh was pretty sure he'd be a wreck. Even with her there, though, he felt like he was teetering on the edge most of the time.

Hugh's own birthday, two weeks before midsummer, barely managed to distract him. Ironically, all his friends had, without consulting one another, bought him books.

He ended up with several new volumes from Sabae and Godrick on wardcrafting to add to his rapidly growing collection, a volume from Avah containing biographies of a few of the more famous crystal mages, and a hilariously inaccurate book from Talia filled with rambling conspiracy theories about how Emblin secretly ruled the world.

Apparently, the reason there was no magic in Emblin was because Emblin had a massive enchantment using all the available aether there that erased the memory of anyone who stumbled across their secret rule. Which sort of begged the question of how the author had managed to write about said conspiracy.

Even when the five of them were laughing about Emblin's secret invisible armies and mind control cheese, the threat of Midsummer still loomed in the back of Hugh's mind.

"You're not paying attention," Kanderon said, lightly tapping Hugh with her paw.

Well, relatively light— Kanderon's paw was considerably larger than Hugh, and even a light tap was enough to send him rolling across the sand.

"Sorry," Hugh said, after he spat sand out of his mouth. "Midsummer's less than a week away, and we still haven't…"

Kanderon shot him a glare, and Hugh stopped himself before he could blurt out anything. It was important to be extra careful around Kanderon— unless they were in an adequately warded location, odds were she was being scried on by someone. Great powers like Kanderon, Ilinia, Chelys Mot, or Indris were watched carefully most of the time. Which made sense to Hugh— any of the great powers were about as dangerous as an army, and far more mobile. Not the sort of thing you'd want to be lax about keeping your eyes on.

It made sense in retrospect, at least— Hugh hadn't ever thought about it until Alustin started training Hugh and the others as prospective Librarians Errant. To his irritation, however, he'd been the only one surprised by that revelation.

Hugh whistled, and the sand a few feet away started churning, and a patch of green poked out. "Could you do the thing?" Hugh asked his spellbook, trying to send it the mental image of what it had done to block Alustin's scrying attempt.

The book shot a few nervous looks at Kanderon— it was still skittish around her after she'd manhandled it. It finally seemed to decide she wasn't going to shove her claw in its extraspatial cavities, and the labyrinth stone's pattern began spreading across the cover of the book. Hugh could feel that odd feeling of tightness spread through the aether around him again.

"It's safe to talk now," Hugh said.

Kanderon eyed Hugh and his spellbook intently, then finally nodded.

"We still haven't caught the traitor," Hugh continued. "I don't suppose any of your agents have had any luck?"

"I'm afraid not," Kanderon said.

"So what then? We just go into the labyrinth and hope Bakori is feeling merciful?" Hugh said. He couldn't help but feel embarrassed at how whiny his voice sounded.

Kanderon opened her mouth, as if to say something, then closed it, an odd look on her face.

"Do you trust me, Hugh?" she finally asked.

"Of course," Hugh replied, without hesitation.

The odd look on Kanderon's face deepened, and the silence dragged on for quite some time.

"Then, when Midsummer arrives, Hugh, you and the others need to go into the labyrinth again."

Without another word, Kanderon turned and launched herself into the air.

The most terrifying part to Hugh was the fact that he couldn't remember another occasion where Kanderon had ever cut a lesson short.

If Hugh hadn't been so distracted, he might have been able to avoid Rhodes. He'd barely even managed to pay attention in Emmenson's class, though, and Emmenson had a way of holding your attention. Given that it had been the last spellform construction lecture before Midsummer, though, Hugh had hardly been the only distracted student.

After class, Hugh had just wandered off, down one of the usually empty hallways that he preferred to take back to the library. He'd been so lost in his head that he didn't see or hear Rhodes approach, and he'd left his spellbook back in his room, so it wasn't there to warn him.

Rhodes didn't say anything this time, he just walked up while Hugh was staring off into space and grabbed him by the shoulders.

"I need to…" Rhodes started.

Before he could get farther than that, Hugh grabbed Rhodes' arm in a hold Artur had been drilling them in. "Yeh don't want ta be helpless if yeh run out a' mana in a fight," Artur had said. "And sometimes yeh jus' don't have time ta cast a spell."

Time seemed to slow down for Hugh as he sent Rhodes crashing into the wall, and turned to flee. He'd only made it a few steps, however, when Rhodes called out again.

"Please!"

Almost against his will, Hugh came to a stop, and made himself turn to look at Rhodes. Rhodes had sounded… desperate, almost.

He didn't say anything, just stared at his former bully. Rhodes… didn't look great, honestly. His usually impeccably groomed appearance had gone far downhill. His hair was a mess— and not a carefully cultivated one. His expensive clothes looked disheveled and wrinkled, as though the noble had slept in it. Rhodes looked like he'd lost weight, and he even had deep bags under his eyes.

The silence stretched on for an eternity before Rhodes finally spoke. "I'm not a coward," he blurted out.

"What?" Hugh said.

"I'm not a coward," Rhodes repeated, but he didn't seem sure of it. "I... I've never run before."

"What?" Hugh said. Rhodes couldn't possibly be talking about their encounter in the labyrinth, could he?

"In the labyrinth," Rhodes said. "I didn't... I'm..."

The noble wrapped his arms around himself, and slid down the wall. "I shouldn't have run," Rhodes said. "I shouldn't have left you and your friends in the labyrinth."

He was much bigger than Hugh, but he looked broken and small sitting there on the floor.

Hugh felt a surge of joy rise up in him at the sight. Part of him felt viciously happy at seeing someone who had caused him so much misery and suffering looking so unhappy. He wanted to laugh, to crow, to mock Rhodes, to let the noble know that he was indeed a coward.

And then Hugh remembered sitting against a wall of Skyhold in an almost identical position, crying.

He sighed, crossed the hallway, and sat down facing Rhodes.

Neither of them said anything for several minutes. Rhodes looked to be trying to regain his composure, while Hugh struggled with his own thoughts.

"I was the golden child," Rhodes finally said. "I could do no wrong. My parents thought they couldn't have children, and when I showed up they and my uncle doted on me. There was nothing that didn't come easily to me. Arithmetic, letters, archery, falconry— it was all easy for me. Everyone expected great things of me even before my magic showed up. Then it arrives, and I have five affinities.

My family was talking about me becoming the next great power of Highvale before I even left for Skyhold. They even arranged for Aedan to return to Skyhold from his travels to take me on as an apprentice."

Hugh raised an eyebrow at that, but didn't say anything.

"Everything went my way here, too. Magic came easily to me, and people flocked to me just as they had in Highvale."

"If everything was going so well for you," Hugh interrupted, "then why did you feel the need to make my life hell?"

"Because it was funny," Rhodes said. "Some peasant brat who couldn't do magic and shouldn't even be able to afford Skyhold? Even if you hadn't just folded over to the slightest pressure it would have been easy, but you were guaranteed entertainment."

Hugh just stared at him, his mind racing in circles.

"Then you just seemed to vanish off the face of the planet," Rhodes said. "Some of us legitimately thought you'd finally given up and left Skyhold, until someone saw you get chosen by some nobody library mage— who, I suppose, turned out not to be a nobody after all."

Rhodes snorted in amusement. "We spent quite a while looking for you, but you're good at hiding, I'll give you that."

His expression turned somber again. "Then I finally found you again, entirely on accident, and your friends intcrfcrcd."

Rhodes seemed to collect himself again. "I still don't know why I got so angry at you and your friends after that. They kicked my ass and mocked my family, so of course I'd be angry, but looking back… I've never been so angry as I was then, or as I was in the labyrinth. It's like I was a totally different person. Messing with you was fun, but I was actually trying to hurt you in the labyrinth. I thought I was better than that, that I had more control than that. I thought I actually deserved all the praise, that I wasn't just another spoiled noble whose family thought they shat gold."

Rhodes laughed bitterly. "I thought wrong, though. Aedan's made sure to remind me of that daily. I've gone from golden child to the shame of the family— the apprentice that dishonorably attacks others in the labyrinth, then flees like a coward and leaves them to die. I'm not even sure why Aedan bothers to keep me on anymore. He keeps talking about earning my redemption, but every time the goal seems to have moved a little bit farther away."

Rhodes folded in on himself even more. "I think he enjoys my misery. Fitting, really, given how I treated you. Aedan loves talking about you, by the way. The apprentice I abandoned in the labyrinth has become the famous one, while I'm just known as a coward. Not a day goes by that I don't hear about the deeds of the Stormward."

"So, what, you're here to apologize for the way you treated me last year?" Hugh said, his mind still racing. It couldn't be that simple, could it? He didn't even mind that damn title for once.

"Honestly, I really don't feel bad about that," Rhodes said. "It really was funny. What I feel bad about is abandoning you in the labyrinth. I could have easily made a couple more trips down to retrieve you, but the instant we landed, all my wrath dissolved into cowardice. I couldn't think of anything but getting to safety. I'm shocked I even rescued my own teammate. And this after you saved all of us with that levitation spell."

"Bakori probably wouldn't have let you," Hugh said distractedly.

"Who?" Rhodes said, visibly perplexed.

"The demon lurking down in the labyrinth? The one who had spent the year manipulating us?" Hugh asked.

"There's a demon in the labyrinth?" Rhodes asked, his face pale.

Hugh nodded vaguely. "Yeah, and he was probably manipulating you too to ensure I'd end up in the depths of the labyrinth. You're an awful person, but you attacking me was somewhat out of character, as was you just fleeing." Hugh didn't bother mentioning *why* Bakori had wanted him in the depths of the labyrinth.

Rhodes worked his jaw as though he was incapable of forming words.

"I'm pretty sure Aedan was briefed on Bakori, if not why he was luring us down into the depths," Hugh said. "He was in the party that rescued my friends and I, right? So I really don't know why he wouldn't have told you, unless he's just that cruel."

Hugh stood up to leave. "Oh, and don't tell anyone I'm a warlock. You owe me that much."

He strode off down the hallway.

"Wait!" Rhodes called out, sounding desperate and hopeful. "You're not lying to me?"

Hugh stopped and turned, looking Rhodes in the eyes. "I'm not lying to you."

Rhodes was shaking, though from what emotions Hugh couldn't tell.

"There's really a demon in the labyrinth?" Rhodes asked. "I'm not a coward?"

"There's really a demon in the labyrinth," Hugh said impatiently, and turned to go. "You're probably not a coward, you were probably being manipulated by the demon."

He'd only made it a few steps farther when Rhodes called out again. "Why are you telling me this? After everything I did, you could have just left me to suffer."

Hugh turned to look at him. "Two reasons. First, because I'm a better person than you. Second, because you just solved a problem for me entirely by accident."

He turned on his heel and strode off down the hall.

"What problem?" Rhodes said, the confusion audible in his voice.

"I'm about to add another deed to my legend," Hugh said.

He might be a better person than Rhodes, but that still left room for a little gloating, and even if Hugh hated being called Stormward, he couldn't help but think that Rhodes had to hate it even more.

Rhodes called out something else behind him, but Hugh ignored it, sending frantic mental signals for his spellbook to find Godrick and Talia and drag them to his room. He managed to keep to a brisk walk until he was out of sight and earshot of Rhodes, then burst into a run, heading towards Ilinia's guest rooms to find Sabae.

If he was right, Rhodes had just blown the investigation wide open. Hugh knew who the traitor was.

CHAPTER TWENTY-FIVE

Departures

"So… what, you're just leaving like that?" Sabae demanded. "You've spent a paltry few weeks here, and you're just going to up and leave just like that? Did your negotiations even accomplish anything?"

The winds in Ilinia's suite continued blowing, picking up the archmage's clothes and folding them. Globules of water darted between them, washing the clothes and then draining away their moisture before the winds settled them into her grandmother's bags.

"They were mostly just an excuse to visit you, dear," Ilinia said distractedly as she shuffled around the massive suite of rooms that had been assigned to her, packing documents and ordering her aides around.

Sabae stared at her in disbelief. She'd spent the past few weeks being dragged in her grandmother's wake, but she'd had precious little time to actually spend with Sabae, apart from a few sessions of Ilinia criticizing the magic Alustin had been teaching her, and a few interrogation sessions about Kanderon, the Librarians Errant, and the events in Theras Tel.

Ilinia reached out and pushed Sabae's mouth closed. "Don't gape, dearie, it makes you look like a fish."

Sabae pulled back and snarled. "I told you what's waiting in the labyrinth for us, and you're just going to leave us to our fates?"

"I'll be a hundred leagues away by the time you enter the labyrinth," Ilinia said cheerfully. "Your friend Hugh is on his way here. He seems like he's in quite a hurry."

Sabae ignored that for now. Her grandmother loved showing off her windtalking abilities. Hugh probably wouldn't be here for a good few minutes yet.

"There's a literal demon down in the labyrinth!" Sabae shouted. Several of her grandmother's aides gasped, but both Kaen Das ignored them. They were all loyal, and Ilinia had her ways of ensuring her security from scrying. "It survived battle with Kanderon, what could we possibly do against it?"

Ilinia waved her hand in the air dismissively. "Feh. Kanderon's not so impressive."

Sabae just glared at her. She'd seen her family assessments of the local great powers, and Kanderon had sat atop the list for centuries. Ilinia, Indris, and a few of the more reclusive Skyreach Range powers were the sphinx's only real competitors in the southwest of the continent. Anything that could survive battle with her was far out of Sabae's league.

"Everyone out!" Sabae snapped. Ilinia's aides weren't technically obligated to listen to Sabae, but considering her tone of voice, they moved almost as fast as they would have for her grandmother.

Ilinia just raised her brow at that, but didn't contradict her.

Once the door closed behind the last of the aides, Sabae turned and glared at her grandmother. This was a calculated risk, but...

"There's a traitor on Skyhold's council, Grandmother."

Ilinia chuckled. "I'm well aware, dearie. I've spent more than enough bribing them."

Sabae rolled her eyes. Of course she was. "I need to know who it is."

"...So you can report them to Alustin? That would be cheating, wouldn't it? I thought you were supposed to discover the traitor yourself," Ilinia said, sipping from her flask.

Sabae actually snarled out loud at that. Of course Ilinia knew about the investigation.

"The traitor is working with the demon Bakori," Sabae said. "If we can unmask him or her, we can get out of having to go into the labyrinth again."

Ilinia chuckled. "You don't listen well when you're in a mood, Sabae. I won't be helping you cheat, nor do I approve of a Kaen Das backing down from a challenge."

Sabae made a high-pitched noise. Facing certain death at the hands of a demon was hardly a reasonable challenge.

"You'll be fine, dear. I have faith in you. Enough that I'm not going to be worried about you, even from a hundred leagues away. Now, your short little warlock friend will be here soon, give your grandmother a kiss before she leaves."

Sabae opened her mouth to argue, but the air in the room seemed to constrict, locking it back shut again. Her grandmother pecked her on the cheek, then the wind opened the door and sent Sabae stumbling towards it.

"Good luck with your finals!" her grandmother called out behind her.

The wind propelled Sabae straight out the door and into Hugh. Before they could pick themselves up off the ground, the door slammed shut behind her.

"I figured it out!" Hugh hissed. "I figured out who it is!"

Sabae clamped her hand over Hugh's mouth automatically, before he could say anything else. "Not here. Let's head to your room."

As they strode off, Sabae couldn't help but glare back at the door to her grandmother's room.

She hadn't even managed to work up the nerve to ask her grandmother about arranged marriages. Part of her was daring to hope that the fact that it hadn't been brought up yet meant that Ilinia didn't have marriage plans for Sabae, but she did her best to suppress that part— Ilinia wasn't the sort to let go of any advantage, and there was too much political value to be gained for the family from arranged marriages for there to be any chance of that.

Godrick and Talia met them on the way to Hugh's room, and they didn't look pleased to Sabae. Well, Talia didn't look pleased, at least, since Hugh's spellbook was literally hauling her down the hallway by her hair. Godrick was visibly torn between concern and struggling not to laugh.

"I'm going to blast this stupid book into bits, Hugh," Talia said, staggering behind the book as it floated down the hall.

"Let go of her hair," Hugh ordered.

The book let go, then dodged behind Hugh to get out of Talia's line of fire.

Sabae rolled her eyes at that. "No time for book burnings, Hugh has had something of a revelation, apparently. The sort of revelation we should only talk about privately."

Talia and Godrick immediately grew serious at that, and no one spoke again until they reached Hugh's room.

Where an unpleasant surprise was waiting for them.

"Hugh, you are an idiot," Talia repeated. "A complete idiot."

"It's not Hugh's fault I was snooping through his stuff," Avah yelled.

"It's his fault he left sensitive documents where you could find them!" Talia yelled back.

Sabae pulled at her hair in exasperation as she watched *That Old Pile of Junk* leave the harbor. This was seriously the last thing they needed right now.

"It's not that we don't like you, Avah," Sabae said, turning away from the window and kicking Talia's shin discreetly when it looked like she was about to comment, "it's that they're secret documents that we're literally not allowed to share with anyone. We could get in a ton of trouble for this. And not just academic punishment sorts of trouble."

Avah stared at her in shock. "Wait, this isn't just some sort of exercise? There's actually a traitor in Skyhold?"

Hugh, who was helping Godrick collect the scattered suspect dossiers, made a quiet, unhappy noise.

"Why would anyone let apprentices participate in this sort of thing?" Avah demanded. "This is way, way too dangerous!"

"We can handle ourselves just fine!" Talia snapped.

"I've seen you go up against Anders in training!" Avah snapped back, "and you sure can't handle him. What's he going to do if he finds out you know he's selling out Skyhold?"

The room got quiet as everyone stared at Avah.

"Anders isn't the traitor," Hugh said.

"Of course he is," Avah insisted.

"What, you figured that out from ten minutes with dossiers we've spent a year looking through?" Talia demanded with a nasty look.

"A few hours, but yeah," Avah said. "Haven't you ever wondered how he can afford it?"

"Afford what?" Godrick asked.

"The silk!" Avah said.

"He's from Tsarnassus, isn't he? They're the biggest suppliers of silk on the continent," Sabae said.

Avah rolled her eyes. "And what, you think they just give it away to their citizens? Silk of the lowest quality is still absurdly expensive, and Anders is *not* wearing the lowest quality. Any one of his outfits is probably worth as much as a small sandship, and I've seen at least three of them. This dossier has assessments of his finances in there, and there's absolutely no way he could afford them on his own without taking bribes or embezzling or something."

No one spoke for a moment.

"Ah think she might be right," Godrick finally said.

"And I have a few suspicions where the money came from," Sabae muttered.

Talia's mood had taken an astonishingly fast turn for the better. "I told you it was Anders," she told Sabae with a gloating smile.

"You thought it was Anders because that's how it would have played out in one of your novels," Sabae pointed out, "not because of any decent investigatory technique."

Talia stuck out her tongue, still smiling broadly.

"It's not Anders, though," Hugh said.

Avah and Talia both shot Hugh glares.

"Or… oh, no. It might be Anders, but it's not just Anders," Hugh said, clutching at his hair.

"Wait, I thought you called us here because you figured out who it was," Talia said. "But you were just wrong about it, and your girlfriend just had the answer ready to go?"

"I did figure it out!" Hugh said. "Or, well, Rhodes sort of accidentally figured it out. It's Rutliss!"

"Wait, how is that pompous jerk Rhodes involved in our investigation now?" Talia asked. "Are you just letting everyone find out about our investigation?"

"He's not! He just mentioned something when he cornered me earlier— that part of why he treated me the way he did was because I never could have afforded Skyhold's attendance on my own," Hugh said.

"He cornered you?" Sabae asked, a little alarmed at that.

Hugh's spellbook poked out from under the bed, looking a little alarmed as well. Well, alarmed at something other than Talia's future vengeance— it had been hiding under there since they got back, though it had at least listened when Hugh had asked it to help prevent them from being scryed on.

"It's fine. I'll tell you about it later. It's not important right now," Hugh said in a rush. "He was right, though, I couldn't have afforded Skyhold, and nor could my family. They could barely afford my ticket here. So far as I know, *no-one paid for my tuition at Skyhold.* I think Bakori must have arranged it— and, since Rutliss is the Bursar, he must have fudged the books to make it look like I'd paid."

Avah raised her hand. "Who is Bakori, and how exactly could you not notice that you hadn't paid anything to go to school?"

Sabae opened her mouth to try and offer a reasonable but not alarming explanation, but Talia beat her to the punch. "Demon, lives in the labyrinth below the school, has mental manipulation magic, had plans for Hugh that he disrupted, and now he has a grudge against Hugh and probably means to kill him."

Sabae sighed in exasperation as Avah turned pale. That little revelation really wasn't going to be great for Hugh and Avah's relationship, but now was hardly the time to worry about that. Sabae would be having words with Talia after this was all over, though.

If they made it through, anyhow.

"There's a problem with yer theory, Hugh," Godrick said. "Even assuming it wasn't one of Rutliss' underlings who did it— and we have no idea how many of them have been influenced by Bakori— his department isn't the only one that could have gotten you in."

"Wait, there's really a demon below Skyhold?" Avah said. "Talia isn't just messing with me because she doesn't like me?"

"Talia likes you just fine," Hugh said.

Sabae rolled her eyes at that.

"Abyla's department could a' slipped you in as well," Godrick continued. "Admissions is actually responsible for collectin' tuition for new students. It's a telling piece a' evidence, sure, and it could give up the game, but not without a bit a' further research."

"So there's two traitors, and we don't know who one of them is, then," Talia said.

"At least two," Sabae said. "Both Abyla and Rutliss could be traitors, even if only one of them is being manipulated by Bakori. Hell, the fact that we know there are multiple traitors even casts doubt on Tarik being innocent, so we could have all four suspects as traitors, though that seems unlikely."

"I read a book once where all the suspects turned out to have worked together," Talia said.

Sabae rolled her eyes. "We're not basing our investigation off the novels you enjoy, Talia."

"It worked for Anders," Talia said.

"That was pure coincidence," Sabae replied.

Talia stuck out her tongue at Sabae.

"Can we talk more about this demon thing?" Avah said.

"We will," Hugh said, "this is just really urgent. Actually because of the demon thing. If we can show who the traitor is, we can get out of having to go into the labyrinth. With the demon."

Sabae had to struggle not to shake Hugh for that. If he was trying to comfort Avah, he was going about it in the worst possible way.

"Midsummer is in two days. We need to get this information to Kanderon *now*," Sabae said. She stood up to go.

"That… might be a bit of a problem," Godrick said.

Everyone turned to look at him.

"Kanderon and over half the full council just left Skyhold a couple hours ago," Godrick said. "Apparently, some giant volcanic elemental is wakin' up in the Skyreach Range, and it's goin' ta' take that many mages ta' put it back ta' sleep."

"Jaskolskus?" Hugh asked. "It's an ash elemental, but it lives in a volcano. Though some people think it created the volcano, which kind of tells you how powerful it is."

"Ah think that's what me dah called it," Godrick said. "The remaining councilors are all up in arms. They're not supposed ta skip the traditional Midsummer and Midwinter meetings for any reason. Been that way fer centuries."

"Shouldn't you be keeping track of Kanderon?" Talia demanded of Hugh.

"It's more the other way around," Hugh said. "Still no word from Alustin?"

Everyone shook their heads, except for Avah.

"This is insane," Avah said. "This is way more insane than last summer. How do you keep getting in these situations? Alustin I understand, he seeks them out, but you all?"

"So we go to your da," Sabae said to Godrick. Part of her mind inanely pointed out that she'd pronounced da just like Godrick did, which would have been amusing at literally any other time.

He shook his head. "He's already in the labyrinth. The school sends faculty mages into the labyrinth a couple days early to make sure that nothing too dangerous is in the testing levels."

"What do you want to bet that doesn't keep Bakori out?" Talia muttered.

Avah made a whimpering noise.

"What about your grandmother?" Hugh asked Sabae.

Sabae shook her head. "Look out the window, tell me what you see."

"Her ship's gone," Hugh reported.

"She literally just left a few minutes ago while we were talking," Sabae said. "She made it clear that she'd be a hundred leagues away when we entered the labyrinth."

"So literally every adult that we could potentially trust with this information is missing right now?" Talia demanded.

"Tarik?" Godrick asked.

Sabae frowned and shook her head at that. "Too much of a risk."

There was something deeply wrong with all of this. There'd been something deeply wrong with this investigation from the very beginning. No matter what excuses Alustin gave, this wasn't the sort of thing you entrusted to apprentices. You didn't just casually leave apprentices at risk of being murdered by a vengeful demon. You didn't act so casual about it.

Sabae's frown deepened. The disturbing part was that all of those arguments applied to all the adults involved. Not just Kanderon and Alustin, but to Artur and her grandmother as well.

In fact, it almost seemed like…

"I think Kanderon knew from the start that we'd have to go into the labyrinth," Hugh said.

"That's insane. Why would she want a demon to get you?" Avah asked. "Is she insane?"

"I think she's been planning this," he said. "At the last lesson we had, she told me that we probably wouldn't catch the traitor, and we'd probably have to go into the labyrinth again, and that I needed to trust her."

"And you didn't say anything?" Talia demanded.

Hugh looked at his feet, turning red. "I didn't actually want to believe it," he said in a small voice.

Sabae interrupted before Talia could start yelling at Hugh and send him into a downward emotional spiral. That was the last thing they needed right now.

"I think my grandmother wants us in the labyrinth too," she said. "When I told her about the situation, she just insisted I not back down from the challenge, which I thought was ridiculous, but…"

"Am I literally the only one taking our secrecy seriously?" Talia demanded.

Godrick made an affronted noise.

"Are Godrick and I literally the only ones taking our secrecy seriously?" Talia demanded.

"I was trying to find us a way out of this whole situation," Sabae said. "My grandmother apparently even knew there was a traitor this whole time, and even already knew about our investigation somehow, and she still wouldn't do anything. I think she wants us in the labyrinth too."

"This is all absurd," Avah said. "The people that are supposed to be protecting you all are not only forcing you into a dangerous situation, they're actively removing themselves from positions where they could help you?"

"Sabae's grandmother, maybe," Hugh said, "but Alustin had a mission, Artur had his own duties, and Kanderon could hardly help when Jaskolskus decided to wake up. They wouldn't deliberately abandon us for no reason."

A part of Sabae couldn't help but feel a little cynical about that. Still…

"There's no way Artur would have agreed to us being put in a situation with more danger than he thought we could handle," she said. "Even if we can't trust anyone else involved, we can trust him."

"We can trust Alustin and Kanderon," Hugh insisted. "And you should be able to trust your grandmother, right?"

Sabae gave him a flat look. "I trust the other three not to actively have it out for us, but all three of them would sacrifice any of us if they thought it necessary to achieve their long-term goals. Artur wouldn't."

Hugh crossed his arms and gave her a defiant look. "I can't speak for your grandmother, but I trust Alustin and Kanderon. I think you're just letting your cynicism do your thinking for you."

There was no faster way to pull Hugh out of one of his emotional spirals than to insult someone he cared about. It didn't necessarily leave him in the most helpful mood, though.

Sabae raised her hands in a conciliatory gesture. "At the very least, I don't think they're going to put us in a hopeless situation here. I think that they're trying to get us in the labyrinth for a reason."

"I have a better idea that doesn't get you all killed," Avah said. "Run away. Come join the Radhan. I can guarantee you'd all be welcome. Please."

That... was actually tempting. Sabae couldn't deny that her family's demands on her were onerous at times, and while she'd learned an incredible amount at Skyhold, it didn't exactly hold the fondest place in her heart.

Sabae shook her head. "I owe it to my family to keep going."

Talia snorted. "I don't run away."

Sabae knew that wasn't true— Talia was belligerent, not foolhardy, but the redhead would hardly admit that to Avah.

Godrick patted Avah gently on the shoulder. "It really means a lot that yeh'd offer— ah know how much that means ta the Radhan— but ah can't disappoint me da like that."

Avah looked on the verge of tears. "Hugh?"

Hugh looked torn, but Sabae already knew which way he'd jump. As much as he cared about Avah…

"I'd be nothing without Kanderon and Alustin," Hugh said. "They made me a mage, rather than a failure. I need to trust them. We're going into the labyrinth."

CHAPTER TWENTY-SIX

Return to the Labyrinth

When you made a momentous, important decision, it should really be followed by important preparations.

Not dealing with your friend's hysterical girlfriend.

It had taken hours to calm Avah down, and Talia was far from pleased about that. That was time they could have spent preparing for the labyrinth, and now Hugh was sulking instead of focusing.

"She's going to break up with me," Hugh was muttering.

Talia rolled her eyes and stared resolutely towards the doors that led into the labyrinth, trying to ignore the conversation that was rehashing itself for the twentieth time behind her. She started double checking her armaments.

Magical dagger that could suspend itself in midair, check. Drinking water, snacks, check.

"You had your first real fight. That doesn't mean she's about to break up with you," Sabae said tiredly.

Clan Castis dagger, check. Newest enchanted dagger, check.

"First fights in a relationship aren't usually multi-hour affairs revolving around literal life or death situations, are they?" Hugh muttered.

Lock pick hairpins, check. Enchanted pins stuck in the heels of her shoes, check.

"If ah told yeh that she was goin' ta break up with yeh, would that help yeh focus any?" Godrick asked.

It really said something that even Godrick was getting impatient with Hugh— the big apprentice usually had seemingly endless patience when the rest of them were concerned. Though, admittedly, a lot of Godrick's current mood probably had to do with pre-labyrinth jitters.

Enchanted gloves, check. Portable ward Hugh had made her, check.

Hugh made an unpleasant noise in his throat.

Throwing knives, check. Bone shards in belt pouch, check. Bone necklace, check.

"Is this really the best time to have a conversation about your dating lives?" someone in the group behind them asked.

Talia smirked a little at that.

The four of them had been placed at the front of the line at this labyrinth entrance, just like last year. The second years, however, entered earlier in the morning, far before the first years did. The third years had entered even earlier, apparently.

A faculty member had covered the rules with them again, but little had changed since last year, other than the fact they were going as deep as the second level now.

"What if..." Hugh started.

Talia turned back and glared at him. "Equipment check, Hugh."

"I already…" he started.

"Doesn't matter," Talia said. "Do it again. You need to know exactly what you have on you going into this, and exactly where it all is on your person."

Hugh frowned, but he began patting his pockets and belt pouch. His spellbook shifted sleepily from where it was slung over his shoulder.

At least someone was getting enough sleep, even if it was that annoying book.

Talia turned her gaze on the other two. "Equipment check."

Godrick opened his mouth to say something, but Talia just glared at him. He closed his mouth sheepishly and began going over his own gear, starting with his massive warhammer.

Sabae gave Talia a knowing look, then she patted her shield and her big canteen. "Check," she said.

Talia rolled her eyes at that. Sabae was a competent enough leader once she was in the thick of things, but if given time to worry beforehand, she was as bad about overthinking things as either of the boys.

This wasn't, of course, something Talia had to worry about at all. She was utterly calm and prepared, and she had no need to overthink anything. Everything was going to turn out fine.

"First team, it's time to go!"

As the massive enchanted quartzite doors swung open, Talia began unconsciously patting herself down again in what, if she had been counting, was her eighth equipment check of the morning.

Godrick activated his hammer's silence enchantment as they strode into the labyrinth. He'd gotten better at using the enchantment more selectively— they should be able to talk fine without it carrying, but it should dampen their footsteps entirely.

He'd gotten some pushback on his choice of enchantment from a few people, but he didn't need to hit harder or set fire to things when he hit them or anything like that— Godrick was already plenty destructive enough with his bare hands, let alone when he put his attunements behind his blows.

No, Godrick had done enough sneaking around over the course of the last year and change to know its value, and he was quite happy about anything that would make that easier.

Hugh and Sabae summoned lights to guide their path.

No one spoke as they strode deeper into the labyrinth, save for Sabae giving off the occasional direction. Even Hugh's spellbook seemed alert and ready.

The first attack came fifteen minutes or so into their trek. They'd been trying to head for the center of the first floor as quickly as possible this time— a viable strategy, but one that was noted for attracting more attacks and traps than usual.

Alustin's explanation of what the labyrinths were answered a lot of questions, but far from everything. It did not, for instance, do a lot to explain the oddities of the floors, the variety of the traps, or even exactly what their purposes were. It also didn't explain many of the stranger behaviors of the labyrinth, like why it responded differently to people using different strategies to move through it.

When pressed, Alustin just admitted that he didn't know. Godrick would have preferred it if Alustin did know and was just trying to keep it a secret.

The attack was over before Godrick even realized it had started. Some sort of spined snake came slithering down a nearby passage, and Talia immediately blasted it with dreamfire. The snake rapidly shrank in size, coiled around itself, and then formed an eggshell around itself.

Within seconds, the egg had vanished as well.

Godrick was fairly sure he'd seen dreamfire do something similar before.

He was fairly sure that his hammer enchantment would reduce the number of attacks they'd suffer, even taking the more dangerous route, but even if it didn't, he wasn't overly worried about most of the stuff on the first floor. They'd handled it relatively easily last year, and they were far more capable this year.

Honestly, if anything on the first floor made it past Talia, he'd be surprised.

Hugh had thought he'd be stuck thinking about his fight with Avah until he saw her again, but he found the labyrinth to be an excellent distraction.

Somehow, the enchantment on Godrick's hammer made the labyrinth more ominous. Their clothes didn't rustle, their footsteps were silent, and their breath hardly seemed to stir the air around them. They could still speak, but they were avoiding doing so to keep from attracting trouble.

So there simply wasn't anything to hear, save for their own heartbeats. The first floor was, as always, deathly quiet. Something about the spellforms on the walls and the layout of the halls dampened sound. This near complete silence disturbed Hugh more than any noise he could think of— it was what he imagined being deaf must be like.

Something else about the labyrinth seemed different to Hugh. It felt larger, more watchful. He wasn't sure whether it was because of his fear of Bakori, his knowledge of what lurked in the depths of the labyrinth, or his new knowledge of what the labyrinth was.

Or if it actually was different, somehow.

His spellbook felt alert, but not nervous. It felt... comfortable, somehow. Not the sort of comfort you felt in a safe place, but the sort of comfort Hugh remembered from wandering the woods of Emblin, being in a place where you knew the dangers and could be ready for them.

He'd found the labyrinth stone here, after all. Who knows how long it had laid in the labyrinth, attuning to its aether?

Hugh kept his sling ready in one hand, a warded slingstone in the other.

After the snake, nothing attacked them for some time as they wandered through the labyrinth. This didn't comfort Hugh much. Last time they'd been in here, they'd been repeatedly confronted by packs of Bakori's imps— guided by them, though they hadn't known it at the time.

This time, with Bakori actually out to harm them, the lack of imps was somehow more intimidating than their presence.

As the group advanced, Hugh abruptly felt alarm from his spellbook.

"Stop!" he hissed.

Even trying to be quiet, Hugh's voice sounded alarmingly loud after the silence.

The others halted immediately. Hugh carefully crept past Godrick and Sabae at the front, and crouched to look at the floor.

It took Hugh a second, but he found carefully hidden spellforms underneath the dust of the floor. He took a second to study them— like most of the spellforms in the labyrinth, they worked in a fundamentally similar manner to wards.

He pointed out the spellforms to the others. "It wouldn't have killed us, but it would have hurt. It would have temporarily altered gravity so that the way we just came from was down. Would have slammed us into that wall hard."

"Can you break it, or should we find a way around?" Sabae whispered.

Hugh didn't respond, just crouched down. He reached out with his crystal affinity sense to the rock around it and prepared to break it, but then paused. A grin crossed his face, and he carefully made some more complex alterations.

It took less than a minute, then he moved forward and gestured for the others to cross. They got back into formation, Sabae and Godrick at the front.

"I didn't break it," Hugh said quietly. "I altered it so that it would let humans past without triggering, and I changed the function of the spell so that it would alter gravity upwards instead of sideways for anything else that passed."

Sabae nodded at him, looking pleased.

They reached the center of the first floor without any further incident.

"Trying to set a speed record?" one of the mages guarding the entrance to the second floor called as they approached. "We only got the signal that the doors were opening twenty minutes ago. You're the first team here!"

"How close ta the record are we?" Godrick asked.

"Not even close," another mage said. "The record is four and a half minutes. A team of third years set it seventy years ago— they were all fliers of different types, and they blasted through the labyrinth at high speed. Half the monsters on the floor chased them to the center, too."

Talia snickered at that.

One of the mages touched an amulet to the dome shaped shield over the stairwell down, and an oval door opened in the shield.

Godrick went first, and had to duck through, but the rest of them passed through just fine.

Hugh was last, and he could feel a crackle behind him as the barrier shut.

CHAPTER TWENTY-SEVEN

Twists and Turns

Hugh had never seen the second floor of the labyrinth before, though he'd been far below it. He'd technically been on the second floor too, but he'd been unconscious then. It looked remarkably different from the first— the walls were still stone, but instead of the square granite tunnels of the first floor, limestone walls arched overhead. It was tall enough that Godrick couldn't reach the ceiling even with his hammer in the center, but he'd have to crouch if he wanted to move closer to the sides.

Hugh and Talia, as the shortest members of the party, had considerably more room to maneuver in the tunnels of the second floor.

Unlike the other floors they'd seen, there was light down here that emanated faintly from this floor's spellforms. It was dim enough that they'd need to resummon light cantrips to read by, but they could maneuver down here well enough without them.

The spellforms on the walls weren't carved in stone. Instead, finger-thick streams of water flowed, twisted, and interconnected across the curving arch of the tunnels, in a constantly shifting, gravity defying web of spellforms.

The whole floor echoed with the gentle sound of water.

"It's beautiful," Hugh said.

The others nodded.

"Doesn't make it less dangerous, though," Sabae said. "You've read about this floor. Stay alert."

The second floor had a number of peculiarities all its own. The passages shifted and changed far more rapidly than any other floor, and the main stairs down were never found in any consistent location.

That didn't mean the floor was impossible to navigate, though— in many ways, navigating it was a fairly direct process. The water in the spellforms tended to flow away from the exit, so you could find it without too much difficulty, so long as you stayed alert.

The dangers of the second floor were numerous, however. The monsters that dwelled in the thicker aether down here were far more numerous, powerful, and aggressive than their upstairs neighbors. The traps down here were much more likely to maim or even kill, and there were other, unique hazards to the floor.

The liquid spellforms frequently varied in width and volume, but sometimes they would begin to massively expand. When that happened, you had only minutes or seconds before a flood of water would pour through the tunnels, dashing you against walls, dazing you, and usually separating you from your party. Drownings were rare, given how short-lived the floods were, but they were hardly unknown.

Other times, the spellforms would begin to peel away from the walls, forming liquid webs of spellforms stretching across the corridors. They didn't pose any threat to life or limb, and would reform when you passed through them, leaving you just a little wetter, but the monsters on this floor seemed to be able to sense when you did so, so it was best not to walk through them.

There were also deep pools of water in many of the intersections of the tunnels, as well as even larger caverns with pools approaching the sizes of lakes. Dangerous creatures often dwelled within them, so apprentices were advised to stay away, but many other explorers and mages specifically sought them out— this floor was the first where items of real value started to be regularly found.

Rare, aether-sensitive freshwater corals glowed in the depths of the pools. Exotic fish found nowhere else lurked in the depths, and mysterious objects were often found half-buried in sand at lake bottoms.

Of course, now Hugh knew that all the residents of this floor were just inhabitants of other worlds that had slipped into the labyrinth when it overlapped their world, permanently or temporarily.

Most of the dangers of the floor could be handled easily enough if you stayed alert, but that was the trickiest part of the floor— something about it calmed and soothed you. It was easy to relax, to forget your fears. It was a subtle danger, by all accounts— it's not easy to fear peace.

On this floor, however, you needed to, because if you were relaxed here, you weren't nearly alert enough.

They found the current in the spellforms easy enough, following them down the tunnels. Within a few twists and turns, Sabae had lost all track of which direction they were going, but she just focused on following the current upstream.

The light was dim enough that she was relying on her water affinity sense as much as her vision to tell which way the current was moving. Hugh, oddly, seemed to be moving much more confidently in the dim light than the rest of them— perhaps he was using some sort of cantrip to help him see in the dim light?

Godrick's hammer definitely gave them a major tactical advantage— she was still in shock at how easily it had let them pass through the first floor— but the dead silence it had created for them had been more than a little creepy. Here, at least, the sound of water was always present.

It reminded her a little of the waves in the harbor at Ras Andis. Most children had preferred playing there at low tide, when the ships sat on the sand at the bottom of the cove, but Sabae had always preferred high tide, when the water was several building heights higher, lapping at the lowest tier of the city.

Sabae saw a flicker of color out of the corner of her eye and shook her head. She'd known about the soporific effect of the floor, and it had still managed to mess with her head.

The flash of color had vanished, but several more were approaching along the walls. As they drew closer, Sabae saw that they were tiny brilliant red and yellow fish swimming through the strands of water that made up the spellform.

"Look at that," Sabae whispered.

The others seemed to wake up from a daze when she spoke, and she realized that they'd fallen prey to the floor as well. She felt a brief flash of irritation, but dismissed it. She hadn't done any better, and lecturing them wouldn't help.

"There wasn't anything about them in the guides," Talia said.

"They're probably new to the labyrinth," Hugh said. "They probably slipped in from some other world, somehow managed to survive here."

"Where do they find food in the spellforms, do yeh think?" Godrick asked, bending down to get a closer look at the fish as they passed.

"They probably use the spellforms to move from pool to pool down here," Sabae said.

"There's a lot more fish coming," Hugh said nervously, looking down the tunnel "I don't think that's a good sign."

A lot more was a gross understatement. The spellforms were flooded with the tiny fish— there were so many they'd

249

begun falling out of the strands of water, flopping on the floor.

"If we get eaten by a school of minnows, I'm never talking to any of you again," Talia said, pulling a pair of daggers. One was Talia's familiar magic dagger, but the other looked suspiciously like it was carved out of bone.

"Armor up, Godrick," Sabae said, and began spinning up her own armor. She almost drew on the water around her to do so— water armor had proven more mana intensive and less mobile in most situations than wind armor, but it was also significantly harder to penetrate.

Considering they were under potential threat from fish, however, it might not be the best idea to surround herself with their element.

Sabae had her wind armor most of the way spun up when the leading edge of the school reached them, but to her great relief, they simply flowed on past the apprentices. She began to let her wind armor dissipate.

Godrick, who had only covered his torso and one arm with his stone armor, let out a sigh of relief. "I guess that was…"

He froze, sniffing the air, then his stone armor rapidly resumed assembling itself. "Something's chasing them," he hissed. "Something foul."

A few seconds later, Sabae caught the sound of something striking stone. She cursed, and spun her wind armor back up to full speed, readying her buckler on her arm.

The creature came into sight around the corner a moment later.

It was a bird, but it was unlike any bird she'd ever seen before. It towered over them, its head nearly scraping the ceiling in the center of the hallway. Its beak was longer than her leg, and it looked like it was meant to tear and shred at meat. The bird's wings were vestigial things that fluttered close to its body. Its talons looked sharper than swords, and Sabae seriously doubted her armor's ability to fend them off.

The bird was dragging its beak along the wall, scooping up the fish by the dozen, and spilling even more on the floor, where its talons smashed and shredded many of them.

The stench hit Sabae a moment later. The bird reeked of rotten meat, blood, and urine, even through her wind armor. She could hear Hugh gagging behind her.

None of that was the worst part of the bird, however. The worst part were the feathers.

They didn't hold to a single color— they shifted between colors constantly. The colors were each and every one vile, however— a yellow that reminded her of pus, a blue that made her vision waver and feel like a migraine was coming on, and a mottled orange that somehow *tasted* of rot to her eyes. The colors didn't shift smoothly, either— they jerked and twisted, tore viciously into one another, and flickered in and out in eye-aching patterns. The color of bruises was devoured by a grey that made her insides *itch* somehow, and Sabae had to look to the side before she vomited.

It was a little better when she could only see it through her peripheral vision, but it still hurt to look at.

Abruptly, the thing's smell seemed to roll away from her, and she breathed in a sigh of relief and sent a nod of thanks in Godrick's direction.

That motion, unfortunately, finally drew the bird's attention towards them. Its beady black eyes glittered in the low light as it cocked its head first one way then the other to get a better look at him.

Then, with a vicious, ear splitting shriek, the bird charged them.

Talia blasted bolts of dreamfire at the creature, but as soon as the purple-green flames approached it, the hideous colors of its feathers seemed to reach out into the flames and disrupt them. The colors of the feathers dimmed for a moment, but quickly returned to full strength.

Hugh's attack had a bit more effect— one of his warded slingstones slammed into the bird's hip, detonating with a sharp crack. The creature stumbled, and a splatter of blood and feathers went flying, but the bird didn't stop.

"Aim at its feet; I'm going in high!" Sabae shouted. She detonated her wind armor around her feet, sending her blasting towards the creature's head.

It didn't even hesitate before trying to impale her with its beak in midair, but Sabae twisted her body and windjumped using one arm, sending her just out of the way of the strike, and slamming her shield against the bird's head.

Before the shield had even struck, Sabae was already flooding it with mana.

She'd spent months training to use the shield properly— a process that had involved dislocating her shoulder and breaking her wrist more than once during training before she figured out how to control her body and her wind armor to keep the impact and the sudden halt from injuring her. The medical wing had not been pleased about her repeated visits.

The bird, however, was definitely not prepared for this. It might massively outweigh and outmuscle any of them, save for maybe Godrick in his armor, but the full force of of Sabae being propelled by a windjump was more than the bird was prepared to handle.

The instant the shield struck, it glued itself to the head and beak of the bird, and the trajectory of Sabae's flight just yanked the bird over. One of Hugh's slingstones detonating at its feet sent it toppling completely over, and it hit the ground with a thunderous crash.

Sabae's windshield collapsed on hitting the ground, and she quickly stopped channeling mana into the shield as she pulled it from the bird and rolled away. She immediately began spinning her wind armor back up, hoping she could get it up fast enough.

The bird had started climbing back to its feet when Godrick's sledgehammer slammed into its side, sending it sprawling. The bird let loose a pained, ear-splitting screech.

The stone mage, completely armored in stone and looking like someone had brought a statue of a suit of armor to life, reared back, bashing the creature a second, then a third time.

When he reared back to hit it a fourth time, the creature twisted onto its back faster than Sabae would have thought possible. The talons of one foot wrapped around the handle of the sledgehammer, stopping it in mid-swing. The creature's other foot shot out almost faster than Sabae could see, slamming into Godrick's armored chest.

Sabae could see the stone actually crack, and Godrick went flying back towards Hugh and Talia. Sabae cried out, thinking that her friends were about to be crushed, but Hugh and Talia fell upwards against the ceiling, crashing into the flowing spellforms above them and sticking there.

Part of her wanted to laugh at how many situations Hugh solved with levitation cantrips, but most of her was feeling utterly terrified as her cry drew the bird's attention, and as she realized she could smell the creature again.

She'd mostly spun her armor back up, and she detonated it around one leg to send her skidding along the floor away from the bird, just in time to dodge its beak, which fractured the limestone floor when it struck.

The bird recovered faster than she thought possible, and lunged for her again. She just barely dodged by blasting herself backward across the floor.

Just when it looked to be ready to lunge again, the bird froze in place and screamed— louder than it ever had before, enough that Sabae thought her eardrums were about to burst. It cut off as soon as it had started, however, and the stench of burning meat poured off the creature.

It collapsed to the ground, and Talia rolled off its back, holding a dagger that was burning almost too brightly to look at. Spellforms on her gloves and jacket were glowing brightly as well, and Sabae could see a hazy heat shield emanating from them, protecting Talia from the dagger.

The back of the bird was charred to a crisp where Talia had dropped from the ceiling and stabbed it.

Talia, apparently deciding she wanted to be sure it was dead, stabbed it again. This time, a blast of flame tore out of the dagger, ripping a wing and part of the torso off the bird.

Sabae took a shuddering breath and stared at Talia.

"Dragonbone dagger," Talia said cheerfully. "Works even better than expected."

Godrick, thankfully, was only bruised and winded— the outer layer of his armor was apparently designed to break under strong enough blows, which apparently provided better protection than just making the whole thing as sturdy as possible.

Talia tried to act confident and relaxed, but she was still on edge from the battle. The bird's feathers had been packed with dream mana, and it had shrugged off her dreamfire with terrifying ease. She was insanely lucky that her dragonbone dagger had been so effective, and she knew it.

The terrorbird— Godrick had claimed naming rights, since he'd been the only one injured, however lightly— had been far more dangerous than anything they should have encountered on this floor. It had been at least as dangerous as the massive crab they'd battled in the depths of the labyrinth last year, and even with how much more powerful they were now, it had been a close call.

It wasn't so much fear of the terrorbird that had gotten under her skin— though you'd have to be a fool not to respect that thing— but the helplessness she'd felt for a moment when her dreamfire failed. She was terrified that she wouldn't be able to help her friends.

She'd felt that fear before, of course— as wonderfully effective as dreamfire was, there were creatures that could withstand it and defenses mages could use against it— but it never got any easier.

Bonefire was even more destructive in many ways, but using it in cramped tunnels with her friends around was an awful idea.

The dragonbone dagger, though, had worked beyond her wildest expectations. It had cooked the terrorbird from the inside out— she probably hadn't even needed to shed the excess heat inside of it, she doubted it had even survived the first strike.

Though she still would have had to shed that heat somehow. It would linger for ages before it dispersed otherwise— that was one of the two big downsides of using her abilities on dragonbone.

Well, that and the fact that she could only safely use it with clothing enchanted to protect herself from the heat.

It took them almost an hour to make it to the center of the maze. They were attacked three more times after the terrorbird— once by a swarm of flying carnivorous fish that Sabae knocked out of the air with a gust strike, and that Talia then slaughtered with a rain of dreamfire; once by a slow-moving armored creature that they hadn't even gotten a good look at before Talia turned it to seashells with dreamfire, and once by some sort of vicious lizard-wolf whose back Godrick had broken with his hammer.

Hugh also detected and disarmed a half-dozen traps, though he gave most of the credit for detecting them to his spellbook.

They also survived a couple of the flash floods common to this floor— they caught one with enough forewarning to escape into another hallway, while Sabae managed to part the second around her, sheltering the others behind her until it passed.

Talia had to admit, it had been a really impressive sight.

Standing with the other mages at the exit to the third floor was a familiar figure— Artur himself. The big mage wrapped each of them in bear hugs in turn when he saw them— Talia was pretty sure she'd come close to suffocating from her hug.

"Ah'm glad yeh made it fine," Artur said. "Yeh're the fifth group ta get here, and ah've heard some real horror stories from 'em. Somethin's got the labyrinth all good and riled up today."

One of the other mages nodded as she handed out the tokens that proved they'd been to the second floor exit.

"Zzh... Zyzzi... the big spider didn't show up at the third floor exit this time," she said.

"Zzthkxz?" Hugh asked.

"Right, her," the mage said. "She usually lurks below the shield we set up and asks riddles of the students before we let them have their tokens. She'd eat them if she could, but she enjoys the riddles for their own sake, and we usually leave her a goat or two as a token of thanks. She just didn't show up this year, and it's been at least a decade since she's missed a Midsummer test."

Talia exchanged serious glances with her friends.

"Ah can't keep yeh, or ah'd get in trouble, but be careful," Artur said. He gave them each another hug, but Talia couldn't help but feel that Sabae had been right— Artur knew Bakori was somewhere down here in the labyrinth, but he wasn't acting nearly as nervous or stressed as he should be.

An unpleasant suspicion came over Talia— what if Bakori had been meddling with Artur's head?

She promptly dismissed it, since there was no way the demon could also have successfully done the same to Alustin, Sabae's grandmother, and Kanderon, but she couldn't manage to entirely dismiss it from her head, unfortunately.

At least, she couldn't dismiss it from her head until something else showed up to distract her.

About ten minutes into their trek back, a single one of Bakori's imps was waiting for them in the center of the hallway.

CHAPTER TWENTY-EIGHT

Imps

Next to him, Hugh could see Talia getting ready to attack the imp, so he reached out and touched her shoulder. When she gave him a questioning look, he just shook his head.

"Hugh of Emblin," the cat-sized creature said, in a voice deeper and more resonant than Godrick's.

The imp looked like a miniature version of Bakori, bat-like face and all. The only things missing were the protuberant belly that looked like a transparent sack full of tadpoles and the tail with the venomous stinger.

"Or should I call you Hugh Stormward now?" the imp said with a chuckle. It didn't look at him, idly inspecting its finger talons.

Hugh didn't respond, just eyed the imp warily. None of the others said anything.

"It's been an entertaining year, for me, I must admit," the imp said. "Watching your desperate, doomed little hunt for the traitor."

Hugh could see Sabae stiffen at that, but he didn't say anything and just kept his focus.

"Ah smell a lot more a' these things," Godrick whispered. "In every direction."

The imp tilted its head, focusing on Sabae. "You were so desperate to figure out why your little investigation seemed so strange, Sabae Kaen Das. Why apprentices would be put on such an important investigation. Why they'd be given oh so little support. Why nothing seemed to add up."

Another imp wandered around a corner, trailing its fingers through the streams of water running along the walls.

"Would you like me to tell you?" the second imp said. "It's a much less complicated answer than any of your theories."

"I wouldn't trust anything you have to say, demon!" Sabae snapped.

A third imp chuckled from behind them in that too-deep voice. Hugh didn't turn to look, though, keeping his eyes on the original imp.

"Everyone always speaks of demons as creatures of lies, as though we live for that, but that's hardly an accurate depiction," it said. "I won't claim that I don't lie— it's a necessary talent for any sophont— but in all my centuries of life, I've found that the truth can so often be far more devastating than any lie."

Hugh noticed Sabae clench her fists at that, but he just kept his eyes on the first imp, focusing intently.

"The reason the investigation seems so strange to you, Sabae? I hate to break it to you, but it's because no-one who matters actually cares about it. Kanderon, Alustin, your grandmother— they're all focused on events of far greater import. The world's changing, and you're all just a side-note."

"You're trying to sell us painted crap and call it gold," Talia snapped. "Alustin never would have spent as much time and effort on us if he didn't care."

Several more imps had casually wandered into the corridor around them, but Hugh paid them no attention.

"I never claimed they don't care about you, little weapon," another imp said. "I claimed they didn't care about your little investigation."

"Are yeh trying to convince us it was just somethin' ta keep us busy and nothin' more?" Godrick asked.

Two different imps chuckled, then spoke in unison. "No, I think they would have been quite pleased if you'd solved things. I'm saying there are bigger things in play than poor, innocent Bakori. They're just not worried about little old me, and I can't say I blame them."

At least twenty imps had wandered into the corridor at this point. One imp, who had been picking through the fur of another for lice, found one and held it up for inspection. "The world's about to change in a big way, and everyone wants their piece of the pie," it said, then ate the bug.

The original imp spoke up then. "More fool them. It's truly astonishing to me how foolhardy the mighty can be when they feel safe. Do you know why Kanderon never took on a warlock pact before, Hugh?"

He didn't respond, just stayed focused.

"It's because, in the right hands, a warlock pact is a point of vulnerability. A weapon to be used against its signatories."

The imp chuckled as it slowly approached them. "Now, it would be truly absurd to think of someone using Kanderon as a weapon against you through your bond, but the other way around? You've put a chink in her armor that can be exploited. Admittedly, those who have both the knowledge and ability to do so are rare, but you have the luck of speaking to one of those few. What an interesting coincidence, isn't it?

There had to be at least fifty or sixty imps in the corridor with them now, and Hugh's spellbook was letting him know it could sense hundreds more within its range.

Hugh didn't respond to Bakori's taunts, though. He just stayed focused.

He was not, however, focusing on Bakori or any of his imps.

"If you've got anything to say, Hugh, I might suggest you…" the original imp said, and then stopped.

Not a deliberate stop, or even a surprised stop. No, it stopped in the way that a bird does when it runs into a pane of glass it didn't see.

Hugh let a slow smile spread across his face. "You talk too much, Bakori," he said. "You could have had us if you'd tried to surprise us, but you're a gloater."

The four of them might have thought they could escape entering the labyrinth again, but that didn't mean they hadn't spent any time planning, and one of the foremost possibilities they'd foreseen was an attack on them by Bakori or his imps *after* the demon gloated over his victory. It wasn't just their previous encounter that made them expect this, but every known encounter others had had with the demon.

Bakori seemed constitutionally incapable of not monologuing.

Hugh had spent the entire conversation focusing not on Bakori, but on the ground around them. More specifically on the crystal structures in the rock around them. He'd put his crystal training with Kanderon to good use, crafting intricate wards running through the entire hallway around them and arch above them. The ward could probably hold out against Bakori's imps for hours. Not that Hugh intended to use it for much longer.

Bakori was saying something through one of his imps— probably something menacing and knowing— but Hugh ignored it. He also ignored the dozens of other imps clustering around the ward, testing and pushing at it.

"Ready?" he asked the others.

"Ready," said Talia with a grin, a dagger in one hand and a shard of bone in the other.

"Ready," said Godrick, as his stone armor closed back around him, and he slipped the warded faceplate Hugh had made him into place.

"Ready," said Sabae, as streams of water were absorbed into her new water armor.

Hugh detonated the ward he'd just built.

CHAPTER TWENTY-NINE

Race to the Top

Godrick had used his affinity senses to watch Hugh grow the ward just below the surface of the floor, and it had been a genuine pleasure to watch him work. Hugh's wardcrafting skills had been impressive even when Godrick had first met him, but over the last year and change Hugh had grown preposterously skilled with wards.

Even for a ward only meant to last a couple of minutes, Hugh didn't take any shortcuts. His ward lines were elegant, clean, and immediately recognizable as his work, even for someone as relatively unversed in wardcraft as Godrick. (Though, being friends with Hugh, you couldn't help but pick up a few things.)

Watching Hugh detonate the ward was a pleasure of an entirely different sort. Rather than the side of him that appreciated skilled craftsmanship and scholarship, it was the side of Godrick that still held onto a childlike love of fires, explosions, collapsing structures, and other such destruction that found joy in the ward detonation.

His da claimed that everyone had that side to them to one degree or another, but Godrick liked to privately call it his Talia side.

The physical part of the ward exploded a fraction of a second before the magical part. There were, Godrick was sure, more precise names Hugh would use for them. Shards of stone and crystal spellforms blasted out of the ground and into the air around the four of them, and a fraction of a second later the shards were met by an expanding wave of force that sent them blasting out into the ranks of imps.

It was messy, to say the least. The imps that weren't shredded immediately by the shards of stone and crystal were sent hurtling back by the blast, splatting against the walls, floor, and ceiling.

Talia was laughing maniacally next to him.

"Let's move!" Sabae yelled, charging forward.

Godrick followed her with a broad grin.

Moving in his stone armor was a singularly impressive experience. He'd always been big— huge, really, just like his da— but with the armor on, he couldn't help feeling like a force of nature. His foot came down on a still-moving imp, and he barely even felt any resistance. Godrick might be strong, but his sledgehammer was still no small burden— in his armor, it was as light as a feather. When the four of them turned at an intersection, rather than slowing down, he just reached out and sunk the fingers of his armor into the corner of the wall to let him corner more easily.

Godrick could hardly imagine what his armor would feel like to wear when he was able to construct it as large and effectively as his father could.

Hugh still struggled with his self-esteem, but, if he had to admit it, not with his wards any longer. When it came to his battle magic, though, he counted himself entirely outclassed by his friends.

Considering the situation they were in, however, Hugh was quite happy his friends were so dangerous.

Godrick's hammer slammed into a dog-sized imp, hurling it into the wall at the same time that his massive armored stone foot came crashing down onto another imp. When a whole pack of imps charged Godrick, the stone at their feet softened, letting them sink into it, then hardened, trapping the imps up to the waist in solid stone.

Talia sent finger-size bolts of dreamfire scything through crowds of imps. They boiled, dissolved into liquid musical notes, and in one memorable case, turned into a pinecone. When they rounded a corner, Talia hurled a shard of bone from her necklace back around it. The whole corridor shuddered from the detonation, and burning oil shot out into the intersection behind them, blocking it off.

That had been the whale bone, Hugh assumed.

Sabae seemed to be everywhere at once. One moment she'd be launching back a group of imps with a water equivalent of a gust strike— a geyser strike, maybe? He'd have to talk over its name with Talia and Godrick. The next moment she'd launched herself up to the ceiling, using her shield to crush an imp that had been preparing to drop down on them. Then, rather than dropping back down, she stuck herself to the ceiling with her buckler and detonated her water armor, sweeping every other nearby imp off the ceiling as well. By the time she dropped back down to the ground, she'd already spun up her wind armor.

Hugh did his best to keep up, but the others— especially Talia— were killing imps at an astonishingly fast rate.

Still, he wasn't feeling useless, by any means. He didn't have unlimited slingstones, but their explosions were effective against dense groups of imps. He'd brought out his trusty chunk of quartz, and was sending it hurtling into nearby imps whenever he got a chance.

Hugh was also crafting quick and dirty— by his standards, at least— wards on the fly, funneling the imps into more manageable sections of the corridor and letting his friends carve through them much more rapidly. Hugh couldn't be grateful enough for his will-imbuing ability at the moment— it was letting him put exceptions for himself and his friends into his wards far faster than it would have been possible to do otherwise.

Down one corridor, Hugh saw a swarm of imps clambering all over a pair of terrorbirds, and he was more than happy to leave both sides to it.

Hugh had just started to feel like things were going their way when the first of the bigger imps started arriving.

Until then, the only imps they'd encountered had been dog-sized or smaller. This one, unfortunately, was taller than Hugh or Talia, though still shorter than Sabae or Godrick.

It probably outweighed all of them save Godrick combined, though. It was wide and stocky, and its limbs rippled with muscle. Massive plates of chitinous armor grew from its chest and shoulders, and smaller ones were scattered across its body, like someone had haphazardly glued scales all over it.

And, of course, it was charging straight at them.

Talia was distracted clearing an intersecting hallway of imps, so Hugh launched a slingstone straight at its chest. The explosion didn't slow it at all, and barely fractured its armor.

Which was when Godrick slammed into it.

The impact between the two was hard enough that it actually shook the corridor around them. Chitinous plates and stone armor both fractured.

It was the imp that went down, though, and Godrick's hammer followed it.

Even as the big imp stopped moving, two more rounded a nearby corner— one armored like the first, the other covered with spines and thorns. The river of imps flowing at them continued to thicken, and the apprentices' forward momentum began to slow.

"I've got an idea!" Sabae shouted. "This way!"

She sent a massive gust strike into a side corridor, clearing a path for them. Hugh sprinted after her, Talia and Godrick close behind him.

Hugh focused his attention towards the end of the short side tunnel they were in. The wards he'd been crystallizing in the stone of the tunnels were effective, even as hastily crafted as they had been, but they simply weren't cut out to handle the sheer mass of the imp swarm. An explosive ward would take out a big chunk of them, but their numbers never seemed to end. A barrier ward would only hold them back for a few seconds before their weight overwhelmed it.

So Hugh tried something different with the ward he was crafting ahead of him. Something that he thought Talia would quite approve of.

With his affinity senses so focused on the ward he was crystallizing in the stone ahead of them, he didn't notice the trio of imps plunging down towards him from the ceiling until they were almost on him.

His spellbook, however, did.

It shot up from where it hung at his side, clamping its cover shut around the torso of one of the imps. It didn't even make a sound as the book bit down.

The book's lunge dragged Hugh to one side, making him stumble and almost fall. This pulled him out of the way of one of the other imps, which hit the ground and rolled.

The third, however, landed on Hugh's shoulder, and immediately bit down.

Hugh screamed in pain— the imp might be the size of a cat, but its teeth were viciously sharp. To make it worse, something in its saliva made the wound *burn.* Hugh could only think of a handful of things in his life that had hurt worse.

Hugh grabbed at the imp, only to receive a nasty scratch across his forearm. It burned as well, though not nearly as badly as his shoulder.

The imp lunged for his ear, only to have its head dissolve in a shower of wooden coins.

Hugh glanced back to see Talia shoot him a wink.

He was definitely happy she had good aim.

Hugh pulled his focus back towards the ward, and it finished crystallizing just before he passed through it. He skidded to a halt on the other side. Godrick and Talia sprinted through it, the swarm hot on their heels. Several of the imps were actually clambering over Godrick, trying to find a way in through his armor.

Each of them burst into flames the instant they passed through the ward.

It wasn't enough to kill them immediately, but all of them dropped to the ground, screaming in pain. Several more sprinted through the ward as well before they could stop, bursting into flame as well.

The imps behind them tried to stop in a panic, but at least a dozen more were forced through by the ranks behind them. Soon they were clambering over one another to try to keep from having the weight of the swarm push them over the ward.

"That," Talia said, "might be the most beautiful ward you've ever made."

Hugh shot her a grin, then turned to catch up with Sabae. He'd only stopped part of the swarm, and if they were really determined they could still make it through.

Sabae pushed her water affinity sense as far as it would go through the tunnels, seeking out what she was looking for.

An entrance to one of the big lakes on this level opened up on her right side. She glanced in, seeing part of the imp swarm engaged in battle with what looked like a school of horse-length lampreys.

Sabae shuddered. Definitely not that way.

Another of the big imps rounded a turn straight ahead of her. The nasty thing began giggling as it braced itself to catch her.

She smiled, and picked up the pace. With every step she took, she detonated a fragment of her wind armor, until the tunnel walls were blurring past her.

She rammed her shield right into the imp's stupid smiling face. She hit it so hard that the impact collapsed half her wind armor, but she could feel something crunch in the imp's head, and it flew backward a limp tangle of limbs.

If she'd hit it in a full windjump, it probably would have broken her arm at the very least.

It also would have completely collapsed her wind armor, which would have ended badly for her, as one of the big thorned imps lunged out at her.

Sabae dropped to the ground as the imp swung a massive spiked fist at her. She caught the glancing blow on her shield as she did so, latching onto the imp's fist.

Then she detonated the remainder of her wind armor, sending her flying straight between the imp's legs, dragging its arm with her.

The imp's head slammed into the tunnel floor with an audible crunch, and Sabae immediately let the shield unglue itself from the imp's fist, promptly starting to respin her wind armor around herself.

Sabae twisted to her feet as a regular imp launched itself at her face. She lashed out with her arm, sending it flying against a wall, and then stomped on the spine of another imp.

A third big imp came running out of a side passage, reaching out towards her with foot long, razor-sharp claws.

Sabae detonated the wind armor she'd managed to spin up so far. It wasn't enough to windjump far, but it was just enough to get her to the ceiling.

The clawed imp spun, obviously intending to disembowel her as she dropped.

It was too bad for it that she was still stuck to the ceiling by her shield.

The clawed imp stumbled, not meeting the expected resistance.

Sabae smirked, then dropped from the ceiling towards it.

She'd spent the precious few seconds on the ceiling spinning up water armor, but only around one leg.

She kicked the clawed imp, detonating her leg's water armor as she did so, sending it hurtling into the corpse of the thorned imp.

It didn't make for a soft landing for the clawed imp.

Sabae stretched and spun her water armor fully up as she waited for the others to catch up.

"This way," she said through a gap in the water around her face, waving them down a tunnel in the direction her affinity senses were pointing her. "Godrick, drop the armor."

"That doesn't seem like a…" he started.

"Just trust me," Sabae said.

Godrick gave her a doubtful look, but his armor dropped off him in chunks of stone onto the ground, though he snagged the faceplate Hugh had made him out of the air.

Sabae hauled them to a stop in a new tunnel that split off from this one, examining the walls carefully. She smiled grimly, then stuck her shield to Talia.

She ignored Talia's loud protests as she stuck the shield to her own back. Talia weighed hardly anything, so she wasn't too much of a burden.

Given how dangerous Talia was, that might actually make her the deadliest mage in Skyhold by weight.

Not that she'd say that out loud, Talia's ego and love for bad jokes were already both far too swollen.

"Uh, Sabae?" Hugh said uncertainly. "The spellforms on the wall are flooding."

The chittering of the swarms pursuing them were growing louder, but there was another noise that was starting to drown them out.

"Exactly," Sabae said, and grabbed each of the boys by the hand, just before the flash flood hit.

CHAPTER THIRTY

Out of the Labyrinth

Hugh hacked up water as he hauled himself to his feet.

Sabae had somehow managed to guide them all the way through the floodwaters, getting them back to the entrance to the first floor. Hugh had lost half the contents of his belt pouch, his sling, and half the warded slingstones, but he supposed it was a small price to pay for traversing the floor so quickly.

Hugh frowned at his clothes and cast a drying cantrip on himself, then repeated the process for the others, except for Sabae— who was, of course, perfectly dry behind her water armor, as annoying as that was.

"Something's wrong," Sabae said.

"Yeah," Talia said. "I'm missing my throwing daggers, half my hairpins, and a bunch of bone shards. I'm still amazed Godrick managed to hold onto that hammer."

"Mah shoulder's not happy about it," Godrick said, rubbing the body part in question. "That flood did *not* want me ta keep it."

"No," Sabae said. "The shield between the floors is down."

The four of them exchanged glances, then sprinted towards the stairs.

Well, jogged while hacking up water, at least.

The entrance to the second level was a battlefield. There were at least two dead students and a mage lying on the ground, surrounded by literal mounds of imps.

To their relief, the rest of the mages were all still alive, along with a crowd of students. They'd reformed the magical shield to one side of the room, packing everyone else into it.

One of the mages opened up a hole, and gestured for them to join them. "Quick, get in, before that *thing* comes back!" she called.

"What thing?" Sabae asked as they approached, but Hugh felt like he already knew what the answer was going to be.

"I think it was a demon," the mage said, as though she didn't believe her own words. "At least two or three times taller than a person, bat face, scorpion tail, and a gut like a translucent bag full of tadpoles?"

"Bakori," Hugh muttered, rubbing his wounded shoulder.

"Where'd it go?" Sabae asked.

The mage replied, but Hugh didn't hear what she said—his spellbook was sending him the image of a battered down labyrinth door.

"Sabae!" Hugh said, interrupting the mage. "The book's telling me that Bakori's already escaped the labyrinth!"

Everyone swiveled to look at him.

"Isn't that the Stormward?" he heard a voice in the crowd under the shield whisper.

Hugh winced at the sudden attention.

"There's no way even that thing could batter down the labyrinth doors by force," another of the mages said. "And even if it could, invading an entire mountain of mages isn't going to go well for it. Right now, you need to get under the shield. There's nothing you can do about it."

Sabae's face turned abruptly thoughtful.

"I thought he was after you," Talia hissed. "Why's he leaving the labyrinth? He can't survive out of it for long, right? Isn't the aether too thin?"

"You need to quit ignoring me and get under the shield, NOW!" the same mage ordered. "You're just apprentices. There's nothing you can do."

A nearby apprentice grabbed the mage's sleeve. "They're the ones who helped stop Ataerg's attempt on Theras Tel this summer!"

Hugh winced again. He had to deal with this sort of attention *now*, of all times?

"I don't care who they are, they're apprentices, and they're not going anywhere but under this shield."

"Wait, what about my da?" Godrick asked suddenly, grasping Hugh by the shoulder.

The spellbook sent Hugh a mental image of an enormous suit of stone armor crushing an imp bigger than Godrick beneath its foot, an equally colossal hammer smashing down into a crowd of smaller imps.

Hugh blinked at that. "He's about twenty feet tall right now and wrecking a small army of imps single-handedly."

Godrick smiled. "He's not even in enough trouble to go all-out, then."

Hugh gave Godrick a startled look at that.

"You all need to quit ignoring me and get under the shield," the irritated mage said.

"What in winter's frozen arsecrack is Bakori doing?" Talia demanded. "What could he be up to?"

"He's heading to the council chamber!" Sabae blurted out.

Everyone turned to look at her.

"Why would he be heading towards the council chamber?" Talia said. "It's guarded by a group of the most powerful mages alive. Most of them individually are powerful enough to be able to survive at least a while in battle against one of the great powers, and together..."

"Have you ever wondered why they need to be so powerful, though?" Sabae demanded.

"Because they're the Council?" Godrick asked, as though that were obvious.

Sabae shook her head. "Magical might doesn't make you an effective ruler or administrator. Do you know how many great powers' territories have fallen not to outside threat, but due to mismanagement? There are countless archmages and great wryms out there that couldn't govern if their lives depended on it. No, they're all effective administrators as well, but the magical might bit would only make sense if..."

"They're guarding something!" Hugh blurted out.

Sabae nodded at him. "And most of them, including Kanderon, are out of Skyhold. I'd guess that Midsummer and Midwinter are some sort of vulnerable time as well, given that the council is normally required to all be here then. Bakori must be trying to get at whatever the council is guarding."

"You're all going to stop him, though, right?" one of the other students called out.

"No, they're not going to stop him," the irate mage snapped. "They're going to wait this out under this shield. Even a partial council is more than capable of taking on nearly any threat."

"Except that at least one a' them is a traitor," Godrick snarled. "All they need ta do is wait fer just the right time, and…"

Hugh hadn't seen Godrick look angry often before, and it was always terrifying.

"Weren't we supposed to be keeping that a secret?" Hugh managed to ask him.

"It hardly matters now, does it?" Talia muttered, blasting a group of imps with dreamfire before they could fully exit the nearby tunnel.

One, Hugh noticed, was entirely sucked into its own mouth by the dreamfire. He really hadn't needed to see that.

She wasn't the only one muttering now. Most of the students were clustered around the entrance of the shield, eavesdropping on their conversation.

"Enough of this nonsense!" the mage bellowed, striding towards the four of them. Misty tendrils started forming in the air around the mage, and Hugh could feel the ice crystals comprising them growing.

He frowned, and visualized a pattern unlinking spellform. The ice crystal patterns collapsed immediately, drenching the mage in water.

None of the other adult mages under the shield made any move to help the spluttering man.

"Someone needs to warn them," Sabae said, biting her lip.

Hugh sighed. "Why do I gain the impression that you have us in mind?"

Talia smiled at that.

Godrick put his shoulder forward and charged straight into the crowd of imps. These ones were pushing nine feet tall, but were skinnier than Talia. They had particularly nasty looking claws and fangs, and they had unpleasant looking slime dripping off them.

None of that helped them much when Godrick slammed into them.

With his armor at its current full size, Godrick weighed in at a solid third of a ton. While the terrorbird might have been able to knock him around, these imps went flying with satisfying crunches. Imp limbs shattered beneath Godrick's feet, and his hammer crushed another of the tall imps against the labyrinth wall.

He didn't bother slowing down to get any of the imps that survived or dodged his rush. The others were more than capable of handling them.

As he broke through the pack of tall imps and into another swarm of regular imps, Godrick checked on the spellforms running his armor, making sure the links to his body weren't fraying.

Satisfied his work was holding up well, he drew another spellform in his mind's eye. It was a particularly complex one that had taken him ages to master. It linked to his armor spellforms, drawing much of its energy from the mana that bled off his armor.

The next time his foot descended, the floor nearby rose up into a thin stalagmite, impaling a nearby imp. It happened again with his next step, and again with the one after.

The part of the stalagmite stride spellform that crafted the actual stalagmites was the easiest bit. The part that made sure none of the stalagmites would rise up in his path was tricky, but there was nothing more to it than memorizing a particularly complex spellform piece. The part that let the spell know what to target— now that was tricky. It basically amounted to spellform construction each time he used it, but his da had already done most of the footwork— Godrick had only needed to memorize a series of rules for how to redesign the targeting lines.

He'd always known his da was brilliant, but he hadn't realized exactly how brilliant until he started seeing Hugh learn spellform construction. Artur's spellforms were designed to be easy to combine and easy to scale up and down, and they were incredibly reliable. Armor spells were hardly unknown, but his da's armor was leagues ahead of anything else Godrick had ever heard of.

Godrick burst through the imp swarm and found himself in the labyrinth entrance hall, the exit door ahead of him.

The remains of the door, at least. The massive quartzite door was lying in shards across the hall. Sparks of mana dripped from the door's broken spellforms, and char marks radiated out from it.

In between the labyrinth entrance and Godrick was another armored imp, surrounded by a swarm of regular imps. It dwarfed the earlier armored imp, even towering over Godrick.

Godrick slowed his charge as he approached, but didn't stop. He'd barely knocked down the previous armored imp, and this one had to weigh twice as much, not to mention being much more heavily armored.

As he slowed, less mana bled off his armor, and the stalagmites didn't grow as large, but they still were quite effective at impaling the smaller imps. One rose up beneath the armored imp, but just broke against it.

He rolled his shoulders and grabbed his sledgehammer in both hands. The imp bared its teeth in a maniacal grin as it trotted forward.

Moments before they impacted, Godrick dropped the stalagmite stride spell and crafted another, much simpler one in his mind's eye, also of his father's invention, then linked it to his armor spellforms. This one just altered the stone he trod on, making it shift in response to his steps. It slowed him during a long-distance run, but when maneuvering during a fight, it made his turns, sidesteps, and shifting his center of gravity far more responsive.

Godrick leapt to his right as he approached the imp, swinging his hammer in a massive arc towards it. He drew a simple steel spellform in his mind's eye that amplified the force of his strike.

Which only served to remind him again of his father's brilliance— so long as his other active spells remained linked to the armor spell, they ran independently, without any conscious effort on his part. They still drained his mana reservoirs, of course.

His sledgehammer hit one of the imp's armor plates with a boom— he wasn't wasting mana on its silence function in the middle of all this. The armor plate shattered, but the impact vibrated the hammer so hard he almost dropped it, even through the stone armor.

At the same time, one of the imp's fists slammed into his shoulder, cracking his armor in turn. Godrick could feel the armor on his left arm grow less responsive, as its link to the rest of the armor was weakened. If he hadn't dodged, though, the blow probably would have taken him in the neck or head.

The two of them stumbled past each other, both reeling from the hits they'd taken.

Godrick recovered first, thanks to his ground-altering spell. He whirled around, delivering another blow to the armored imp, cracking a bone plate on its back. He pulled back to hit it again, but the smaller imps around him swarmed up his armor before he could.

Godrick snarled as he tried to swat the little things off. He managed to crush a couple as the armored imp scrambled to its feet, but more piled onto him, until he started to worry they'd actually knock him over by sheer force of numbers.

So he changed tactics. He dropped his hammer entirely and quickly lunged forward towards the armored imp. He drew another spellform in his mind's eye, but didn't link it to his armor just yet.

The armored imp was taken entirely by surprise as he wrapped his arms around it and began to squeeze. One of its arms was trapped, but it battered at him with the other, and bit at his helmet with its fangs.

Godrick pumped his mana into his armor at a faster and faster rate— even as dense as the aether was down in the labyrinth, his stone reservoir was running out quickly. It could only refill itself so fast, after all. He amplified his strength through the armor as much as he safely could as he squeezed.

Several unlucky imps who hadn't gotten out of the way simply popped between Godrick and the armored imp. Most were clawing at his back and shoulders, slowly clawing away the stone, but they wouldn't get through in time.

Godrick felt the imp's bone armor begin to crack in his grip. He continued to squeeze as more and more bone plates broke, and even as his own armor began to crack.

Finally, when the bone imp started hacking up ichor onto his faceplate, Godrick linked the new spellform to his armor.

It was a relative of the stalagmite stride spell, but it didn't affect the ground— it affected his armor. Stalagmites erupted out of his armor, drawing their mass from it. They impaled nearly all of the imps clambering on him, and plunged deep into the broken armor plates of the big imp.

Only a single smaller imp survived, chewing on his faceplate. Godrick tried to reach up and grab it, but his arm was anchored to the big imp.

Godrick sighed, and head-butted the big imp, smashing the smaller imp between them. It whimpered and fell to the ground.

Godrick disconnected the spellform, and the stalagmites shattered off his armor. He disentangled himself from the armored imp and let it drop to the ground.

His armor was battered, thinned, and cracked, but Godrick didn't hurry while he rebuilt it. Rebuilding the armor slowly was much more mana efficient. Not to mention that the room was clear, and he wanted to fully refill his stone reservoir before exiting the labyrinth. Not that the aether wasn't still absurdly dense in Skyhold, but better safe than sorry.

The whole fight had taken considerably under a minute, so it was quite gratifying to see the expressions on his friends' faces as they followed him into the room. Talia and Hugh let out simultaneous, impressed whistles.

Godrick realized that they were probably whistling at the broken door, and not at him, and his ego deflated a bit.

Sabae pursed her lips as well, and Godrick briefly thought she disapproved for some reason, until he realized she was trying and failing to whistle yet again.

He did his best to keep his amusement off his face.

"Hugh, can you get your book to scry for Bakori?" Sabae said, clearly pretending she hadn't just been trying to whistle.

Hugh scrunched up his face in concentration, then shook his head. "However my spellbook is doing it, it can't scry outside the labyrinth."

"I think we can probably just follow the trail of wreckage," Talia said dryly.

Sabae nodded. "Hugh, have your book shield us from scrying as we leave. I don't know how much it will help against Bakori, but better safe than sorry."

The four of them slowly picked their way through the shattered wreckage of the doors. Any of the crystalline chunks they stepped between and clambered over were large enough to have smashed Godrick, even in his armor.

By the time they exited the labyrinth, Godrick had fully rebuilt his armor.

The entrance hall to the labyrinth was a disaster area. Huge craters had been torn in the walls and floor. Drifts of imp corpses littered the hall, and Godrick could spot at least four dead humans. He didn't look too hard at them, or try to spot any more. Vines covered one corner of the room, where a plant mage had apparently made their last stand.

The four of them stared in shock, until Godrick managed to clear his throat and speak. "Ah didn't think it would be this bad," he said hoarsely.

Hugh's head jerked up. "Avah!" he said, almost yelling. "She's not a combat mage! I need to go after her."

"She'll be fine," Talia said, rolling her eyes. "There's probably a thousand mages in between her and the imps."

Sabae grimaced. "Actually, it makes sense that Bakori would send his imps after Avah. He has more than enough to spare, and it would be an easy way to get back at Hugh for scorning him."

"I need to…" Hugh started, but Sabae interrupted him.

"Not a chance," she said. "You're powerful, sure, but you're also the least capable of the four of us in a fight by yourself. I'm not letting you run off on your own just to impress your girlfriend. I like Avah, but the council is more important. We can only spare one of us. I'll do it, I'm the fastest here."

Hugh started to open his mouth, but Godrick spoke first.

Godrick shook his head. "Yeh can't. Yeh're the one who's goin' ta have ta persuade the council that one a' them is a traitor. Yeh're by far the most articulate and persuasive a' us. Hugh or Talia certainly can't handle that part. Ah'll get Avah."

Hugh was looking mutinous at this point. He opened his mouth to speak again, but this time he was interrupted by Talia.

"By that logic, I should be the one to go," she said. "I'm by far the least persuasive of us three."

"Godrick and I have armor to protect ourselves when we're on our own," Sabae said. "You don't. It's a major risk for you to go on your own. As much as I hate to admit it, Godrick's probably the best one to do it."

"Armor," Talia said dryly, "is for people with insufficient firepower."

She reached out and hugged Hugh. "I'll rescue your dumb girlfriend, Hugh."

"Hold on just a second, Talia," Sabae said. "We need to talk about this."

"No time!" Talia said, walking away.

"Talia!" Sabae yelled after her.

Talia just made a rude gesture.

Hugh stared after Talia, looking like he wanted nothing more than to go with her.

Sabae sighed, and leaned towards Godrick. "Are you sure it's the best idea to send Talia after Avah?" she whispered.

Godrick considered that carefully for a moment, then nodded. "It'd wreck Hugh if somethin' happened ta Avah, and Talia's way too protective a' him ta' let that happen.

He shouldered his hammer and walked over to Hugh, resting his hand on the smaller apprentice's shoulder. "We've got a job ta' do, Hugh."

Hugh gave Godrick an uncertain look, then nodded.

CHAPTER THIRTY-ONE

Wreck the Halls

Hugh sometimes forgot how enormous Skyhold was. Even ignoring the numerous extradimensional spaces riddling the mountain— like the labyrinth and the Grand Library, and who knew what else— the tunnels carved through its granite stretched farther than the streets of any city Hugh had ever seen, with the exception of Theras Tel.

Most of Skyhold's tunnels were abandoned and often sealed off. A few were sealed off due to magical experiments gone horribly wrong or structural instability, but mostly the population had just shifted through the mountain over time. Not because its population had dropped— Skyhold's population currently numbered in the high tens of thousands, nearly as high as it had ever been— but because of a long history of digging new tunnels whenever you needed a new classroom, workshop, dormitory, or any other sort of room.

Unlike other universities, there was no need to wait for an older scholar to die or retire to get their office space— just find a nearby empty office and claim it for your own.

This led, of course, to all sorts of bizarre situations. There were countless stories of stubborn academics and researchers who claimed an office ahead of the crowded regions, then were left stranded through miles of empty tunnels when the crowds decided— through whatever mechanism crowds made any decision— to resettle an entirely different section of Skyhold.

Over the past two years, Hugh had grown used to Skyhold's size, and he had stopped really considering it.

Sprinting up through the corridors and stairwells of Skyhold towards its highest peak, however, was giving him a new appreciation of its immensity.

Awareness might be a better word than appreciation, really.

The fact that they were having to fight their way through swarms of enraged imps on the way up didn't help Hugh's mood.

Trying not to worry about Avah— and Talia, for that matter— Hugh reached out with his affinity senses into the stone of a nearby cross-tunnel. A particularly dense swarm of imps poured down it towards them, trampling one another in their haste to get to the three of them.

Hugh found the crystal patterns stretching through the hall's stone ceiling, and began unlinking them.

The hallway roof collapsed, crushing the swarm underneath it and sealing the hallway.

Even considering how many tunnels Skyhold had to spare, collapsing tunnels was definitely more than frowned upon— but, given the chaos in Skyhold right now, Hugh doubted anyone would be investigating where specific instances of damage came from.

He glanced over at the other two. Sabae had stuck a small, white furred imp to her buckler, which she was repeatedly pounding against the wall until the imp stopped moving. They'd run into a few of them— they weren't any more dangerous than other small imps, but they were inexplicably harder to kill.

Godrick, meanwhile, was rebuilding his armor from scratch. They'd run into a morbidly obese large imp that had projectile vomited some sort of caustic bile all over his armor. It wasn't an acid, so far as they could tell— it appeared to be digesting the rock, not dissolving it.

Rather than close with the thing, Hugh had crystallized wards buried in the rock above, below, and to the sides of the thing that trapped it in place and deprived it of fresh air. He'd had to continuously build new layers of ward against the encroaching bile eating through the stone until the imp had finally collapsed. The instant the imp died, the bile stopped devouring the stone around it.

"How much farther?" Hugh asked Sabae, trying not to sound irritable, and doing a bad job.

"We're more than a third of the way there," Sabae said, "but if we keep running into all these imp swarms, it could take us hours to get to the top. Plus, we keep missing shortcuts that I know should be there."

"Why haven't we seen more people?" Godrick said, somewhat distracted with his armor.

It was true, they'd hardly seen anyone. A fire mage incinerating imps across a large dining hall, a weaver mage binding and suffocating imps in fine tapestries, kitchen rags, and wool blankets, and several guardsmen simply hacking their way through a swarm with swords, but they should have seen dozens of people at least in this section of the mountain. Rather than go through one of the abandoned sections, Bakori had taken an odd path that led through several inhabited sections.

"They must have all been driven away by the swarm," Sabae said, a little uncertainly. "Better than the alternative."

Hugh's spellbook sent him a hesitant feeling, as though it felt something was off. Hugh thought about mentioning it to the others, but decided against it. They needed to be heading for the council chamber, not investigating every oddity they found on the way up.

"We should get after Bakori," Hugh said impatiently. He didn't want to be waiting around doing nothing while Avah was in danger. He needed to do something, even if he wasn't going after her.

Sabae shook her head. "We need to stop following Bakori," she said. "We're trying to get to the council chamber first, and following behind him just forces us to battle every swarm trailing behind him. We need to cut around him."

"And where are we supposed to find a shortcut past him?" Hugh snapped.

Sabae and Godrick gave him odd looks, and Hugh felt momentarily ashamed.

Then he just felt puzzled. Sabae was making perfect sense, why had he been so resistant.

Something clicked in Hugh's mind then. He shut his eyes, turned, and walked exactly in the direction he didn't want to go.

"Hugh?" Godrick said. "Where'd yeh go?"

Hugh opened his eyes and looked back. He was standing in a narrow side passage, and he could see the other two plain as day, but it was clear they couldn't see him.

Hugh looked down at the lines drawn on the floor and smiled.

While most cantrips Talia tried to use tended to fail catastrophically, or just set things on fire, there were a few that worked much better than normal for her. Unsurprisingly, they were all cantrips that mirrored fire-like effects.

One cantrip that worked particularly well for Talia was designed to evaporate small amounts of liquid— spilled drinks, for instance. When Talia used it, the liquids tended to flash into steam on the spot— a trick that Talia fully intended to use in combat someday.

For now, though, it was doing a great job of clearing her path of gallons of imp ichor. Her shoes weren't even getting wet.

Talia delicately stepped over the bone-splinter ridden corpse of a thorned imp, humming a jaunty marching song Clan Castis sang on their way to battle. She couldn't remember all the words, but the tune itself was easy to remember.

An armored imp charged at her from straight ahead, bellowing in rage. One of its arms hung uselessly at its side, having been turned into a drawing of an arm by dreamfire.

Talia drew her enchanted dagger from the labyrinth— it really needed a better name— and threw it at the charging imp.

It had taken a lot of practice to master this trick. The dagger wasn't weighted as a throwing dagger, and it was extraordinarily hard to time exactly when to pump mana into the dagger.

Talia might not be the most patient person in the world, but she always had more than enough patience to practice new combat techniques.

Talia pumped mana into the dagger in midair, and it froze just a couple feet in front of the charging imp, point angled forward and up. Talia frowned a little at that— she'd intended for it to angle straight forward— but it still worked well enough.

The imp didn't even have time to slow down or dodge. It rammed straight forwards against the dagger at full speed. Its thick chest plate actually splintered against the dagger. Its back chest plate didn't break, but actually partially tore off its back as the imp passed through the space where the dagger was hanging, completely immobile.

The imp, its momentum lost by the impact of the dagger against its armor plates— and its insides— stared at Talia for a moment, then collapsed to the ground.

She aimed the evaporation cantrip at the dagger to clean the ichor off it. She wasn't worried about damaging it— it was absurdly durable. It never needed sharpening, and she'd wager it hadn't even chipped punching through bone plates.

The dagger did heat up quite a bit from the cantrip, but Talia's gloves would handle that.

Talia smiled as she delicately stepped over the armored imp and snagged the dagger from midair and sheathed it while firing a dreamfire bolt at another stray imp.

If only she'd had an audience for this.

The hallways grew much more crowded once Hugh led Sabae and Godrick past the wards.

Someone had, so far as Hugh could tell, constructed a series of attention wards meant to limit Bakori's movement choices through Skyhold. It wasn't a full path, but instead merely blocked off key hallways from notice.

Whoever had drawn them appeared to be trying to mitigate the damage Bakori was doing in Skyhold without preventing him from reaching the council chamber.

What was even more interesting was the fact that the wards were built to decay. Hugh would wager money that if he returned to look for them an hour from now, he wouldn't find a trace of them, or even of the chalk they'd been drawn in.

Hugh grudgingly had to admit— to himself, at least— that they were probably better than anything he could do yet.

Even if that didn't massively limit the field of possible suspects, he was fairly sure he recognized the style of the wardcrafter.

He still hadn't met his wards teacher this year, but Loarna's wards were memorable, to say the least.

Mages were running around in a frenzy, trying to frantically establish order. There had been breakouts from the labyrinth into the mountain in the past, but never on this scale before.

It didn't help matters that the imps weren't nearly so focused on the council chamber as Bakori was, and were all over the place.

Hugh launched another slingstone at a pack of imps. It detonated, pulping most of them and cracking the stone beneath them. He'd packed a lot more power into these new ones than the old ones last year— not to mention getting rid of the risk of them just randomly exploding.

He was starting to run low, however. Hugh had calculated how many he'd needed for the labyrinth, then doubled it, but he'd never expected a situation like this.

Off down a hallway, he could see a shadow mage strangling imps with their own shadows, while someone Hugh guessed was a pollen or flower mage, or both, had put a few dozen to sleep and was— somewhat gruesomely— turning them into flower beds.

Magic was a common sight in Skyhold, but never on the scale he had seen since they passed the wards. The aether was noticeably thinner than usual from all the magic being used.

He'd seen a lot of mages clustering up and simply blasting fire, lightning, ice, or whatever else at imps. Nothing fancy, but for all the complaints Alustin had about the Skyhold curriculum, massed ranged attacks by groups of mages were both terrifying and effective.

But, then, Alustin almost always worked alone, and the standard Skyhold combat style wasn't necessarily the best for that.

There had been plenty of more unusual mages to be seen.

There'd been a light and stone mage riding a stone bull and filling a cafeteria with illusions of herself riding the bull as she trampled imps.

He'd spotted the angry journeyman girl from Emmenson Drees' class. His suspicions about her had been correct—she was a hair mage. Not only was she strangling imps with her hair, which had grown to a good twenty or thirty feet long, she was also using her hair to construct spellform glyphs, casting as many as a dozen spells at once. It had been more than a little impressive.

It had grown even more impressive when Hugh led them on a quick detour to give his classmate copies of some of the wards he'd been using against the imps. Hair made for a pretty decent material to craft wards out of, it turned out.

They'd seen a mage surrounded by a whirling cloud of metal shrapnel. Lightning periodically erupted from his hands and arced through the cloud of metal. Imps that drew too close got shredded and charred.

A couple of their instructors had shown up as well.

The fire illusionist Talia had been working with on and off, while he'd had little luck with Talia's training, was proving quite effective against the imps. He'd marshaled an army of foot tall soldiers made of fire against the imps.

Their cryptography teacher had made an appearance as well, battering and throwing imps with a localized windstorm.

The most impressive sight they'd seen so far, however, had been Emmenson Drees.

They were battling their way through a particularly thick swarm of imps when they saw him. The three of them had actually gotten bogged down in the swarm, to the point where Hugh had actually had to crystallize them a series of defensive wards from the rocks around them, and Godrick and Sabae were still having trouble keeping up with the imps making it through.

Hugh had known that Talia was the most offensively capable of the four of them, but not having her around really drilled in how much they depended on her.

The noise had been nearly inaudible at first, drowned out by the chittering, laughing, snarling imps. It quickly swelled— an off-tone, low pitched hum that seemed to resonate in the bones. It gave Hugh an immediate, low grade headache.

It did quite a bit worse to the imps. The vast majority collapsed on the ground writhing, save for a few of the odd white furred ones and one larger imp with four extra-long tails and proportionally bigger stingers.

Then Emmenson rounded the corner into the hall.

As the spellcrafting instructor stepped forwards, his metallic tattoos glimmering, the imps nearest to him began to vibrate harder and harder, until they simply… exploded. As Emmenson strode confidently but unhurried through the room, he was accompanied by a wave of ichor and bits of imp.

Hugh couldn't help but notice that none of it landed on Emmenson. He quickly crafted a variant on a levitation cantrip and began channeling mana into it. As Emmenson approached them, the exploding ichor hit Hugh's levitation cantrip and was levitated not upwards, but away from the three of them.

Emmenson had stopped next to them.

"A clever use for a levitation cantrip," he said, "though I'm using a cleaning cantrip instead to keep the gore off me."

"I thought about using a filth-repelling ward," Hugh admitted, "but this was faster to put up, and I have almost as many wards layered here as it's safe to use. Besides, levitation spells are one of my specialties."

Emmenson nodded at that. "It's good to know your strengths, but also good to know when not to depend too heavily on any one of them. Will you be needing any assistance?"

"We're trying to get to the council chamber," Sabae said. "We need to let them know there's a traitor among them who is working alongside the demon that broke out of the labyrinth."

For the first time that Hugh could recall, Emmenson actually looked shocked. He'd seen Emmenson mildly startled before, but the only strong emotion he'd seen from the instructor otherwise had been irritation.

"Best you get on that, then," Emmenson said. "I'd offer to accompany you, but I've been sent to rescue a large group of first year apprentices besieged in a cafeteria where they'd been eating breakfast before their labyrinth final."

"Also," Emmenson added, almost as an afterthought, "the council chamber is warded quite thoroughly against sound magic. Quite sensibly so, if you ask me, but I'd be of limited help. And I'd keep that news to yourselves, if I were you— if there's a traitor at the highest level, there are almost certainly more wandering the halls right now."

Emmenson turned to go. With a casual wave of his arm, the small number of imps that were still standing exploded.

As the sound mage walked away, they just stared after him.

"Why would the council chamber be warded against sound magic?" Sabae asked.

"There's no better affinity for ward-breaking," Hugh said. "A sound mage can shake most wards apart with little difficulty. It's also one of the most difficult affinities to ward against. I'd bet they have some wards that they really, really want to stay intact up there."

"Remind me," Godrick said, "never ta' pick a fight with a sound mage. Bloody terrifyin'."

"Good plan," Emmenson's voice said from the air next to them, despite him already having passed out of sight around a corner.

Even with the impressive feats of magecraft they encountered, however, there were still more than a few non-demon bodies littering the halls. No matter how weak most imps were individually, numbers still counted for a lot.

Even if a mage could kill hundreds of imps on their own, that wasn't much good against thousands.

CHAPTER THIRTY-TWO

Confrontations

The entrance to the council chamber was in a broad, circular chamber, with a massive stone spiral staircase in the center leading up to and through the roof. The room was normally full of functionaries, clerks, and scribes, tending to the massive amount of paperwork generated every day by Skyhold. Offices normally full of clerks branched off from the chamber, along with hallways leading to the councilors' chambers and offices. Even when the council wasn't in session, this hall was usually packed.

It was even busier than usual today, but not with clerks and scribes.

The chamber was a battlefield. Dozens of battle mages held a fortified circle around the base of the stairs, while a sea of imps battered against the defensive ward they'd established around themselves. They'd had a windshield earlier as well, but it had already collapsed.

Sabae stared out into the hall from her concealed perch. She could spot at least a dozen different types of imp, everything from armored imps to thorned imps to types of imps she hadn't even seen before.

Worst of all, Bakori was on the battlefield. He stood just outside the range of the battle mages, laughing and taunting them.

He wasn't making any move to attack them, but then, he didn't need to.

Sabae had been watching the assault for about ten minutes now. She'd stuck herself to the ceiling where a minor hallway entered the circular hall at an odd angle. Godrick had silenced her movements with his hammer from where he and Hugh waited, about fifty feet back.

Bakori had shown up halfway through her scouting mission, and the battle had immediately turned against the mages. Ranged attack spells had started failing rapidly in Bakori's presence— his reputed ability to decay spellforms used multiple times in his presence, apparently. The windshield had collapsed quickly, and the wards around the staircase had likewise begun to visibly decay.

She was hoping that the fact that she used formless casting rather than spellforms would prevent Bakori's disruptive aura from interfering with them, but she didn't want to test that until she had to.

Sabae, having seen enough, dropped from the ceiling. She twisted as she fell to face back down the hallway, and detonated her wind armor to send her back towards Hugh and Godrick.

Hugh was rubbing his shoulder again. She'd done her best to heal it when they'd had a quiet moment, but he'd need a fully trained healer to look at it later on.

After rolling to a stop, she quietly relayed her findings to the others, then told them her plan.

"Talia," Godrick said, "would have absolutely loved this."

Talia poked her head around the corner towards Hugh's hidden room in the library. There were a good dozen bigger imps in front of the door to Hugh's lair— mostly armored ones, with a couple thorned imps and a particularly nasty variety she'd encountered a couple times now that spat wads of caustic mucus. There were more smaller imps than Talia could count clambering over the bookshelves.

Talia had checked Avah's assigned room, but hadn't found her there. She was guessing the Radhan girl had returned to Hugh's room— probably to apologize or something after Hugh finished the test.

The fact that there was a swarm of imps attempting to batter down the door of Hugh's hidden room somewhat confirmed that guess. Hugh's wards were still holding strong, and Talia could see several charred, broken imps that had clearly failed to breach the ward, but who knew how much longer the wards would last?

Talia retreated back around the corner, then carefully sorted through the remaining bones on her necklace.

Birdbone wouldn't do enough damage to take down all the imps. Birdbone was for when you needed explosions fast.

Cuttlebone would be far too likely to set the library on fire. Same with her one remaining piece of whale bone. While Talia enjoyed burning most things, books were assuredly not on the list. She was willing to sacrifice the dry legal textbooks and other boring tomes around Hugh's room, but she didn't want fire to spread.

Squid bone… now that was a distinct possibility. Though it was really better for heading off pursuit or defending than attacking— she'd have to fight through the smoke as well.

Sunmaw bone… now that was an interesting option, but she still wasn't entirely sure what situation that would be useful in.

Next was a fang the size of her little finger. She wasn't entirely sure what the fang was from, but it was hollow, clearly meant to deliver massive amounts of venom. She'd plugged the hole near the tip of the fang, then capped the open top, forming a convenient little bone vial.

A vial filled with a very carefully measured mix of powdered bone of several sorts, along with a healthy dollop of powdered magnesium.

Talia smiled, yanked it off the necklace, and began charging it with bone mana. After a couple of seconds, she hurled it around the corner, pulled back, cast a cantrip, and covered her eyes.

Even behind a stone wall, with her arm over her eyes, a cantrip over them to shield them from light, and them simply closed as well, she could see the flash of light.

She quickly dropped the cantrip— it worked, but it also tended to uncomfortably heat up her eyes if she left it on long, something you generally didn't want to do.

Talia would rather not become known as the mage who boiled her own eyeballs.

Then she rounded the corner and got to work.

She hadn't had a ton of luck learning from the fire illusionist, but she had figured out one or two neat tricks.

A spider web of purple-green dreamfire burst into existence above the main group of imps. They were all staggering about, clutching bleeding eyes, so they didn't see it gently drifting down onto them.

Talia didn't waste her time watching the mad burst of colors, shapes, and bizarre dream figments erupting from the remnants of the imps, though she did have to shoo away several butterflies made of imp ichor as she hurled dreamfire bolts at the imps that had survived the blast.

It didn't take her long to clear the room of opposition entirely. She'd definitely have to make more of those flare teeth. So useful.

Also, that was a great name for them, she'd have to remember that.

She was stepping over the remnants of the bookshelf that had hidden Hugh's door when Bakori spoke up.

"Hello, little weapon."

Talia whirled, ready to hurl a bolt of dreamfire, but only a single small imp sat in the center of the room, its eyes bleeding and one leg a broken mess. It must have been trampled by a larger imp after she set off the flare tooth.

"What do you want, demon?" Talia demanded. "And why do you keep calling me that?"

"Because that's what you are, little weapon. Your family started shaping you in that direction, but failed. Alustin took that failure and forged it into an even greater success. You have no other purpose but to destroy, and only at the command of others."

Talia glared at the imp, considering whether there was really any point to listening to Bakori.

"The librarians have also trained your friends to be weapons, but they at least have other uses. You only exist to destroy, little weapon. You have no other use, nor will anyone ever want you for anything else," Bakori said. "And once you're no longer useful for that— once your edges have been dulled— you'll be cast aside like a broken dagger. You…"

Talia sighed, loudly. "You know, Sabae's always telling me that real life is nothing like the novels I read, but I've got to be honest, you talk just like a villain from a particularly melodramatic novel."

"…What?" Bakori said, sounding a little confused.

"You're going to go through this whole, long-winded argument that tries to show why I can't trust my friends in order to, I don't know, try to recruit me, or sow the seeds of doubt between us, or give you information you badly need, or maybe just delay me so more of your forces get here," Talia said. "It's really sad, because I was hoping an actual demon would have something more interesting to offer. Like promises of otherworldy power or something."

"You already have plenty of power," Bakori pointed out, seeming quite taken aback by this angle of conversation "and it's only going to increase in the future. Besides, you're not a warlock, so there's less I can do."

"Well, sure, but it still would have been polite to offer," Talia said. "Anyhow, you're kind of showing your hand here, because your whole sowing doubt thing kinda shows how much you actually know about me. It's clear you know a decent bit, but not enough to try for anything more specific or focused. Or would it be showing your talon?"

"More specific?" Bakori said, ignoring her wordplay. "How about the fact that you're trying to rescue the girlfriend of the boy you…"

Talia blasted the imp with a dreamfire bolt, then turned and strode over to Hugh's door.

She pulled it open, and was promptly greeted by a terrified scream and a thrown knife.

"It's me, Avah," Talia said, picking up the dull butter knife from where it had bounced off the doorframe. "I've come to rescue you."

Talia was, to her irritation, promptly hugged by a weeping, terrified Avah. She awkwardly patted her back.

"Come on, let's get you somewhere safe," Talia said. There was a dead-end hallway full of classrooms she'd passed a ways back that a group of teachers had barricaded to guard students. It should work to keep Avah safe.

Just in case, she'd also leave Avah the portable ward Hugh had given her for her birthday— the merchant girl would need it more than Talia.

As she tried to convince Avah to leave Hugh's room, a whisper drifted into Talia's ear. A whisper from a very unexpected source.

"I hate this plan," Hugh whispered, from where he was lying on the ground.

"You came up with half the details," Sabae said, also laying on the ground.

"It's not so much the details I hate as the general shape of it," Hugh said. "And how much of it relies on me. Why do so many of our plans end up relying so heavily on me?"

"Because you're the most versatile mage in our group," Sabae said. "The rest of us are mostly just here to hit things."

Hugh was fairly sure Sabae was stretching the truth a little bit there. She had her healing affinity and her maneuverability, and Godrick had his stone and metal reshaping, and Talia…

Well, Talia basically just hit things, yeah.

"Yeh'll do fine, Hugh," Godrick said, as he laid back and set his hammer on the ground beside him. "Yeh're sure my part will work?"

Hugh nodded. "It should."

"It should?" Godrick asked. "That's really not comfortin'. And ah wish yeh didn't make me drop my armor for this."

"Too heavy," Hugh replied.

"On three," Sabae whispered.

Hugh definitely wasn't ready for this.

"One," Sabae said.

He could think of a whole long list of reasons why he wasn't ready for this.

"Two," Sabae said.

He wasn't even sure if he had enough mana in his reservoirs for this plan.

"Three," Sabae said.

Hugh prepped the spellform in his mind's eye, then waited for Sabae to say go.

And kept waiting.

He realized the other two were staring at him.

"What are you waiting for, Hugh?" Sabae whispered.

"I thought you were going to say go," he whispered. "You know, one, two, three, go."

"I said on three," Sabae hissed, "not on go."

Godrick rolled his eyes. "Go," he said.

Hugh channeled mana into his modified levitation cantrip spellform from his spatial mana reservoir, and the three of them fell upward onto the ceiling.

Hugh caught himself on his hands and feet. They stung with the impact, but it was better than dropping head first onto the ceiling.

He briefly panicked that Godrick's hammer would give away their plan, but he relaxed when he realized the hammer had made no sound whatsoever.

Hugh was continually surprised at how useful that silence enchantment was. Though, considering it basically mimicked a sound affinity, he shouldn't be too surprised.

Hugh could already feel his spatial mana reservoir draining, so he clambered to his feet, trying to ignore the fact that the floor was above his head. The others did the same.

Sabae nodded at both of them, then burst into a sprint.

Godrick and Hugh followed.

Right into the circular hall.

It was several seconds before anyone noticed them. Several seconds of sprinting what felt like downhill, but was actually them running *up* the upwards curving roof. The farther down— or up, Hugh was having a lot of trouble with adjectives at the moment— they ran, the more mana it took to keep them on the ceiling.

It was also several seconds of trying not to stare at the writhing sea of imps that looked like they were about to fall on their heads.

When the imps did notice them, however, that started happening.

Or, rather, the larger imps started hurling smaller imps at them.

Hugh's spellbook lunged off his shoulder, the strap coming loose, and battered against a shrieking imp, sending it hurtling back up against the floor. Godrick smashed another out of the air with his hammer, then a second he smashed downwards against the ceiling. When he took the hammer away, its remains dropped limply back upwards. Sabae hit a whole group of them with a gust strike uppercut, sending them flying back up.

Quite a few reached the ceiling, however. Many dropped right back down, but a few clung to it and began crawling towards them.

Hugh just tried to focus on his spellform and running towards the stairwell.

"Well, well, well," Bakori said. "Look who's decided to join us. Kanderon's little pet and his friends."

He just focused on the spellform and the running. Ignore the imps screeching above— below?— their heads. Ignore the fifteen foot demon taunting them. Ignore how quickly his spatial mana reservoir was running low.

"I honestly thought you'd run to save the girl," Bakori said, "not throw your life away in a useless attempt to… what? Try and better serve a master who abandoned you in your time of need? Who left Sk…"

Bakori's voice cut off abruptly, and Godrick chuckled.

"Silence enchantment," Godrick said.

"Did you really think you could silence me tha…" Bakori began to say through a nearby imp, but Sabae launched a blast of water from her flask right into its face. Not enough to knock it off the ceiling, but enough to make it splutter and shut up.

Enough to know it was an insult, not an attack.

The imps below shrieked, redoubling their efforts to get to them. Hugh's spellbook was darting around in midair gleefully, knocking thrown imps out of the air.

To Hugh's distress, however, imps had begun to pour up the walls and onto the ceiling from all sides. Some of the smaller imps were moving faster while crawling along the ceiling than the three of them were while running on it.

He just focused on the spellform and the running. Ignore the imps screeching above— below?— their heads. Ignore the fifteen foot demon taunting them. Ignore the fact that his spatial mana reservoir was most of the way empty. Ignore the rapidly constricting circle of imps rushing up the ceiling towards them. Ignore the way his spellform was…

No, Hugh decided, it was definitely *not* a good idea to ignore the way his spellform was degrading and falling apart in his mind's eye.

Hugh desperately started designing a new levitation spellform to hold them on the ceiling, but it was like wading through mud. He could feel Bakori's influence seeping into the spellform, like corrosive gas.

He was so focused on maintaining the failing spellform and constructing the new one that he didn't even notice when Godrick's hammer passed right in front of him, sweeping an attacking imp off the ceiling before it could get to Hugh.

He just barely managed to draw the final line of the spellform and start channeling mana to it in time. He felt a brief lurch upwards— or downwards— he supposed— as the first spellform collapsed and the second took over, but he recovered with hardly a stumble.

"Now, Godrick!" Sabae shouted, blasting several more imps off the roof.

Hugh really hoped his guess about the wards ahead of them were correct. The battle mages had established a cylindrical barrier surrounding the central spiral staircase, stretching from the floor to the ceiling. There were couple ways they could have done it. First, they could just have the ward spellforms describe the barrier as going up to the ceiling. It was the easiest and most reliable way to pull off a ward of that style, and Hugh was betting that they'd used it.

That would make it easy enough to pass, with Godrick on their side— he just needed to sculpt the stone of the ceiling ahead of them into an arch right along the ward line, and the ward should just recognize the top of the arch as the ceiling, letting them run straight through.

Of course, they also could have just defined a specific height for the ward, which would mean that raising an arch would do nothing, and they'd be stuck on the ceiling, running low on mana, with an army of imps about to descend— or ascend?— onto them.

Ahead of them, the stone started to shift and twist as Godrick began lifting the arch.

Which made for a perfect time for a massively obese imp to projectile vomit caustic bile ahead of them.

Hugh cursed as he and Godrick dodged around the patch of bile dripping up towards the floor. He really hoped the lost second or two wasn't going to cost them.

Sabae, however, took a different approach.

She windjumped straight up to the floor. Hugh could feel the drain on his mana increase as she did so. She slammed into the obese imp, detonating her wind armor and releasing a burst of wind that send dozens of imps hurling outwards in a shockwave, crushing the obese imp against the floor.

One particularly heavy armored imp resisted the shockwave and tried to grab at Sabae as she fell back towards the ceiling. She twisted out of the way as she fell, spinning her wind armor back up.

A particularly inane thought ran through Hugh's head— if he was going to spend much time upside down in the future, he should really develop an absolute, rather than relative, system of terminology for vertical directions and movement.

Hugh could feel the second levitation spellform failing as they approached the almost-completed arch. He frantically drew a third spellform in his mind's eye as he maintained the second, and prepared to switch from his about empty spatial mana reservoir to his stellar mana reservoir.

He failed. Both the second and third levitation spellforms collapsed as his spatial mana ran out. He felt normal gravity reassert itself, and Hugh's feet slipped out from above him as he started to plummet headfirst towards the floor.

Which was when Sabae jammed her shield against the ceiling and kicked Hugh and Godrick through the arch with a gust strike. The shield stuck to the ceiling kept her from flying backward.

Hugh and Godrick hurtled through the arch and crashed down onto the broad spiral staircase with bruising force.

Sabae gracefully jumped onto the inside curve of the upside down arch, then jumped onto the staircase. Hugh's spellbook flew in behind her, chewing on an imp.

"Collapse the arch!" Sabae said to Godrick.

Godrick groaned, but the arch exploded out into the room, sending chunks of rock hammering into imps. Several imps on the ceiling that had been about to pass through the arch slammed into the reformed ward instead, and were sent tumbling back into the sea of imps.

Hugh could hear shouting from the battlemages below. He wasn't sure if they were angry at them for going through the ward, or happy they'd made it through, but waiting around to find out probably wasn't a good idea.

"Let's go!" Sabae said.

Godrick and Hugh picked themselves up from where they were lying on the staircase with almost identical groans of pain, then followed Sabae up.

The last sight Hugh saw before ascending out of the circular hall was thousands of imps clinging upside-down on the ceiling, staring at him hatefully.

CHAPTER THIRTY-THREE

The Council Broken

Sabae had warned Hugh and Godrick about how intimidating the council chamber was, but they still gaped in shock at the chamber's agoraphobic grandeur.

Which meant they didn't see the lightning bolt coming.

Sabae lunged for the lightning bolt, knowing she wouldn't make it in time.

A long strip of spellform embroidered silk got there first instead. It burned up in the process, but completely blocked the lightning.

"Those are students, Dyne, not demons!" a familiar voice shouted.

Anders Vel Siraf.

Several councilors strode out from the circle of thrones in the center of the vast open space that was the council chamber. Sabae recognized Anders, Tarik, and Dyne Sul, the head of internal security for Skyhold.

While the councilors were bickering, Sabae confidently strode forward towards the circle of thrones, ignoring Hugh and Godrick's whispered questions.

Before the bickering councilors even took note of them, she was already into the circle of thrones. She gestured at Hugh and Godrick to wait for her between two empty thrones. She came to a halt atop the massive, spellform enhanced seal in the center.

The plan wasn't done yet, and Hugh and Godrick still had a part to play, but all Sabae could do was hope they pulled off their part of the plan correctly. If they didn't…

Sabae cleared that thought out of her head. She just needed to focus on her end of things, and trust the other two.

The three councilors followed her into the ring of thrones, still arguing. Dyne demanded to know what the students thought they were doing here, but Sabae just ignored them.

Anders, catching on quickly, seated himself in his silk-draped throne. Tarik quickly followed, seating herself on her massive, undressed stone seat.

Dyne glared at Sabae for a moment longer, looking like they wanted to yell more, but one of the seated councilors— Rutliss the Red, Sabae noted with dislike— interrupted.

"Just sit down, Dyne. We're in the middle of the biggest labyrinth breakout in Skyhold's history and half the council is gone. Now's no time to engage in petty games of protocol," Rutliss said.

"Now's no time to indulge some apprentice with an overlarge ego, either!" snapped Dyne.

While the two of them argued, Sabae slowly turned, taking stock of the councilors that were there.

Headmaster Tarik. Probably not a traitor, but Sabae wasn't quite willing to risk her life on that. She looked exhausted and stressed.

Anders Vel Siraf. Definitely a traitor, but it was an open question whether he was working with Bakori, or just selling out Skyhold out of greed. He looked genuinely curious at why she was here.

Abyla Ceutas. A strong chance of her being the traitor. She was glaring at Sabae like she'd like to attack her here and now. She probably did actually want to, most likely.

Rutliss the Red. A strong chance of him being the traitor as well. If Sabae was being honest with herself, it was hard to say whether she would rather Abyla or Rutliss be the traitor. He was still caught up in his silly argument with Dyne.

Yves Heliotrope. Staunch opponent of Kanderon's on the council, in charge of the Skyhold docks. Almost certainly not a traitor, from what the Librarian Errant analysis claimed. Light, shadow, and force affinities. A particularly dangerous and versatile combination— her illusions could actually pack a punch.

Dyne Sul. Notoriously paranoid and foul tempered, Skyhold's internal head of security was pretty conclusively not a traitor, but most people considered their appointment a serious mistake. Sabae couldn't say she disagreed. Dyne had lightning, venom, and gravity attunements. An odd combination, but one that had proven extremely effective in battle.

The instant Dyne and Rutliss' argument ended, Sabae spoke up. She didn't even wait for the two of them to finish seating themselves. Best to hold onto the initiative for as long as she could.

"Isn't it strange that Jaskolskus would stir himself so suddenly?" Sabae asked the council. "That half of Skyhold's council, including Kanderon herself, would be called away on Midsummer to put him back to sleep? On the day you can least afford to have half the council gone?"

"What do you know about Midsummer, girl?" Dyne snapped.

Sabae smirked at her, hoping it looked knowing and not like the bluff it was.

"I'm a Kaen Das," she said. "That should tell you everything you need to know."

Sabae actually had no idea what they were guarding up here, or why Midsummer was so important, but she knew it was important.

Abyla actually growled a little bit at that. "I bet your grandmother would have loved to have still been here for this. The old harridan would have loved the opportunity to seize a little more power in the chaos, wouldn't she?"

"I, for one, would be happy to still have Ilinia Kaen Das here," Rutliss said. Storms, he irritated Sabae. "Kanderon abdicated her duty dragging the others on the council to try and put Jaskolskus back to sleep during Midsummer. It left us vulnerable, and now Bakori is taking advantage of the chaos. The fact that thing is even still alive is just another of her failures coming back to bite us."

Sabae couldn't have asked for a better set-up.

"You have it backward," she said. "Bakori isn't taking advantage of Jaskolskus' wakening, he set it up."

That did the trick. The assembled immediately began erupting into shouting, arguing, and questions.

Sabae waited patiently for the councilors to settle down. Well, she at least tried to look patient. There was no telling how much longer the battle mages below could hold off Bakori.

She felt a momentary twinge of guilt at that— part of her still thought that she should be convincing the councilors to go help hold the stairs, to not sacrifice the mages below while they argued like children.

But if Sabae was right about what was going on— what had been going on all year, what Kanderon and Alustin had lied to them about, and what was about to happen— that would potentially risk everything.

She glanced over at Hugh and Godrick, who both nodded. Sabae tried not to sigh in relief at that.

"How," Yves said, once order had been restored, "could Bakori have possibly arranged that, child? Up until today, he's been trapped in the depths of the labyrinth for centuries. He's powerful, but his influence can't reach all the way out of Skyhold and across half a hundred leagues of mountains."

"It doesn't have to reach past Skyhold," Sabae said. "Bakori is a schemer, a manipulator. He prefers to send others to do his work for him. And I'm not talking about his brood right now."

"What are you saying, girl?" Dyne asked.

"That seems obvious," Yves said. "She's saying there's a traitor in Skyhold."

The councilors grew quiet at that.

"Not just in Skyhold," Sabae said. "On this council."

You could have heard a pin drop in the resulting silence. Sabae surreptitiously checked to make sure she was exactly centered on the great seal.

"That's a serious accusation," Anders said. Sabae had to admire his cool. "Do you have any evidence?"

Sabae forced herself to smile at that.

"Even better. One of you has evidence that outs the traitor, and they haven't even realized it," Sabae said.

She could see a drop of sweat running down Anders' face, though it remained impassive.

Tarik was remaining silent, Sabae noted.

"Rutliss, when we last spoke you mentioned that Kanderon had already broken quite a few rules for Hugh, didn't you?"

Rutliss nodded.

"Why would Kanderon violate rules she helped establish for some backwoods rube?" Dyne demanded. "I can't stand her, but I've got to respect her for being even more of a stickler for the rules than I am, and almost as much as Tarik."

"She has a warlock pact with him," Rutliss said, with visible relish.

Hugh shifted uncomfortably under the sudden attention of the council.

Rutliss shot Hugh a nasty look. "She smuggled him into the school without paying Hugh's entry fee, to keep anyone from realizing her connection to him. She was forced to disclose her pact with him to the academic council after the incident in the labyrinth last year. I tracked down the discrepancies in the paperwork myself."

"And you haven't reported this to the council why?" Dyne asked with irritation.

"I was waiting for an opportune moment," Rutliss said. "Kanderon is too entrenched in Skyhold for an accusation like that to matter if brought out carelessly."

Sabae snorted. "You weren't waiting, you just didn't have definitive proof that Kanderon was responsible for the discrepancy, no matter how hard you looked. And that's because Kanderon wasn't the one to alter the paperwork. I doubt Kanderon even looks over the initial test results for applicants when they arrive. You're right that someone broke the rules getting Hugh in for the purposes of pacting with him— the size of his mana reservoirs are going to make him attractive to any entity looking to pact with a warlock— but it wasn't Kanderon."

Sabae stared directly at Rutliss. "You were told this last year, and you didn't listen. You know who else wanted to pact with Hugh before Kanderon did, and you didn't think the implications through in the slightest."

"Bakori," Anders said quietly.

"Bakori," Sabae agreed. "And who on the council looks through the new admissions first? Who is positioned perfectly to look out for prospective warlock candidates for Bakori?"

Abyla chose that exact moment to release the magma she'd been brewing up beneath the surface of the council chamber.

Straight at Sabae.

Well, at everyone else too, but Sabae was mostly concerned with the cresting wave of molten stone about to crash down on her.

Sabae had taken quite the risk, pointing the blame on Abyla. Their case against her was part speculation, part intuition, and only a little bit of evidence.

Ultimately, though, three things had convinced Sabae it was Abyla.

First, she didn't think that Bakori would be foolish enough to work with someone who was already selling Skyhold's secrets, no matter how hard Alustin and Kanderon had tried to convince them of that. Too much of a risk of exposure there. So that ruled out Anders.

Second was the whole mess around Hugh's enrollment. Abyla and Rutliss were the ones who had the best chance of altering those records. It wasn't impossible that Tarik could have pulled it off, but she was also famously rigid and rule-following— even if Bakori had manipulated her, it was unlikely that he could have forced her to break Skyhold's regulations.

The final clue also revolved around Hugh's enrollment. It was convoluted enough that whoever was behind of it *had* to be aware of Bakori's existence. Not just being subconsciously manipulated by him, but actively working with him.

And though Sabae wouldn't ever rely on Rutliss' virtues, she would absolutely rely on his flaws. His greed, his pride, and most importantly, his hatred for nonhumans.

There wasn't a candle's chance in a hurricane a human supremacist like Rutliss would knowingly work with a demon.

Sabae's plan, Godrick reflected, had gone almost perfectly. Godrick had spent Sabae's entire show in front of the council carving messages into the stone of Tarik's throne for her to read, with her responding in kind in the stone beneath his feet.

Tarik hadn't wanted to believe that Abyla was a traitor, but she'd agreed the evidence— which Godrick was presenting to her ahead of time— was at least compelling enough to warrant being ready to defend the council from assault by Abyla.

When Abyla had started brewing magma in the stone below them, Tarik had changed her tune fast. She wouldn't have even noticed if she hadn't been already on the alert— Abyla was somehow concealing the magma, most likely with spellforms built into her obsidian throne, since the magma stretched up to its base. It was enough to fool passive affinity senses, but not enough to fool Tarik actively looking.

The wards Hugh had constructed during Sabae's conversation had only held for moments— Abyla's magma might be fluid, but it was no lighter than the rocks it was melted from— but those moments had been enough. Tarik and Godrick threw their magic against Abyla's, and Hugh threw his against the remaining minerals in the magma that hadn't melted yet.

Even with all of Tarik's might, and the power Hugh and Godrick could add, they hadn't been able to keep the magma underground, and they'd barely held back Abyla's magmatic assault.

It wasn't just that Abyla had the affinity advantage— though she certainly had more control over magma than they did— it was her sheer skill at manipulating it. Abyla wasn't just pushing at the magma, she was building currents in it, transferring the heat to the stone around it in an effort to generate more, hurling lava bombs in high arcs at the others, and even shaping disruptive glyphs on the crust of the magma.

On top of that, the heat from the magma was truly punishing, even from cross the circle of thrones. It felt like he was standing inches away from a forge fire, and he was having trouble catching his breath.

Abyla still might have won if the other mages on the council hadn't stepped up. Sabae hadn't counted on them intervening, but it was a good thing they had. They were, one and all, archmages or the next best thing to it. Perhaps not on the level of the great powers, but none of them were weak enough to be dismissed by the great powers.

Anders sent a cloud of silk ribbons fluttering towards Abyla. Most of them burnt to a crisp in the heat of the magma, but enough approached Abyla to divide her attention and make her fight back.

Yves simply hammered force against the magma. Cunning illusions wouldn't do anything against molten rock— though Godrick was sure that the Yves he could see was an illusion, and that she'd already moved elsewhere— and Abyla was somehow standing on the surface of a patch of brightly glowing magma, meaning she didn't have a shadow for Yves to work with.

Dyne increased the pull of gravity on the magma, and tilted it back towards Abyla. They also launched lightning bolts and clouds of toxic gas, but the latter just dissolved in the heat. As for the lightning bolts, Abyla somehow drew up rods of molten metal from the magma to divert the lightning.

There shouldn't be *any* metal in granite, so Godrick suspected that she'd smuggled metal ore up here in the past— most likely hidden in the base of her throne.

Even Sabae was hitting the magma with gust strikes and bursts of water, the latter of which just erupted into steam.

Godrick was happy to see that their guess about the seal had been correct, though— the splatters of magma bounced off a dome rising up from the metal. Whatever was under there was well defended.

If it wasn't for Rutliss, though, Abyla still might have won.

Water rose up in spouts from Rutliss' pool, and spun towards the magma. Godrick would have sworn there wasn't enough water in the pool to make a difference, but as it approached, he could feel an impossible chill emanating from it. When the water struck the magma, the magma almost immediately began hardening into rock— obsidian, ironically, given the speed of cooling.

The water barely even steamed.

Godrick and Tarik immediately began applying pressure to the obsidian. Abyla was on better than even footing with them when it came to obsidian, but that was a lot better foothold than they'd had before.

"How are you doing that?" Abyla screamed at Rutliss. "You're supposed to be useless in combat! You never should have been accepted as a vault guardian!"

Godrick made a mental note to ask Alustin what a vault guardian was at some point.

Rutliss laughed. "Everyone assumes I have a saltwater affinity. I don't. I have salt and water affinities."

"What does that matter?" Abyla screamed.

"A fun little side effect of mixing salt in with water," Rutliss said, "is that it drops the freezing point considerably. Having separate water and salt affinities lets me increase the salt concentrations to otherwise impossible levels, and lets me supercool the water faster than the magma can heat it. You'll note that my throne is dissolving— it's fashioned of sylvite, a naturally red variety of salt."

Godrick had never even met Rutliss, but he was already forming a strong dislike of the academy's bursar. What kind of pompous ass lectured on their magical techniques in the middle of a fight? For that matter, what kind of idiot talked during a fight more than they had to at all? It was a great way to distract yourself.

Still, their combined efforts were working.

Slowly but surely, the magma started retreating, leaving huge gouges where Abyla had melted the stone. Godrick's stone mana was running perilously low— and, for that matter, probably would have run out already if not for the mana efficiency techniques Tarik had taught him earlier in the year.

That was, unfortunately, when Godrick realized that his spellforms were decaying rapidly, and when he felt Yves' force spell pressing against the magma vanish.

Godrick whipped his head around to see Bakori ascending the staircase up to the council chamber, carrying an impaled Yves on his tail. Imps flooded up the stairs past Bakori's feet.

"I'd like to request an audience with the Council, if I may," Bakori said, chuckling.

That was why Sabae's plan had worked almost perfectly instead of perfectly.

They were supposed to have subdued Abyla *before* Bakori arrived, not after.

CHAPTER THIRTY-FOUR

Bakori Ascends

Hugh's crystal reservoirs were almost completely tapped out by the time Bakori arrived. He'd been pushing them hard since he'd first entered the labyrinth, and he had hardly given them enough time to recover. They felt scraped raw from the heavy use he'd put them through today, and keeping the pressure up on the few mineral crystals he could find floating in Abyla's magma was exhausting.

Not to mention the fact that the heat from the magma was literally cooking Hugh's skin. He hadn't gotten closer to it than twenty feet, and it still hurt worse than any sunburn he'd ever had.

So when Hugh saw Bakori again, his instinctive response was to reach for his only full mana reservoir— his stellar affinity. He dropped his already decaying spellform pushing against the magma, and constructed the starbolt spellform in his mind's eye.

The spellform collapsed instantly, but his stellar mana reservoir still drained as though he'd cast the spell.

Bakori chuckled, even as one of Dyne's lightning bolts hammered into him. It tore open his arm, exposing and burning bone and muscle, and boiling the ichor in the demon's veins.

"I felt that, Hugh. I've battled your master before, and she used more than her share of starbolts on me. That trick's never going to work on me again."

Nearly a dozen imps near Bakori simply *dissolved*. Streamers of vomit-hued energy flowed from their dust into Bakori, and his arm knit itself back together as though it had never been injured in the first place.

Bakori whipped his tail, sending Yves' corpse flying at Tarik. The headmaster tore a boulder out of the ground and blocked the corpse with it, but at a cost— the magma had begun to creep forward again.

Hugh was frantically wracking his mind for ideas when Godrick wrapped an arm around Hugh's waist. "Hold on tight," the big apprentice said. "All that magma is about to break loose in a moment."

It was barely a fraction of a moment. With Yves dead, Hugh and Godrick running out of mana, and the other councilors distracted, the magma exploded outwards.

At the same moment, though, the stone underneath Hugh and Godrick erupted, sending them flying backwards towards the edge of the mountain.

Hugh barely caught them with a levitation spell before they crashed down. At least his stellar mana was still useful for this.

Hugh had several smoldering patches in his clothes from the close escape, and he could feel one especially bad burn on his back.

The levitation spell had just barely managed to set them down when the spellform Hugh was visualizing simply dissolved.

The council chamber had erupted into complete chaos. Dyne was floating fifty feet above the floor, cycling through lightning and venom spells as fast as they could. They'd even drawn out the venom from Bakori's tail to launch at Abyla, which mostly seemed to amuse the demon. Dyne's aim, however, was being thrown off by dozens of lava bombs shooting up at them.

Tarik had given up on trying to hold off the magma. She'd lifted herself and the throne on a massive column of granite over the battlefield, and was levitating and dropping immense boulders. Bakori caught one boulder twice his size with his hands, and then simply shredded it like fresh-baked bread. Abyla deflected several boulders with magma and simply surfed out of the way of others atop a current of magma.

Rutliss had just surrounded himself with a sphere of super-cooled saltwater and was rolling it off the side of the mountain to escape.

Which, given what Hugh knew of Rutliss, didn't surprise him at all.

Most of the thrones had already been destroyed or melted, several detonating in magical explosions.

Hugh caught a brief glimpse of Sabae crouching down in the center of the metal seal, which remained untouched by the violence around her. She'd spun up her water armor to protect her from the heat, but Hugh could see the surface of the spinning water starting to steam.

Bakori's laughter seemed to hang over everything.

Hugh was desperately trying to eke his last remaining crystal mana from his reservoir to construct a ward around himself and Godrick, who was looking distinctly unsteady on his feet, when his spellbook sent him an image.

The image was vague and tinted with fear, and Hugh could actually feel the book trembling at his side, but he felt a smile creep across his face as his hand dove into his pocket for something that he always made sure to keep there.

The image had been of a piece of chalk.

Just as Hugh's chalk touched the ground, though, Dyne's gravity-based flight spell failed, and they plummeted. Tarik stretched out a granite fist to catch them, and streamers of silk raced towards the falling mage.

One of Abyla's lava bombs got to Dyne first.

Then Abyla turned her gaze towards Hugh and Godrick. Even from here, Hugh could see her smile as she launched a whole barrage of lava bombs at them.

Sabae hunched down lower, focused on maintaining her water armor.

Another wave of magma crashed over the magical field surrounding the metal seal, and Sabae could feel more of her water armor flash into steam from the heat. None of the magma got through the shield, but plenty of heat did.

As the wave passed over her, Sabae realized that the metal disc was actually floating above the magma— the stone beneath it had been completely eroded away.

She huddled down lower.

She'd been so sure that she was right about Kanderon's plan, but the longer this went on, the more and more she was becoming convinced that she'd gotten it wrong, and that the three of them were going to die up here.

At least Talia would be safe.

Hugh was convinced he was about to die. Abyla's lava bombs were descending through the air towards him. A wave of magma was racing along behind them, even if he and Godrick could survive the lava bombs. Past all that, he could see a flood of imps flowing up Tarik's granite column, and her spells had begun visibly failing under Bakori's influence.

Abyla's spells weren't being affected by Bakori's field at all.

Hugh wasn't even bothering to try and finish his chalk ward. He simply wouldn't have time. Even if he still had crystal mana available, he'd...

Next to him, Godrick bellowed, and the head of his sledgehammer *cracked.* It started to shake, and a brilliant white light poured out of the cracks.

Godrick threw the hammer with all the force his arm and steel magic could provide. It flew so quickly that Hugh was buffeted backward by the wind generated by the hammer's flight.

The hammer exploded just before it reached the descending cloud of lava bombs.

A massive shockwave surged forward, catching the lava bombs in midflight, scattering them off their paths and breaking them into droplets. It actually pushed the lava wave back a few feet, and knocked Godrick and Hugh back farther towards the edge of the chamber, even though the blast was directed away from them.

It took a second for Hugh's hearing to come back, but when it did, Godrick was laughing.

"Me da's goin' ta kill me fer losin another hammer," Godrick said, then started laughing harder.

Hugh couldn't help but chuckle too.

As Godrick and Hugh stood up, Hugh glanced behind them, looking for a way to escape. He still had stellar mana left, maybe even enough to levitate them down the mountain safely.

There were imps waiting on the edge of the mountain. Hundreds of them. They must have escaped out of Skyhold's windows and climbed all the way up.

There's no way the imps could get to them here— the weird distance manipulation shield Kanderon had crafted for the council chamber meant that they were effectively leagues away from the apprentices, even though they could reach the imps in just a few steps.

The imps didn't need to get to them, though. The magma would do for them just fine.

Hugh turned back in time to see Abyla recover from the blast and launch another wave of magma in their direction, followed by another barrage of lava bombs.

He was fairly sure the back of his shirt was on fire, that spot on his back was burning so bad, but he didn't make a move to put it out.

He opened his mouth to tell Godrick goodbye, but before he could say a word, a figure plummeted down from the air, catching themselves on extended strips of silk.

Anders glanced back at them and smiled. "It looks like my lessons came in handy for you three, doesn't it?"

Anders' robe exploded outwards into a massive cloud of silk.

Everywhere Godrick looked, streamers of silk danced in the air. Dozens of them shot up towards the descending lava bombs, embroidered glyphs flaring to life along their length. Lava bombs froze and shattered in midair or were thrown off course.

More silk streamers wrapped themselves around Hugh and Godrick's legs and waists, then *lifted* them into the air fast enough that Godrick felt slightly nauseous. The wave of molten rock crested only a few feet below them, but Godrick didn't feel any heat at all as more silk streamers hovered between them and the magma, glyphs glowing brightly even compared to the magma, creating a visible heat shield between them.

The streamers creating the heat shield quickly smoldered and burst into flame, but by the time the heat shield dissolved, they were already far above it.

Imps screamed as the wave of magma poured over the edge of the mountain.

Tarik's granite column collapsed completely, but she had already been borne aloft by more silk streamers.

Abyla and Bakori were suddenly dealing with a plague of magical attacks from silk glyphs. Firebolts, ball lightning, frost spikes, and at least half a dozen other types of energy attacks bombarded them. None of the attacks were especially powerful, but there were enough of them that Abyla had raised a shield of magma to protect herself, while imps were dissolving at an astounding rate around Bakori as he drained their essence to regenerate his wounds.

"It turns out Bakori doesn't decay glyphs or enchantments," Anders shouted back at them, "but I don't have enough silk to keep this up for much longer! I'm going to try and rescue Sabae, then we're retreating!"

More streamers were trying to reach Sabae, but most of them were simply bursting into flame in the heat from the magma.

A web of silk threads descended towards Bakori, then simply passed through him. The demon collapsed into a pile of what Godrick could only describe as chunks, none bigger than Godrick's fist.

Within seconds, half the imps in the council chamber dissolved, and Bakori was already climbing back to his feet, looking unamused.

Godrick glanced over at Hugh, only to see Hugh pawing at his back urgently, muttering "ow" over and over again. Finally, Hugh's hands closed around something in his shirt, and he yanked it loose.

Hugh spent a moment looking at it, then began to chuckle. He opened his hands to show the object to Godrick, not dropping it even though it was visibly burning his hands.

When Godrick saw it, he started laughing too. Not the despairing laugh from earlier, but a genuine laugh this time.

It was a metal pin covered in spellforms.

Talia's tracking pin.

A massive explosion tore out of the stairwell, sending imps and chunks of imps flying through the air. Through the smoke, Godrick could see flashes of purple-green dreamfire.

Talia fired a couple more dreamfire bolts at imps that hadn't died in the blast. At the same time, she pumped mana into her dragonbone dagger and charged through the scattered corpses her bonefire blast had left. Nothing fancy this time, just regular mammal bone. Cow, she thought. Sometimes all you wanted was a good old-fashioned big explosion.

Well, a lot of explosions, really. She'd burned through the majority of her bones fighting her way through the hall below.

The magma raining down through the ceiling of the big circular hall hadn't made things easier in the slightest.

When her dragonbone dagger was charged enough, Talia hurled it towards Bakori, who had just recovered from the blast and was turning to face her.

Unlike her other enchanted dagger, this one *was* weighted for throwing.

It sunk deep into Bakori's side, and immediately began to cook a sizeable chunk of Bakori's torso. Imps simply started dissolving around Bakori, erupting into weird vomit energy and flowing into the demon. His flesh started to heal as fast as the dagger could burn it, and Bakori laughed as he stepped towards her.

Talia had wondered why imps had kept doing that down below.

She ignored Bakori striding towards her as she searched for her friends.

There was Sabae, sitting on some sort of hovering magical disc over a lake of lava, wearing a thin, visibly evaporating suit of water armor.

Headmaster Tarik was floating through the air, borne by silk streamers.

Talia focused her senses back on the tracking spell and…

There was Hugh and Godrick, being held in the air by Anders. All three were being targeted by misshapen, spinning spheres of lava being launched through the air.

Godrick had told her the proper names for all of Abyla's known combat spells when they were studying her, but right now, Talia couldn't care less about spell names.

The damn woman was trying to kill her friends.

Bakori was halfway to Talia when he simply exploded in a shower of ichor and flames. All that remained was a pair of crisped, barely connected legs.

Talia smiled grimly at that as she readied a spellform in her mind's eye. She hadn't stopped pumping bone mana into the dagger, and when dragonbone was filled past capacity, well…

Boom.

She paid no mind to the ichor misting down on her from blowing up Bakori as she pumped her dream mana into the spellform she'd envisioned.

All of her dream mana.

A writhing column of dreamfire as thick as her torso shot out of her outstretched hands. Talia felt like it should make a noise, but it was utterly silent as it stretched towards Abyla.

Talia could feel… not heat, but *something* radiate off the beam of dreamfire. She'd never used this much dream mana at once, or attempted a spell this large before. Ripples of hallucinatory nonsense pulsed out from the beam. The lava below it bloomed into fanged flowers and oatmeal shoes, and the air around it began to turn blue and sparkly.

Abyla desperately lifted a wave of molten rock to block the oncoming beam, but it punched through without slowing or shrinking noticeably, and the wave dissolved into butterfly winged fish, which in turn simply faded into mist.

The beam struck Abyla, and the woman erupted into a burst of caustic sounds, tastes heavier than stone, and colors that rasped across the skin like a cat's tongue, even from where Talia stood.

The magma— that was what Godrick had called it, magma— simply collapsed to the ground instantly, splashing and rolling. The lava bombs already in the air kept flying, but Anders was already deflecting them easily.

Talia's mana reservoir emptied completely, and the beam flickered out like it had never happened.

The instant it did, she sagged, almost collapsing to the ground. She forced herself to stand, however, and started sprinting towards Hugh.

She dodged around puddles of magma and leapt over rivulets. She could feel the heat even through her enchanted clothing.

Talia just needed to get in earshot of Hugh.

Behind her, Bakori's torso had already grown back up to his ribcage, streamers of energy rushing into him from inside the mountain.

The instant Anders lowered Hugh and Godrick to the ground, Hugh started running for Talia. Not fast— the imp bite and his countless bruises and burns, not to mention his exhaustion, were finally catching up to him.

"Hugh!" Talia yelled, but the rest of her words were drowned out by a bellow as Bakori stood back up, all regenerated save for a single arm and some skin, and a few rents in his distended, transparent stomach.

Hugh unwillingly came to a stop at that.

"Hugh!" Talia yelled, as Bakori began to run after her, "Make your book stop blocking scrying!"

What? Why would…?

Hugh shook his head and relayed the message to the book. Behind Talia, more of Anders' silk glyphs began launching magical assaults at Bakori, but the demon barely slowed.

Hugh's spellbook dropped the scrying shield it had been holding since the labyrinth.

A cool breeze immediately picked up, and a shadow rose over the peak of Skyhold.

"**What a proper mess this is**," Ilinia Kaen Das said, and in a burst of wind, Bakori was yanked into the sky.

CHAPTER THIRTY-FIVE

Don't Forget to Chew Your Food

Hugh turned around, and the view of the Skyreach Range gave way to what should be a view of the Endless Erg.

Ilinia Kaen Das stood in the way.

Or, rather, a stormcloud in the shape of Ilinia stood in the way. It towered over Skyhold, idly bouncing something tiny in the palm of its cloudy fist. With a start, Hugh realized it was Bakori.

"**It's about time you dropped that scrying shield, Hugh.**" Ilinia said. When the stormcloud spoke, lightning crackled in its mouth. "**I couldn't interfere so long as it was blocking me from seeing into the council chamber. And Talia, well done, dearie!**"

"I couldn't have done it without you!" Talia said as she came to a stop next to Hugh. He silently handed her the still hot tracking pin with a smile.

In the center of Skyhold's new lava lake, another breeze picked up Sabae and flew her towards them.

"She basically flew me most of the way up through the mountain," Talia confided to Hugh, "until we got close to your book's weird scrying shield."

She took the pin, tucked it away in her shoe, and then grabbed Hugh in a bear hug and squeezed. A moment later, Sabae was set down next to them, and unsteadily staggered over to join their embrace.

Bakori's voice drifted to them on the wind, despite the distance. "How is this possible? You're hundreds of leagues away!"

"I'm exactly a hundred leagues away, little demon," Ilinia said. **"Well within my range, but far out of the range of your vile little spellform wrecking field."**

Hugh and Sabae exchanged smiles at that. Ilinia had told Hugh, right in front of everyone, how she'd enjoyed watching Hugh protect Theras Tel from the sandstorm, and Theras Tel was a hell of a lot more than a hundred leagues away from Ras Andis.

Godrick limped up to them— Hugh had no idea when Godrick had hurt his leg, but then, Hugh was feeling a lot of aches and pains right now that he didn't know the origin of as well— and wrapped all three of them in a hug.

And squeezed.

"Too hard, too hard!" Hugh managed to wheeze.

Godrick chuckled, and eased up a little.

"Who do you think you are?" demanded Bakori. "Under what right do you…"

"You know damn well who I am," Ilinia said. **"And you know damn well how long of a list of titles I have. Right now, though, all you need to know is that I'm the woman whose granddaughter you just tried to kill."**

Bakori barely had time to scream before the stormcloud shaped like Sabae's grandmother tossed the demon into her castle-sized mouth and began to chew.

Streamers of vomit-colored energy began to pour up from Skyhold to regenerate Bakori's wounds.

Sabae slowly disengaged from the hug. "You all smell awful," she whispered.

Godrick snapped his fingers, and the smell vanished.

Hugh frowned suddenly. "It's my fault backup took so long to get here. If my book hadn't been blocking scrying, your grandmother might have…"

Sabae covered Hugh's mouth with her hand. "No. I was the one to order you to shield us from scrying, the responsibility lies with me. I honestly never thought your book would prevent the jaws of the trap closing on Bakori."

"Also," Sabae added, "I kinda expected it to be Kanderon who'd be the jaws of the trap, and I guess I thought my grandmother was just doing some sort of information exchange or something. A bit obvious in retrospect, I suppose."

Hugh started to say something, but Sabae hushed him as a pair of figures approached. Best not to give away incriminating details.

"I've got to admit," Anders said as he helped a wounded Headmaster Tarik towards them, "This is the most unusual exam day I've ever experienced."

The six of them turned to watch Ilinia chew on Bakori.

No one left the mountaintop while regeneration energy was still streaming up from the mountain to Bakori, though Tarik was kind enough to sculpt chairs out of stone for them to sit on.

When mages came up from below to investigate the council chamber, Anders just shushed them, and told them to send a message to the council members who had gone to deal with Jaskolskus.

It was sunset when Bakori finally died in a vomit-shaded explosion that punched out from between the storm's lips.

"That," Ilinia said, **"was disgusting."**

Talia sighed. "I want to be your grandmother when I get old, Sabae."

Alustin returned a day later, and Kanderon and the remaining councilors soon after that. The mountain was still a hive of activity, with mages repairing the damage, healing the wounded, and going over Skyhold with a fine-toothed comb for any more traitors.

Over two hundred people had died, most of them trained battle mages. Amazingly, less than a tenth of the casualties had been students, despite the huge number of them in and near the labyrinth during the breakout.

Sabae had strong suspicions regarding that, but she hadn't voiced them to anyone yet.

It had been a week, and Alustin had just now found the time to meet with them, apart from a long debriefing in front of the remaining council members, which hadn't given them a chance to ask any sensitive questions of Alustin or Kanderon.

Sabae had managed to sneak a letter to Alustin informing him of a few more sensitive details, like the fact that Anders was selling Skyhold secrets.

"You used us as bait," Sabae said, the instant the apprentices had settled in the comfortable, battered armchairs in Alustin's office.

The paper mage gave her a pained look and sighed. "It wasn't my idea, but I'm not going to argue I don't share responsibility. I could have told you what Kanderon was planning from the first, but I didn't."

"You knew exactly who the traitor was from the start, didn't you?" Sabae said angrily.

Alustin nodded. "We did. Well, we didn't know that Anders was selling secrets, but Kanderon knew Abyla was working for Bakori the instant he sent her the order to vote against the alternate test."

"Wait, what?" Talia demanded angrily. "You *knew?* What was even the point of the investigation, then? You and Kanderon almost got us all killed!"

"Like I said," Sabae replied, still staring at Alustin, "we were being used as bait. The whole investigation was a sham, meant to put pressure on Bakori to accelerate his plans."

"I mean, we already guessed that Kanderon was trying to lure out Bakori," Hugh said uncertainly. "Is this really that much worse?"

"Yes," Talia snapped. "We wasted how many hours this year on this stupid investigation, and it was all for nothing?"

"Also, yeh know," Godrick said, "there were all the people that died."

"It wasn't for nothing," Alustin insisted, pushing his glasses back up his nose. "Again, you figured out that there was a second traitor…"

"Avah figured out what Anders was doing," Talia interrupted irritably, "not us."

Alustin paused at that. "Wait, Avah did what now?"

Sabae rolled her eyes as Hugh and Talia gave a somewhat garbled explanation of that. She could see Godrick smirking at their divergent explanations for the situation.

Alustin lifted his glasses and rubbed his eyes in exasperation.

"Alright, alright, let's just not mention that part to Kanderon?" Alustin said. "And please ask your girlfriend not to tell anyone about any of this, Hugh."

Hugh grew a little quiet at that. Things had been a little... strained between them since the battle against Bakori. There had been quite a bit of crying, though no fights.

"I seem to recall you predicting exactly this outcome, Talia," Alustin said. "Two traitors, one of whom was Anders. I really don't think you need to be grumpy about Avah figuring it out."

Talia brightened up immediately. "Oh yeah, I did, didn't I? I guess life does turn out like in stories after all, doesn't it?"

She said that last with a smirk at Sabae, who struggled not to roll her eyes again. Talia was going to be insufferable about that.

Part of Sabae didn't mind that at all.

"In addition, your investigation served its intended purpose quite well," Alustin said. "It was the stick that pushed Bakori into moving early by threatening to expose his ally on the council, with Kanderon's absence on Midsummer serving as the carrot luring him up. He moved far ahead of when we anticipated him to, based on our scouting of his forces in the labyrinth. If he'd waited a few years, he could have flooded Skyhold with more imps than Kanderon and the full council could have dealt with easily, at least not without far greater casualties in Skyhold."

Talia brightened at that.

"Ah'm a little shocked yeh got me da to go with this plan," Godrick said. "He seems... rather angry with yeh right now."

Alustin gave another pained look. "So... things might not have actually worked out quite like we planned. The four of you were actually supposed to be shadowed by a team of Librarians Errant that had been hiding in the labyrinth, but you somehow managed to give them the slip minutes into entering the first floor."

If Sabae had to guess, that had probably been thanks to Godrick's enchanted hammer and Hugh's spellbook helping guide them past dangers in the labyrinth.

"The four of you were never intended to…" Alustin sighed, taking off his glasses again, "fight your way through an army of imps out of the labyrinth, engage in a running battle with said imps all the way through the mountain, break through both a besieging horde of imps and a military grade magical barrier, confront the council, expose a traitor, engage in combat with said traitor, who happened to be one of the deadliest battlemages alive, somehow manage to kill said traitor after she eliminated multiple other council members, accidentally delay Ilinia from arriving and destroying Bakori, and then survive a confrontation with a demon who could easily have been counted among the great powers."

Alustin closed his eyes. "No, you were supposed to just be escorted to a hidden safe house we'd established in the labyrinth after you picked up your tokens at the entrance to the second floor, and guarded there until Bakori was dead and the threat was over."

Everyone was silent for a little bit. When put that way, their actions might be… a little on the absurd side. It might have been a little more sensible to hide, rather than… well.

"You forgot kill a giant awful nightmarc bird…" Talia said.

"Terrorbird," Godrick interrupted.

"And rescue a damsel in distress," Talia finished, ignoring Godrick. "Also, it should be pointed out that one of the councilors actually ran away, unlike us."

Their teacher sighed and opened his eyes again. "No, let's not forget any of that."

"Has Rutliss shown up at all?" Sabae asked.

"Nah, still missin'," Godrick said. "Me da reckons he's ashamed ta show his face and ran fer it."

Alustin sighed even louder. "I have a lot more work to do, do you have any other questions?"

"It doesn't seem very responsible of Kanderon to put that much human life at risk," Hugh said uncertainly.

"Kanderon doesn't care that much about human life, to be honest," Alustin said, "save for on the scale of cities and civilizations. I doubt she generally notices much of a difference between a human dying of old age and a human dying young in battle."

Sabae had basically suspected as much, but it was still a sobering thing to hear from Alustin.

"What is the council guarding?" Talia asked. "What's with that weird metal seal?"

Alustin actually seemed a little relieved at this question. "It's the entrance to an extraplanar vault Kanderon built soon after the founding of Skyhold, with the assistance of several other archmages. It can only be opened on Midsummer and Midwinter, and… well, it contains things too dangerous to use and that, for one reason or another, can't be destroyed."

"Like what?" Talia asked, visibly excited at the thought of weapons too dangerous to use.

"The only known egg of an Issen-Derin queen, held in stasis. Some sort of Ithonian artificial plague engine. A red aether crystal sword that generates uncontrollable, nigh-inextinguishable wildfires. A sphere that corrupts and twists people's affinities permanently and horribly. A four-foot-long tuning fork that can generate mana deserts lasting decades. A pair of sentient leather boots that has a habit of assassinating rulers in ridiculous ways." Alustin had an odd look on his face. "And those are just some of the tamer items near the entrance."

"I feel like it would be easy to destroy a pair of boots," Talia said.

"You'd really think so," Alustin muttered irritably. "I'll lend you its file sometime."

"What was Bakori after? Ah highly doubt it was a pair a' boots," Godrick said.

Alustin snorted. "No, indeed. Near the back of the vault is a rather delicate wand made of some sort of chitin. Kanderon believes is an artifact of the Labyrinth Builders. It… well, she's fairly convinced that Bakori could use it to destroy the labyrinth."

No one commented on that.

"Any more questions?" Alustin asked, rubbing his eyes again and yawning. "I have a lot more work to do today."

"What has Kanderon had you and the other Librarians Errant looking for all year?" Sabae said.

Hugh's spellbook suddenly hovered up a few inches from his side, looking oddly interested.

"Looking for the lost city of Imperial Ithos," Alustin said, sounding almost bored. He didn't even look at them. "The weapon that Kanderon and the other Skyhold founders built to exile it out of our universe and make the entire world, including themselves, forget its location, is failing. We expect the city to return to our world in a matter of just a few years. Half the nations and great powers on Ithos are scrambling to figure out where it will reemerge, while the other half have realized something is going on and are trying to figure out what has everyone else so worked up."

Alustin sighed when no one answered him. "I literally can't tell you what we're looking for," he said.

Hugh's spellbook was shifting its gaze eagerly back and forth between the apprentices and Alustin.

"But… yeh just told us what yeh were lookin' for," Godrick said.

Alustin went perfectly still, then slowly looked back up at them, fixing his glasses once more. He didn't even look remotely tired now.

"What did you just say?" he asked in a quiet voice.

"You just told us you were looking for the lost city of Ithos," Hugh said, sounding confused.

Sabae felt confused herself. Had she really never wondered where Imperial Ithos was? The most powerful city in the history of the continent? The center of an empire that had ruled almost the entire continent, and that the continent was still named after?

She honestly didn't think she had.

Hugh's spellbook seemed… relieved somehow.

"Hugh," Alustin said in a very quiet voice, "please ask your spellbook if it did something to break the Exile Splinter's hold on your memories."

Hugh gave Alustin a slightly nervous look, but turned and stared at the book intently. After staring intently at it for a time, he turned back towards Alustin and shook his head.

"My spellbook doesn't seem to have any idea what an Exile Splinter is, and that it didn't do anything. It did send me what feel like memories of you telling us all this before, and it being really confused about why we kept forgetting it," Hugh said.

Alustin didn't react for a moment, and then grabbed a book off his desk and threw it at the wall. Hard.

The apprentices all stared at Alustin in shock as he began pacing around the room, muttering frantically to himself and clutching his head.

Eventually, Alustin seemed to gain control of himself again.

"I'm sorry about that," he said. "I thought we had more time, but it seems Imperial Ithos is going to be returning sooner than we thought, if you're starting to remember conversations about it. Normally you can only remember if you've got some way to block the Exile Splinter's power, as Kanderon did for me, and even that doesn't do much more than let you know it exists and what its purpose is. The damn thing is powerful enough that it even purged every map of Ithos' location, and any clues to Ithos' location in nearly every book on the planet."

Something seemed to occur to Hugh.

"Nearly every book?" he asked. "What about that book you got from Indris?"

Alustin gave Hugh an appraising look. "There were a small number of books that, for whatever reason, were in different universes or were otherwise shielded from the Exile Splinter when it was activated. *Grain Shipments to the Imperial City of Ithos, the Year 378 After Its Founding* was one of those books. Kanderon had been trying to retrieve it from Indris for most of a century, but it didn't become urgent until recently, when the Exile Splinter began failing. Before, when you read one of the books that escaped its influence, its information just slipped out of your mind. As it started failing, though…"

"You were able to start actually reading the books," Talia said.

Alustin nodded. "We already had three others, and the one we got from Indris has gotten us closer than almost anyone to figuring out the city's former location."

"Almost anyone?" Sabae asked.

Alustin scowled. "Imperial Havath is at least as close to finding it as we are."

Sabae decided not to comment on that. She still wasn't entirely sure why, but Havath was an extremely sensitive topic to Alustin.

The paper mage shook his head. "I need to alert Kanderon to this development immediately. I'm going to have to answer any more questions you have at a later point."

He sat back down at his desk and began writing.

Hugh, Talia, and Godrick all stood up to go, but Sabae stayed seated. They gave her uncertain looks, but she gestured at them to go.

Then she just waited.

Alustin was usually uncannily observant, but he actually jumped a little in surprise when he looked up and saw Sabae was still there after he finished writing the letter.

"Sabae, I'm sorry, but…" Alustin started.

"We're not done yet," Sabae said, her voice absolutely flat.

Alustin blinked, then seemed to really focus on her, rather than everything else on his mind.

"You have questions you'd rather the others not hear," Alustin said.

"Observations, mostly," Sabae replied.

Alustin seemed to consider that for a moment, then gestured for her to continue. He folded his hands in front of him as she began to talk.

"It seems interesting to me that all the councilors that Kanderon left behind were either her enemies, traitors, or politically unreliable," Sabae said.

Alustin said nothing, his face entirely expressionless.

"All of Loarna's wards seemed designed to lead Bakori and his imps through sections of the mountain filled with members of her rival councilors' factions," Sabae said. "And so far as I can tell, no one else seems to know about them, and we wouldn't even know if Hugh hadn't figured it out during a very, very narrow window of opportunity after they activated— presumably by Bakori breaking out of the labyrinth— and before they faded away. I also feel quite confident that it wouldn't take very much digging to find that Loarna has ties of some sort to Kanderon, or at least the Library."

Alustin said nothing.

"I think there's a reason why so few apprentices and students died," Sabae said. "For all your claims that Kanderon doesn't care overly much about human life, she has an obvious soft spot for the young, and I think she arranged for as few of them to die when Bakori broke out of the labyrinth as was possible."

Alustin said nothing.

"I think that your most recent mission might have taken you on a path quite close to a certain sleeping elemental's home caldera, just a short time before it mysteriously started waking up," Sabae said.

Alustin said nothing.

"I have a lot of doubts about whether this was the least bloody way of baiting Bakori out of the labyrinth Kanderon had available to her," Sabae said.

Alustin said nothing.

"I think that this outcome, or one like it, with her enemies and unreliables on the council either dead or discredited, was exactly what Kanderon was aiming for. She knew what everyone wanted— Bakori, her fellow councilors, even us apprentices— and she used that knowledge to manipulate all of us. She was cleaning house— not just of Bakori, but of any resistance to her dominance of Skyhold."

Alustin said nothing.

"This was a coup," Sabae said. "I've been convinced of it for a while, but until just now, I had no idea *why* Kanderon would launch a coup like this. It seemed completely illogical to me. But now…"

The silence hung thick in the room.

"Now, it makes sense," Sabae said. "Kanderon wanted to make sure her affairs in Skyhold were all in order before Imperial Ithos returned, so that she didn't have to worry about threats within and without."

Alustin said nothing, just carefully stood up and picked up his letter to Kanderon. He slowly walked around his desk. As he passed Sabae, the blue tattoo around his arm flared into existence, and he pulled something out of midair, and set it down on the desk in front of Sabae.

It was a deck of cards.

Sabae turned around to watch Alustin as he walked towards the door of his office. The chalkboard walls, the crowded bookshelves, and the dozing origami golem on top of one shelf… they all seemed out of place for a moment, as though they were just window dressing. As though the excitable, learning obsessed scholar; the dashing, confident spy; and the deadly battlemage were all just costumes Alustin wore. For a moment, Alustin just looked… sad. Lonely. As though he bore a weight on his shoulders that was crushing him.

Sabae spoke up one more time, just before Alustin left the room.

"What is it?" she said. "What's in Imperial Ithos that has everyone so up in arms?"

Alustin turned back to look at her. For a moment she could have sworn she saw something like fear in his eyes.

Then he slipped out of the room and was gone.

Anders Vel Siraf shifted nervously on the blue crystal platform, trying not to look at the figure at Kanderon Crux's feet.

Not that looking at Kanderon's baleful gaze was much better.

"I never meant any harm," Anders insisted. "I never sold any truly sensitive information."

Kanderon shifted forward slightly, and Anders tensed. He looked around desperately, but there was nobody down here in the depths of the Grand Library save for himself, Kanderon, and…

"I don't especially care how you rate the severity of your betrayal, Anders," Kanderon said. **"I care that you did it at all. Count yourself lucky that you're alive at all right now. As far as you're concerned, Anders, you're my devoted servant now. You vote how I want you to vote, and you leap when I say jump. You'll keep selling secrets, but you're going to be selling whatever I want my enemies to hear from now on, Anders."**

Anders opened his mouth, then closed it again when he couldn't find anything to say.

"If you hadn't kept the children alive during the battle in the council chamber," Kanderon said, **"You'd already be sharing our friend here's punishment for fleeing and failing in his duty as a vault guardian. If you ever disappoint me again, Anders, you *will* end up sharing his fate. You can't escape me and you can't defy me. All you can do is obey me."**

Kanderon reached out with her paw and delicately picked up the bound figure off the floor of her aether crystal platform. He was wrapped in bonds made of more of Kanderon's aether crystal, engraved with spellforms that made Anders queasy to look at.

Kanderon smiled at Anders with closed lips as Rutliss shouted incoherently through his gag.

Then she opened her mouth the rest of the way, revealing her massive, man-sized fangs.

She leaned forward and bit down.

Rutliss' incoherent shouting ended instantly, and Anders shut his eyes, doing his best to ignore the horrible chewing noises.

CHAPTER THIRTY-SIX

Breathing Room

Talia, Godrick, and Sabae were walking up to Hugh's hidden room when Avah came out, her eyes red from crying. She stormed directly past them, not saying anything.

They glanced at each other, then rushed to get behind the repaired bookshelf and through the door.

Hugh was lying on his bed, staring at the ceiling. It was pretty obvious that he'd been crying as well. His spellbook was sitting next to him, gently nudging his side.

"Avah just dumped me," Hugh said.

Talia stepped towards Hugh, her first instinct to hug him, then stopped. The other two were looking at her oddly, as though unsure what she'd do next.

Talia strode over to Hugh, gave him a quick hug, then turned and walked out the door.

It didn't take her long to track down Avah.

The Radhan girl glared at her.

"What do you want?" she demanded. "Are you here to mock how useless I am? Gloat about how you knew I wasn't good enough for Hugh? Or are you here to punish me for hurting him?"

Talia just stared at Avah, trying to think of what to say.

Avah burst out crying again, then hugged Talia out of nowhere. Talia awkwardly patted the taller girl on the back as she wept.

That sarcastic little part of Talia's brain, the one that always had to needle at her in vulnerable moments, made a crack about how Avah was, by any reasonable standard, still really short. She was only tall in comparison to Talia.

Talia dismissed the thought easily. That was hardly the worst thing her mind could throw at her.

"I'm sorry," Avah said, once she'd calmed down a little. "You saved my life, and I just said all those awful things to you, and…"

Avah pulled away from Talia, and wiped her nose on her sleeve.

A nasty, jealous little part of Talia gloated about how Avah wasn't so pretty right now, but Talia shoved that thought aside too.

"Do you know why I broke up with Hugh?" Avah asked.

"Because… he lied to you about the investigation?" Talia ventured. "Because he risked his life in the labyrinth?"

Avah shook her head. "I was mad about both of those things, but I honestly get why he did them. No, I broke up with him because I was afraid."

Talia gave her a confused look.

"Back in Theras Tel, I was terrified," Avah said. "We'd just gotten caught up in this terrifying situation that made absolutely no sense, and the four of you were all just… so confident, so capable, and I just got dragged along in your wake."

Avah sniffled, and wiped her nose on her sleeve again.

"When it was over, though, I thought it was over," Avah said. "That it was just some freak, uncontrollable occurrence. Then I found those files in Hugh's room, and everything started going sideways again, and I realized that this is part of your lives. Part of Hugh's life. He's going to keep getting drawn into these situations— he's even going to seek them out. I'm not brave like you, Talia. I can't do this. I can't deal with the fear and the danger and the uncertainty."

Tears were starting to well up in Avah's eyes again.

"Hugh's a wonderful person, and he deserves someone braver than me," Avah said. "I'm just a merchant girl who got a crush on a boy just because he was a great mage. He deserves someone like you."

Talia opened her mouth to argue, but Avah shook her head. "I've seen the way you look at him, Talia. It's obvious to everyone but Hugh how jealous you were of me, and how much you disliked me. How much you were convinced that I would hurt him. And look, you were right. You, though— you're fearless, you're loyal, and you're a terrifyingly powerful mage. You're perfect for him."

Talia shook her head and laughed bitterly.

"I'm not fearless," she said. "I'm constantly afraid that someone's going to realize how insecure I am about nearly everything. About my height, my tattoos, the way my hair is constantly being difficult, and the way I always feel like everyone's running circles around me. The only thing I'm really good at is destroying things."

Avah started to speak, but it was Talia's turn to cut her off. "I don't mind that about myself. I'm good at it, and I like the fact that I'm good at it. I killed someone for the first time when I was just a girl— another clan was dumb enough to raid us, and I got one of the raiders with a rusty old spear I'd found behind the woodpile from behind. She never even knew who killed her. I had a few nightmares afterwards, sure— I'm not broken inside or anything— but I was ultimately fine with what I did. I've got no problem with being good in battle, Avah. But sometimes I feel like it's the only thing I'm good at, like it's the only worthwhile thing about me, and I start lying and acting like it's the only thing I really care about. Not just to the outside world, but to myself."

Talia could feel her eyes watering a little, and she surreptitiously wiped the corners of her eyes.

"I'm terrified to talk about my emotions even with my friends, to be vulnerable with them, and to be honest with them, Avah. You, though... you're open with your feelings like it's nothing, like it's the easiest thing in the world. I wasn't jealous of you because of Hugh, I was jealous of you because you're confident and brilliant and not a giant ball of insecurity like me, and you just walked into our little group of friends like it was nothing."

Talia wasn't exactly sure how, but Avah was hugging her again, crying onto her shoulder, and Talia was crying into her tunic, and some apprentice walked by staring at them, and Talia shot a few dreamfire bolts near his feet to encourage him to move along and stop staring at them, but doing it carefully so Avah didn't notice that she was doing it.

Eventually, both of them stopped crying, and started wiping away their tears.

Talia, rather than use her school uniform, used a bit of cloth she kept on her for cleaning off her knives if they needed it.

"You were definitely a little jealous of me dating Hugh, though," Avah said.

"I don't know," Talia said. "Sometimes I think I like Hugh like that, and sometimes I think I'm just feeling protective of him and getting that confused for... liking him,

344

and sometimes I have no idea what I think and I go and cause lots and lots of explosions and fires."

Avah giggled a little at that.

"I always thought I'd fall for some invincible warrior," Talia said. "Some invulnerable mage that was an immovable object to my unstoppable force. And Hugh might be my best friend in the world, but he's far from invulnerable, if you know what I mean."

Avah grinned, a little sadly. "He's brilliant, brave, and loyal, but if someone he cares about shows him the slightest bit of disapproval, he turns into a kicked puppy."

Talia nodded at that. "Pretty much. Not that I blame him, considering how rough he's had it much of his life."

Neither said anything for a while after that. Finally, Talia broke the silence. "I should probably get back to the others," she said. "They probably think I'm disposing of your body right now."

Avah laughed at that. They hugged one more time, and the Radhan girl turned to head towards the docks.

"Hey, Avah," Talia called.

Avah stopped and looked back.

"If you tell anyone I have emotions and insecurities, I'll blow up your family's ship," Talia said.

Avah laughed at that, but there was an uncertain note to it.

Talia turned to head back to Hugh's lair, feeling like she could breathe a little easier.

"No, Hugh's a complete mess right now," Godrick said. "Yeh can hardly mention sandships without him mopin' about Avah."

Artur sighed as he chopped vegetables. "Poor kid. First breakups are tough. Ah wish it had at least come at a better time."

"How would yeh know how a breakup feels? Yeh only ever dated Mum," Godrick teased.

"Ah'm not an idiot," Artur protested, "Ah've had more than enough friends go through breakups ta know what they put yeh through. It's not exactly hard ta figure out—breakups don't inspire particularly subtle emotions."

Godrick chuckled at that.

"But jus' because they're not subtle emotions doesn't mean they're easy ta get a grip on," Artur said, dumping the vegetables into the frying pan. "Ah've known a lot a' folks who just lock 'em away and hope they vanish."

He looked straight at Godrick at that.

Godrick rolled his eyes, wadded up a nearby sheet of paper, and lobbed it at Artur.

"Ah'm fine. The breakup with Irrick wasn't bad," he protested.

Artur chuckled. "Alright, alright, yeh can't blame me fer worryin'."

"Yeh're more worried about that than the giant battle ah barely survived?" Godrick joked.

Artur rolled his eyes and threw the wad of paper back at Godrick. "There'll be plenty of yellin' and lecturin' yeh all about that this summer. Fer now, though, yeh all deserve a little break."

Godrick groaned theatrically as Artur adjusted the enchantment that heated the oventop.

"So there was never an arranged marriage?" Sabae asked.

"Feh," her grandmother said. "No point! Your mother already ruined the bloodline, marrying that healer. You can marry whoever, doesn't matter. You have more than enough cousins for me to marry off, even after losing half of them in the Blue Plague. Get over yourself, girl."

Sabae folded her arms and glared at her grandmother.

Well, at the human-sized stormcloud her grandmother was projecting onto the peak of Skyhold.

The peak was a mess. All the lava had drained down through the holes ripped in the peak of Skyhold, dried, or been cleaned up, but almost all of the thrones had been shattered, and the wards guarding the peak had mostly failed, save for Kanderon's spatial defenses.

Finally, Ilinia sighed and rolled her eyes. "You're no fun, girl. I thought about finding you a marriage, but I just didn't have the heart for it. I lost my daughter for years over trying to force her into a marriage she didn't want, and I missed out on so much of your childhood. I just don't have it in me to arrange a marriage for you too."

"But you're fine with it for my cousins?" Sabae asked.

Ilinia waved her hand in the air, tiny lightning bolts trailing her cloud-fingers. "Feh."

Sabae eyed her dubiously, but she let that one pass.

"You still owe me great-grandbabies, though," Ilinia said, jabbing Sabae in the side with a cloudy finger. A tiny lightning bolt leapt out and jolted her. "Lots of great-grandbabies."

Sabae threw her hands up in the air and stormed off. "I'm going to sell all your secrets to your enemies, Grandmother," she yelled. "All of them! Even the name of that little shop you buy all of your awful romance novels at, and the guy who brews that awful rotgut you drink."

"I can still drop a lightning bolt on you, ungrateful little girl," Ilinia said, laughing.

Ilinia watched her granddaughter descend into Skyhold. Once the girl was out of range, her smile faded, and she turned away from the stairs down.

"You can both come out now," Ilinia said. She pulled out her flask and sipped from it, and hundreds of leagues away, her storm body atop Skyhold copied the motion.

The air just above the ground rippled, and the immense body of Kanderon Crux emerged from nowhere, settling gently to the ground.

Ilinia wondered idly how many people had noticed that the depression Kanderon had worn in her spot for council meetings had remained almost entirely untouched, save for a little dried lava that had been scraped out easily.

Skyhold was as much a part of Kanderon as Kanderon was a part of Skyhold.

A breeze began blowing sand up to the top of the mountain, and it slowly consolidated into a small sandstorm the shape of a dragon.

Well, not that small— still a good fifty feet long— but it would be rude for Indris Stormbreaker— ridiculous epithet, that— to craft a storm body larger than Kanderon for herself.

The three of them each stood equidistant to one another. You could draw a perfect triangle between them, if you were one of those ridiculous idiots that were always pestering Ilinia about the need for some new breakwater or drain system for Ras Andis, with their exhausting little papers full of math.

She kept a perfectly good prince around just to deal with that sort of nonsense. She couldn't be bothered with the absurdities of ruling a city herself, not at her age.

"Indris, how did things go on your end?" Kanderon rumbled.

The sandstorm rustled its wings as Indris took her time responding. **"Chelys Mot still refuses to join us, but he did at least agree to keep the peace in the Endless Erg if the situation requires,"** the dragon said. **"The lesser powers of**

the Erg have all agreed to behave themselves over the next few years."

Ilinia snorted. She'd believe that bunch of fickle idiots would behave when she saw it. Still, if anyone other than the three of them could keep that bunch in line, it was Chelys Mot. The big turtle might be utterly disinterested in politics or ruling, and he might not be as powerful as the three of them, but he was reliable. And he was more than enough to deal with the assorted archmages, dragons, sphinxes, and whatever elses always stirring up trouble in the Erg.

Well, except maybe for that damn giant sunmaw, but for all its power, it was just an idiot beast, and the spells keeping it asleep should last for decades yet— enough time that Ilinia's successor should have already claimed the Storm Seat.

"Indris made sure things will stay nice and peaceful," Ilinia said, "and I've dealt with your nasty little demon problem. It's time to fulfill your side of the deal."

"Very well," Kanderon said, not seeming overly pleased about it.

A rush of light flowed through Kanderon's massive crystal wings. Ilinia turned towards the Skyreach range, and watched with pleasure as answering blue lights flashed on several nearby peaks as, for the first time in the history of the Kaen Das family, Skyhold's great weather wards came down.

Ilinia reached out on the wind, her perception rushing over hidden valley after mountain after waterfall. As the great barrier fell, it felt like an itch she hadn't been able to scratch had vanished, like a box that had been around one limb her whole life had been removed.

She could feel Indris' power reaching out alongside hers as they both stretched towards the lands east of the Skyreach

Range, to extend their unending rivalry over the winds to whole new territories.

Ilinia grinned in anticipation of the contests to come.

Before she got too caught up in expanding her power, however, she turned to Kanderon.

"Do you think your little pet paper mage suspects our plan?" Ilinia asked.

Kanderon snorted. **"I've burdened him with enough harsh truths that he won't reach for this one. That one will chase a lie to the ends of the continent, and an unanswered question even farther, but leave a truth in plain sight, and he won't even glance twice at it."**

"Cryptic twaddle," Ilinia said. "I don't know why so many people get all pretentious when they get old."

Indris chuckled at that. **"As opposed to turning into a trashy old harridan?"** she said.

Ilinia made a rude gesture at the dragon, who just chuckled harder. Ilinia shook her head and turned towards Kanderon.

"Alustin is fashioning my granddaughter and her friends into weapons," Ilinia said, her voice suddenly serious. "I'll tolerate it for now, because I had thought her broken, and he's given her a new path, but I won't see her thrown away."

"You're not the first one to notice what he's doing," Kanderon said, her expression as serious as always. **"For now, his aims serve our own."**

Kanderon rustled her wings, setting off a cascade of gentle chimes.

"And what if our fears for Imperial Ithos are realized?" Indris asked.

Ilinia shuddered a little at that. As powerful as she was, as powerful as the three of them were together…

Power didn't mean much in the face of the Cold Minds.

"Then none of our plans matter," Kanderon said. **"But the Cold Minds don't think like we do, and it's entirely likely they didn't even notice the bubble containing Imperial Ithos. Five centuries is a blink of the eye to them while they sleep in their dead universes."**

Ilinia hoped Kanderon was right. The sphinx was far more knowledgeable about the multiverse than either of the others.

If Kanderon was wrong, though, Ilinia had no intention of sticking around, or leaving her family to the ministrations of the cold minds. She'd already plotted out routes through several labyrinths to likely new worlds.

If their world was going to die, Ilinia Kaen Das, Stormguard of the South, Protector of Ras Andis, Kraken's Bane, and Hammer of the Sky was going to make damn sure the Kaen Das line didn't die with it.

Appendix: Galvachren's Guide to Anastis
Annotated by [Redacted]

The world of Anastis should, by any account, be a hub for multiversal travelers. *([Redacted]'s note: Isn't it, though?)* There are more mana wells than nearly any other known inhabited world, with a preponderance of them being junction wells.

For some reason, however, the labyrinths on Anastis have run amok. They're far deeper and more tangled than any others I've encountered, going far beyond the original design of the Weavers. Whether this is a result of the unusual characteristics of this universe's Aether, or a result of how close to going aether critical this world is, is unknown. It's also possible that the labyrinths are evolving over time. I'm curious what the Weavers would think of that, but, alas, we'll never know. *([Redacted]'s note: Galvachren is, so far as we can tell, the only scholar to refer to the Labyrinth Builders as Weavers. We have no idea why. We remain fairly confident that he's not old enough to have encountered the Labyrinth Builders— Galvachren might be ancient, but he's no Cold Mind.)*

Physical Overview: Anastis is disproportionately geologically active, even for a young world. Much of this can be attributed to Anastis' preposterously large moon. Moon is a poor name, really, since Anastis and its moon actually orbit one another— it's not significantly smaller than Anastis itself. This also results in the massive tides of Anastis, which have resulted in the unusual population distribution on the continents— sapients on Anastis only inhabit the coast atop seacliffs or other raised landforms. Atmospheric pressure is also marginally higher than most inhabited worlds— in combination with Anastis' moon, this results in some truly impressive storm systems.

([Redacted]'s note: "impressive storm systems" is understating it.)

Anastis has recently exited an ice age, but it doesn't seem to be thanks to interference by *[redacted]*.

([Redacted]'s note: The ice age is only geologically recent. To anyone else other than Galvachren, recent is a terrible adjective. And of course there's no [redacted] presence— Anastis is one of our strongholds, not theirs.)

Ecological Overview: Anastis' ecosystems are, to say the least, a mess. Remnants of the original ecosystem can still be found in some parts of the world— Ithos' Endless Erg, Gelid's great mudflats— but for the most part, it has been supplanted by invasive species that have poured out of Anastis' countless labyrinths over the eons. I've personally identified species from dozens of known worlds, and countless more I don't recognize.

There are at least a half dozen tool-using sapient species, and half again as many non-tool using sapients present. None are native to Anastis. This doesn't count the numerous members of the "Great Powers" of Anastis that are the only representative of their species on Anastis. It also doesn't count Aether mutations and [redacted] that can't properly be counted as members of their species any longer.

([Redacted]'s note: Our assessments of the count differ from Galvachren's, but this is, as usual, thanks to differing definitions of what counts as a species. Our official nomenclature also differs with who counts as [redacted]— while many of the Great Powers of Anastis can go toe to toe with [redacted], there's more to becoming [redacted] than mere power. Galvachren, after all, is no [redacted], and, well... Anyhow, by our definition, there are no [redacted] on

Anastis. Which is one of the reasons we established this as one of our stronghold worlds.)

The strangeness of what native life is still present leads me to hypothesize that Anastis originated in a relatively distant habitable reach of the multiverse, and that its connections have shifted over time.

There is a truly splendid diversity of spiders on Anastis. I could fill entire volumes on them. None are native, however.

Aetheric Overview: The Aether of Anastis is singularly unusual. While in many respects its Aether resembles a fairly typical liquid Aether world, there appears to be some process interfering with the free flow of Aether. Aether density is radically variable across Anastis, something usually only found in gaseous Aether environments. Even then, however, it's seldom even close to the Aether density variance of Anastis. There are a few rival hypotheses as to why this occurs.

The most popular hypothesis points to the unusual number, depth, and complexity of Anastis' labyrinths as the cause. While plausible sounding, an actual mechanism for this is seldom put forwards.

Another hypothesis claims that the Anastan Aether is thixotropic— that it responds to shocks by changing its viscosity. Shocks in this sense, of course, being heavy draws upon the Aether. The downside of this analysis, of course, is that no-one has ever felt said viscosity change.

There are a few other minor hypotheses to consider, ranging from the eccentric to the insane, but the last I find worthy of inclusion is that there is some sort of substrate through which the Anastan Aether flows. This is controversial, to say the least— there has never been direct evidence of any such substrate, and solid Aether is, to say the least, quite easy to perceive. Still, there is a marked similarity between the Anastan Aether flows and the movement of liquids in aquifers. *([Redacted]'s note: So far as we can tell, Galvachren was the originator of this hypothesis, but he shows his usual reticence in claiming credit for anything.)*

Regardless, as a consequence of this, Anastans tend to do well as multiversal travelers. They tend to recover from Aether sickness far more quickly when traveling between worlds than natives of worlds with more stable Aether. It seems likely that the variable Anastan Aether density has acclimated their systems to an extent.

As an added benefit, Anastis is far less prone to Aether exhaustion than many other worlds. One city-state overusing its Aether will seldom even affect many of its neighbors.

The magic of Anastis is also unusually versatile in function— not on an individual level, where mages tend to have quite specific portfolios of power, but overall, it's astonishingly diverse.

Political Overview: Thanks to the variable Anastan Aether density, political organization tends to lean towards smaller nation states and city states. While a few empires exist, they're far less common on Anastis than other worlds. The lack of Aether exhaustion as a major threat to civilization also changes political interactions, though in a perhaps less easily definable manner. *([Redacted]'s note: What a polite way to say that Anastan politics are an unstable, constantly shifting mess of coups, civil wars, and assassinations.)*

There is relatively little organized multiversal presence on Anastis. [Redacted] have planted none of their [redacted], [redacted] incursions are unknown, [redacted] has built no [redacted] *([Redacted]'s note: We most certainly have, and*

Galvachren's visited them. What's he up to? Perhaps he thinks he's doing us a favor by not letting others know we're here? We might be one of the weaker multiversal powers, but we're not that weak], [Redacted] infections are a non-factor, and there are few [redacted] on Anastis. *([Redacted]'s note: there are no true [redacted] on Anastis. Again, it's why we made it one of our stronghold worlds. Anastis' Aether is inherently hostile to those belligerent, imbecilic godlings.)* The [redacted] are, as with most human worlds, present, though as is often the case, they have no idea how far their own [redacted] extends. There are a larger than normal number of demons on Anastis, but that's simply a consequence of the numerous labyrinths. *([Redacted]'s note: It is, as always, exasperating trying to figure out who Galvachren considers to be a multiversal power. His list is considerably shorter than expected, and excludes quite a number of powers that we'd include. Most notably of course, Galvachren himself.)*

Afterword

Thank you so much for reading A Traitor in Skyhold, Book 3 of Mage Errant!

This was a tough one to write— not so much the actual writing, but life around it. Illness, personal drama, and over a month of traveling this year. Plus, the transition into writing full time was a tough one. Before, I'd just come home from my day job and immediately start writing. Having to manage my own schedule again was tricky.

I'll be taking a little break between books 3 and 4 to write a standalone epidemiological fantasy novel that follows the course of a plague across a continent. It will be very different than Mage Errant in both tone and content, and is set in an entirely different world, but if you keep your eyes open, you'll almost certainly notice a few details that will be of interest to Mage Errant fans. (Though, again, it will be a very different beast from Mage Errant- it's going to be pretty depressing, and not have much in the way of action scenes.)

If you have any questions or comments, please feel free to contact me at john.g.bierce@gmail.com, or on reddit (u/johnbierce). For news about the Mage Errant series, other upcoming works, and random thoughts about fantasy, worldbuilding, and whatever else pops in my mind, check out www.johnbierce.com. The best way to keep updated on new releases is to sign up for my mailing list, which you can find on my website.

I've also started a Patreon, which can be found at patreon.com/johnbierce. There, I'll be posting monthly short stories set in the worlds of my books.

Cover art by Tithi Luadthong.

Cover design by James of GoOnwrite.com

Edited by Paul Martin, of Dominion Editorial.

Special thanks to my beta readers, F James Blair (you should totally check out his Bulletproof Witch series), Sam Juliano, Gregory Gleason, Pierre Auckenthaler, Sundeep Agarwal, Adam Skinner, and Garret Miller.

If you're looking for more reading material similar to Mage Errant or that I think readers of Mage Errant might enjoy, and you've already read the suggestions at the end of the first two books, well, I've definitely got more suggestions for you!

- *Street Cultivation*, by Sarah Lin— The first book in Sarah Lin's new cultivation fantasy series. Unlike most cultivation series like Cradle, however, Street Cultivation is set in a fantasy world at our level of technology. Heavy focus on training.
- *The Daily Grind*, by argusthecat— A bored call center IT support guy finds a dungeon that only appears at a specific time each week, and starts delving into it with his friends. Instead of the usual monsters you'd encounter in a dungeon, there are living staplers and other office supplies. It sounds weird, but it's an absolute blast.
- *Twelve Kings in Sharakai*, by Bradley P. Beaulieu— If you're craving more sandship action, look no further. *Twelve Kings in Sharakai* is the first book in

the excellent Middle Eastern-flavored Song of Shattered Sands series.

- *A Thousand Li,* by Tao Wong— Another cultivation series with a heavy focus on training. This one is the one that is by far the closest to being like actual medieval China- even compared to any of the translated Chinese cultivation/xianxia novels I've encountered. (Except, you know, for the magic and demons.) There are even footnotes explaining various units of measurement, foods, and other parts of medieval Chinese culture.
- *Kill Six Billion Demons,* by Abbadon— I've often described this webcomic as the cyberpunk Bhagavad Gita, directed by Akira Kurosawa and starring Buffy the Vampire Slayer. I stand by this description. Image Comics is responsible for releasing the print version. (To give you an idea of how good it is, *they* approached the creator. That's… unusual in the comic book industry, to say the least.)
- *The Forbidden Library,* by Django Wexler— Aimed at a slightly younger age group than *Mage Errant* or the other entries on the list, but still well worth your time. An orphan girl is sent to live with an uncle she'd never heard of before, and, well, of course he has a magic library.
- *Six Sacred Swords,* by Andrew Rowe— Prequel to Rowe's *Arcane Ascension* series. Much faster paced and action packed.
- *The Immortals,* by Tamora Pierce— Though not my favorite Tamora Pierce series (that would be *Protector of the Small,* which I've already recommended), *The Immortals* is absolutely fantastic. Follows a wild mage with power over animals as she tries to learn to control her powers

and help fight an escalating magical threat against the kingdom of Tortall.

I only set up the aforementioned Patreon a short time before release day, but I've already got patrons backing me! Special thanks to Adam Milne, Cortney Railsback, James Titterton, Josh Fink, Reudiger Pakmor, and Ryan Campbell.